Born in 1955, Fiona Cooper lives in
Northumberland. She is the author of *Rotary
Spokes, Heartbreak on the High Sierra, Not the Swiss
Family Robinson* and *The Empress of the Seven
Oceans. Jay Loves Lucy*, a novel, and *I Believe in
Angels*, a collection of short stories, are also
published by Serpent's Tail.

A Skyhook in the Midnight Sun

· ·

Fiona Cooper

First published in 1994 by
Serpent's Tail, 4 Blackstock Mews, London N4
and 401 West Broadway #1, New York, NY 10012

Phototypeset in 10pt Galliard by Intype, London
Printed in Great Britain by Cox & Wyman Ltd of
Reading, Berkshire

For Jean
and all the dreamers
in love and joy

With thanks to Sarah Lefanu, for her inspired editing and thanks always to my mum and dad, Sara, Dee, Barry, Kitty, Molly, Elsie, Marion, Margo, Marion, Jamie, Sharon, Caroline, Mary, Tenebris, Linda, Elaine, Jenny, Shena, Christie, Fizzy, Rosemary, Alison, Winston, and of course, Pete, for all your love and support.

Part one

1

Standing on Balcony D, Caz had the topmost branches of a flowering cherry at eye-level and wonderful fresh air gusting from the Tyne. Someone was mowing the green way down below and children played hide and seek among the bushes. Two little girls had made a house of three huge lumps of stone quarried from the site and settled into the grass specially for them to play with.

There was a suggestion of buds swelling on the cherry-tree branches and every flat had a long deep tub of earth outside it. Some people had ignored this, others had cacti and daffodils and geraniums; one flat had hanks of spindly wallflowers.

'A garden already!' said Caz.

She opened the door.

Seventy-seven was filthy. Shredded wallpaper on wallpaper on grease on wallpaper. Layers of lino stratified with grime. Every ledge thick with grease, a sticky fountain of coffee stains hurled up the wall and across the ceiling, stains like dog piss – probably the real thing – against the skirting board. Dead cockroaches. Caz held her breath and opened every window in sight, retching at the stench.

Think of it as a challenge!

The voice of her gym teacher rang in her mind.

In one of the cupboards was a Christmas card: 'To Dorrie and Family this Season'. There was a certificate of marriage for June 29th 1933 under the sink.

Caz sat on the top step and wrote a list.

Bleach.

Scouring pads.

Sandpaper.

Disinfectant.

Scrubbing brushes.

Cloths.

White paint: gloss and matt.

Sugar soap.

Paint brushes.

Candles.

Masking tape.

Cassette player.

Cassettes.

Batteries.

Sandwiches.

Overalls.

Soap.

Swarfega.

Energy and patience!

All the things one needs to make one's little home a home. Ha ha. She had just a fortnight to make it all habitable, February 1st, the official key day.

She walked to the window and looked out across the valley. It had been years since she bothered thinking of where she lived as a home. Not since Trimdon House, a spit from East India Dock Road, London E14. After college, she had spent the five, nearly six, best years of her life there. They all had.

Caz and Alex and Andy and Charlotte and David and Jay and Ben.

They'd been a group since the first term at art school, they ate and talked and stayed up all night together. None of them had ever met anyone else who *understood*. One of their tutors with a big red nose tried to get rid of them. He said they were disruptive, disaffected, anarchic, idle. He said they were unteachable, unreachable, but the other tutors said they were the only ones likely to bring the art school any glory, and he failed. They called him The Dong and flyposted caricatures of him all over.

Came the third year and the need for deciding what on earth they would do next. It was obvious that they'd stay together for the rest of their lives. Caz and Ben were a couple, they vowed it was written in the stars: they swore they were each other's first, last and only lover. Charlotte and David didn't need no piece of paper from the city hall keeping them tied and true. Alex and Andy were gay virgins, blood brothers terrified into celibacy because of AIDS: their ambition was to turn into a more brilliant copy of Gilbert and George. Jay was in love with all of them and looking – not too energetically – for Ms Right. Which was hard when your essential baggage in life is six other people.

And where are they now? Full fathom five . . . Caz pushed the thought away.

They'd wanted a huge place: seven rooms and seven studios as a minimum. They were some years too late to slide into their dream: a riverside warehouse squat. The yuppie developers had put paid to that.

Then they found Trimdon House, a Victorian block built for the deserving poor. It had been condemned as unfit for human habitation and everything about it suited them down to the ground. The staircases were lined with shiny bricks the colour of toffee or shit, depending on how cheerful you felt. The balconies were wrought iron worn to spider's legs of rust. Amazingly the council suggested they form a co-op and granted them a renewable five-year lease, charging only rates. A proper lease! In their eyes it was a bit of a comedown from squatting, but it made life wonderfully simple. They qualified for decoration and modernisation grants and within a year, Trimdon House was an urban palace. They filled the window-boxes with geraniums and painted the doors brilliant yellow and scarlet.

Caz had been drawing a cartoon for all the years she'd been at college. It was three hundred and seventy yards long. It was the story of a creature who'd stuck its head up a sooty chimney and wanted to get clean again. It roamed through jungles and swamps and pirate caves and she wasn't done with it yet. She started to transfer it on to the glazed brick stairwells.

Andy and Alex turned the courtyard into a garden.

Charlotte made flags for every festival and season.

David had found electric blue slates and planned to retile the roof between money-making graphic design work.

Ben was rewiring so that the courtyard could be turned into fairyland at the flick of a switch.

Jay had an advertising job which took most of her time but paid her a ridiculously high salary.

They pooled the money, shared the food and dressed erratically from a communal wardrobe.

And so it continued.

Caz snapped out of her memories and checked the time: the woman had said they closed at twelve. She had twenty minutes. She walked through the rooms once more, picturing it finished and furnished.

Her own little maisonette, deep in the heart of Miston.

Maisonette? She cringed at the word. It was so . . . dinky. Maisonette, kitchenette, dinette, Tammy bloody Wynette. Duplex?

'Split level,' she thought, 'I can handle that.'

She squeezed the amethyst crystal she carried like a talisman.

She went down to Anchorage Point housing office and told the woman she'd take the . . . flat.

'This is your tenancy agreement, lass,' the woman said. 'No pets, keep your rent up to date and come and see me if you've any problems.'

No pets? Caz had seen half a dozen cats and heard three dogs on her balcony alone. She read the leaflet: she had security of tenure for life. This made her grin absurdly. 77, Galleon Heights was hers and nobody could throw her out ever. She was going to make it beautiful.

After Trimdon House, she'd never made a home again. Where she lived was just somewhere to sleep and keep things and have people to stay. And of course to paint – canvasses, not walls or window frames. It was never worth painting walls, you just covered the worst bits with posters and postcards. She'd taken accommodation furnished and unfurnished and put up with whatever the landlord had dumped there. Three wheels on my wagon, three legs on the table, bow-backed books to prop the bed more or less level.

She felt that her thirties called for a little comfort. Like carpets, like bought furniture, as opposed to the weird and wonderful *objets trouvés* she'd found skip-diving. A series of wooden crates and cushions and the obligatory Indian rug just didn't do as a sofa any more: they always came adrift and had to be remade daily until you moved again, and sent them back to skip-land for the next treasure-seeker.

Galleon Heights was going to be different. She planned murals: serpents and dragons and sea-beasts swirling exotic tails over the ceilings, fins and scales flowing through doorways, a dash of bubbles on the bathroom door. When the money came. Meanwhile, everything would be Mediterranean white and the huge windows downstairs and up gave the effect of even more space.

Mrs Beeton said first catch your hare, before you jug it, and *first prepare your surfaces*, muttered Caz, before you juggle with your decor. She pushed a trolley round the Miston DIY megastore, where they had background muzak of songs she liked cut by static announcements of today only unrepeatable bargains, and a bored cashier calling in vain for Mr Hanson from gardening to come to the check-out please. *You are the sunshine of my life*, come to the check-out now, come immediately, come urgently. *The first time ever I saw your face*, Mr Hanson, please, check-out three, my customer is waiting!

Back at the flat, she piled up tins, bottles, trays, cartons and canisters, cursing the dead power points. Washing the walls raised swirls of dry grime and she longed to damp her throat with tea, coffee, anything. Maybe she'd get a six-pack of Ace, the cheapest lager, to help her through the dusty days ahead.

By the time she'd purged and scoured the moth-wings of wallpaper upstairs, glow-worm trails of neon had started across the valley and the lamp on the green was an unlikely nightclub pink. She dumped the filthy rags in the sink and scrubbed her hands clean. It was going to take longer than she thought and she locked the front door until the morning. Tonight she was clubbing and for the first time, she wouldn't bother creeping in quietly. Let the ratbag landlady have broken sleep for a change!

An old lady came out of the flat two doors down and clutched her arm.

'Moving in, pet? You'll like it here. It's a good place.'

2

Day Two
      Was sweltering at 8 a.m., a giddy heat blasting out of February nowhere and straight into every smeared window of number seventy-seven. Caz propped the door open while she worked. Five buckets of grey-brown ooze later, she threw her bald sponge into the black dustbin bag and ran icy water over her wrists. She popped a can of lager at ten and sat outside with a cigarette. On the green below, children chased and whooped and captured each other in the bushes. A big red-gold dog, somewhere between a setter and a labrador, ambled across the grass wagging its fat tail. It collapsed into one-eyed sleep by the monolithic trio of golden stones.

'Working hard, pet?'

'I am,' Caz said, and squinted a smile at the old lady of the evening before.

'Yes, you'll like it here. Some people don't live here properly, like, just use it as a giro drop. Him next door – we haven't seen him in months. But I love it. It's warm, yes it is, and the view! You couldn't pay money and see better. I'll give you some cuttings for your box if you like.'

'Well, thank you,' said Caz, 'that's kind. I was going to ask you – who was here before me?'

The old lady smiled vaguely and nodded. Was there a mystery about the last tenant of seventy-seven? No! Caz noticed the pink plastic hearing aid at her ear and nodded back.

She was at the top of the steps, gouging at polystyrene tiles and the filth of abandoned spiders' webs when somebody knocked at her door. Two somebodies, old ladies in well-seated hairy coats, one grey and blue criss-cross, the other brown and bobbly. They smiled with eyes darting beyond her. Grey and blue criss-cross was tall and thin, brown bobbly was dumpy and wore a hat like a woolly Christmas pudding.

'There's some work to be done here,' said tall and thin.

'Oh, yes,' said dumpy.

'But you're doing it properly,' tall and thin approved, 'that's the way. A place is never your own until you've cleaned it, my mam always said.'

'Cleaned it, oh yes,' the woolly hat said cheerfully.

'I'm over there, aren't we?' criss-cross stabbed her gloved finger over the green. 'Lovely. What age would you say I am? I've been here sixteen year, mind. Seventy-nine, that's me. Put something in your window-box and forget about it. The sun just brings it out. I've got roses – do you see?'

'Yes,' said Caz, 'beautiful. I thought about sweet peas.'

'Sweet peas,' said the woolly hat, 'we never thought of them, did we?'

'That'll be lovely,' criss-cross approved and mustered her hand-bag and shopping bag to shepherd her friend away. 'Good luck with it. You want to get your young man up that ladder.'

Caz went back to the slush-storm of foam on the ceiling.

One of her older and wiser friends had written to her last month, saying: 'Everyone is breaking up. Everyone is going bankrupt and moving and changing. It's a terrible world. No stability. People are awful to one another. The only way to live today and have a certain degree of peace is to live alone. I *love* it. I wouldn't want anyone in my space *ever*. This space is still and dependable and it is me. A big balloon of my very own air.'

Caz liked that, though she gave a wry smile at the next paragraph asking her to come down, to stay as long as she liked: her friend even enclosed bus and train timetables.

'*You*, of course, would be *very* welcome.'

That was one of the tricks of living alone – to share the time and space selectively. Since Trimdon House, she'd found there were fewer and fewer new people she could really be bothered with. There was nothing wrong with them, just they didn't suit her. She had a couple of friends, the sort you see every year maybe, odd friends from odd jobs. There were friends for coffee, a drink, a phonecall. The bread and butter of being a social animal with anti-social tendencies. She had a number of friends through the mail. Charlotte wrote regularly.

The one person close to her now was Josie and she'd only known her for about four years, since she'd come to Newcastle. Josie suited her because she was the least curious person she'd ever met. No one had ever been family like Andy and Alex and Jay and Charlotte and David and Ben. Sometimes she missed that like the ghost ache of an amputated limb. Champagne friends, people who walked in like they belonged. Josie was almost that, but they didn't have the day by day year after year intimacy of old friends. Caz felt that they would: it would take time, which is easy, and trust, which is not.

Often she met new people who excited her, but even then, she kept a distance. She'd come to accept that their contact might be for three days, a few weeks, sometimes even months. Then there would be just a nod and a smile in the street, a chat in the bar.

She felt that these people had come into her life for her to learn something, to remind her of some useless pattern she was sliding into. Example: Wosh the mad artist. Duration of friendship: five months. Nature of meetings: platonic evenings, filled with outpourings from the soul about the agony of trying to keep one's vision clear and steer a course for which there are no maps: your very own life.

Wosh threw in his job towards the end of the five months and went to Central America via Mexico, to wow his muse among Mayan temples. Caz finished her off and on project about masks and skyscrapers: she'd said all she had to about both, for the time being. She drank a cocktail with Wosh at the airport and waved him off on his plane. There were illegible postcards for a while from Teotihnacan, Chichén Itza, Belize, Mayapan. No doubt they'd meet for a drink if he ever came back. Their process was finished, the meeting of frightened and crazy creative fires, a mirror of each other's vision. Here endeth the lesson. She would tell strangers stories about him and he would tell other strangers other stories about her.

And what had she learnt in the weird wild hours with Wosh?

A definition of happiness. Happiness is perfect work and perfect work is the best you can do at the time. Keep on keepin' on, dude!

It filtered back to her that the arty scene thought of her as loftily self-contained and she accepted that with a slashing indifference courtesy of Dorothy Parker. It hurt, but so much less than the pain of opening up enough to let someone under your skin. Getting real. She'd learnt that her safest place was inside a shell since most of the time the tides were simply too dangerous to venture out.

Her task was to make the flat a coral garden sheltered from sharks and tempests. She shucked off her overalls and decided to eat lunch on the High Road, find out a bit about where the storms had blown her, who lived here, what drove them.

77, Galleon Heights was a big balloon of her very own air and nothing would cross her threshold wishing her harm. She touched her lips and brow with salt water and dashed salt along the doorway to seal the spell.

3

The housing complex was called Anchorage Point for the days when ships sailed down the Tyne rich with cargo. Men came rolling home with a pocket full of money and a head full of adventures after months at sea. Heydays and yesterdays. Now there were grey queues at the job centre and the grocer-cum-video-hire-cum-newsagents had packets of tea and cheap biscuits piled up like gold bars. Shops were dusty with bankrupt stock, dirt cheap and still unaffordable: there were sales, end-of-line clearance, interest-free credit, nothing to pay for six months, once-in-a-lifetime trade-in offers. Shops closed every week in spite of it all. The inhabitants of Anchorage Point were geniuses at make do and mend and barter took over from buying and selling. Money changing hands? They barely had enough to hold on to.

To reach the High Road Caz had to cross the green to an archway. Galleon Heights rode its full seven stories above her. The archway was called Starboard Cross and led to a windblown vertiginous bridge across four lanes of traffic dashing for the city centre. She passed thin mothers blowing smoke into the wind and skinny children in pink and green shellsuits piled into pushchairs. The supermarket windows were plastered with bright orange signs offering processed peas and family packs of own-brand tea-bags at rock bottom prices.

The pub at the corner puffed gravy-scented steam from a rusted pipe on the wall and her mouth watered automatically. A shabby greyhound shivered on its rat-tail leash tethered to a spike. She wondered about lunch there, proper dinner, turnips and mash and meat, but the saloon door opened belching out big unshaven men and stale beer and an oily swell of tarnished ashtrays and she went by.

Caz needed to find her caff. It had to be an egg and chips caff with decent coffee and space enough for her to read the paper. Maybe a juke-box, definitely chairs and tables rather than benches. It was important who worked there: they didn't have to be chatty or charming; her favourite caff in London was run by a manic depressive Italian couple who sighed and screamed and cursed and laughed like souls lost in the third circle of Hell. Always the same words as she left: *See you tomorrow, Caz, if God saves us so long. Me, I pray for a quiet death!* Breakfast at Alphonso's was pure theatre. A caff could make or break the day: it was where she woke up and ate before the total isolation of her work. Sometimes it was the only time she saw people from morning till night.

The first café she saw was The Ritz, its sixties bubble-writing sign quivering alight only on the 'it'. Two kicked-to-bits fruit machines stood like shabby sentry boxes inside the door and as she hovered, a waitress passed by with pallid chips and grey peas steaming dismally on a plate. Oh well.

Past the electrical stores and shoe repairers While U Wait she came across Dennis's Den. Red plastic benches crammed against formica tables ringed with tea stains and charred by smouldering cigarette butts. Sometimes a place like this could be surprisingly good, but the man behind the counter had a face white as lard, mouth clamped shut, chin tethered to the counter by lines of dissatisfaction. Hell, Caz didn't expect anyone to whistle while they worked, but she couldn't stand surliness louring behind her while she ate.

If she dithered much longer, the flat would never get done. She bought a newspaper and tobacco in a shop where the card racks were empty and dusty little plastic bags of sweets cost ten p. She'd mooch for two blocks more and if they yielded nothing, she'd settle on The Ritz for today.

The only gloriously happy windows in the High Road fronted Earl's Amusement Arcade And Grills, foot-high letters embellished with gold. Glossy statues of elephants trumpeted over crystal vases and bowls, and a huge china tiger snarled at a pink and gold cupid. These were the star prizes, highlighted by a rainbow of neon. Well, why not. She pushed the saloon-style doors open and went in.

Earl's was dark inside, nightclub dark with spotlights on the chance-your-arm machines where pale hands ladled out silver and pulled a handle to make the fruit wheels spin. They didn't even look at the win lines, these people, carrying on dismal conversations about the weather and the government (both terrible but as good as you can expect these days), while their hands and arms worked independently, ladle, pull, ladle, ladle, scoop. You've cleaned that one out, shuffle, shuffle, ladle, ladle, pull, pull, ladle, ladle, must keep enough change for a cuppa. Cherry, orange, bonus, cherry cherry twenty p. Nobody bothered feeding the log-jam of coppers slumped around Niagara Falls. Apple banana mystery, double or nothing, grapes grapes nudge nudge lose. A dyed blonde in uniform leaned against the glass, hands stuffed into her change pouch, pink lips working a mouthful of gum, pink nails flicking the tip of a filter cigarette. Plum orange pineapple, shuffle plum plum plum. twenty p, bank or gamble, Hi or Lo. Aces High and the Jack of Hearts hologram flickered hopelessly: *pet, can you kick this machine or something, it's not right*. A pale youth in monogrammed overalls unplugged it and pulled it out, drawing a screwdriver from the navy blue sheath of his skin-tight pants. Back to normal in no time.

Double or nothing. Shuffle and spin. Win some, lose most.

The local radio station told everyone to sit back and relax while Jim Reeves brought them days of wine and roses; a barker's voice cut in to remind them that he was Happy Henry, their host and one till two was Super Win bingo hour, when the star prizes could walk out of the windows straight into your sitting rooms. Happy Henry came from the Teddy-boy era, a smirk hanging between mutton-chop sideburns, a bootlace tie, a ruffled shirt, an electric blue jacket.

Caz went to the Snak Bar and stood until two women came out from the back. Their overalls were the colour of pumpkins and one said Wendy, the other Donna.

'I think we should throw out those sandwiches,' said Wendy, 'I'm not happy about them.'

'Well, ah dunno,' Donna said, 'they were fresh this morning. Ah'm pretty sure but I couldn't take an oath on it.'

Bleach white and sweating margarine, the sandwiches lay under a heat lamp, tomato juice staining the bread like blood, processed cheese oozing.

'Ah think she shouldn't have put them under the heat,' Wendy said, 'I'd not be happy selling them, like.'

'Hoy them out. She'll never know. I like a sandwich made fresh, me, and here's us standing talking while this poor lass is waiting on being served. Yes, pet?' Donna looked at Caz.

'Do you do – like, breakfast?' Caz asked.

'Er, Wendy, do we do breakfast?'

'Well, what's breakfast, like?'

'Oh, you know,' Caz said, 'eggs and chips? Bacon? You know.'

'Oh, like a fry-up sort of,' said Donna. 'We can do you one of those. Toast? Tea or coffee?'

'Yeah. Toast. Coffee, please,' Caz said.

She sat at one of the orange-topped tables and unfolded the paper. She was, as always, absurdly pleased that just paying money got someone else to cook your breakfast and wash up for you.

'Have you got a light, pet?'

Caz looked up. A little old lady at the next table was turned awkwardly towards her, gold rings worn thin on her extended left hand. She took the lighter and puffed and slid round to Caz's table to hand it back.

'I'm eighty-one this year,' she announced.

'Never,' Caz said, smiling. This wasn't to be a newspaper breakfast after all and she swept aside her instant irritation. Let life happen, she'd met so many people that way.

'I am,' said the old woman, 'eighty-one, uh huh. And I've always lived in Miston. Not in the same house, mind, but always within a few streets. The young people, they move all over but it wasn't our way, you see.'

'It's nice here,' Caz said.

'Do you like it, do you? Ee, I'm glad. Of course it's changed. You don't mind me talking to you, do you?'

'It's nice,' said Caz, 'it's my pleasure. Changed?'

'Oh, yes,' the old lady's lips threatened to engulf her cigarette. 'Everything's closed down these days and there's no work. Can only get better, I say. And I've known it worse. Eighty-one, pet, I've seen it all come and go and come back again. Yes.'

Donna dumped a bowl of grey water on a table and slopped a cloth around, carefully lifting the plastic sign advertising Froffee Coffee. She dabbed at the cracking plastic chairs.

'Aye,' the old lady said, 'Donna could you do us a coffee pet? And I've paid me poll tax. Council tax, Ah dunno.'

'Well now,' said Caz.

'I've never owed any bugger owt. Always paid me bills on time, me. Ee, it was a struggle, but you know how I did it? Young 'uns are soft.'

'Mm,' said Caz.

'Bread and jam for a month, pet, get it all out of the way. They say you can pay every week, but you always wind up paying more, they get it somehow. Bread and jam and a week or two just the bread, but it didn't do me any harm.'

'It's a bad tax,' Caz said, 'not that I can think of a good one.'

'That's right and all,' said the old lady. 'Still, mebbes I'll hit the jackpot today! It's been nice talking to you, lass.'

Caz ate the fry-up quickly, paid and escaped back to the task of the day: her nest, her eyrie, her cave. The poor thin little old lady had rattled her somewhere deep inside. Where Joan of Arc raged and fought for liberty, Violetta Parra sang her heart out for freedom and Harriet Tubman laughed aloud in the face of oppression.

Someone had been going on about the starving millions in Africa once and Ben leant over and said very quietly: 'Name five.'

In the awkward silence, she added that Mother Teresa didn't own an armchair: you put up or you shut up. That was Ben's way.

4

Her head agreed with Ben, but somewhere in her guts she yearned for a flaming sword of justice. It was a good thing number seventy-seven needed so much done to it. No time to waste on memories or a soapbox rant.

She cleared the kitchen ceiling of its limp polystyrene scales and fought against her screaming spine to stuff the debris into a black sack. She swept up the drifts of foam and dust, already noting the broad stripes of black sweating filth hanging behind the heating pipes.

'Pack your bags, scum,' she threatened, making a fist of a scouring pad, 'Super Caz versus the Grime Monsters of Miston! I'll make you eat mat!'

The first few days at Trimdon House, they'd all gone flat out, scraping and washing through the night, grabbing a few hours of sleep and staggering upright to start again. Charlotte had been the first to crack.

'We're not enjoying this,' she said, one grey 5 a.m. 'We've got to get a balance. A method. Work, rest, learning, leisure.'

'Rise with speed and rest with dope,' David said, mocking her seriousness.

After that, they gave eight hours a day to nest-building, punctuated by tea breaks, wine breaks, huge bowls of salad, bags of chips. The first job was to get a bath working and then at the end of the day, they could soak the aches from their bodies and go to the pub for lazy rounds of pool and darts. Saturday and Sunday were rest days.

'Not slob days,' Charlotte said, 'time to admire what we've done and congratulate ourselves a bit. And plan the next week.'

'Vive the protestant work ethic!' Had Ben said that? Had she?

Caz smiled. She must write to Charlotte and tell her about Galleon Heights, bring back the memories of those lovely days.

'Days of wine and roses,' she said out loud.

Balance. She could do the flat room by room, or task by task. Best to vary the movements: Caz was not given to exercise by choice and all too soon she felt every muscle and every tendon screaming in outrage. At least there was constant scalding water in number seventy-seven. She decided to buy exotic bubble bath and make a point of changing into paint-free clothes every night.

Method. Scraping with her right hand brought to life a sheath of muscles right up her arm, across her shoulder and up her neck. Muscles grumbling awake after a long hibernation, grouching at her with stale acidity. Cleaning in great wide sweeps with her left hand made her aware of a whole system below the skin, blood pulsing as her muscles contracted, the million different connections of bone and tissue.

Left hand, right hand, giving one aching shoulder a reprieve while the other gathered its own painful threat of stiffness. And when she'd pushed herself past pain and her blood flowed like setting lead into red mists before her eyes she'd stop, stagger to a seat, drink a lager, smoke. Her head would cease to throb, the fresh air and stillness let her body reassemble itself from the isolation of limbs, the domineering thud of physical exhaustion.

Andy and Alex had talked about satisfaction. 'You've got to feed the five senses,' Andy said. 'Good food, mega incense, something soft to sit on. Fabulous music. And something good to look at.'

They'd bought a potted passion flower vine which lived on one of the balconies and Andy insisted on taking tea breaks beside it. When it rained, they huddled under bright golf umbrellas.

'If you sort of unfocus your eyes,' Alex said, giggling, 'it sort of masks out the urban squalor.'

Galleon Heights came up trumps again with everything laid on. Today was another gusty sunshine extravaganza, haze sweeping from the horizon, surprising birds into a gusty dawn chorus well into mid-afternoon. The heating tower to the east was studded with pigeons and as she watched they all took off at once. The sun turned their wings to glass and the sound echoed against every wall of the courtyard like windblown paper falling on a polished floor. Three times they wheeled over the green, then the formation divided and seven of them landed on the clear corrugated roof above her. She swivelled her neck to see the dark blobs slipping and sliding on rattling claws.

'Get out of it!' A small and bristling shape stumped towards her, swinging a handbag as if it was a lasso. Four times round her head and she leapt two feet into the air to thwack the roof with a sound like cannon-fire. The pigeons flew away. Beauty and live theatre already!

'You want to keep a stick behind your door,' the woman gasped, pulling her coat straight, 'hit it every time you hear them. Filthy things!'

She was scarlet with the effort and glowered into the sunshine.

'There's some here that feed them, more fool they! Vermin they are. The mess! The flies! Diseases: worse than rats they are, nesting all over! Whoever built this place was crackers, a real crackerjack. It's nothing but a great big ugly pigeon loft. I hate them!'

Caz liked the idea of birds nesting. When she was a little girl, house martins had nested in the eaves outside her window and she'd learnt complete stillness so she could watch them. She guessed it was not wise to say any of this to the pigeon hater.

'Moving in, are you? Well, I wish you luck!'

It was delivered as a threat and Caz watched her stotting down the balcony, belting the roof every few yards. Well, it made a change from *I'm eighty-one two three four five years old*, which seemed to be second to hello on most people's lips. And why not: their parents would have been proud of seventy after a lifetime of scrimp and save and wear yourself out.

She wouldn't whack away the pigeons: there must have been trees before Anchorage Point started its mile long sprawl of bricks and the pigeons no doubt saw the whole complex as a shanty town of human squatters robbing them of perches and nests. You have to share.

You also have to keep on working. More than twenty minutes' break and her body would assume that she'd declared a holiday. Getting it out of its happily slumped-on-deckchair mood would be nigh impossible. She stood up, grinning at her toes' surprise: they'd been wriggling in anticipation of sand and sea. Tough.

She dawdled in the doorway: yes, there was definite progress, a fresh smell albeit still dusty. She wedged the windows open with cans of paint, let the breeze clear that.

Halfway down the stairs a curl of mustiness hit her. She slid the huge picture window wide open in the living room, and pinned back the window in the bathroom. The whole flat was made for light and air – even the bedroom had its own pocket-handkerchief balcony – and she wedged the glass door open, dreaming of tubs and hanging baskets full of scarlet geraniums.

She brushed the walls and the ceiling in the living room, more cobwebs and sighs of dust everywhere. Heavy duty gloves and a bucket of steaming foam followed. The floor first? It was boarded over and every board had a relief map of stains. Scrubbing brush time. Rather, scraper time. How the hell had someone managed to leave a coating of yellow-green grease on the skirting boards and wedged between each board? Don't ask.

Caz measured time in taped music, and chose an hour-long Fats Waller tape for the floor. She was halfway through the second side with the knees of her overall black and shiny before she reached the last filthy piece of boarding. She had gone through nine buckets of water. She sat against the wall and smoked.

Done.

The walls and ceiling arched over her in mucky magnolia splendour. Christ. Fats Waller swore he couldn't give her anything but love and she hauled herself up the steps. Washing the sour-cream paint left waves of grey just beyond her reach. Up the steps and down again, she targeted the ceiling and the first two feet of the walls before she'd let herself stop. She couldn't even drag herself up the stairs and on to the balcony for her legs were shaking. She sat against the back wall, popped a can of lager and rolled a cigarette. The unwashed height of the walls stood around her, a palisade of grime. She crawled on all fours towards the tape machine and hunted for something to make her get up and boogie just one more time.

The Pointer Sisters chugga-boom chugga-boomed, *I'm so excited!* It was wonderfully infectious and she straightened up, wincing. Outside the window, bands of sunlight lay like snow on the bare branches of the cherry tree. Beautiful! Half robot, half cowboy, she swaggered exaggeratedly slowly to the bathroom and swung the bucket into the bath and turned the taps on full. Rivers of panhandled grime swirled down the plughole.

Caz versus twenty years of neglect: it was germ warfare.

Mentally, she added a surgical mask to her list.

And two smoke alarms. Better to be safe.

Much much better.

The battle was over as the lamp on the green glowed pink. She turned the tape over for a final onslaught and flew at the decayed teeth of the radiators by way of establishing victory.

A good day's work. She hung her overall on the bannister, slopped brushes and cloths into the bucket. From the balcony, she saw children were getting shouted for their tea, the soppy old dog stood wagging its tail at its master and shuffling amiably after a tennis ball. *You want to keep throwing it away? Fine, I'll humour you and keep fetching it back.*

'All done for the day are you, pet? Well, well.'

It was the deaf old lady taking the evening air.

'I am,' Caz said.

5

Day Three
'Cigarette ash, biscuits and coffee, I guess,' said Caz in the carpet shop, 'let's be realistic.'

It was the sign reading DALY'S FAMILY BUSINESS – FREE ESTIMATE AND FITTING that decided her on this particular carpet shop. And a woman on the bus saying *I divent care what ye say, ye cannot go wrong with Daly's, mine's been down ten year and it's as good as new.* That was better than a centre page spread in the local free paper.

Josie had promised her ten days' decorating serfdom. She'd only held back until she knew the shape of her own work for the next fortnight. Josie was a landscape gardener, meticulous and visionary and much in demand. She never broke promises.

Suddenly there seemed to be an end to painting and decorating. Josie worked like she did, always pushing herself a little bit further before collapsing in a heap. It would be brilliant working together, devising carrots to keep each other going. One of the best was a must-finish-by date. Caz ordered her carpet for two weeks ahead.

And? Oh yes: two surgical masks, one for her and one for Josie, who'd be arriving at eleven.

She whizzed around the DIY store, no time for browsing; she flew into the off-licence and lugged her treasures up to seventy-seven. The pigeons rustled and rattled over the door: she smiled. Last night they'd been cooing a lullaby as she left. Someone in the pub had called them ratti flottati, shoot the buggers, Caz, but she'd given them a silent pledge of peace. Now she was working out how to stop them huddling right next to the balcony window and shitting down the glass. Without hurting them or scaring them. Someone else had suggested a model of an eagle to fly like a balloon from the edge of the balcony, but Caz had grown up in the countryside and knew that rooks and the like come to see scarecrows as little more than a halfway house between hedgerow snacks. Pigeons weren't daft.

She'd just buttoned her overalls and put the radio on when Josie knocked.

'Well, this is going to be lovely,' she said, dumping bags on the floor. 'I've got my brushes, my overalls, my fags – I've even made sandwiches.'

'I'm getting total sympathy with workmen,' Caz said. 'When I'm sitting outside and people say ooh, you'll never get finished that way, I just nod. It's bloody exhausting. Thank God I'm only a dilettante painter of pictures. I'd want a hundred quid an hour for this.'

'You need muscle, my girl,' said Josie, strutting all her five foot two like a bodybuilder. 'Give us one of those cans and show me the worst.'

'I haven't touched the bathroom,' Caz said, 'or the passage or the bedroom.'

'Christ,' Josie said, leaning into the passage, 'what do they call this colour? Tandoori orange?'

'I call it twice over with Domestos and five coats to cover. I'm just going to whitewash the lot,' said Caz. 'I mean paint. White everywhere. Good taste and low budget in total harmony.'

They decided to attack the folds of filth up behind the kitchen pipes. Josie didn't mind heights, so Caz started to sand the skirting boards. They played the Gipsy Kings until aching arms dictated a smoking break.

'Let's sit on the balcony,' said Caz, 'it's beautiful.'

'Working hard, girls?'

They smiled up at the thin wispy-haired woman who'd spoken. Arms folded, she pulled at her fingers and rubbed the nails nervously. She was pretty, but looked like she'd been out of the sunlight for a long time: there was a dustiness on her pale skin, and her grey eyes were huge and bright as a bird. There was something waif-like about her, her grey-lipped smile flickered on and off, showing strong teeth.

'Yes,' she said, stretching her thin neck to see into the flat, 'you're doing it nice. They offered this one to me, but I wouldn't take it, you see, I'm a very clean person and I can't work hard like I used to. My health, girls. I could see a month's work just clearing up, but yes, yes, there's two of you and you're young, young. I'm not so old, but don't you feel it sometimes?'

'You do,' Caz agreed, wishing for calm. She hated agitation and this woman was never still, almost hopping on the spot. A caged bird, jumping from one claw to the other, darting its beak at the wire, clashing a wing at anyone who came close.

'I'm at seventy-four – until the people at the office find me a better place, you see. Seventy-four, just down there,' the bird woman said. 'If you need anything, just knock, I'm not being funny. Only make sure you don't knock next door to me. Mad.'

She nodded and winked and stretched her neck to bring her face close to Josie.

'There's some strange people round here,' she hissed, one eye rolling as if she feared something wicked sneaking up behind her, 'you have to be careful. That's my mistake, you see, I always think the best of people and then they go and do the dirty, the bastards, excuse my language.'

'That's always the way,' Caz said.

'Ah, you understand,' said the woman, nodding wildly. 'Yes. But I like to help. Now if you need to leave your key, I can let people in if you need to be out. I don't mind. I like to be friendly. Your key would be safe with me, you see. There's some you can't trust. Safe with me.'

'Well, that's kind,' Caz said, 'thank you.'

'I must get on,' the woman said. 'Don't take me wrong and don't forget about that neighbour of mine. Neighbour! Well, she lives next door . . . she's dangerous.'

She showed no signs of getting on beyond dancing backwards and forwards, flicking the ash from her cigarette over the balcony. Another woman came towards them and the bird woman drew herself up and turned her back with disdain. The woman passing by smiled at Caz and Josie and tapped her head at the rigid back.

'That's one of them,' she said, when the woman had gone, 'I know all about her. She steals from the window-boxes at night. Oh, hers is lovely thank you very much and everyone else's is a mess after she's been by. Thinks she's something clever. We'll see.'

She pulled faces like a child in a playground, then smiled beatifically. 'But you're nice, good class of girl, I can tell,' she crooned. 'Don't forget, number seventy-four.'

'Seems harmless,' said Josie when she'd gone.

'Yeah,' said Caz.

The day raced by, all the old ladies clucking that it was a lot of work and glad there was someone to help. Such a lot to do.

6

Caz went back to South Pendleton, declining Josie's invitation to the pub. There were only three days to go before the removal men would come. She'd found them in the local free paper, Dose of Salts: *'We'll get you shifted – FAST!'* Dose of Salts was Ted and his brother Gary and they assured her she wouldn't have to lift a finger, leave that to the men, pet. Which was fine by her since she was paying the men. Tonight was for packing.

Two women sat on the bus in the seat next to hers, both holding shopping bags like awkward children on their laps. One wore pearly rimmed glasses and a hat whose single blue flower waved like an antenna. The other had purple hair and was straining to light the cigarette she'd jammed between frosted apricot lips. The lighter slipped in her blue net gloves and she sighed.

'*Every time you say goodbye . . .*' her friend's voice and the blue flower quavered out of sync. '*I die a little*,' she stated out of the side of her mouth.

'I *cry* a little,' the glasses glinted. 'I'd put money on it.'

'Well, I'm sticking wi' die,' the blue net gloves dropped the lighter into her handbag. 'Don't forget there's *wonder why* as well and where would you stick that?'

'Reet,' said her friend, flower bobbing like an exclamation mark, 'Ah'm going to run it right through. Divent interrupt us, man, it's hard enough with all these bags.'

'Ah told ye we'd be best wi a taxi,' the smoker exhaled, 'but ye wouldn't have it. Naa, ye says, we'll spend all the money we've saved.'

'Had yer wisht,' said blue flower, 'listen to us, man.'

'Well,' smoke rose in a derisive puff, 'Let's hear it.'

'*Every time we say goodbye, I cry a little*,' she nodded more or less in time, '*Every time we say goodbye, I* – ye knaa, I'd forget me head! – naa, I've got it! *I wonder why a little. Why the Gods above me* . . . what are ye laughing at?'

'This lass'll think we've a tile off,' her friend wagged her cigarette at Caz. 'She'll have us down for out on a day pass from St Zach's. It's a song, pet, one of the old ones. "Every Time We Say Goodbye". Ye'll not remember it, a bit lass like ye.'

Caz smiled. She'd always been taken for ten years younger than her age. Her and Ben, both. Half fares on the buses, the Spanish Inquisition in pubs and clubs . . . she carried her birth certificate for years. In spite of everything, she still didn't look her age and now she always carried her passport, just in case.

'I know it well,' she said, 'I've got Ella Fitzgerald and Dinah Washington singing it. But I can't think is it cry or die. They both sound right. Maybe there's three verses. With an instrumental bit.'

'Well, our instrumental'll be David on the piano and it's not fair. David'll shite himself. We don't have to do it at all,' the blue flower bobbed, 'we could do that one we did at Christmas.'

' "Son of a Preacher Man," ' the smoke came through a smile.

'Not that I'm saying ye're right,' the petals were a blur of indignation, 'but David couldn't play without us to follow. Do ye knaa "Son of a Preacher Man", do ye, lass? It's a bit more modern, like. It's for the old people in Chicago. I think they'd like a bit laugh.'

'What we dee, lass,' the smoker leaned forward, 'it's a duet like, the two of us. And we crack on we've both been seeing the same lad. The son of a preacher man.'

'I know,' Caz said, smiling, 'I saw Julie Andrews and Ethel Merman do it on the telly, years back.'

'I told ye!' the blue flower was pizzicato with excitement, 'I said to ye, it was Julie Andrews and ye said she'd never sing a song like that. And I told ye it was Ethel Merman and ye said was I right in the head?'

'Well, ye can be Ethel Merman, man,' the smoke came out in a long stream. 'I can just see meself in one of them habits, ye knaa, like a nun, running over the hills . . .'

'What's she like? This is Chicago Con Club, a bit stage ye couldn't hang yer washing across and she's away with "The Hills are Alive"! Did ye ever!'

'Well, ye knaa, I can get into the spirit, can I not? No, lass, I sing the bit *he was, he was, the son of a preacher man*, and she goes, all hands on hips, *he was, was he? Son of a preacher man? I'll have him hung* . . . It's a bit fun.'

'Well, it's my stop,' Caz said, 'good luck!'

'Take care, lassie!'

Caz swung down the stairs to the lower deck.

'I don't know why they dress like that,' said the blue flower, craning to watch her walk down the street, 'nothing but black. It was only widows had to wear it in our day.'

'It's the fashion, man, it's in,' she-who-would-be-Julie-Andrews stubbed out her cigarette.

'Aye. Our Julie's Elizabeth's the same. I said to her, yer nanna'll get ye a new outfit, pet, I know it's hard making ends meets. A grandbairn of mine dressing out of Oxfam! She laughed, she says, oh, Nanna, I like me clothes. Clothes? I says, ye're only wearing tights wi the foot gone and a T-shirt. She says I'm out of date. And ironing? They wadn't knaa which side of an iron to use!'

7

Caz and her unironed/Oxfam/nothing-but-black clothes walked up the garden path with all the panache of Ethel Merman: '*I can hear a lark somewhere, begin to sing about it . . .*'

Bugger the landlady! She stomped upstairs.

Inside her flat, she dropped the sneck. There was a letter from Charlotte, her only regular correspondent. She'd have to let her know about the move pretty damn quick: no way did she wish to leave a forwarding address. She put on a Dolly Parton tape, smiling at how much she liked Dynamite Dolly and how uncool that was. She popped a can of lager and sat on the floor. Let the packing wait a while. She opened Charlotte's letter.

Well, Caz!
Don't worry about the letter imbalance! I have, after all, bugger all else to do here. That's not a guilt trip, by the way, I know what you're like! I've actually been very busy. Some sort of fellowship has adopted our sheltered wing of Elm Villa and our lives are radically changed. They've taken me swimming.

That was strange: I felt self-conscious, pathetic to need two grown people to help you into a pool, but there were five of us, so it didn't really matter. It was more the physical weakness that got to me. I'd had this absurd idea that flexing my arms along with Lizzie at eight in the morning was keeping me fit. I loved it when she did exercises for arthritic people, you know, stuff like putting your fingertips together, drawing a figure of eight with your nose. I was feeling ready for an arthritic Olympics. Just getting into a swimsuit brought me out in a sweat.

But the water was wonderful, I felt weightless, I felt like a dolphin that's been in dry dock. Do you remember when we went swimming in Limehouse Basin and Jay insisted on greasing herself all over against pollution and couldn't get out? Well, our little quintet of crips was in the same situation. It's something that makes people wince, the way we joke.

Daisy started it – her bedsit's next to mine. I told you we play poker and she smokes little cigarillos? She calls Mick Long John Silver: he came off his Harley. She's got nicknames for all of us. I'm Sweet Legless Charity – supposed to have a drink problem. She's Armless Anna. She says, 'Don't mind me, I'm armless. My bike had a run in with a bus and I've got the stump to prove it.' As I say, people wince, but it's cheered us all up. I can't stand hallowed tones of compassion. The League of Friends specialises in that, they talk to us as if we're slightly deaf and retarded.

Daisy gets furious at that, she shouted at one of them the other day. 'So I've got a bit missing and I'm waiting for spare parts! At least it hasn't hit my brains.' Exit one distressed League of Friends lady, snuffling into her Jaeger scarf.

It's attitude, isn't it. I mean, you took the bull by the horns and moved away. So brave! It is, Caz, you didn't know anyone in Newcastle four years ago. I often thought – hours and hours of it, my dear! – that Trimdon House was my life. When it ended, so did my life. I think we had everything; well, we did, and we thought it would last forever . . . But at the same time, everything we did was betting on a future, all the painting and sculpting, even my flags were waving and saying, hey, notice me, I'm here.

Since then, I've just lived as if there is no more tomorrow. The dawn comes up and I'm awake, thinking, so fucking what? Jay said she wanted that on her grave. Jay Martin, the dates and *then SO FUCKING WHAT? But since Daisy's been here, I've started making plans. Just little things, like tomorrow morning, I'm going to feed myself breakfast. Tomorrow evening I'm going to play backgammon. It was Daisy that got hold of the worthy fellowship to adopt us all. So now it's, 'Next week I'm going swimming.' Small steps, if you'll pardon the expression. Daisy is cheerful, foul-mouthed, flirtatious: alive. She won't be here long, but then again, I can see an end to being here now. Out of my shelter and into the real world again.*

What a lot about me. Thanks for your cuttings about the Gardez! Gallery, everybody here was v. impressed by my mate in a Real Newspaper. Come and visit. Mick thinks you look like Ulrike Meinhof, which is a compliment from him. Daisy says you sound like a right hard case, ditto. My League of Friends lady wondered if you always painted pictures 'like that'. She was a bit thrown by the references to S.E.X. That's another thing we're supposed to have lost. Daisy's been threatening to snog Mick, just to keep in practice, she says.

But you looked wonderful. So fierce! Ben used to say you looked like a giant otter, your eyebrows give you that surprised, questioning air. But such a softie!

I'll write again soon. You must be feeling a bit lost, now the exhibition's over. Any plans? (Like visiting moi?) We're going to The Rocky Horror Show tonight, courtesy of Daisy who's got a friend in the cast. So I'm actually going to try some make-up.

Well, what about this, Caz? A happy letter from Elm Villa! Miracles will never cease, fortunately.

Charlotte. Take care.

New beginnings all round, Caz thought.

And time to pack.

There wasn't a lot, really. Caz didn't acquire or collect very much. It was more that things were delicate or awkward shapes. The most difficult things were the models. Merrilegs the roundabout horse, for example. And Gladys the pantomime dragon. Demelza the flying pig would need careful handling: they were all too big to even try and cover. She wondered how Dose of Salts would manage.

She settled to tissue-wrap the seventy-seven porcelain fungi she'd made one year, each one finer than an eggshell, so fine that on the wide attic windowsill the sunset glowed through them like fire. That had been a pottery class two winters after Trimdon House, self-chosen therapy. The tutor was brisk and enthusiastic, but he gave up with her after three sessions, when it became clear that technique and texture and throwing on the wheel didn't interest her. All she would do was fungi, she didn't know why, and when they were done, she left the class.

Seventy-seven fungi . . . she paused with recognition. 77, Galleon Heights! But why fungi? Well, why not. She had a passion for miniatures – she and Ben had sat up stoned all night once modelling a herd of Das dry-fast elephants, twenty-one of them, from four inches high down to three millimetres. Jay had joined them after the clubs had closed and made wellington boots, four for each elephant, in case of floods. *What did you do in your youth, Caz?* She shook her head.

Oh, the ladies on the bus. She got up and found her Dinah Washington album, *The Swingin' Miss D*. 'Every Time We Say Goodbye' had just two verses. The pizzicato flower would have lost her bet: the word cry didn't feature at all.

8

Next day in Miston, it was mid-morning when the bird woman rattled at the door.

'Your electric's not on,' she said, peering downstairs, 'I've brought you a thermos. Mind what I said, they're not to be trusted, all nice to your face, and nyah nyah nyah about your business behind your back, in and out of each other's houses with it all day, I can't effing stand them.'

She swayed in the middle of the floor, eyes screwed up then bright and wide open. 'It's lovely to plan a home, isn't it,' she said, lighting a cigarette.

'Yeah,' Caz said. 'I mean, I know this is hard work and everything, but it's better than having to make do with someone else's idea of decoration. And furniture.'

'Private landlords,' the bird woman twisted her mouth as if spitting, 'they give you the old rubbish they don't want and charge you for damaging it. I know, mind, since I've been back in Miston, I've always been council. But I was in London, girls, many years ago. I'll tell you about it sometime. Tottenham. Tottenham. Tottenham. Do you know it?'

'I know Stoke Newington,' Caz said, 'I used to go to the Jewish bakery at Stamford Hill – Grodzinski's?'

'Yes, yes,' the bird woman nodded. 'Well, I was married to an Egyptian, oh I could tell you stories, his family was cruel to me, set him against me. My little boy lives down there, the family wouldn't let him go and I had to, you see, for my nerves. I was glad to be rid. Not my little boy, well he's grown up now, but the family . . . They didn't want to lose him, their son, my husband, their grandson, my little boy, and they didn't care. I'll tell you about it sometime. I never trust foreigners now, and it's better that way. I must be getting on.'

'Well, it's kind of you to bring us a thermos,' Caz said.

'Just pop along and knock when you've finished with it,' the bird woman said. 'Seventy-four. Or if you want a refill. It's nothing to be friendly and helpful. And remember what I said about next door to me. She's trying to drive me round the bend, I'll give her a fight one day and then we'll see.'

She clenched her pale fists, then tottered to clutch Caz's arm, gasping out rattling laughter.

'I'm Serena,' she said, suddenly standing upright and dignified.

'Caz, Josie,' Caz said.

Serena shook their hands formally; her hand clasp was limp and damp. 'I'd better get along,' she said, 'my Friend should be calling in any moment now. You know what men are like, can't be kept waiting. But Lennie's a gentleman. I'll tell you about it sometime.' She winked and left, smiling ferociously.

'Do you think she's nuts?' Josie asked.

'Probably,' Caz said. 'Seems harmless. I wonder what the gentleman friend's like. Do you think it's true, about Tottenham, Tottenham, Tottenham and the Egyptian husband and the child?'

'What, do you think she was lying?' Josie said.

'Necessary fiction,' Caz said. 'You know when I was working with the prison rehab group? My dear, the tales of tragedy! She, he, it, done me wrong, but *good*! Bastard lovers, bastard screws, bastard DHSS. Sometimes they'd forget they'd told me one thing and tell me another. Always worse than the last. There was always a grain of truth there, but people get fed up with hearing the same tale of woe long before the hurt has gone. I mean, how do you deal with real deep pain?'

'Get blasted,' Josie said, 'drown your sorrows and bore your friends all over again. It's no solution.'

'Yes,' Caz said, laughing, 'if reality offend thee, pluck it out. Invent another disaster. Serena's probably had an awful life and no one around who cared enough. She's probably said it all so often now she believes it anyway.'

'I wonder what her life's been like,' Josie said.

'No doubt she'll tell us about it one day,' Caz quoted her anxious new neighbour.

'Yes,' Josie said, 'it's always been little things with me. When little things go wrong and you feel like they're too much, you feel like a fraud for moaning about them, you almost wish something major had gone wrong. Last year, my tap was leaking and I just lay on the floor and howled. People said, oh well, get a new washer. Which was perfectly reasonable.'

'But you didn't feel perfectly reasonable.'

'No. I wanted someone else to get a new washer and put it on and I felt stupid, because it was the last of a whole series of silly little things: my bike had a puncture, the electricity bill was huge, the latest job was turning into a pain, the cat wouldn't eat, I'd burnt the toast that morning, the big job I was counting on fell through. Nothing catastrophic, just all too much. Things can get out of proportion when you live on your own. The tap was the last straw.'

'What did you do?' Caz asked.

'I had that party, remember? That cheer-me-up-party? Everyone had to be nice to me all evening.'

Caz nodded. She'd thought it was a brilliant idea, this invite from out of the blue, demanding that she cheer up her friend. Everyone who'd come had been lovely, not just to Josie. And all because of a last straw leaking tap.

'Cuppa tea?' Josie said, unscrewing the thermos. 'Courtesy of Serena in the middle of her troubles. That was kind of her.'

'How nice,' Caz said, then as she sipped, 'oh dear, sterilised milk.'

'Yuk,' Josie sipped too, 'never mind, it's the thought that counts. You can't look a gift horse in the mouth and start questioning its parentage. Count your blessings.'

'Every silver lining has a cloud,' Caz said, pouring the rest of the tea down the sink. 'A job worth doing is worth doing badly. We should be mixing paint, not proverbs.'

'Yes,' Josie said, levering off the paint-tin lid with a screwdriver, 'any colour you like so long as it's white.'

9

The carpet was going down first thing Sunday and Caz decided to spend the night – her first – at Galleon Heights. She brought a sleeping bag and a blanket, a candle, a torch, books. She feared sleeplessness, not knowing what night-time sounds her flat would make. Night-time was the acid test of a place – would there be drunks howling at 3 a.m.? Did Serena have an after-the-pub row with Lennie, her gentleman friend, as yet an unknown quantity? Did the quiet daytime green erupt with brawls and slammed doors all night?

Police sirens wailed after screeching tyres at about midnight. Uh oh, thought Caz. Earplugs. She looked out of the window. Two couples lurched along the path, eating chips and cackling over the night they'd just had. Otherwise, silence. She settled down to read and woke when someone next door went out at seven. It was weird to wake in a new place without a stick of furniture. No phone, either. All alone in a crow's nest. She had a bath and waited.

The men came to do the carpet at eight, as promised, three of them. Two grown men, Paul and Martin, and a wisp-chinned lad who was learning the trade. They refused tea.

'Take more than tea to shift this head of mine,' said Paul.

'Good night out?' Caz asked.

'One of the best, pet,' he said, laughing. 'Ah remember it all, that's the difference. He doesn't.'

Martin smiled under his Burt Reynolds moustache. He'd

already started measuring. She'd told Josie to come over about two: she guessed they'd be through by then.

Paul unrolled a length of carpet. Oh dear.

'Um,' she said, 'that's not the carpet I ordered. I mean, it's the right colour, but . . .'

She'd gone for the cheapest, foam-backed cord, cheap enough to replace when it wore through. This was upmarket, Berber effect, with small raised diamonds all over. It was beautiful.

'Lady says it's not what she ordered, Martin.' Paul was an expert lounger, an adept roller of convict slim tabs.

'It isn't,' said Martin, teeth gleaming a smile through the shaggy moustache. 'Tell her.'

'Wor gaffer,' said Paul slowly, 'she's a good gaffer. She has an agreement with the warehouse. If they cannot supply the carpet you order, then they put one on that's the right colour. You ordered that needlecord, didn't you, pet?'

'I had to,' Caz said, 'it was what I could pay for.'

'Ah,' said Martin, 'This is seven pound ninety-nine you've got here. Your needlecord's one pound ninety-nine. Of course, if you divent like it, we'll be on our way.'

Jesus! I do believe in fairies, Caz thought. And magic. And Father Christmas.

'Oh,' she said, 'I think I'd better keep my mouth shut. I just didn't want to suddenly get a bill . . .'

'Wor gaffer's done you a favour,' Paul said, shoving himself upright.

'She has,' Caz said. 'Lovely carpet I chose, isn't it.'

'The stuff you thought you were getting,' Martin said, 'it's rubbish. We sell a lot, but you'd be through on the stairs in no time. This needs underfelt on the stairs, mind.'

'Right,' Caz said, 'what's that cost?'

'Ah, we'll do it for six pound,' Martin said.

'Are you trying to bankrupt us, like, man?' Paul sounded tragic.

Caz laughed with Martin and the wisp-chinned youth sniggered.

'Well, we best get on,' said Paul.

'I'll get out of your road,' Caz said and went on to the balcony. She could have kissed them, stubble and hangovers and all.

It had been this way many times since she'd come to Newcastle. The first week she'd taken a drive with a stream and a rowan tree in mind. Away from London at last, the sea at her feet and the hills at her back in half an hour. Zig-zagging through villages and hamlets, she'd seen a dozen smallholdings where she could live. Then, at the foot of a long curved stretch of road, she'd been stopped in her tracks with the beauty of a giant beech tree by a deep golden river. She went there a lot: she'd seen an otter, a heron, she'd sheltered under the cat's cradle of roots and smoked in the rain one drizzly grey day. No one else ever went there: it was hers.

And now low budget cord had turned into luxurious diamonds. If she ever doubted her move from London, things like this came along like a caress, out of the blue. Gifts. Just what she wanted, only much much better.

'Are you the YTS trainee?' she asked the youth, hunched in a corner, watching the expert slashing and tacking as Paul and Martin worked.

'Summat like,' he said, 'they're always having a go, so I must be. I divent get paid, like.'

'Listen to the little toe rag,' Paul said. 'You're wanting paid now, is it? Martin, this lad of yours is getting out of hand.'

'He'll do,' Martin said. 'Go down the stairs, son, and see what a hash you can make of the bathroom.'

Caz lounged on the balcony and let herself feel Lady Gracious rich. Workmen already. Carpets. She smiled: she'd never had new carpets before, always raised an eyebrow at people who talked about their houses as if it mattered. Now she was one of them. In the pub last night, they'd laughed at the paint in her hair and her anticipation of what was happening now.

'Lost to the cause,' boomed Wayne, professional drunk and poet, 'buried in a welter of ideal home catalogues. Caz, shall I rescue you?'

She'd just stubbed out her cigarette when Paul and Martin and son joined her. 'Tea break?' she said.

'We're done,' said Paul, 'go and see.'

She walked in as if it was a strange land. The stairs felt springy, the living room was complete. Jesus, they'd even carpeted inside the cupboards and there was enough left over for mats and repairs.

'Gob-smacked,' she told the men, 'thank you. You're amazingly fast.'

'Aye, we're quick on the job,' Paul said, gentle flirting his stock in trade.

She gave them a tenner, said, get yourselves a pint.

They went and she closed her front door. It was ten o'clock. The only thing to do was lie in the middle of the living room, staring at the ceiling. God, she was tired. So tired, she was only aware of a dull ache and the sluggish heat of her eyelids closing. Almost asleep. Half fighting it: the feeling was delicious and the white ceiling swam overhead and soothed her.

Sleep possessed her, and she was lifted into the brand-new space, drifting against walls, riding invisible waves. Weightless. The lightbulb hung by her shoulder. As she floated there, a foot from the ceiling, she wondered if Michelangelo had lost all sense of gravity, lying flat in mid-air for years, dabbing paint on plaster only inches from his eyes. Lying so long his body and the scaffolding would be one, so familiar he'd forget both, only his moving fingers and the pictures in his soul would be real.

Her eyes were drawn to the boxed-in corner and she was suddenly alert. The tacks holding it were loose: Josie must have painted this bit, for she hadn't noticed it before.

She pulled herself along the fresh paint and climbed down the wall. She could see her body lying perfectly still and composed on the carpet. Sh! The baby's asleep. She inched towards the corner and pulled herself down to hover beside it. Her fingers rapped its surface and it rang hollow, nothing more than plywood.

10

Caz prised the plywood away and looked down into an empty shaft. Odd how plaster and paint turn bricks into a room, when just inches away there is a well of naked brick, and naked brick always means wind and weather: outside. She'd assumed the boxed-in corner masked down-pipes – why down-pipes? after all they went upwards as well – but there was nothing to be seen by craning and peering upwards. She found a torch in her hand. Why was that corner boxed in?

About a foot above her head she saw a metal bar clamped to the wall, another just within reach – and another. And so on as far as her beam could waver. Turning the beam, she could see none leading down.

Climb me, said the rungs.

She grasped the first one and climbed, feeling like Alice in Wonderland gone topsy turvy. There was just enough room for her shoulders to clear the walls and suddenly she wondered – were the rungs safe, why didn't they go downwards, should she have tied a piece of string to her waist before she leapt so blithely into this dark labyrinth? But what could she tie it to in the fresh-painted newly carpeted space? Who else – if anyone – had used this secret spine rising through Galleon Heights?

She heard voices at one point and held her breath until she was past them. Did the speakers have any idea that someone was climbing up the corner of their living room for no good reason other than to find where the shaft might lead?

Finally her head knocked against wood. Wherever she was going to, this was a door and maybe she'd almost arrived. She gripped the last rung with her right hand and her left fumbled and shoved at whatever was above her head. It gave as easily as the panel in her living room, with a squeak of small nails in old wood, and she pushed it back.

She was in daylight, under a bluer sky than she'd seen from her windows five floors below. She'd been expecting to be on the roof, or in some outraged someone's flat, improvising an explanation. Neither was right. Had someone made a roof garden? All around her was grass embroidered with daisies dipping and rolling away as if she was in the middle of the countryside. It felt firm enough as she scrambled out of the hole. It wasn't possible, but here it was.

Her feet felt light, the way they do walking in a park after city pavements. She could taste the sweetness of clover in the air and the grass held the scent of early morning dew. A bee buzzed towards her, hovered at the square hole at her feet then flew on with fat globs of pollen golden on its legs. Over the rise she could hear birdsong. There were grass stains on her hands where she'd pulled herself upright.

Where was she? Logic said she was hallucinating or mad, but her senses were more than satisfied. All that really worried her was walking away from the hatchway to Galleon Heights and not being able to find it again. Logic would have written off the iron rungs as access for workmen doing structural repairs and maintenance. She'd never forgive herself if fear stopped her exploring now she'd got this far.

She put her amethyst crystal beside the hole. It was the best common sense could come up with. When she reached the top of the rise, she looked back and it winked a rainbow her way – it said *go on, Caz, it's safe.*

At the top of the rise was a view like fairyland: the nearest she'd seen to it was when she climbed the Malvern Hills years before. She'd stood in a get-out-of-my-way wind, looking down from such a height that sheep were grains of rice and houses were monopoly pieces. Blank them out and the landscape was alive with *once upon a time*.

The land at the top of the ladder had a horizon peaked with soft blues and indigos, floating in strips of silver. Mountains sealed the limits of a valley and from their soft green roots to her feet, she could see nothing by way of a landmark. No roads, no pylons, no clusters of roofs, just woods and grass and a lake with a heart of black grass lapping waves of gunmetal gray and molten silver.

She ran down the hill to a rocky ellipse of shore and stood to catch her breath. The mountains stood closer now, and mist smoked the foothills, puffing upwards as if from the heart of a subsiding volcano. Only wisps of white rose as high as the bluffs, scarred with silver falls and shadowed scoops where rocks lay tumbled like coal.

The lake went as far as any ocean from where she stood. She had no idea where she was, or even when she was. The grass was soft green and though the trees were bare of leaves there was a haze like spider webs around the branches. Sunlight flowed along every twig, tripping at the suggestions of buds nudging through the bark. Birds were darting at the lake and diving from bushes to meadow grass and back to the trees: it was a busy time. Maybe it was early spring. That would be the same as Galleon Heights, a thought she found absurdly comforting.

She had every twentieth-century woman's fear of lonely places, raging that it should be so, but she couldn't detect any danger in this place. Someone had asked her once if she thought feminism had achieved its aims and after she'd got over laughing she said no. How could it have, when women shouldn't go out on their own; even broad daylight in a crowded street could lead to robbery, rape, attack, murder. She'd thought about it and decided that she had a simple solution to life: Everyone should be able to go wherever they want to and whenever they want to and be absolutely safe. That was her manifesto.

'Womanifesto,' Ben had said, laughing after a draggingly serious political dyke had been visiting. 'Christ, it sounds like you've got nits: is this a perwomanent problem?'

Absolutely safe. Up here in the land in the sky, she felt it had never been otherwise. She imagined the lake at night and could conjure up no sinister shadows beyond owls and foxes. No danger to her under the soothing shush of night-time branches. She loved walking in the woods by moonlight or clouded starlight, she and Ben had often done it. Since then, alone, she'd raged that it wasn't possible. Up here it would be as natural as breathing.

But there was more than safety. All her adult life she'd been wanting to belong somewhere. Since Trimdon House, her times of greatest ease had been travelling, when she spent a day or a week in one place, sometimes even a month if it felt right. Unless the people who lived there got too curious or too friendly and panic got her feet and thumb itching for a new road. A whole new set of unknown faces, a bed where a thousand faceless strangers had rested, before moving on.

Only once had somewhere felt like home. That was with a woman who'd given her a lift and said *stay with me for a while if you want to*. She lived miles from anywhere and played Billie Holiday and had a pond in the garden and didn't talk much. A week later, she'd kissed Caz goodnight. Caz didn't sleep after that kiss, her arms ached to hold someone, her body ached to be held. She left before dawn, she just couldn't handle it.

Out of the blue, she'd been given 77, Galleon Heights, hers for as long as she wanted. And beyond all reason, she'd strayed up an abandoned shaft into a land of lush untrodden grass, a silver lake and wild indigo mountains. Wherever this place was, she knew she could sleep without waking in the woods on the other shore. She could even curl up right here beside the flat rocks and sand and doze off if she wanted to. She'd never had such a strong feeling of *déjà vu*, everything in her knew this place by heart. It felt like home.

The mountain shadows flowed over the lake towards her and a breeze rustled the bullrushes and fluttered the reeds on the shore. It was time to go back and unquestioningly she turned and climbed the hill to – reality? She felt her heartbeat race as she neared the top of the hill; what if she couldn't get back down again?

But the square hole was there with its splintered cover lying beside it, her crystal was in the grass and she turned to see the view once more. To say goodbye? Who could tell. She could only wish for au revoir and she said it out loud.

Au revoir.

She wanted to pick a flower or a blade of grass as a charm, but this place was not to be violated. She wished she'd washed her hands in the waters of the lake, then they at least would hold a memory. Oh, peace to the fretting. Let her eyes store it, let her legs remember the spring in the turf and the solid shift and settle of damp sand under her feet at the water's edge.

She knelt by the hole and her hands and knees felt grass and earth as her foot searched for the first rung. She leant back in the shaft and pulled the board back into place.

The metal ladder seemed longer on the way down. Perhaps it was the open lightness of the air that exaggerated the darkness of the descent. She'd have to count the rungs next time. Down and down until her foot reached and found only bare bricks where light came in. She swung through the hole, not even fully expecting to be in her living room. But she was, standing on her new carpet with the smell of fresh gloss paint rising from windowsills and frames and skirting boards. Still floating, slightly dizzy.

All at once, she was lying on the floor, blinking herself awake. Her shoulders registered hard floor, her legs tingled with cramp. The corner was still boxed in and there was a loud knocking at the door, with Josie's voice shouting her name through the letterbox. She ran up the stairs half awake, confused that there was no trace of sand on her shoes, and her wrists were clean: surely there had been a grass stain?

Had she really been there?

Only the feel of fresh lakeside air lingered in her cheeks. She felt that she'd been torn away too fast. *I am not yet born . . .* She couldn't tell anyone, not even Josie. If she said anything, Josie wouldn't rest until they opened up the corner and explored. Loss was all too often the price of sharing.

Would she ever be allowed back?

'Caz? Caz! Are you there?'

Josie's voice through the letterbox hit her in the gut.

She opened the door.

11

'**M**y God, it's a palace,' Josie said, bouncing on the carpet and strolling around as if the ceiling had suddenly shot up three feet higher. 'You're just about done. You've got the all spills carpet, you just need a spills and thrills rug – a red wine rug? – and you can have parties. Soirées in Galleon Heights, what will the neighbours think!'

It was true. Paint and carpets had turned seventy-seven from an abandoned shell to a place where someone lived. She lived. Caz's place. Anything else was sheer luxury. Caz switched off her mindbending dreams dazzling around the valley and the lake. She knew as sure as breathing that getting there was a gift to her, a gift from God knows where and God knows why. It was a gift and also a secret.

'*We're* just about done,' she said, finding herself trying to block Josie's view of the boarded corner. No good. Josie crossed over and rapped on the panels.

'This is a bit of an eyesore,' she said, 'I suppose it's for heating pipes and things.'

'I had a look inside,' Caz said, faking a yawn and strolling over to the window, 'I can't say I recommend it.'

Josie stopped and backed away.

'There's things in there, moi dear, as a nice young lady like yourself wouldn't be too 'appy about,' Caz said, all wise Dorset yokel.

'Do I wish to know?'

'No,' said Caz.

'Spiders? Beetles?'

'Worser en thaaat, ooh arr,' Caz said, 'there's THINGS, moi dear and Oi caan't shock 'ee by sayin' what.'

'Right!' said Josie, wrinkling her lips, 'I'll leave it unexplored. But what are you going to do about it? Paper it over might be an idea. Stop the THINGS getting out.'

'No,' Caz said, her heart racing, 'I mean, what if they have to get into it to do maintenance and I have to rip me nice contour to bits? I'll just leave it for now and maybe do a fabbo *trompe-l'oeil* and make it vanish.'

And maybe she would. If the focus became the outer shell, people would concentrate on that and forget anything that lay behind. The main thing would be to make it look solid, all of a piece, rather than a trapdoor to magic. Now that every wall and ceiling was white and the all-stain camouflage carpet lay beautifully new, she could start dreaming about real painting; the fiddly layer upon layer of dragons and birds and sea-horses that swam through her mind most of the time. And of course, her things, those objects she'd made, or chosen from shops and barrows and markets, that would imprint a character on each room.

In a way she'd already begun, by painting her bedroom ceiling heaven blue, picturing wisps of sunset cloud and glow stars to lift it sky-high in the darkness. She wanted to use a lot of gold everywhere, Hundertwasser-inspired spirals to make the square cupboards elastic, turning sharp-angled corners fluid.

For now she stood looking out of the window. Just three weeks' heat had massaged the bare cherry-tree branches alive. Dark pointed studs were splitting into soft green folds of leaves and soon there would be tassels of flower buds before the sunshine explosion of popcorn blossoms in white or pink. She hoped for pink, pink was carnival.

The grass was new-mown, and the trio of gold stones looked bare, like ears under a ruthless haircut. The floppy gold dog yittered across the grass on its back, its happy owner calling it every nuisance under the sun as he stood enjoying the warmth and his pet, his friend.

A little Chinese girl pushed a pram along the path, scolding her doll to sleep. 'All right, I'll sing to you,' she said, exasperated. 'But just one song and you must be a good girl. I've got a lot to do apart from seeing to you. There, my baby, don't cry.'

'Bet her mum says just that to her,' Caz said, lounging over the balcony. 'I don't feel like working today, Josie, shall we go to the coast?'

'Yes,' Josie said, 'let's go on strike. Down tools and out.'

'Everybody out!' Caz laughed. 'Out – quick now, before Serena gets us.'

She locked the door and they ran along the balcony like kids bunking off school.

12

You could get a little overland train from Miston right to the coast. Part of the reason Caz had decided she was happy to live there. The next stop was Hollywood, a village that had sprawled into the town, much as Miston might have done but for The Drop. Spanned by three bridges – road, rail and metro – The Drop was a daunting moat, a natural boundary and maybe why Miston had kept its own ways when the rest of the villages clustered along the banks of the Tyne were colonised by high-rise estates and hidden under flyovers. Miston, Hollywood, Copperfield, Clay Bank, Harbour Point, Yard, Paris, New Orleans, Stoneburgh, Florida: glamorous names masking the suburban sprawl. And then the coast, Tynemouth. The little train hummed along, sometimes right on the banks of the Tyne, always a hint of the river in sight. Past Hollywood the track ran through an abandoned housing development, where the cheap pink buildings stood boarded up, scorched by wanton fires, tattooed with the graffiti of angry years past.

JIMMY HAYNES IS INNOCENT

FUCK THE POLL TAX

SANDRA WALTON IS A SLAG

LEGALISE POT

TROOPS OUT OF IRELAND

PEACE

Injustice, rage, jealousy, escape: the letters were black and blue, dripping and jagged. Jimmy Haynes was doing life, the Poll Tax was dead, Sandra Walton was married with three children and the police turned a blind eye to small amounts of cannabis. Those wars were over. Ireland still had roadblocks and terrorist murders. Peace was just a five-letter word.

Most of the glass in the windows was gone, but here and there a pane gaped black, where someone had lobbed a brick to leave a spider web of cracks. Some windows were whole and one still had a net curtain, now grey. Caz always wondered about this place. Years before, it was wild, copses and streams, lovers' lanes and a wild never-never land for children. Maling Woods.

Word was that property developers had wanted the land for factories. A mild protest from nature lovers, loud support from the Nanny knows best brigade deploring crushed cans, condoms and dirt-track scramblers: Maling Woods was under the hammer. But not for factories, oh no, the developers creamed off an EEC grant for housing creation. They called it River Mansions and twinned it with Berlin. They built dangerously and welcomed the worst of all Tyneside's council list: the drug-runners, the joy-riders, those in chronic rent arrears. Within eighteen months, the new estate was a leper colony where policemen and firemen feared to tread. Within two years, it was condemned.

The developers rubbed their hands.

But the late eighties brought bankruptcy, leaving only vacant squalor as an ugly testimony to greed. Even squatters hadn't bothered moving in. It was that bad. The final nail in the coffin for River Mansions was a gangland kidnap and murder: a gruesome sculpt of two burnt-out cars bit into the masonry of one building and another was acned with police bullets. Rumours and ghosts more powerful than barbed wire and snarling dogs scared off even the boldest and wildest intruder. Hollywood faced away from it, Copperfield drew its terraced skirts firmly to one side and built a wall twenty feet high. River Mansions was dead and hopeless, as likely to come to life again as the poisoned acres of Vietnam sprayed by Agent Orange.

Clay Bank was a different story. Cheerfully criminal, resisting all attempts at high rises with a year's rent strike culminating in a truce where Brussels arbitrated and signed cheques. Then an amnesty and every back-to-back was given an indoor bathroom and a redecoration grant.

Caz could have got a house in Clay Bank and had toyed with the idea. Clay Bank was colourful. An evening in the local pubs put an end to that. You had to be hard as the hobs of hell to live here, not flicker an eyelash at the Dickensian thievery and whoring that passed for a night's entertainment. She'd stick out like a sore thumb, be a target for curiosity and housebreaking unless she could trade something with the local mafia. She didn't imagine that murals and portraits would come high in the barter stakes. She sat out the evening with Josie and her pint with every eye and every mouth working overtime at sussing them out.

Caz needed to be anonymous where she lived, or rather, as anonymous as she chose. She had nightmares about Clay Bank and being forced to live there. The next day she went back to the housing office and they sent her to Galleon Heights. Every time she went on the train through Clay Bank she smiled – a mixture of relief and self-ridicule. Newcastle Council wasn't in the business of forcing you to live anywhere.

13

Harbour Point was a snooty little place, white walls and landscaped gardens sandwiched into a dip between two shoulders of rock: natural boundaries again, dictating the shape of it, protecting it from zealous suburban reform. She'd had upmarket Sunday lunch here, luxuriating in cobblestones that looked newly swept and Victorian lamp-posts bright with new paint. Like most rich areas, Harbour Point had an air of sterility: children and dogs didn't feature and the streets were clean and empty like the Disneyland version of an English village.

Caz had often fantasised about living somewhere like Harbour Point. Her time in South Pendleton under the eaves of Mrs Greatheart was the closest she'd got. Apart from a stifling two months nannying in Hampstead. Both places were full of arty-looking types who had Jaeger written all over them. Hampstead had actors and writers and wannabes: she'd been jostled by Bill Oddie in the post office and once, she'd sat in a café at a table next to Peter O'Toole. South Pendleton had acupuncturists and psychotherapists, moneyed eyes burning with religious fervour. Wealth recreated 'natural' bliss: to Caz, it felt like Versailles when Marie Antoinette became a shepherdess. Good clothes and even better accents projecting all over the supermarket. The upper middle classes with their absurd rules and snobberies, armchair socialists, leafleteers: she summed it up as the lady prison visitor attitude to life.

Harbour Point station was ornate Victoriana, wrought iron roses painted white and gold, a ticket collector oozing with self-importance and cap-tipping subservience.

The train pulled away.

All the dinky cottages in Harbour Point used to be worker housing; some were fishermen, some were sailors. Most rose in the dark and climbed the cobbled road to the dry docks to weld and rivet, refit and load. Yard had built some of the finest war-ships and freighters this century. Now wire-netting sagged upwards to a rusty twenty feet and barbed wire marked the edge of Yard. Peeling notices warned of security patrols. For now the ships went to Malta, to Tunisia, anywhere that people worked cheap and long, like the people of Yard had to before the unions. The skyline was pinked with cranes, pulleys swinging in the wind, rust streaked blue and bleached turquoise, like children's toys abandoned in the rain.

The River Tyne was screened by warehouses, high windows hanging from one bolt, iron doors bent with their own weight and stillness. Only thirty years ago, this place was alive with buses bringing in the workers, tea chests and containers heaped to the roofs, men swarming over decks with brushes and blow-torches. There had even been a tram to service the docks: now the tracks were edged with tufts of grass and wild cats sprawled across the rails bickering.

Paris and New Orleans merged in a waterfront of frenzied entertainment. Some canny someone had seen the slump coming and no sooner was a warehouse empty than they turned it into a pub, a restaurant, a waterfront hotel. One was an ice rink, another a roller skating rink. Paris had a funfair open all year on the site of Magnum Shipping. '*For the Time of your Life, bring your Kiddies and Wife.*' New Orleans had Big Mama Murphy, a real Mississippi paddle-boat holding a disco, restaurant and cinema. Twice a day, every day but Christmas, Big Mama wallowed out into the middle of the Tyne and cruised all the way along to Tynemouth decked with fairy lights, pounding out steam and music. The owners had wanted Big Mama to go inland, past Miston and Lower Pendleton to the heart of Newcastle, but the residents of Harbour Point had campaigned so furiously that they were stopped. Yard they would tolerate, a sad memorial to the great working class and the past, but the present-day fiesta of Paris and New Orleans was unspeakably vulgar, a sad sign of the times. To be shunned and scorned.

'We could get off 'ere, chérie,' Josie said, ''ave a leetle wander in Gay Paree?'

'It's better at night,' Caz said, 'I always feel cheated in the daytime when there's roundabouts and rollercoasters. It's the lights I love, and they just get swallowed in the daytime. Maybe on the way back?'

'You're right,' said Josie, 'only it always feels dangerous, me duck, all them boys.'

'I like to live dangerously,' Caz said, 'makes me feel tough. Swoon away, my girly, big Caz is here.'

'Well, that makes me feel better,' Josie said, giggling.

'Oh, don't let the hippy drag fool you,' Caz said, 'I may have the body of a twelve stone weakling, but I have the heart of an old fashioned butch.'

14

The train terminated at Stoneburgh and they waited on the platform. Every station had the studded iron pillars and ornate arches of a more elegant age and Stoneburgh had copied Harbour Point with a lick of paint on its ancient finery. Only it was municipal red and municipal green rather than upmarket white and gold.

'If we were abroad, this would be colourful,' Josie said.

'Well, I feel like I'm permanently on holiday since I moved here,' Caz said. 'Everyone in London keeps saying, Caz, what do you DO in Newcastle, isn't it all flat caps and whippets? They think I'll be growing leeks soon. I might, if I get an allotment. They still think I'll go back to London, you know.'

'It's what you're used to,' Josie said, 'I was born here, did college, came home. What's your excuse?'

Caz thought for a moment to hide her panic. That was as close to a personal question as Josie had ever come. Keep it light, she ordered herself.

'Well, I did college in London,' she said. 'People tend to hang around the place where they've had their first years of freedom, so I did. You know. Then, well, it just got a bit flat. After years in the Great Metrollops, I got an overwhelming desire to reduce the stress factors.'

'You always seem pretty laid back,' Josie said. 'Wayne says you're so cool it's alarming.'

'Camouflage,' Caz said dramatically. 'The inner me bubbles

with uncertainty and fear, my dear. Where's your violin? No, it was London really. When your greatest moment of joy is finding a broken parking meter or getting too much change because the pub's busy, then I say Koyaanisqatsi.'

'That's impressive,' Josie said, 'what's it mean?'

'It means "a way of living that calls for a change in your way of life". It was a Hopi Indian word; Philip Glass made a movie of it. Just images, speeded up, slowed down, countryside, city, industry, amazing images and music. I saw it a thousand times, blew my crazed artistic brain apart.'

'Have you ever been into Stoneburgh?' Josie said. 'It's like that. Used to be based around a quarry, hundreds of little men carving gargoyles and tombstones. They did the restoration work for St Paul's, I think. Now it's a marina, windsurfing and hot dogs, part of it's got simulated waves for surfing.'

They stood for a while in silence. Josie had been surprised when Caz had become a friend. After all the build-up about Caz Hewson, a real London artist, coming to Newcastle, she'd been intimidated. Caz dropped in to the arty pub frequently, her dry one-liners only adding to the hype. They thought of her as a recluse, then Caz had phoned her one day and said, hey, let's meet for coffee? Josie found that the brittle one-liners were a shield for shyness. She played with the idea that it was a chat-up; she wouldn't have minded, but relaxed when it wasn't. Over the years, they'd become best mates, but she wondered if she'd ever known very much about Caz: mention of London brought only slender anecdotes that revealed little. Even talk of romance Caz fenced expertly, deflecting the conversation on to anybody and everybody else. A neat way of saying shut up and mind your own business. Well, it suited Josie. She'd given up with close encounters of the human kind: roots and leaves were much more responsive.

A new train pulled in.

'Well, Koyaanisqatsi,' Caz said.

Josie laughed as the doors hissed open.

'To the coast, my man, and don't spare the horses!'

15

A roguish old fellow boarded the train at Florida, the next stop, eyed up the empty carriage and came and sat opposite Caz and Josie. Caz liked this as well: in London, he'd be a flasher or a loony. On Tyneside, he was just friendly, carrying his history around with him and wanting to share it. He wore a dandyfied velvet jacket and thick velvet cords tucked into his boots, the old leather polished like wood, reheeled, resoled, so long on his feet they were part of him. He put a carrier bag on the seat beside him.

'Florida,' he said, 'ee, how my son laughed when he heard his father was gan to live in Florida. I said to him, mind son, there's nae orange groves and sunshine here. Well, we're not so bad for sunshine, like, these days. It's five year since we had what I'd call a winter. Snaa as deep as yer windies, and ice fit for polar bears! There was wan winter ye could skate across the Tyne, save yerself a canny bit boat fare, like. I've known years when it wad keep ye locked behind doors till February. Ye'd come oot of yer hibernation and lookit the sky, see a big shiny thing up there and ask yerself, what the hell's that? The sun I'm meaning. Aye.'

'No, it's been mild,' Caz said, 'there's daffodils all over where I am.'

'Ye're not from round here,' said the old man, nodding.

'Miston,' Caz said.

'Oh, Miston,' he nodded, 'I've a sister there. Used to be in Bell Court, thirty year she was living there. Then her man, ye knaa, passed on and she was put in Anchorage Point. Barquentine Walk, she is. Lovely flat, mind.'

'I'm in Galleon Heights,' Caz said, 'it's good.'

'Won an award, that place,' the old man said. 'I visit her, like, for me dinner every couple of weeks. She's geet happy there. Seventeen years she's been in. No complaints. I'm a fisherman, meself.'

'Are you fishing today?'

'Naa, naa,' the old man laughed, 'I was out on the trawlers, me. I had a coble and all, used to get crabs and lobsters till the wife was sick of the buggers. I sold them to the hotels all along from Tynemouth to Yard. Made a bit coppers, like. You had to. And then I had the allotment. My family was Lower Pendleton. We'd a bit allotment in The Drop. But I cannot climb up from it, these days. I can get down, but as for up! I might as well think o' flying! Naa. And I'm too old to start sleeping in the shed. The wife'd gan light. I'm off to the wherry, and along Jack's Beach if there's nowt there. There's a bit beach there, all rocks and I'm after winkles. Ye'll not eat stuff like that now, will yez?'

'No,' Caz said, 'seafood's fine if it's prawns and shrimps and lobsters. Not crabs. Nothing slimy.'

'Haddaway wi ye,' the old man chuckled, 'they're a delicacy these days, ye knaa – winkles. I saw a feller with a stall outside the pub, selling seafood. This is in the town, me wife likes going in and I'll gan wi her. Well, he wanted fifty pence for a thimble full of winkles. Fifty pence, I says to him, that's ten shillin old money! I can remember when I was earning ten shillin a week, and I wouldn't have called the Queen me auntie. I couldn't bring meself to buy the buggers, but I've had a taste for them ever since. The wife says to us today, get out the house and gan get yerself some winkles, I'm sick wi hearing you wanting them. So that's me. The bairns are the same, winkle daft every one of them.'

Caz and Josie laughed. The old man nodded and laughed with them.

'Aye,' he said, 'I'll gan along the wherry and fill me sack then out on to the rocks for a bit smoke. That's wan thing I cannot stand wi these trains, no smoking. Ye'll be against it, any road, will ye not, smoking?'

'No, we both smoke,' Caz said.

The old man smiled. 'And are yez just out for the day? Are yez working?'

'We're just out for the air,' Caz said. 'Nothing like the sea air to blow away the cobwebs. I'm a painter, she's a gardener.'

'Is it,' he said. 'My daughter's a teacher down in London, ye knaa. Tries to get home when she can. Well, here's the station. Take good care now, lasses. Goodbye now.'

'Tarra,' Caz said, 'hope there's lots of winkles for you.'

'No bother,' said the old man, striding ahead of them and up the iron stairs two at a time.

'By, it's good to be alive,' he thought, 'me own dad was in his grave thirty years younger than me.'

He passed a Daily Star billboard that threatened MADONNA REVEALS ALL.

Lasses these days! Clarting about on stage in their underwear until his wife called him a dirty old man. Just teasing, like. He smiled, thinking of the wind-up he'd give her about the lasses on the train. *I'm not safe out of me own, ye knaa.* That'd get her laughing. They all looked so young these days and it was only when they spoke you got an idea they were years past being students. A painter and a gardener those two, funny jobs they went for. And living in Miston! By, when he was young, if you lived there it was because you'd been born there, you were dirt poor and all your dreams were of leaving.

'Young uns!' the old man thought, 'those two would be about our lass's age, thirties. And our lass a teacher, she's worked for her promotion. Our lass ganna be a headmistress! That's something to be proud of.'

When he was thirty, there were three bairns to feed and a look of worry in his wife's eyes every night in case he brought his tools home. And when he was young, his father was an old man, spent and bent like a used matchstick at forty.

'I wonder if they know what worry is, these young uns,' he told the wide horizon. 'It's a different world these days.'

Caz and Josie watched his busy figure striding ahead of them. 'I think maybe it'll be OK,' Caz said, 'getting old, I mean. What a nice bloke.'

'Blimey,' Josie flourished the words, 'I'm not even half his age and I couldn't get up the stairs like that.'

'Not enough winkles, my dear,' Caz said.

16

The station was in a tree-lined cul-de-sac, where the houses had leaded window panes, carriage lamps, yellow plastic boxes warning burglars that the property they were eyeing up was seriously alarmed. Privet hedges grew in severe rectangles, snow white nets said keep your eyes off our fixtures and fittings, thank you very much. It could have been any suburb anywhere, but for the airborne hint of the open sea. And the Venetian wash of sky that umbrellas the north east with its unique wide-eyed clarity.

The cul-de-sac ended at the main road to the sea and a steady gust of salt blew in their faces and drew them on. The tang of the sea spells adventure, even beside a tarmacked promenade and terraces of bed and breakfasts. It was the beginning of the season proper and the rooms would still have a winter mustiness and chill. By high summer, all the bay windows were wide open and the borders of every garden paraded ranks of bright plumed flowers.

Caz liked the haphazard feeling of off-season. People bent against the wind, trying to stroll along the promenade in winter coats blown tight as bandages round their legs. The Welcome Café all shuttered, last year's menu a spidery bleached parchment behind salted glass. Only a few amusement arcades were buzzing and even these hadn't bothered to light up their come-into-my-parlour neon arrows and flashing dollar signs. Summer, and the whole sea-front was alive with glitz: lights lit up to make dancers, pink bulbs flickering a tireless high-kicking cancan. The Lee

Marvin growl of a holographic cowboy goaded people into hopeless duels. Hundreds of fluffy turtles and kittens and gorillas were a squashed scrum inside a glass tank, glass eyes twinkling under the lights. A silver crane juddered above them, its mechanical claw lurching down in one empty grab after another. Father Christmas nodded and clapped with every try, booming *ho ho ho, boys and girls, have another go*.

The bingo boards glittered night and day in the summer months, women perched on shrunken cocktail stools feeding them with coins. The floor was riddled with stiletto prints and cigarette burns. They could win tins of skimmed milk powder, processed peas, corned beef, tinned ham, fruit bowls, vases, and even a six-foot-high fluffy Pink Panther if they gambled seven full houses. If anyone had gambled no one had won, for the Pink Panther's head was grey with dust, its nose and paws tarry yellow as if scorched.

Going into an arcade off-season felt like slipping into a speakeasy during Prohibition. In the summer, the doors were fastened wide open, you and your day-glo pink stick of candy floss swaggered into the mêlée, jostling for the machines. Off-season, the wind bowled you hard against the Las Vegas-style door handles and you had to push hard against heavy plate glass to get in. There was only a gaggle of school truants languishing between the buzzes and pings and simulated racing car noises. Pale youths, punching buttons and swigging Coke, practising smoke rings and passing the tab on; sub-James Dean acned faces dreaming of grown-up glamour: money, cans of lager, drugs, girls. For the moment they played electronic roulette and gawped at the page three blow-ups stapled to the walls. It beat dropping into school.

Caz and Josie didn't merit more than a glance: women, yes, but too old to even think of, hopelessly unfashionable, nowhere near the pale teenage dreams of pouting lips, upthrust breasts and powerful welcoming thighs.

Their favourite game was Dead Man's Gulch, a fantasy shooting range with a saloon and a forest clearing straight from a B-movie western. You could shoot the piano player and start a frenzied honky tonk as his wooden hands beat mechanically up and down. Ping the cooking pot and a red-eyed possum head-butted the lid, waving its claws and screeching. Dead centre on a roulette wheel jerked the glass-eyed croupier alive to scoop up all the chips, nodding and grinning while the two gamblers beat their painted brows on the table.

Caz had played Dead Man's Gulch every time she'd been down to the coast and she grinned as she peppered the cooking pot until the possum was a jack-in-the-box blur. The gamblers bit the dust and the piano player out-gladded even the mighty Mrs Mills.

On to the papier-mâché splendours of the great outdoors! Much more of a challenge. A row of beer cans clattered off a log but only if you scored a direct hit on the label. In a tree stump, a psychedelic woodpecker shot out with eyes and beak a flashing staccato. If you kept your fingers pumping at the trigger a brown bear lurched side to side behind the trunk, growling. Dead drunk or dead, a panhandler lay face down at the stream and raised his head when you hit the stack of golden nuggets by his shoulder. The most difficult target was the owl, swooping jerkily from a tree to the saloon doors. For Caz, winging the owl was the grand finale: its horrified eyes flashed green and yellow, its wings flapped and it went HOO-HOO as loud as a train. HOO-HOO, HOO-HOO! and unseen motors whirred and unseen wheels clicked and the whole spectacle came alive again, swept by beams of red and green and lilac and yellow, like fireworks, like carnival.

'My shoulder's aching!' said Caz. 'Phoo! I love that.'

Dead Man's Gulch waited, silent and still. Josie slid coins into the slot and raised her gun, thundering away at the owl like a one-woman firing squad.

'Show-off, that's me,' she said, when the time was up.

'Let's go to the beach,' Caz said. 'Enough of man-made delights, I want to say hello to the ocean.'

17

Caz and Josie struck out separately. Caz's goal was the furthest rock she could reach – just to sit and smoke and absorb. Everything on the way fascinated her.

There were two wooden jetties whose dark skeletal arms reached across the sands. They had been deemed dangerous and wired off. The massive supports were squared tree trunks marching across the harbour. A crescent of giant Xs with the tops bleached by sun, sucked dry in the salt winds, furrowed like the hard bed of an extinct stream. Here and there, an arm was missing, a gashed stump remained and a log lay like a crocodile in the sand. They'd crowbarred the planks from the top to stop people walking there, but three teenagers were playing dare, leaping and shrieking as they almost lost their balance. The dregs of low tide sat around sunken rocks, dampened heaps of seaweed, sly tongues of water melted the sand from the feet of the jetty, barnacled and black with age. Seaweed hung from the legs in shaggy brown bunches and slime-green fronds clung to the wood just above the tidemark.

Between the jetties, the sea had left a lake where gulls floated calm as ducks on a pond. That peculiar northern light – eggshell blue, wild-rose pink – streaked the ripples into painted glass. The furthest jetty was a silhouette backdrop, a natural frame that held the salk lake and the birds perfectly. She stood until the whole scene was fixed in her mind.

On to the sea. Under her feet, she felt seaweed pop: bladder-wrack. She liked that name, a glutinous word with a whipcrack K to match the snap of bursting pods. She remembered summers at the seaside with her mum and dad, dipping in rock pools.

'What's that?'

'Anemone, crab, hermit crab, limpet, mussel, sea anemone, seaweed, bladderwrack.' Her mum knew everything.

She'd squatted, fascinated by the brown warty pouches, giggled because bladder was rude, wrack was rack and ruin; the rack was where hooded figures stretched twisted truths from their helpless prisoners. Sea thistle was Eeyore's thistle patch dusted with powder blue, sea anemone was a flower come to life, seashells were every colour and shape. Sea-horses came from a fine fairytale tapestry. *I do like to be beside the seaside*. Seaside was next to the sea where it all happened. *Beside the seaside, beside the sea*. Mrs Mills was gaudy summer razzmatazz.

Sea-water was slatey and blue, marvellously clear close to, whirling with grains of sand like gold dust.

Brownian motion.

Caz thought of a microscope where random dots dance forever. Invisible to the naked eye – a microscope was magic! Her mum and dad had bought her one, but it worked with a mirror and there was never enough sunlight. School microscopes were electric. She wished she'd told them, not just let it lie in the cupboard unused with them thinking she was frivolous and careless. She'd wanted it so much. Her dad would have worked out something with lights: when she was four, he'd made her a huge doll's house with papered bricks and real bulbs in the plywood ceilings.

Oh well, here she was, thirty years on with it all sitting in her head as bright as day. Walking on a beach hardly noticing how her feet found dry rocks like stepping stones on the way to the edge of the ocean. It was second nature.

18

She crouched by a rock pool garnished with sea-plants made of pink lace. Tassels of underwater grass gave sanctuary to crabs the size of her thumbnail. As a child she spent hours lying by rock pools with a magnifying glass, watching sea-snails toil along the rock, antennae finer than hairs sensing the way. Dozens of clear bodied creatures smaller than the eye could see, legs a silky fringe whirring through the water. Round glassy shapes in a dizzy whirligig, huge alien heads hovering then shooting away from shadowy danger. The water was alive.

Benthos.

They had been on the sea-shore, her and Ben, crouching by rock pools, eyes and lips saying *look*. A rock pool like this one, maybe a little more lush and lavish, for they were in Cornwall, where the sand is licked by the Gulf Stream and you can sit outside under palm trees.

'Look,' Ben said, 'benthos.'

'Uh?'

Ben's eyes were dancing. 'The flora and fauna at the bottom of the sea,' she said, mock teacher. 'It's Greek. Benthos, the depths of the ocean. So maybe this is benthos minor, a shallow little splash of benthos. Th'ocean bed, Caz.'

And when she spoke, they giggled and called it *benediction*. *If you take benzedrine, you'll find Ben's a dream.* Caz was more difficult. Casablanca, for example.

Give Caz a blank canvas and she'll be happy for hours.

Cazanova: PMT gave Caz an ovarian spasm.

Come with me to the Cazbah!

It was all play, word play, love play, playing new tunes. Sometimes they'd be playing at being workers for money to go and play on holiday. You sell minimum time for maximum money so that you can play better when your time's your own. Thinking about Ben now was like rereading a favourite book with a cracked spine and pages whose edges are golden brown. She knew every twist in the plot, she loved every phrase, and somehow every time there was something new.

Ben's words never intruded. Caz would have given anything to hear that voice again. She'd give everything, but what good would it do?

'. . . *his bones they are of coral made* . . .'

Oh well.

She walked further, the gravelly feel of limpet shells and barnacles under her feet. A dip in the rocks might hold water, but no canny little marine community would try to fix itself here. Four times a day the rising falling tide swept these rocks and they'd be as crazy as people building a village in the path of an erupting volcano. Down in the dark cracks between the rocks there was seaweed and mussels gathered like a clutch of eggs in an underwater eyrie. So small, yet their wiry roots had wedged into the sheer rockface and tethered them safe against anything the ocean could toss their way.

She was just a few rock leaps short of the shifting edge of the waves now. It was low tide and salt spray slapped over the edge of the rocks playfully. Or so a fool might think, for every so often the spray reared up like a phantom and flung down across the rocks as hard as hailstones.

Caz watched for twenty-one waves and noted where the fiercest spray could reach. She sat a careful foot away from its darkening stain and lit a cigarette, wasting three matches before she huddled round the flame and scorched her nose. The wind ripped the smoke into extinction and took her breath away. She pushed her hair out of sight and squinted at the horizon. She could almost see islands . . .

It had been one of the candlelit late-night dreams of Trimdon House. Ben had seen a colour supplement feature on islands for sale. Everything from a tropical white-beached paradise to a sparse atlantic outcrop of rock no one wanted and somebody owned. If they all got jobs, Andy and Alex and Charlotte and David and Jay and Ben and her, they could just about run to the wild bleakness of cold mid-ocean.

'Let's be practical,' David said. 'We'd need a boat and a generator, something to live in, boatloads of dried supplies, a radio . . .'

'Months of back-breaking labour against the elements, months of ice and rain,' Alex said softly.

'We could do it,' Andy said.

'Of course we could do it,' Ben said, 'if we want to. We can do anything we want. The worst bit is deciding.'

Caz could see her speaking, the firm way she moved her hands to go with the words, the flicker of amusement in her eyes. The island remained a dream for all the years they stayed together, and even afterwards, it haunted her. Maybe if they'd done it they'd all still be together. If only, if only and all too late.

It was strange and there was a kind of peace in it, but since she'd come to Newcastle, she no longer wanted an island. The sea was just a whisker away after all.

Josie squatted beside her and won the fight with tobacco and cigarette papers. The wind caught her long hair and blew it upwards. It whipped across her face like a giant spider in a horror film and she tugged dark strands from her mouth and tucked the whole mane firmly under her chin. Her lighter threw out a sheet of flame like an Olympic torch.

'Zippo,' she said, puffing, 'nice 'ere, innit?'

19

At three in the morning Caz sat with a cigarette, looking at the boxes. Glass. Glass. Records. Tapes. China. Kitchen. Books. Food. Paint. Paint. Paint. Shelves. Canvas. Her place never looked crowded and only when she had to pack did she realise how many objects simply accumulate. Pebbles, feathers, shelves, leaves, leaf skeletons . . . ordinary objects that spoke to her from the sea-shore or a hedgerow, *take me with you.* And immediately became magic, a whisper of the time she'd been there. Postcards, photographs sent in letters . . . *just thought this might amuse you . . . do you remember?*

She walked round the four rooms of the flat and was pleased that the wonderful arching beams looked in need of a coat of paint and the lino in both bathroom and kitchen was tacky. The decor gave an overall impression of elegance, but close to, with nothing personal to say anyone lived there, it was shabby. Dreck. The landlady's bobbly green three-piece suite was hideous once more, now that she'd folded away her tapestry shawls and silky rugs. Mrs P. Greatheart! Caz hoped her landlady really suffered with the next tenant!

Cleaning. She wasn't going to risk a speck of dust to give the wretched woman an excuse for keeping her deposit. She gave a wry nod of thanks to modern technology for cure-all easy cleaning sprays: hell, she'd purged 77, Galleon Heights until she was screaming. But to squander t.l.c. on the old bastard's beloved Property? She resented every sweep of the cloth. As she wiped

and scrubbed, she dreamed of a hundred and one ways to unsettle
Mrs P. Greatheart. God, she hated the woman! Slow down, she
told herself, she just ain't worth it. The moral of this story is two-
fold, my dear. One: don't rent a place where the landlady lives on
the premises. Two: avoid having your anti-establishment work
shown at the Gardez! Gallery and yourself publicised all over the
north east as a l-l-l-l-lesbian artist. *I am the monster!* No wonder
poor old Philomena Greatheart wants you out.

And there are ways and ways . . .

Caz smiled, paying particular attention to the bathroom.

It was a pleasant surprise when Josie rang at six thirty: she'd
promised to, but Caz wasn't holding her to it.

'I'll come over,' Josie said. 'I'll pick up bagels and bring a
family-sized thermos of coffee. You have to take care of your
workmen.'

Caz had saved her Fela Kuti tape for farewell music, pretty sure
that the wild wall of sound would irritate Mrs P. Greatheart more
than any other music she owned. Seventy drums and seventy
voices beat out defiance.

Zombie no go unless you tell im to go . . .

I am no zombie – but I'm going!

She grinned.

Dose of Salts was due at 10 a.m. sharp. She wanted to hand the
keys back at twelve o'clock midday, not a second before or after.
The doorbell rang. Ping pingi ping ping ping PING! Josie. They'd
reckoned that would rattle the landlady out of bed with annoyance.
For the first time in three years, Caz thundered down the stairs to
open the door with a loud *hi, baby!*: she used to pad around and
whisper *come in . . . be quiet*.

Josie set out breakfast.

'Bagels,' she said, 'smoked salmon, cream cheese, grapes. Plastic
knives, paper plates, a paper tablecloth, everything disposable.
And real glasses for juice, but then we break them. New
beginnings.'

'Oh, we can beat juice,' Caz said. 'I've got champagne.'

'When we get there,' Josie said, 'don't you think? Celebration?'

'You're right, Josie, would you do me – yet another – favour?'

'Ask away.'

'Could you pretend to be Mrs bloody Greatheart and inspect this place? I've Mister Muscled it all over, I don't want a thing to be wrong.'

Josie stood up and clasped her hands behind her back, setting her jaw like a monitor lizard.

'You'll have to imagine the tweed skirt and cashmere twinset,' she said, brushing at her burgundy overalls, 'and the rocks. Just remember, my girl, each finger of my hand is worth more than you'll ever earn. Economy and investment, Miss Hewson, economy and investment. Ha ha. How am I doing?'

Caz laughed. It was Mrs Greatheart to a T. The words were a glorious anomaly coming in an Edith Evans quaver from Josie's lips; the saurian jut of her jaw between curtains of thick hair: Josie said if she was blonde, she'd understudy the Swedish singer on the Muppet Show. She walked round the flat and sat down.

'It's fine,' she said, pouring coffee, 'sparkling. We'll get your deposit.'

'You know,' Caz said, 'I read about the most fabulous act of revenge the other day. Seems this airline pilot was playing transatlantically fast and loose and his girlfriend rang the speaking clock in New York and left it on for three days while he was away. Then there was a woman who sewed prawns into the top hems of the curtains. It took her ex-husband six months to find out where the smell came from.'

'Brilliant,' Josie said. 'What are you going to do to the old bag downstairs?'

'Dunno. Probably stick her in a painting somewhere, do a caricature . . . It's not worth the effort. I'd have had to move some time, just the reasons why now, is awful. Not awful. So bloody silly. I could have been on the game, pushing drugs, ram-raiding,

I could have had all-night acid house parties, been the most appalling tenant. But oh no. 'Scuse me, Mrs Greatheart, 'er upstairs is bent. Help me hence, ho, what, in MY house?'

'You must have done something to get at her,' Josie said, 'this is altogether too calm for you. And you've got a wicked gleam in your eyes. What have you done? Tell me!'

'Happen I have, moi dear,' Caz said, smiling, 'happen I'll tell 'ee about it some day.'

There was a sound of air-powered brakes outside and Caz looked out of the window.

'Jesus!' she said, 'I've got a pantechnicon!'

20

Josie sat among the chaos of a lifetime's possessions and smiled. 'Congratulations, Caz,' she said, 'the champagne's cooling. You've done it.'

'Oh, I've done it,' Caz said, 'we've done it. This calls for Tina Turner.'

'Is she coming too?'

'Tina Turner in Miston? I should be so lucky!'

Immortal Tina was belting out 'You're Simply The Best', when they heard a call from the open doorway. An old lady was standing there, one they hadn't seen before, with a huge bouquet all over cellophane, ribbons and bows. Caz noticed her eyes at once: a deep blue, like a willow pattern plate, sparky and alive.

'I'm Carrie, pet,' she said. 'These come for ye. Ah said, Ah think she's moving in today so I took 'em in. Ye daen't mind, do ye?'

'Of course not,' Caz said, 'come in. Have a glass of champagne.'

'Well!' Carrie said, 'Ah'd love to. Only I'm on me way to me club. The bus'll not hang around for us, so I'd best say no. You enjoy it, lasses. Them flowers is beautiful. I'll be seeing yez. Mind and knock if there's owt ye need.'

She went down the balcony, humming.

'Caz!' Josie teased, 'is there something you should tell me?'

Caz opened the card.

'*Welcome home. Thanks for your card! Viva Galleon Heights! I'll write soon, love. Sweet Legless Charity.*'

'Charlotte,' she said, 'she's lovely that way. Just a friend, Josie, I've known her ages. Take that smirk off your mind. Where the hell did I put my vases?'

They sat amid the debris of seven vaseless boxes, pinks and lilies and roses and freesias on every pile. Caz had stuck a rose behind Gladys's ear, and the dragon grinned rakishly from the corner of the kitchen. The champagne cork bounced off the ceiling.

'Cheers, Caz,' Josie said.

'Cheers, duck,' Caz sipped. 'Wondrous. But you have yet to hear the best. Not Tina. The revenge of the bent artist.'

'What? I knew you'd done something.'

'Magic,' Caz snorted. 'Lesbian artist Caz Hewson in Landlady Attack Shock Horror. I got some of that chameleon paint – you know the stuff? It goes on white and changes colour when you wet it.'

'What did you do with it?'

'Pink triangles,' Caz said, 'all over the bathroom, in case she never washes the walls anywhere. The first bath the new sucker has, up they will come in the steam. And GLAD TO BE GAY right across the ceiling.'

'I love it,' Josie said.

'Because I am glad,' Caz said extravagantly, swigging champagne, 'glad to be me anyway. Gay's just a part of it.'

'I don't think I'm gay,' Josie said, 'I think it's people. Only I haven't met anyone I feel like that about.'

'Yet,' Caz said firmly.

'I'm sure you've got a dark secret past,' Josie said.

'Dozens of them, dear,' Caz camped.

. . . those are pearls that were his eyes . . .

'Well, anyone who sends you a flower garden . . .!'

Caz smiled. 'Charlotte's a very dear friend,' she said, forcing her voice to be light, 'but never a lover. We were at college together, you know, we all shared a – house – for a while afterwards. It was good.'

Until it burnt to the ground. But she was not about to lay that one on Josie.

'And then you came up here,' Josie said. 'Why Newcastle?'

'Work,' Caz said briefly, 'a fresh start. There was nothing left for me in London. And look how well I've done! The Gardez! exhibition and eviction in a few short years!'

'Well, maybe you'll meet Ms Right up here,' Josie said, 'get yourself married to a nice Geordie lass.'

Caz's face froze behind her careful smile. 'I think I'm probably past all that,' she said.

'Never say die!'

'Sometimes you have to,' Caz said, 'but not today. Let's indulge our champagne tastes and bugger the beer bottle income!'

'To Galleon Heights,' Josie said, 'and new beginnings!'

Caz raised her glass. 'Galleon Heights!'

Part two

21

Carrie lived along the balcony from Caz. She might have been eighty and she might have been seventy for her soft elegant bulk moved like a dancer. Her dresses had gentle folds crossing the bosom and she clipped a small brooch above her left breast: a twinkly-eyed squirrel, a silvered basket of jewel-like enamel flowers. Her hair was the shampoo and set you get down at Doreen's by the post office, special prices for pensioners on Monday afternoons. She had dark hair, almost black, with maybe a dozen strands of silver. She was one of those unblinking people only with her it wasn't unnerving, there was a wealth of compassion and humour in her Celtic blue eyes. Her mouth had done its full share of laughing and crying and keeping mum, and tiny lines gathered her lips with dignity. She came into Caz's flat and smiled when she saw the postcards and the pantomime dragon who lived in the corner.

'You're artistic, like me,' she said. 'Do you find people get awkward and have to make a joke of it? Ah. So do I. But it's my place and I couldn't care. You get past bothering what people think – you probably never did, pet. It's a different world.'

She told Caz she was eighty-three and expected her surprise, people always said she was marvellous for her age.

'You come and see me any time,' she said, 'I'm just sitting, pet, a bit company makes a nice change.'

Decorating her own flat made Caz notice other people's decor like she never had before. She joked with Josie that she was turning into the DIY home furnishing bore you always avoid at parties. She wondered what Carrie's place would be like, clean as a new pin, no doubt. Flowers? Photos? Carrie had said she was artistic.

She walked along the balcony, light turning the cherry blossoms into clusters of butterfly wings. Carrie's door was propped open and when Caz knocked, she peered round the door frame from her chair.

'Come in, pet. Isn't it a lovely day?'

'Beautiful,' Caz said, sitting in a cushioned kitchen chair, relaxing, looking round the room.

She was delighted by the mix of subtlety and opulence. She hadn't been expecting soft greys and blues for wallpaper, still less the way everything in the room caught the light and twinkled. There was a crystal menagerie on a glass-topped table, grouped round a crystal ball shot with rainbows, just like the prize in the Crystal Maze. One wall was mirrored in squares of smoky blue, framed by glass whirling with soft gold.

'I did that meself,' said Carrie. 'Me friend said, ee, Carrie, you're daft, them's for a bathroom, but I said a bathroom you go into maybe twice a day, I want it where I can enjoy it.'

And that was the feeling of the room: a gentle delight. Carrie had a porcelain clock which wouldn't have looked out of place in Versailles, a languorous youth sighing after a come-hither shepherdess, hands clasped across her bosom, lilies and irises at her feet.

'She's a right tease, that one,' Carrie said with approval. 'She'll lead him a merry dance, you know the sort.'

'I do,' said Caz, laughing. It always pleased her when old ladies talked dirty. It wasn't in the words, more the knowing look, a wry half smile. It was as if Carrie was saying, do you know, I fell for all that, every girl falls for it and now it just doesn't matter.

'Aye,' Carrie said, 'I had a sister like that, ye knaa, had the lads flocking round like a swam of bees. She could make her cheeks go pink just thinking about it, and make-up! Me dad strapped her more than once, *go and wash yersel', ye hussy*, ye knaa. She had her choice of lads and she picked a bad un, one of those fellas that's in love with himself. Ee, Carrie, she said, he's so handsome. Handsome is, they say, but never mind. We'd all do it right if we knew then what we find out. Me, I picked a right ugly one, married him and the life I had, pet! I didn't know any better. It was no life at all. These days I'd have been in one of those refuges, but we didn't have anything like that. If you had a wrong un, you were stuck with it. Where could I go, with four bairns? Me mam was, well, you know, a bit simple, I brought up her family when I was a bairn meself, but I was the oldest, so I thought that's the way it was. But never mind.'

She settled in her easy chair, a can of pop in her hand, a stack of large print books at her feet. The television was on, 'Today in Parliament', but Carrie pressed the remote control and dark-suited green-leathered Westminster vanished.

'I cannot stand hearing them, pet,' she told Caz. 'It's all lies and long words, and when ye get the sense of it, there's no sense in it at all, is it? If ye've got a lot of money, ye'll keep it, if you've a little, they'll take it off you and if you've nothing, there's nothing they can do but lock ye up. I manage all right, I don't see why everyone else can't. I have me bit dinner every day, I eat a proper meal. I get me electric paid and there's a bit over for getting things I like. Now if *I* can do that, I want to know what they're all complaining about. Oh, aye, I've known poor. Many's the night I was crying because I was hungry and couldn't have but a cup of water and that makes yer stomach sick after a while. Me throat would close up pet, and it was only knowing the bairns needed me there stopped me putting an end to it. It was awful – but never mind, I'm eighty-three and I'm here and that's what matters.'

Caz nodded. 'Yeah,' she said, 'there's hard and hard. People expect more now, but you know, it's better even than when I was little. People have got more, only it doesn't make them happy. I'm sounding like my own mother. But it's true. You can be happy with very little, and if you're not, having lots more doesn't help.'

'Take me,' Carrie said, 'I never had nowt. Me man was out of work for six years and believe me, there was nothing like the social in them days. There was welfare and they'd come in your house and look round and say, well, Mrs Ives, you've got a table in the kitchen, sell it! They would! Ye were supposed to sell your last stick of furniture before you'd get a penny off them. And the men, they were different. *Are ye trying to starve us, woman?* That was my husband. How was I supposed to make a dinner wi' nowt but coppers and three bairns to feed? That was before the fourth came. We were living in two rooms over the High Road, Hartshorn Terrace. It's gone now. Demolished. If ye couldn't pay yer rent, the landlord would hoy yez all out on the street. When I found I was expecting again, I cried for three days.'

Caz lit a cigarette. Carrie's cheeks were a scorched pink under her eyes and her hands shook as she raised them in a gesture of surrender.

'But never mind,' she said, 'me bairns is all up now, and me man is six foot under and I have a good life wi'out him. I've a good friend in Rose, and the bairns has bairns of their own now.'

'Do they live near you?' Caz said.

Carrie shook her head. 'There was nowt for them here, pet,' she said quietly. 'They're all ower the world, my bairns. They've made something of theirselves, all of them.'

'That's good,' Caz said.

'And they get up when they can,' Carrie said, 'but they can't be travelling hundreds of miles every week to see us. They've been good bairns. Aye.'

She sat in silence, utterly still. A comfortable silence, her eyes far away with memories.

'I'd better get on,' Caz said.

'Mind ye call by soon, pet,' Carrie said, 'I like a chat.'

'I will,' Caz said, 'you take care now.'

'What sort of mischief could I get up to up here and all on me lonesome?' Carrie laughed. 'Get away with you and good luck with yer decorating.'

Back in number seventy-seven, Caz started sketching a dragon on the bathroom door. It would be a comfortable dragon with a knowing gleam in its eyes. An old dragon, nodding at the glittering razzmatazz of familiar treasure scattered around its cave.

22

Later that week, Caz met Carrie and her friend at the bottom of the stairs. She was dressed to go pubbing and clubbing, more or less the same as decorating, really, only ski pants minus paint stains. Given her destination, she'd added a badge which said TALK NORMAL and slung on her Quentin Crisp fedora.

'Where are you off to, pet? This is Caz, Rose, I told you about her. She likes it here,' Carrie said, leaning on Rose's arm. They carried twin handbags, big and flat and beige and navy. They wore identical three-quarter-length coats in beige and charcoal and neither one owed them a penny for wear. But Rose had an enamelled ballet dancer pinned to her lapel and the rims of Carrie's glasses were bright with jewels. Diamanté earrings sparkled above her collar.

It was Saturday night. The girls were on the razz.

'Oh, just into town,' Caz said, 'have a drink with a few friends, maybe go dancing.'

'It does ye good to get out, doesn't it, Rose?' Carrie nodded approval. 'Enjoy yourself, pet.'

'Where are you off to?' Caz asked.

'Ah, just up to The Turk's Head. We go every Saturday, divent we, Rose? They have a bit sing-song, nothing fancy. Sing a song with the piano. They've got a – what is it? – microphone now. You ought to come up one night. It's a bit fun, ye knaa, just a few friends on a Saturday night.'

'Oh, I'd like that,' Caz said. 'Yes. I'll come up next week.'

'Bring yer friend,' Carrie said, 'it's a bit different to town like.'

'Where is it?'

'Up the way,' Rose said, her arm sweeping a circle. 'Where would you say, Carrie?'

'Aye, up the High Road a bit. Past that Bingo that's closed and round the back of Earl's. The Turk's Head. It's got a geet sign up, pet. The Turk's Head, the piano bar's up the stairs. Well, have a nice night, whatever ye're doing,' Carrie said.

'I will,' Caz said, 'you too.'

She watched them walk up the street, arms linked, she heard them laughing.

'Ye knaa,' Carrie said, 'she's always rushing around, our Caz. Looks like a lost bairn to me most of the time. She paints real pictures, Rose. Ah wish I could have done that, I tellt her, and she says, ye can, Carrie, ye can borrow me brushes and that. Ah says, pet, I'm too old.'

'She's a nice lass,' Rose said. 'Ye should take her up on it, Carrie, man, it's never too late. Does she have a boyfriend? I know they don't go in for marrying these days.'

'Not that I've seen,' Carrie said. 'She keeps herself to herself, Caz. Mind, there's a lass comes round a lot.'

'Is it?' Rose said.

'I'm saying nowt, me,' Carrie said, 'it's her business. The day she moved in there was a geet bunch of flowers come for her. Like a wedding. Ah thinks to meself, ah hah, but never a sign of a young man. Her friend was there, they call her Josie, she's a gardener. Lasses these days! Never mind, I give her the flowers and she was over the moon, Rose, her little face was smiling away. It's wonderful what a smile can do, especially if ye look as serious as Caz. They said would Ah hev a glass of champagne! Posh! Well, I divent like the stuff, tell the truth, but I'd have had a glass, ye knaa, to be friendly. Only I was on me way out. Her friend never stops there, mind.'

'Well, like ye say, mebbe she's just a friend,' Rose said. 'Mind, talk about not marrying, there's a lot of women lives together like man and wife these days. Open about it. It makes ye think, ye knaa, them two teachers of ours, Miss Graham and Miss Wood, lived together till they died – well, it didn't cross our minds.'

'Why not,' Carrie said. 'Ye were lucky wi your man, Rose, but if I'd known the life my husband would lead me, I doubt I'd hev jumped in saying I do! But times is different now, they do what they like. There's rotten in men and women both, but women is kinder as a rule.'

'What about the babbies?' Rose said, 'most women wants babbies. Ye need a man for that, even these days.'

'Babbies is easily got, pet,' Carrie said, 'easy as blink. Too easy, sometimes, Ah say, else there wadn't be all this trouble. Half of it is babbies not wanted. Look at her on the green. I cry for them bairns.'

23

Caz stood at the bus stop. Yes, she'd like The Turk's Head a whole lot better than the evening ahead of her. A night on the town, beginning at Lady Emma's Lovenest. The Lovenest was one of those choky smoky pubs with a juke-box that blared out Whitesnake and The Grateful Dead by way of nostalgia. Nauseastalgia, someone was sure to say at least three times a night and wonder why the tired pun didn't even raise a snigger. Wall to wall posers, poets and painters and photographers, the men wild and pissed and arty, declaiming against Fate and shouting about their misunderstood talents. The women pissed and arty and wild, kohl black hair trailing pints of real ale, I love him, I'll kill him, murmured fantasies of romance and murder, bisexual angst dribbling from scarlet lips, scarlet nails tugging hennaed hair. The code of dress was Oxfam reject.

'My friends,' Caz thought, swinging up the pole to the top deck of the bus. 'My milieu. My destiny?'

Christ! She wouldn't have met these people but for the artist's residency that had brought her to Newcastle. She'd only applied as a joke, feeling somehow that her work should provide her with a living even when it didn't. The residency paid her to work with the underprivileged denizens of an area deemed SNPD 17: Social Needs Priority District 17. The post was funded by The Northern Agency for Cultural and Artistic Development, a grandiose title with a suitably daft acronym. NACAD.

'Are ye with Knackered, like?'

That was the most polite comment from her artistically patronised clientele. Taxpayers' money paying for a bunch of drunks and posers to carry on drinking and posing. Those who can, do, those who can't, teach, those who can do neither work for a development agency.

NACAD had a policy of drawing in prestigious artists from all over the globe for the plum jobs. Any painter or writer or playwright who happened to live in Newcastle could hope, at best, for the odd scattering of crumbs. Without the dole, most of them would have starved. Poets did all right: poetry somehow occupied a well-funded niche although no one outside the cliques actually read it. Poetry and cliques and community murals that the communities didn't want or even like particularly once they were done. Subsidised mediocrity, Caz said to Josie, amazed and furious after the one and only policies meeting she'd attended.

When she arrived in the north east, George Tweddle, NACAD's head of visual arts, had taken her under his wing: an uncomfortable position for both of them. He couldn't flirt with her, and since that was his rather bad stock in trade, he blustered with gallantry. He held dinner parties for 'like-minded souls' but once her residency was finished and she'd lost her novelty value, he turned his attentions to the next incomer. Caz was relieved. She was accustomed to paddling her own canoe: somebody like George was useful for work and outside of that, she didn't know what to talk about.

On her first Saturday, he'd taken her to the Lovenest, to 'meet the folks', as he put it. She flustered him, lesbian artist and London and all, and he was out to impress. The north east was his domain and all its artists his *enfants terribles*. She guessed, from the looks coming her way, that 'the folks' all knew who she was and were wary of a southerner camping on their underfunded home territory.

George had been relieved when Wosh the mad artist had latched on to her: Wosh with the Salvador Dali eyes and total disregard for cliques and fashions and worthy projects and everything else about NACAD.

'Look at them!' he hissed at her, 'washed up wankers! Parasites the lot of them. And baa baa baa – here comes George Tweddle, the only sheep who feels a social responsibility for its ticks. Get your jaws into the veins of Knackered, my girl and you've got a place for life!'

Their friendship had confused the Men: clearly there was no sex involved, and the artistic community thrived on its incestuous chain of affairs. They swore they lived for romance, desperate not to sleep another night alone as their eyes roved over the tired and familiar faces. Wosh, untypically, was romantic to the point of celibacy. When he went to the Andes, there was a rumour that she had broken his heart, but she ignored it and it died a lingering death.

Her friendship with Josie was still a talking point. Were they, weren't they. She didn't gossip and neither did Josie and the stories flew and grew around them.

Josie was another enigma for the clientele at the Lovenest. She seldom went there, showed no interest in propositions drunk or sober and worked constantly with gardening. There was no sexual hook to hang her on. And somehow she'd cracked the combination of Being Creative with Earning a Living. And if she could . . . 'the folks' felt uneasy in her presence.

George had introduced them: *another creative lady, Caz, I'll get some drinks.*

'We have so much in common,' Caz said mockingly.

'Of course,' Josie said, flicking her hair back, 'I hate George trying to turn this hole into a cocktail party.'

'He's trying,' Caz said, 'very trying.'

'This must be very parochial for you,' Josie said.

'Don't believe the hype – mine or London's,' Caz said. 'Believe me, it's a relief to know there's just one arty pub. You can't move for them down there. At least here you know where to avoid.'

Josie giggled. 'I'll show you some nice pubs sometime,' she said, 'if you like. Places George wouldn't even think of.'

'I think George is having a hard time with me,' Caz said. 'He can't forget that I'm a woman. Not that he should. But he's got his boxers in a knot about the L word. It would be a breath of fresh air to be a person, wouldn't it?'

'Yes,' Josie said, 'I get so fed up with men talking to my ample bosom. Have you noticed that?'

'Have I not!' Caz laughed, 'whatever you wear.'

'I did think of cutting my hair,' Josie said, 'but why should I? I like it long.'

'Good to see you getting on,' George gave them their drinks. 'Plenty to talk about, yes?'

'Oh yes,' Josie said, 'men, and all that jazz.'

George ho-ho'd and left them to it.

Josie hid her grin behind her hair. She'd given Caz her phone number and one lonely evening a few weeks later, Caz had rung it, ready just to chat and hang up: *we must meet* was Londonspeak for goodbye. But Josie had meant it and, starting with a disillusioned impatience with the scene, they found they liked each other.

Caz was aware that now they all treated her with lightly jeering respect: she'd had that exhibition at the Gardez! Gallery and even sold things often enough not to need or want handouts from NACAD. She missed them when she stayed away for months at a time, forgetting the irritation that had made her vow never again. Sure enough, when she went back, within ten minutes she was on the highway to boredom at how predictable it all was. How stale. They were still drinking the same drinks and holding the same conversations.

I just can't get started. I just can't get finished. That bloody grant never came through. If I had money now I wouldn't know what to do with it. I love her, I'll kill her. I love him, I suppose, why does it all hurt so much?

The names and the gender might change, but precious little else.

Dreary Desirée would be chain-smoking More menthol and mainlining vodka and tonic like it was going out of style.

'What do I do wrong?' she'd be asking someone. 'You tell me. Listen. Just listen, you won't believe what she/he said/did.'

Mad Mark would have filled the juke-box and be pleading with the bar staff to turn it up for fuck's sake, they're all peasants here, I don't want to have to listen to them.

Sadie the whiplash lady would be there with her anaemic band of followers, neck weighted with outsize crucifixes, her pallid bulk swathed in black. Swaying, tapping black leather boots spiked with lethal spurs. Drinking Bloody Marys in pint glasses, lighting black Sobranies with a steel lighter shaped like a gun.

Caz wondered which of the jaded bantering long-lost welcomes she'd get from Mad Mark. He said she was the most intelligent woman he'd met and they should breed geniuses. She told him that she didn't welcome vaudeville into her private life.

'Then I shall languish,' he cried, 'languish until doomsday, oh what a fate!'

She dithered at the bus stop. Look, she only had to cross the road and a quarter of an hour would deposit her safe with Carrie and Rose in The Turk's Head. But that would leave Josie friendless and fuming. Tonight she'd chosen the wild side and she'd just have to walk on it.

One thing you could be sure of in Lady Emma's Lovenest was the chance of work. That, and easy sex, were twin magnets. The powers that be, despised but able to sign cheques, tended to hang out there. A cluster of politically correct funding organisations like a bad hangover from the seventies. NACAD had the most money. Maybe that's why so many posers posed in there. Caz wondered sometimes which came first, the artist or the agent or the collector. Difficult to say. The Lovenest was an unofficial head-hunting ground, and who could tell if there was money around for drunken ranters writing blank verse, dreamers of pictures, conjurers of deathless prose, sculptors of stone and wood. Caz had been offered her most lucrative commissions in the haze of smoke and gin fumes that passed for air.

There was to be an international festival of art on Tyneside next year and Josie was hoping to landscape part of it. She wanted to suss the lie of the land in Lady Emma's and had demanded Caz's company and support.

'Moral support,' she said, 'I realise that's pushing it a bit, but I couldn't stand being cornered by Desirée and her mob. And you know I'm scared of Sadie.'

'You just have to laugh at her,' Caz said, 'I mean, what did he look like, that bloke, you know, the one she brought in on a dog lead. It's a pantomime, Josie.'

'You've not been stuck in the toilet queue with Sadie,' Josie shuddered. 'It was worse than men, you can't just tell a woman to piss off, can you?'

'Oh, you got the *you need to explore your darker side, I can tell* spiel, did you? I thought so. Well, dear, go for it, if that's what you want. I bet you took her card, didn't you? Yes you did, you're so polite – the black-edged, 'call me when you feel the need' card. She'll be expecting you to ring, you know. She's given up on me.'

'How?' Josie exploded, cross and laughing at the same time. 'How did she give up on you? What's your secret?'

'Simple,' Caz said, 'I got the treatment and said yes.'

'Oh, gawd,' Josie said, 'you didn't?'

'No. I *said* yes, I said it has to be now, get a cab. She goes on to The Red Windmill on Saturdays to get her drugs, there was no way she'd pass that up even for me. She said get a cab and I'll join you, so I just stared at her and said, Sadie, I never wait for anyone. You've blown it. Five minutes later, she said, OK, let's go. She'd got the doglead bloke to pick up her smoke. But I just shook my head and told her now means now and you never get a second chance. I said, think about it, Sadie, that five minutes just changed the course of history.'

'Oh dear,' Josie said, 'I don't think I could be that cool.'

'She's quite sweet in a thick sort of way,' Caz said. 'Under all that Leichner pancake and rubber tubing, she just wants to get married and have children. Little house on the prairie with ducks on a pond and a well-stocked dungeon. Relatively normal.'

'Ugh,' Josie said, 'well, I need protection.'

'I'd bring my knuckledusters, but it would only encourage her,' said Caz.

That was three days ago. Caz squared her shoulders and strolled across the road, grimacing at the stench of beer, the deadening bass that thudded in her chest when she opened the door.

24

She walked through the crowd without pausing. Straight to the bar, where the nicotined mirrors would tell her the whole story of the evening. Faces punctuated by glasses, gestures distorted in the ornate wreaths and flowers etched in the glass. Everything back to front, made squat or lean like a fairground hall of mirrors.

'Sol,' she said, 'hold the lime.'

She had never taken to dribbling beer through a slice of fruit. Maybe in Mexico, where the sun burns the salt from your skin, maybe there she'd squeeze a whole lime into an iced glass and slake her thirst on the bittersweet tang. But never in Newcastle, where the sun dropping over the horizon left the streets chilly as winter for three hundred and thirty-three nights of the year.

She clocked the clientele.

The mirror forewarned her of the arm descending around her shoulders. Mad Mark swung her round. 'Light of my dreary days!' he boomed. 'Home is the sailor, home from the sea, Christ, Caz, where have you been?'

'Moving,' she said.

'What? Away from the flinty bosom of Mrs Greatheart? Why?'

'She takes the bloody Thunderer,' Caz said. 'You recall – Gay Glam at the Gardez! – yes? Lurid alliteration equals journalism? Ooh, she's a bent artist, let's ignore the pictures and dig for dirt? My moment of limelight? Mrs Greatheart was not amused. I got a month's notice.'

'Take the bitch to court!' Mad Mark was three sheets to the wind with bluster.

'Unprovable,' Caz said, 'we private tenants have no rights.'

'So where are you staying now?'

Caz drank before she answered.

'Anchorage Point,' she said.

'Darling!' Mark tugged his hair, 'come live with me and be my love!'

'There's nothing wrong with Anchorage Point,' Caz said, 'I like it. It's quiet.'

'So far!'

'You know me, Mark,' Caz said, 'if I want to party I go out. Raise hell in the clubs, my dear, but never take it home. No, it's good.'

'If you moved in with me,' Mark oozed, 'we'd have a colony, woo our Muses from dawn to dusk, booze away the blues until sunrise, recreate the spirit of Bloomsbury . . .'

Bloody Mark, off again, all his dreams came tumbling down in the clear and hungover light of day. She'd worked with him once and found it fascinating. Until then she'd always felt she didn't work hard enough and scourged herself as a dilettante. But Mark! If he'd put even half of the energy he wasted talking about grand schemes into sheer hard graft – but he wouldn't. She could see him at seventy – if his liver held out – wild-bearded and ranting, temporarily impressing callow youth with his gushes and floods of enthusiasm.

'Bloomsbury was a bubble drifting in the river shallows of inherited wealth,' she said.

'God,' Mark said, 'that's brilliant.'

'Uh huh,' she said. And it was equally brilliant all of the times I've said it to you, she added in her mind.

'I must find Josie.'

'Aah,' Mark became cunning, 'how is your *good friend* Josie?'

She could say, how dare you presume I'm sleeping with Josie, she could say keep your voyeuristic mind out of my life, she could say, Mark, Josie and I are just good friends. But why bother?

'Josie's cool, man,' she said, 'real cool.'

Josie, in fact, was sweating when she unearthed her in a corner, gallantly keeping her a seat. 'Thank God you've come,' she said, 'I'm feeling decidedly threatened.'

Caz looked up. Jesus! There must be something in the air. There stood Sadie in red and white, not a smudge of black in sight. Even her gloves were scarlet, spiked like hedgehogs, clutching a glass filled with liquid the colour of a ripe tomato. A pint of Bloody Mary – what else? She raised one glove at Caz and made a coy *moue*. Caz wagged her finger and looked severe.

'Don't encourage her!' Josie giggled nervously.

'Is she really getting to you? Yes, she is, isn't she. OK. Just relax with Auntie Caz and we'll make the nasty lady leave you alone!'

She put one arm round Josie and kissed the end of her nose. 'There you are, duck,' she said, 'peace in our time. And it'll give them all something to talk about for the next year.'

'Thank you,' Josie said.

'My pleasure. Now where are the festival organisers?'

'That lot,' Josie nodded towards a group standing next to Sadie's entourage.

Dreary Desirée had found a backbone somewhere and was peering intently into the face of a small man in a tweed jacket, the sort who jingles coins and keys deep in his pocket and believes that a hand-printed silk tie is the passport to Bohemia. George Tweddle, transformed.

'My God, George has got himself a new wardrobe,' Caz murmured, 'and lost the moustache.'

Two fluffy blonde queens bobbed their heads, laughing eagerly every time he spoke. He knew it and was enjoying himself. George was one of those men who suspect, quite rightly, that people find them ridiculous. His position guaranteed total respect to his face. The queens were Tom and Jasper McVey, landscape *artistes* who loved to talk about Roddy and Mags and Mustique. They flitted between Chelsea and Newcastle scattering swathes of rhododendrons and Japanese follies wherever they went. A bearded figure stood frowning beside them, fingering the buttons of his Icelandic knit waistcoat.

'George is the one to impress with prestige for the region,' Caz said, 'he signs the cheques. Now the beardy waistcoat, he's trying to be incognito. Michael, Michael something, he'll be the one with Vision. That beard means Real Man, he doesn't like queens, so you've nothing to fear from the brothers McVey.'

'Good,' Josie said, 'they terrify me.'

'No need,' Caz said, 'Michael Astrado. Innovation, daring, challenge, accessibility. He's just been an adviser on the Unity Park in Berlin. A little deference is called for. And supreme confidence. Are you up to it, girl?'

'I'm glad you're here,' Josie said. 'I'll get the drinks.'

'Fine,' Caz said. 'It's probably at the stage where George is trying to hook Michael, so we need to be somewhat impressive. Kissy kissy bullshit. I shall drill a few holes in the ice. I think it's time to charm Dreary Desirée out of the picture before she starts on her dismemberment kick. And remember: growing plants introduce a fourth dimension. Get a couple of drinks, mine's Sol – she drinks v and t. Doubles. Think of it as an investment.'

'Sol, v and t double, mine and growing plants are a fourth dimension,' Josie repeated. 'Hey, I said that to you last week.'

'Exactly,' Caz said. 'Michael will love it, *dolling!*'

She set her hat at a Dietrich angle and strolled over to the group.

'Desirée,' she drawled, 'how nice.'

'Oh, hi Caz,' Desirée gave her cheek a sloppy kiss. 'Do you know Caz? Caz Hewson? She just had that fabbo exhibition at the Gardez!'

'Of course I know Caz. I enjoyed the Gardez!' George beamed.

Caz, after all, had stayed in his kingdom, she was some sort of plume in his helmet.

'This is Michael, Caz, Michael Astrado,' George took charge. 'Do you know Tom and Jasper?'

'Yes,' Caz said, using her best handshake for Michael. By now he would have run through his filing cabinet memory and placed her. Pink Triangle, Black Triangle, Rainbow Pentacle Gallery. Beat The Blues Inner City Project. George, with his ingrained system of labels, would probably have mentioned her. Caz Hewson: lesbian artist. Lesbian equals feminist equals stroppy cow equals man-hater equals castrator equals get me *outta* here! It was best to strangle these assumptions at birth. She gave Michael a dazzling smile.

'I saw your work at the Gardez!' he said. 'Very interesting.'

'It's good to be accessible sometimes,' Caz said. 'I've heard great things about Berlin. It's so important to think European, these days.'

'It's coming on,' he said, pleased that she knew about it. 'It all takes time.'

'I'm so impatient,' she said. 'It's always the thing I'm working on that grabs me most.'

Josie appeared on cue. The brothers McVey looked pained.

'Have a drink, Desirée,' Caz said, 'I owe you one.'

'What a memory!' said Desirée.

'The cartoon element at the Gardez!,' Michael said, 'we're trying to do some fun topiary in Berlin. Things that people will like, even laugh at.'

'Yes, yes,' Caz said. 'Accessibility. It's vital. I wanted, was aiming for that. But now I'm knee-deep in a project with Josie. I've always wanted to make my work three dimensional and Josie's a whizz with plants.'

'Growing plants introduce a fourth dimension,' Josie said.

'I'd never have thought of that,' said Michael, obviously pleased, 'but you're right. Can I borrow it for Berlin? It might shift the pen pushers a little nearer to completion. Tell me about your project?'

George shifted a little closer. They were his artists after all, working on his patch.

'Oh you know us free spirits,' Caz laughed, 'it always sounds so pretentious. But it's sort of canvas and bricks and mortar and earth – fusion? Imaginary landscapes with real plants?'

George nodded briskly and Michael looked closely at both of them. 'That's very interesting,' he said.

Gotcha! thought Caz, as Josie fielded his look and went into one of her wonderful raves. Desirée and the brothers McVey had the grace to listen – just.

'I may have something that would interest you,' said Michael. 'What do you think, George?'

'Yes,' George rubbed his hands.

'Let's not talk shop now,' Caz said, laughing, 'this is Saturday night, George.'

'Of course,' Michael pulled out a leather wallet and extracted a card. 'Perhaps you'd ring me on Monday?'

'Give that to Josie,' Caz said, 'I'm hopeless.'

'Make sure you ring him,' George said softly as they left, 'this is going to be very big.'

'We'll ring,' Caz said.

'What do you think?' Josie was anxious.

'Piece of cake, duck,' Caz drained her glass, 'but not more shop, eh, Josie? Let's get another and move on. I want to go dancing.'

Josie went to the bar. There was no point trying to get another word out of Caz about George or Michael or the project tonight. That was work and Caz swore down that the only unpaid overtime she'd ever do was on her own paintings. And that was that.

25

It was five to three and Caz waited for the last night bus home.

The one o'clock and the two o'clock were dangerous, packed to the roof with soused youth, distorted faces jammed against the windows, the aisles a tin-can bowling alley. They were little more than double-decker sardine cans on wheels. The Boys were sitting, standing, sprawling anywhere but on a seat, the air steaming with empty tales of conquest and a fog of cigarette smoke. They would have started the evening with a pocket full of notes and a mouth full of how they'd get laid tonight no bother! Now they were going home again, home with their mates, slagging off every slag who'd ever led them on and said no, boasting over a phone number scrawled on a packet of tabs. There was always at least one who'd try a chat up, nudging his mates and so pissed he thought he was whispering.

You'd think his mates were animals driven wild behind rattling bars, rolling out a chorus of whoops and orgiastic groans. The bold and boozy lad came swinging down the aisle – to cadge a light he didn't want, to ask the time when it was too late to matter. Urban foreplay. Tubes of dull light turned his face fog-sallow and even Caz's city-wise survival techniques were stretched to breaking point. What do you do? Ignore, cajole, giggle with, pretend you're seriously foreign, deaf, drugged, dead? Nothing works. For the demon drink is upon this likely lad and things can get nasty for a hundred different reasons or no reason at all.

Hence the three o'clock bus.

The fight in the club had shaken Caz. Two steps more to her left and she'd have been glassed. Sadie stood watching it all with a fixed smile which had nothing to do with pleasure. Oh no. Whatever cocktail of drink and drugs was keeping her on her steel-capped toes, the fight was just a spectacle, no more than a movie or footage on the nine o'clock news. Sadie probably saw it all in slow motion, glassily admiring the splashes of red dye and realistic sound effects.

After the club, there was vomit splattered right across the pavement outside the kebab shop. Vomit and a snake's nest of piss. A drunk sprawled beside the dustbins groaning. Two men shoving each other, tearing at each other's clothes, banging each other's heads against the wall. Taxis refusing fares, young men and women jeering and barging a berserker conga through the traffic. None of it was unusual for a Saturday night and maybe Caz's distress came from being sober.

Maybe you have to be smashed out of your mind to really enjoy it, she thought. Enjoy it? Because you can ignore it, you're probably in there with it, eight sheets flapping in the wind of 40 per cent proof immortality.

But she hadn't wanted to be drunk. She hadn't wanted to be in town, conniving and manipulating Michael Icelandic Waistcoat Astrado and Tweedy George Tweddle in the Lovenest. On one level, it was worth it because Josie would get her job. But she wanted to distance herself from all that crap, cut free from the clever clever endless round of words. Maybe she was tired, maybe this was middle age.

Whatever.

She went upstairs on the empty bus and sat at the front, her favourite place. The neon-lit inferno of faces and voices receded in a roar of diesel. The city centre streets were empty. Shapes huddled in wide doorways, dustbin bags, crates, people sleeping? Caz steeled herself against guilt: she wasn't going to do anything about the homeless beyond agonising and that didn't help. She'd done soup runs and Crisis at Christmas and that wasn't enough. There was no enough.

Uh oh, stop it, she told herself, before weariness lurched her mind into an insomniac fret of self-doubt. All you have to do in life is find out who you are and be it. If you happen to have chosen painting, do it, love it, do it the best you can and cultivate peace. Not stagnation, peace.

Yes, it was really the farce in the Lovenest that had rattled her. She'd played with those people, unashamedly read their minds and charmed them rotten. Admittedly not for herself, but for Josie and there was a pay-off for her. She knew Josie simply wouldn't push and grab and there would be weeks of shall I, shan't I, until she was ragged with it and any chance of work would have vanished.

She closed her eyes, shook her head and lit a cigarette.

You gotta laugh, innit, else you wind up crying, love . . .

The bus lurched to a stop behind a lorry at the traffic lights on the town side of The Drop. She leaned forward as the slow convoy got the green light.

Deep in The Drop was dark as a well, just three white shapes to be picked out, the goats. All of Newcastle's lights spread out towards the Tyne, ribbons of orange, streamers of white, fairy lights and chimney pots that would never smoke again. The floodlit factory – disused – floated against the night. There was a tall ship on the quayside and she could see the masts and spars picked out in lights like a join-the-dot picture from a child's colouring book.

Up ahead in the sky she saw the illuminated caterpillar of a train flying along the high concrete circle of the railway bridge. A flurry of blue sparks dazzled against the prow of Anchorage Point, riding to the stars. The whole sprawling length of it was an architect's abstract of a massive boat. All the varicoloured bricks swept up to the prow and whoever lived behind the darkened windows had a view over Newcastle that nothing could interrupt. Caz imagined living in the highest flat, sailing above the city: she would be sitting outside under a midnight sky and watching from the crow's nest balcony. She'd see the lurching lights of the three o'clock bus and one or two people getting off to go home. That would be somewhere to live, high above chimney pots and church steeples, keeping watch for Miston over the deep moat of The Drop.

The bus shuddered to a halt outside The Ritz and she got out, very nearly home again and feeling suddenly safe. It was as if there was an invisible barrier on the bridge. She couldn't imagine Sadie and her grotesque sideshow getting through it. Or Tweed Jacket and Waistcoat, they'd all be stranded on the far side of The Drop as the bridge shivered into nothingness. In Miston it was time for sleeping.

26

Morning in Miston brought breakfast and another bit of nest building. Caz got into the habit of dropping in on Carrie most days, for coffee and a chat. Another chapter in Carrie's life, sometimes the same chapter again. Caz didn't mind, knowing Carrie was like having your granny living only doors away. Only this granny never pried and never judged her.

She sat one morning, looking at a photo of Carrie's daughter, the youngest child.

'I couldn't disown that one, could I?' Carrie said. 'She hasn't a bit of Ives in her. She's all Brazier that one – that was my name before I took up with him. Brazier. These days ye can keep yer own name after ye're wed, but it was different then.'

'She's got beautiful eyes,' Caz said.

'Get away wi ye!' Carrie said, 'eyes is eyes. It was me teeth the lads used to notice. Give us a smile, Carrie! I had lovely teeth. Only one time I was in the hospital for a root to come out and they took the lot. The root's still there – it was twisted, they said, and when I come out of th'anaesthetic, I hadn't a tooth in me head. When you think!'

'They took your teeth?' Caz was outraged.

'Do what they like when you're out cold,' Carrie said, quite matter-of-fact. 'Me cousin went in for an appendix and they took the lot out. Hyster-what-ye-call-it. Aye, they did!'

'Blimey,' Caz said. It didn't seem to surprise Carrie one bit.

'No,' she said, taking the photo, 'when I think of the state I was in when I had her! I told ye about the malnutrition, didn't I? It was the worst days of me life.

She settled in her chair and sighed.

'It's a terrible thing not to want a bairn,' she said after a while, 'I was driven nearly mad wi' unhappiness. These days, I'd have had an abortion, I reckon. Well naa, ye see, with the social you get now I'd not have been feeling like that, for I never could take to the thought of abortion. I divent blame a lass if she has to, ye cannot pass judgements on people, well, ye can, but it's no use to ye. I say, walk a mile in her shoes, pet, afore ye start calling her. But there I was, didn't even have a pair of shoes, carrying a fourth when I couldn't feed three and he was a wicked man. All out for hisself. I thought it was because he wasn't working, ye knaa, but it wasn't much better when he did get himself a job.'

Barefoot and pregnant, starving and weeping. Out on the street if you couldn't pay the rent. And Caz thought she'd had a hard time with Mrs Greatheart! Carrie's eyes went distant and she sighed.

'I dragged through them nine months. Couldn't stir meself out of me chair most days. I slept in it, for I couldn't get comfortable lying down. He was shouting at us all the time, but I couldn't care. I didn't listen to him, after a while I didn't even hear him and he stopped. Me spirit was all gone, ye see. Him! He got worried, Ah reckon, or sick of waiting for his food and he'd make bit meals but I said take it away, I cannot eat. I wanted to die, ye knaa, I just couldn't see a way past it. He even called the doctor and that's not like it is these days. Me neighbour's a divil for calling the doctor, even had him out for me. Seven and six the doctor charged for coming out in them days and that was a lot of money.'

Carrie twinkled.

'All doom and gloom, isn't it, pet? Well, it was, like. Them days was terrible. The doctor came and he started shouting at us too, pet, do you want to kill your baby, Mrs Ives, you have to eat. I was crying then, ye see, the doctor was a nice kind man and even he thought I was doing wrong. I didn't know I was crying mind, until I felt me dress getting all wet and he got out his big hanky. He said I'd to go to the hospital and he'd call an ambulance and that was a performance. Me legs had gone with sitting and I knew the ambulance cost ten and six and we hadn't a shilling in the house. He got a police ambulance. That's the only sort there was in them days. The buggers was round every Friday, dole day, for their sixpence until it was paid. They never missed.'

She searched Caz's face.

'But it was like that for everyone, ye see. You hadn't the money to keep well and you hadn't the money to get well once you were sick. Do ye see what I'm saying?'

'Catch 22,' Caz said.

'Aye,' Carrie said, 'summat like. Well, in the hospital, I slept. They wouldn't let me out of bed and the sister used to stand over us to make sure I was eating. She was a tyrant, but I think I owe me life to her. Me own life and me daughter's. I took a little walk one day and ye knaa what they had on me chart? Malnutrition. Malnutrition. I was so ashamed. And I was in a private ward, ye knaa. There was no beds anywhere else, and the women in there used to look at us and talk about us like I was dirt. One of them had a box of chocolates one day and she had the nurse pass them round the ward, but when they got to my bed, she said, OH NO NOT HER, right out loud. I couldn't have cared.'

'That's cruel,' Caz said.

'Well, it worked out, ye see,' Carrie said. 'When the nurse came to give her back the box, she says, oh do have one yourself, nurse. And the nurse, she made a face like this, ooh, she was furious. She threw the box on the bed, threw it, mind, and said, I will not. After that, I got all the attention. The nurses said, Mrs Ives, ye never ask for nowt, and they're ringing their bells all day and all night. They'd bring me a bit fruit, not that I could eat it, mind, but it was something to put on the cabinet. And they give me flowers, I think it was when someone had left or died in another ward, but never mind, I always had flowers after that. Chrysanths, roses, lilies and everything. I divent like cut flowers but it put their noses out of joint. The private patients. I laugh about it now.

'Ye knaa, my little girl was born in that hospital and I couldn't care. I didn't even want to look at her, I'd wished she would be born dead. It's a terrible thing to say, but it's the truth. What sort of a life would she have? They put her in me arms on the second day and I just looked at her and thought, pet, you shouldn't be here. The nurses were saying, oh, come on, Mrs Ives, she's beautiful, what are you going to call her? Three of them, they were angels to me. So I looked at them and said, well, what's your names, lasses? Well, one was Jessie, one was Elsie and one was Patience. So I said, there you are, she'll be Jessie Elsie Patience Ives. Jessie's a pretty name, but I wouldn't give a thank you for Elsie. Ee, she was a lovely nurse though. Patience? It's a bit old fashioned, but never mind I thought, this poor bairn'll need plenty for mine's died a death.

'And Jessie, she's a nurse now. She's got three bairns – look.'

There was a photo of three bright-eyed children on the wall beside the mirror.

'Patrick, he's the eldest, Desmond, he's the middle and Elizabeth, she's the baby. She was born with violet eyes, so Jessie thought of Elizabeth Taylor, but her eyes changed, they're an ordinary blue, like me own.'

Carrie's eyes were anything but ordinary. They were the sort of blue that shifts from summer sky to wild ocean, and all her years floated there.

27

'George was asking after you,' Josie said over the phone.

'Uh huh.'

Caz had the receiver wedged between chin and shoulder as she thinned out nasturtium seedlings. It had taken a hammer and chisel to break up the earth in her balcony tub. The woman in the garden centre had recommended them, she said you can't go wrong with nasturtiums, they thrive on poor soil and neglect. Two weeks later, the earth was alive with rampant discs of green spinning from juicy runners.

'Yes,' said Josie, 'you should have a swelled head, me duck. Him and beardy Michael think very highly of your work. I think they want you to put in a proposal.'

'Proposal?' Caz wondered about planting some fast-growing creeper, something like roses round the door, but easier.

'For the festival! Caz, what are you doing?'

'Pricking out my seedlings,' Caz giggled. 'You should see them, Josie, they're outrageous.'

'Oh. Have you heard a word I've said?'

'George, Michael, swelled head, festival, proposal,' Caz teased two plants from a passionate embrace. 'What grows fast, Josie, up walls, you know? Minimum care, maximum bloom?'

'Russian vine,' said Josie, 'clematis, montana rubens. Anyway, are you coming to the Lovenest this Saturday? That's why I rang.'

'I am not!' Caz sat on the bench and rolled a cigarette. 'Last week was quite enough for a good long time. Disgusting. I lost most of Sunday getting over it. I'm off town.'

'Well, we don't have to go clubbing it. I thought you were pretty cool, though, just swept me away from that awful fight.'

'Yeah, yeah,' Caz puffed her cigarette into life, 'but I don't like it. Come on, Josie, you have to be half-cut to put up with it. And totally smashed to enjoy it.'

'Yes, but . . .'

'Oh, but nothing, Josie,' Caz wasn't going to be talked out of this one. 'I suppose it's just that I've been there, done that and I don't want any more. If Tweed Jacket and Waistcoat want my work they can write and say so. Why should I have to go through all that slaver? Why should any of us? I know art, creativity, is more than a job, mainly cuz you don't get paid enough, but I'm drawing the line at licking arses in the Lovenest.'

'Oh dear,' Josie sounded upset.

'For the time being,' Caz tried to soften it. 'Maybe I'm just tired, Josie. It's just – all those people. Lost, lonely and vicious. The beautiful and the bland.'

'I hope you don't think that of me,' Josie said.

'No,' Caz sighed, then forced some oomph into her voice, 'I don't. You're me mate, ducks, me mucker. Which is why I was going to offer you a Saturday night alternative. Are you game?'

'Try me!'

'The Turk's Head,' Caz pronounced. 'Miston High Road, hubcap of the known universe. Nice people with nice manners. I think.'

'What's The Turk's Head?'

'Well, Carrie and Rose go there on a Saturday night for a sing-along. They said did I want to go, and bring my friend. Which I guess is you. If you have to feather the Lovenest, be elusive! Skip this week. Nothing attracts like unavailability. Are you on?'

'All right,' Josie sounded relieved, 'I owe you one for last Saturday anyway.'

'Josie, this one will at least be different. Remember the F word? F-U-N? We'll go up the coast for lunch, then slob it out here until the evening. Then it's on with the gladrags and up past the Bingo, round the back of Earl's.'

'It sounds so tempting,' Josie was sarcastic, 'all right.'

Lunch was in a restaurant three stories above the prom at Whitley Bay. Family time, where a bored little girl in a pink pastel dress sulked in her chair and her brother made castles of mashed potatoes and swede in gravy moats before demolishing them one by one.

Afternoon they played George Benson and drank white wine and soda on the balcony. For the hundredth time, Caz said did Josie like the nasturtiums, really?

'I really do. Honestly, you'd think they were rare orchids you're so proud of them!'

'You don't realise,' said Caz, 'you just don't know what it is for me to grow something. You do it all the time, I never have. There's just so much of them. They've grown over a foot in four days, Josie, it's magic.'

'Lovely dear,' Josie sounded like a very patient psychiatric nurse. 'I suppose it's therapy.'

'The whole thing is therapy,' Caz said, 'I mean, look! Two months ago, this flat was a tip and I was about to be homeless. Now it's beautiful and there's flowers too. Nearly flowers.'

'Little things,' Josie said. 'Is it time to hit The Turk's Head yet?'

'I think it could be.'

They followed Carrie and Rose's directions, Caz waving her arms with exaggerated delight at the bridge, the motorway, the wasteland, the boarded up Bingo. Last week she'd felt cheated with her forced visit to town. It made her heart race when she thought she was going to miss something, but here they were, her and Josie, seven days later, going to spend an evening with Carrie and Rose.

The windows in The Turk's Head were frosted glass with garlands cut clear. In the centre of Newcastle, it would be a revamped wine bar selling overpriced minimalism to the sort of people who hung out at the Lovenest. There would be no cosiness, no character, maybe a disco floor where you could dance and be deafened. But Miston wouldn't put up with anything like that. Caz had heard people talking up and down the High Road. They didn't like the city, they hardly ever went there.

'Ee, I had to go in, but pet, you wouldn't recognise it. They've got what they call a shopping mall now, instead of the old streets.'

'Mall? Like on "The Golden Girls", is it?'

'Oh aye, American style now. Plastic palm trees and fountains, and I was just leaving when they started rolling down steel shutters. You'd think it was a war zone.'

'They'll make a canny profit, I dare say.'

'Well, I divent knaa about that. Every other shop's boarded over, ye knaa, To Let With Vacant Possession. And the sales! Sales everywhere! Big, huge, giant, mammoth, this month only everything must go sales. They daen't do that unless they're desperate.'

'It's years since I was in town, pet. I used to go and have a bit dinner in Markham's of a Saturday. You got a nice meal there and it was a chance to rest your feet.'

'Aye, well, Markham's is gone now. It's a Virgin Megastore. That's records and tapes: ye cannot buy virgins these days, not for love nor money! Markham's is finished.'

'Never in God's world! Well, I am upset. Me mam used to take us to Markham's. That's going back. Ee, it's all change.'

28

Nothing had changed for many generations at The Turk's Head, Caz guessed, beyond a lick of paint now and again. The Turk's Head was a local, with wide stairs and a hall and a landing bigger than her flat, all brown paint like toffee and red carpets out of an early Technicolour film. She could hear talking and singing, a muffled piano playing as they went upstairs. The room had PIANO BAR etched in the glass of the door and they went in. Everyone looked at them, but it was friendly curiosity.

Caz put her elbows on the wooden bar where people had been leaning since the last century. The lady behind the bar pulled pints with brass pump handles that her great-grandmother probably had polished.

In London, she used to go to The Piano Bar, a subterranean dive near Ronnie Scott's, hosted by a throaty sequinned transsexual called Ritu. It was pure sleaze, the music was a lush medley of nostalgia and The Piano Bar stayed open until 3 a.m. You could meet tired strippers and amiable pimps and larger than life drag queens in their tawdry glamour. Every form of urban life that never went home until the milkman was on his way sipped rotten champagne and sang and danced under Ritu's worldly wise eyes. A pallid blonde queen tinkled the keys of a grand piano festooned with pink and gold, garnished with a rococo candelabra.

This room in The Turk's Head was certainly a piano bar, but

forget the glitz of Soho. She ordered a couple of pints – no Sol here! – and looked around.

There was no one in the room under seventy years old: that was the first impression.

'How nice to be in a pub and feel young,' she murmured to Josie.

She saw Carrie and Rose sitting at a table near the middle of the room. She guessed – rightly – that they sat there every week.

'What do Carrie and Rose drink?' she asked the woman at the bar.

'Carrie has mild and Rose has best nutbrown, pet.'

'Do they drink halves?' Caz was thinking of the Saturday best glitz they wore. She wanted them to feel like ladies – they were great ladies.

'Whey no, pet, pints. But you'll need to take two half glasses and all. They don't drink out of a big glass. They're heavy these glasses. Him downstairs, he says it's so no one pinches them. Did you ever? Can you see anyone in this room pinching glasses?'

There were rogues and rascals, an old man in a flat cap with a devil-may-care twinkle, a big woman in purple silk belting out her own version of 'Love Letters' from her chair, with no need for a microphone.

'*Now my broken heart aches, for every mistake that I've made, I should never have left me mam!*'

'That's enough, Mary, we know you're dying to get up here and rip this out of me hand!' the amplified voice came from a bright-eyed woman by the piano. She was in the upper forty age range, she was in charge and everyone clapped as she silenced Mary – including Mary. She was well liked and there was something of the proud teacher/mother as she looked round the room.

'We'll have a gentleman singer next, Billy, get on your feet now. Come on, ladies and gents, a big hand for our Billy.'

Caz and Josie found seats at the table next to Carrie. She and Rose pushed their chairs back to include them.

'This is Josie, Rose, I told you about her,' said Carrie, while Billy warbled 'Autumn Leaves'. 'Caz, this is Jimmy, he's a bit hard of hearing, and Peter from downstairs. He sees us home, like, me and Rose. And this is Emily, lives down Garton Gardens.'

They must have sat together week after week for years. Deaf Jimmy used to work in the pit. Emily had the sure bulk of old age: small and majestic with moony glasses on a pearly chain. Peter was lanky and grey and his aertex shirts were beige and wrinkled. There was nothing to him but height: the bagged seat of his trousers was empty and his high-shouldered jacket was flat as if it hung on a coat hanger and not on his shoulders at all. Deaf Jimmy was red and randy, his bloodshot eyes twinkling and his mouth throwing lurid compliments at every woman in sight. If he was a schoolboy, he'd be slapped.

'But he's admitting to seventy-odd and you've got to admire him for trying,' said Emily smoothly, swatting his hand from her knee with a beer mat.

They were pleased that Caz and Josie had come. All three women took it in turns to belt Deaf Jimmy when he leaned towards them.

'Divent ye start, Jimmy, give a wrong impression!'

'Can I not say good evening to two beautiful ladies? Can I not? Ye're jealous, all of ye, isn't it?'

He winked at Caz and she grinned back. He was no bother, no bother at all.

'That's Billy,' Carrie said, nodding at the singer. 'Poor soul, used to work at Tanner and Whitleas. Asbestosis, poor man, he had a lovely voice, didn't he?'

'Eh?' Deaf Jimmy cupped one big hand at his ear.

Carrie rapped his cheek with her knuckles. 'Ye have to be right in there, divent ye, Jimmy? It wouldn't be a show without Punch. I said Billy was a lovely singer, now are ye satisfied?'

'Oh aye,' said Deaf Jimmy, serious for a moment, 'lovely voice, Billy, till he got that, what is it? – asbestosis. The little threads get on your lungs, pet. It's wicked. I'll be singing later, me. They save the best till last, divent they, just like in the Bible – will you give over, Rose, have you got bricks in that bag or what – aye. My songs are not for the faint-hearted, lover, I'd be on after eleven o'clock on the telly, wouldn't I? And it'd have to be Channel Four, mind.'

'Terrible what you can see on Channel Four,' said Emily, screeching with laughter.

Peter blushed.

'I'm getting a satellite dish, me,' said Deaf Jimmy. 'Ye can pick up fillums from Italy and Sweden, they say.'

'Now then,' Carrie warned, majestically.

'I don't mean any harm,' said Jimmy. 'Am I all right, lasses?'

'You're all right,' Caz said, relaxing. With a bodyguard of Amazons like Carrie, Rose and Emily, nothing could touch her.

'Big hand for Billy, please, give him a nice round of applause. I suppose we have to have a lady singer next. Oh dear. We'll have riots, ladies and gentlemen,' said the lady with the microphone.

'That's Laura – Laura Anderson, pet,' Carrie whispered. 'She's a lovely lass, keeps us all in order.'

'Aye, Mary, we heard you. How could we not? Ah well, shy bairns get nowt. Will we let her at the microphone and give me a bit peace?' said Laura, rolling her eyes in mock agony.

'Give it your best, Marcia, do!' cried Mary, sweeping the microphone into her hand and boogie-ing away to 'You Rascal You'.

You might as well try to drown out Ethel Merman as talk while Mary was singing. Caz sat back and drank it all in.

There were a few modern features. The round tables and chairs were quite fifties, when spit green was trendy and orange was daring. The piano was an ancient upright and so was Marcia, the player. It was nicotine brown and ringed with glass marks; she was permed in faded gold and her blouse was sage-green, her pencil skirt was bottle-green and her scarf picked up exact shades of both colours.

'*So you think your girlfriend's gone and done you wrong – GOODY GOODY!*' bellowed Mary, swaying like a purple marquee.

The piano player had gold at her powdered neck and gold and diamonds on her fingers, shining like her long, pink polished nails. An engagement ring, a wedding band, eternity rings and rubies. For all there was a score leaning on the piano, she never looked at it: she vamped like Liberace, picking up any tune and bowling it along the keyboard and back again, gathering twirls and ripples of rococo pazzazz. She talked all the time to a woman beside the piano, she slowed or speeded up, jumping ahead of faltered notes and scrambled lyrics and the singers were carried along on the carnival tide of her accompaniment.

'Big hand for Mary,' Laura took the microphone and Mary blew kisses at the applause with one hand, sweeping her skirt into a wide lilac curtsey with the other.

'Ee, she's got a voice,' Emily winced, 'ye cannot hear yerself think wi' Mary singing.'

'Ah, never mind,' Carrie said, 'she enjoys it and we have to suffer it. It's our penance. It's only a bit of fun.'

'She'll ask me any minute now,' Deaf Jimmy nodded, 'any minute now. See, it's a quarter past nine and this is where we start to get the big lads. Mind me cap, Rose, it's not paid for. All right, ee, you're a terror, the big lads and lasses. Are ye happy wi that, are ye?'

'Isn't he awful?' said Rose, shaking her head.

Laura's eyes scanned the room. 'Let's give a welcome to . . . Jimmy. Come on, you old bugger, put your tab out, put down your pint. On your feet, Jimmy. Jimmy, ladies and gents.'

Deaf Jimmy pinched the end of his cigarette and put it behind his ear.

'Cannot waste it, can I, pet?' he said, edging round Caz's chair, his big stiff hands taking him from chair back to table edge until he stood between Marcia and Laura.

'Beautiful lasses!' he said. 'Ahem. Give us the microphone, give us an introduction, ye knaa, ba da ba da, build it up like. I look like Frank Sinatra if yer take yer glasses off. I've got me public waiting and they're thirsty for me. Oh, mebbe they're thirsty for their pints. Give us a kiss, Laura? Ah well, no harm in trying.'

He hoicked up his jacket sleeve and rubbed his nose, while his eyes crinkled delight and wickedness. All week he was just one of hundreds of old men, bodies bent out of shape from years of hard graft, just another old chap living alone, buying a small loaf, a quarter of corned beef, two bob each way on the three-thirty. But on Saturdays he was Jimmy the singer: it was his moment.

'Good evening!' he shouted, cupping one hand round his ear. 'I said Good Evening! That's better, I thought ye were all sleeping. This song I'm going to sing is internationally famous. There's big words. Internationally famous it is, because I've just sold it this week, I have. I've sold it to America! They're slapping us over the face wi' money! They have musical scarecrows in America, I'm told, though what that has to do wi' me! So before I go on me Caribbean cruise with a lady friend – na, Mary, ye're too old for us – before I go out on a geet big liner, I'll sing you this song! Come on, Marcia, do us proud!'

Marcia was laughing so much she coughed and turned to him with streaming eyes. 'You silly sod, Jimmy, I don't know what it is.'

'Ye'll pick it up,' Jimmy said, clapping her on the shoulder. 'Are ye ready? Here it is!'

> '*Heart of my heart*
> *How I love that melody* – get your garters off
> *Heart of my heart*
> *Brings back sweet memory* – I want yer garters now!'

Laura raised one leg with a scarlet and black creation all ribbons and bows just above the knee. Jimmy twinkled and rolled it down her leg and on to his wrist.

> '*When we were kids*
> *At the corner of the street*
> *We were rough and ready guys* – were we not!
> *But oh how we could harmonise . . .*'

Emily took a lilac netted garter from her handbag and Jimmy slid it up his arm. Mary hurled a band of white rosebuds at his head like a gaucho with a bolas. He grinned and waved his stiff hand more or less in time with the music.

> '*But I know a tear would glisten* – I love that bit ye knaa!
> *If I could only listen*
> *To the gang that sang*
> *Heart of my heart!*'

Now his whole arm was covered in net and satin and he raised it in triumph.

'*And the garters are off*!' he hollered down the scale.

'Ah, he's a divil, that Jimmy,' Carrie said, beaming.

Marcia shrugged and thumped away, calling over her shoulder that she gave up, he'd sing what he wanted so she'd play what she wanted, she couldn't do anything else.

'I'm changing now,' said Jimmy, 'I've got me garters. Hasn't the lasses got lovely legs tonight? Never mind, Marcia my love, ye'll catch up with us one day and what a day that'll be! Yes, here's another song I've sent round the world, the known world as far as anyone can tell. I have!'

He bowed over the microphone as if it was a birthday candle and started pianissimo andante, rising to fortissimo bellicoso in seconds.

> '*Da dee dah, dee dah dee dah,*
> *If you don't know the words*

Sing dah dee dah . . .
Because it's raining, raining in me boots.
She said yes and I said NO
If ye've got no sense have a look below
Because it's raining. . . . come on, ye miserable buggers
Raining in me trousers!'

'Isn't he the lad,' Emily said, pinching in a smile.
Jimmy nodded and tapped a rhythm with his free hand. Then
he finished the song with a roar.

'Things are hard, you must admit
When it costs twenty-five pee just to have a . . .
And it's raining, raining in me VEST!'

He nodded at the applause and wiped his brow.
'Me last number,' he said, as static bounced from microphone
to speakers, 'a little tune I'm selling to Libya. I'm getting free oil
for me bike chain for LIFE, people, so it's a real hard bargain I
druv. Ye're a hard man, Jimmy, says Colonel Gaddafi. He did! Ye
knaa this un, Marcia.'
He whispered in her ear and she drew away, shrieking, as her
hands descended on the keyboard like birds.

'I belong to Miston, dear old Miston Town
What's the matter wi' Miston, well,
They've knocked the bugger down!
I'm only a common old working chap,
I'm hiding me royal-teee!
But when I've had a couple of pints on a Saturday night
Miston belongs to me!'

'That lad's a card,' Emily said.
Caz and Josie clapped as loud as they could, while Jimmy made
a courteous circuit of the bar, handing back his sleeveful of garters.

He was a card all right, he was the joker in the pack, he was the saucy knave of hearts, stealing great smacking kisses far and wide.

And when it was the end of the night, Laura Anderson sang. Like many petite women, her powerful voice took you by surprise and first she had the whole bar singing along with 'Goodnight Irene'.

'And this is the last song, folks,' she said. 'We'll be seeing you next week, but just remember this.'

She nodded at Marcia and sang, 'You are My Sunshine'. Caz looked around. Everyone was smiling, nodding, joining in. It was like a lullaby.

'*Please don't take my sunshine away,*' Laura finished, her hand shushing the cheers and whistles. 'Thank you. And thanks to our lovely Marcia, give her a nice round of applause now. And Tom who's been collecting the glasses. And Vinny and May behind the bar. And thanks to all of you, see you next week. Goodnight, God bless.'

'Well, wasn't that amazing?' Caz said as they went downstairs.

'Different,' Josie said. 'I suppose this is where you'll be for the next God knows how many Saturdays? I thought so. Well, tonight, madam, you're staying at my place. We're sorting out this project tomorrow. I won't get any work from you while there's nasturtiums and murals to be looked after in Miston.'

'Oh, you're so tough,' Caz drawled. 'OK, duck. Will you be back here?'

'Course I will,' said Josie, 'it's magic.'

29

Carrie and Peter walked Emily and Rose home for company and safety, though what protection any of them could offer! Emily and Rose went off towards Garton Gardens and Carrie and Peter to Galleon Heights. Carrie saw Peter into his flat and waited for the bolt to fumble into place. Would she take the stairs or the lift? There was enough to climb once she closed her own front door. She pressed the button.

She heard Serena's mad shrieks and murder about the flats every day and the rent office was always full of moaners. For all of that, she was happy here. The place was warm and secure, big enough to move around in and small enough to keep nice. They didn't know they were born, these people, all the hot water they wanted just by turning on a tap: she'd had years of hefting coal – and glad enough to have it! – sweeping grates and putting a paper up the chimney to clean it when she couldn't squeeze silver enough for the sweep.

They grumbled in the supermarket, walking past potatoes and greens to buy frozen chips and baked beans. They went light when those wicked people put glass in the baby food: she'd raised four children years before there was any baby food. Simple: you got a bowl and a fork and mashed it yourself. These people lived out of tins and fridges but they always had enough tabs. She'd nothing against tabs, she smoked herself, but don't cry poorhouse when your first stop is for two hundred king size every giro day.

She couldn't be doing with those silly programmes, either, the ones where they talked about the lives of people like her as if it had been the bad old days. At least you got a smile from your neighbours. It had been hard, every day was a victory once the bairns were fed and asleep, it wasn't easy, but complaining about it didn't help. You made the best. She shook her head: it was too daft to think about.

She leaned on the balcony rail. Ah, it was magic. She could see right over the valley to the pickle factory where her dad had worked. Closed now, it sat like a great floodlit tooth: you could see it for miles around. The valley was strung with orange lights like glow-worms, and the breeze lifted fresh from the river. The green was so peaceful this time of night: the lamp-post glowing pink and the trees shining like wire over a tapestry of shadows across the grass. Where else would you get a view like this?

Nowhere, thought Carrie, taking a last look as she opened her front door.

She draped her scarf over the bannister and climbed the stairs, humming softly. The key to her bedroom hung on a gold chain by the window. After all the two-up-two-down four children and her husband years, she revelled in privacy. Not even Rose had seen her bedroom. She pushed the door and turned up the dimmer switch, smiling with joy.

She had created this room.

The ceiling was heaven blue: the paint tin said High Summer and Carrie had smudged soft clouds of white and gold and sunset rose here and there, masking the harsh line where ceiling meets wall. She'd dabbled with mixers to seep the blue paler and paler through sapphire to scabious to robin's egg to white. When the sun streamed into the room, the light threw the walls back to an endless horizon and she felt she was floating on a magic carpet as she lay in bed. Her bedcover was a tapestry of Hollywood splendour, brought back from Kurdistan by her much travelled daughter. She'd painted all the wardrobe doors with leaves and flowers, smudged a river through the branches, added bright parrots and butterflies from shiny pots of enamel paint, and the sun made them glow. Fairy lights studded the trees: she flicked them on in the darkness and immediately she was in a midnight carnival under a tropic moon.

She had a radio-cassette on her bedside cabinet and she loved to play soft music at bedtime. One of her old-age luxuries was a twin to the bedside model downstairs. Sometimes when she was cleaning she had Acker Bilk in the bathroom and Harry Secombe in the kitchen and she flitted between 'Stranger on the Shore' and 'If I Ruled the World,' dusting and polishing with the changing rhythms. She shall have music wherever she goes.

She'd put spotlights on the ceiling and by turning them and using the dimmer switch she could recreate the changes in light dawn to dusk and moonlight too. Saturday nights she made a promise of sunrise with the fairy lights twinkling like birthday candles. She seldom slept these days and it was lovely to hold the party mood of The Turk's Head until the birds started twittering outside.

30

After a few weeks, Caz and Josie were regulars, greeted and welcomed, a table saved for them next to Carrie and Rose. Let Sadie and Desirée and the brothers McVey swoon among the trendy wendies, the bearded weirdos – Caz was in love with The Turk's Head. One week she'd been asked, wistfully, if she was courting. Her would-be suitor was a melancholy man who sat at one end of the bar with a flat yellow half pint of something all night.

'Courting, like,' he said, 'keeping company?'

'I've given all that up,' she told him.

'No offence?' he sounded anxious.

'Whey no,' she heard herself saying, like she'd been in Miston all her life. She smiled.

That first night in The Turk's Head, she'd got the impression that everyone was at least seventy. Now she thought that was more of an average, with eighties and nineties pulling it up, forties and fifties evening it down. It was a big family of families, generations bearing the same name, the same eyes, chins, noses. An old, waxy white dad with opaque glasses and a trembling chin and his cadaverous son seeing him to his seat, getting his drinks, tossing him a cigarette, taking him home. An old man whose wife was dead. There were a lot of widowers, sitting alone until an old mate came in. Somebody's dad, living by himself, family moved away and not many visits.

There were widows, too, loud and laughing, work over, husband dead, children raised: finally a few years to themselves. Carrie and Rose and Emily were all widows. And Mary. The men flirted gallantly, the women took the piss: at the other end of life, they were like kids in a playground, gangs and games and rhymes and teasing.

No one owned them any more, the widows and widowers, no one could come stotting in the door shouting where's the rent or me dinner's not ready. They were free to be friends if they wanted.

Beyond the banter, men and women didn't speak to each other very much. Women grew animated with each other, men held their own with other men, even though most tables had a mix of age and sex. And there were the loners too, like Caz's suitor, propped at the bar, or sitting against the wall on solitary stools dragged in from the passage. All men.

And there were a few married couples: Laura and Don Anderson, living hatred seething between them; couples who said nothing to each other, beyond what are you drinking. Maybe there were two couples whose life together had bonded them with love. Mostly Caz detected affectionate tolerance and indifference, for where there were groups of couples, they enjoyed each other's partners more than their own.

There were daughters with Bet Lynch perms, sons-in-law mute in their wake. There were grand-daughters chewing gum who'd pop in to say hello to their nanna. There was a little old lady who'd do a cancan, bloomers and all, once she'd had three halves of stout. This was a place where old people partied, their children too old to be nagged at, their grandchildren young enough to adore.

There was the old chap who brought in his own ginger ale to mix with the whisky. Sh! he said to Caz when she noticed. There's a lot do that here, well you have to with the prices. He pulled out a wallet of photos holding all his history. His grandad at Queen Victoria's funeral. His dad in the First World War. Himself and his regiment in the Second World War. His son in the navy.

His grandson, poor lad, dead in the Falklands, such a waste. The end of his line.

Whoever they were, Vinny and May at the bar had a nice word for them. Mary could always find a taunt or a joke to hurl across the room like a brick through a window. But then, that was Mary.

Laura Anderson kept the singers coming, flattering and flirting with men and women alike. Don, her husband, sat near the piano, frowning and chain-smoking. They'd been married for twenty-five years or so. Maybe the first ten, fifteen years they were too busy with children and work to notice that they hated each other's guts. Since the children loafed away from home via the army or a wedding, they'd declared open war. She didn't know why he bothered dragging his miserable face into The Turk's Head week after week and she said so, loud and often. He gave mock Hitler salutes every time she talked into the microphone.

His face twisted into a pantomime sneer when he saw her charming some old boy on to his feet and leading him up to the piano like a shy child at a party. She'd look at him and wipe all expression from her face, the way women are told to if they see a flasher. Everyone in the room caught her bright lively eyes, but his chair held nobody, he wasn't worth the attention she'd give to a bath-stain. Her spine became steel as she told the room: 'We want happy faces in The Turk's Head on Saturdays – miserable buggers should go home and watch the telly. Now, come on, you shrinking violets, I want a big hand for our lovely Emily.'

Emily had one song: 'Hurt'. Each week she demurred, telling Laura to come back to her later, when she'd had her pint. A pint, a few slapped wrists for Deaf Jimmy, a whispered snigger with Carrie and she nodded to Laura: she was ready.

There was a change in Carrie when Emily sang. She turned to see the piano and slung one elbow over the back of the chair to support her body. She clasped her hands loosely and drew everyone's eyes to her friend. Even Deaf Jimmy went silent and

Peter looked like a little boy who's never had a treat in his life or expected one.

Emily bowed over the microphone with its stem of parcel tape and string and her earrings shook and glistened through the smoke and the deeper she sang the lower she bowed. Carrie's head went down with her, then rose again proud as a swan. Laura flicked the dusty volume control higher for Emily – when Mary sang, she'd make a pantomime of agony and threaten to pull the plug.

Emily's voice toppled into the notes and vibratoed every one while the piano player tugged every scale like someone shaking out a sheet in a wild breeze. Between the words, she caught the tune and pleated it, fingertips flying on the ebony and ivory keys. Her touch was light enough to let Emily's trembling lyrics swell through the room. She gathered it all in at the finish, folded its wild edges straight and Emily sang into silence: '*I would never, ne-e-ever hurt you!*'

Carrie was rapt and winked at her friend, smacking her big palms together loudly, leading the applause right until she got back to her seat to a trembling arm-pat from Peter and a leer and knee-squeeze from Deaf Jimmy.

Then Carrie rose like a mer-goddess and sailed to the bar, waving protests aside. 'I'll not sing so there's no good coming to me, Laura,' she said. 'I could mind, but Marcia wouldn't know the song.'

'I know them all,' said Marcia, trilling a laugh like birdsong. 'What I don't know I make up and there's been no complaints so far.'

Carrie laughed and said No, no, no!

'Not tonight pet, you couldn't stand the jealousy once I part my lips, no one would dare follow me.'

'Ye see,' she leaned towards Caz, 'I have a song, "Granny's Hieland Hame". Naebody knows the words, nor the tune and so naebody can tell us I'm getting it wrong. Ah hah! I'll sing it for ye sometime, pet. When they sail the Queen Mary up Miston High Road.'

Caz laughed. She was having a bit of trouble with the project. They were going to stick plastic tulips in the ground, then have a canvas landscape with real flowers growing through it. Only she'd forgotten why. Josie kept having to remind her that this meant enough money to paint whatever she liked for a good few months. She was much more interested in the thirteen feet of nasturtium runners that twined up round her window and threatened to take over the covering of the balcony before the summer was through. She imagined opening her front door one day to find a jungle growth of leaves and flowers blocking her. Anyway, she'd banned all talk of projects on Saturday nights.

'It's me night out, duck,' she told Josie. 'Let me off the leash, girl, eh? Else I'll be pining all week, I might get sulky on you, and honey, when I sulk, the sun don't shine.'

Josie conceded. Every Saturday, Caz stayed with her after The Turk's Head; every Sunday they worked. Getting back to Miston at night-time, she really felt like she was coming home.

31

'I'll thank you to mind your own business!' Serena made her announcement from the balcony in the style of Eva Peron addressing the masses.

Caz was leaning in her doorway enjoying the morning, and ignored the threat. She watched Serena clattering along the balcony, grande dame on acid with a ferocious Lennie humping boxes up to his chin behind her. After the third load, he went back on his own and stopped in front of her, a broken upright clock cradled in his arms like a baby.

'Hot,' he said, his greedy brown eyes over her shoulder: why did she always feel that he was casing the joint? Probably because he was. Always out for what he can get, was Carrie's assessment of Lennie, always got to be into everything and know your business, gives me the creeps.

'Yeah,' Caz said, not shifting, 'you're working hard.'

'Moving,' he said, putting the clock down with an off-key clang.

'Moving?'

'Aye,' he said, caressing his death's head tattoo and flexing his muscles. 'Made an honest woman of her at last, I have. It's Mr and Mrs now so I'm moving into hers. It's a better flat, you know, we laddies just don't have a woman's touch when it comes to homemaking.'

She supposed his smile was meant to be little boy appealing: to her it was just a curved crack chiselled in his red face, his eyes hard stones in a puddle.

'Aye,' he said, stretching and swaggering, 'Mr and Mrs McCulla as of last Thursday morning.'

She guessed she was expected to offer congratulations or express surprise – even pleasure? But Caz wasn't a great fan of the institution of marriage. Who wants to live in an institution, as the lady said. From what she'd seen of Serena and Lennie, they were two oddballs whose insanities happened to coincide. Living more or less together, in and out of each other's flats, well, it seemed to work for them. But in one flat? Ample space for one person, but to share you'd have to be more than fond of your partner. Still, it saved on the rent and the bills. She scolded her cynicism. Maybe they were In Love . . .

'Two can live cheaper than one,' Lennie said, scratching his neck, 'and there's company. Mind, I'm away nights, but I trust the lass. Ye knaa what I mean, eh?'

'Uh huh,' Caz said, 'well, I wish you both luck.'

'My husband and I,' Serena swept towards them breathlessly, 'my husband and I, me and Lennie, we don't need luck. Although thank you, I'm sure. Lennie, the clock.'

'She's the boss,' Lennie said, grinning, 'eh, lass? In our house the woman wears the trousers, do ye not feel sorry for me, Caz?'

'You look like you're suffering,' Caz said drily.

Serena watched him carry the clock towards the flat.

'You have to be careful round here,' she said. 'There's a lot of women who want to get hold of Lennie, he's a good man, I have to keep an eye. He's not got it all up here, you see, I'm the clever one. He needs looking after, yes, looking after, we look after each other. We help each other, not like some I could name, I'll tell you about it sometime. And we'll be neighbours, my husband and I and you.'

She winked at Caz and leant too close. 'I believe our bedrooms are next door, what with the stupid way these flats are designed, so you'll have to be a bit – you know – what I'm saying is, the walls aren't soundproof, ah ha ha!'

She dug Caz in the ribs. Oh. Sex. Mind, if Lennie worked nights, life should continue to be quiet.

All morning, Lennie went from his old flat to Serena's, carrying boxes and ornaments. Finally he took his birdcage and crooned to the pastel blue budgie that she was moving now and he'd a wife and it would be more company for her.

'Won't it, darling,' he said, tapping the golden bars, 'it will, won't it, daddy's found ye a mammy, so he has.'

The next morning, Caz was woken at eight with Serena shouting. 'If you're going to do it, do it properly or don't bother! Put some muscle into it, Lennie, we'll never be finished!'

Caz groaned: was this foreplay? Then she heard Lennie snarling: 'I've been at it all night, woman, is there no bloody peace, I'm doing it, I'm doing it, you don't want a man, you want a bloody little puppy dog, you!'

Caz tensed as their bedroom door was flung wide. She heard the sound of a broom on the balcony: not foreplay but housework. Serena was in full flight, she'd always been houseproud and not about to become a slut just because she was now a McCulla.

'I'll fuckin' belt ye!' Lennie's voice was ugly.

'Oh now, Lennie, let me get you a nice cup of tea.'

'Tea? Bugger tea, Serena, come over here!'

'Oh, Lennie, no. No, no Lennie, please Lennie.'

'Shut it!'

'Oh, nicely, Lennie, nicely.'

'We're married now. Just shut up and come here. Right this minute.'

Caz got up, feeling powerless revulsion. She didn't even want to think about Lennie and Serena and whatever passed for sex between them. It was sordid, didn't sound like there was anything like love in it. If they kept it up, she'd be sleeping in her living room.

But the rest of the week she heard nothing apart from loud Irish folk music and laughter. She didn't see either of them and so she relaxed. Maybe it was OK. One day she spotted Serena coming out of the post office over the High Road and she hid in the gents' outfitters looking at hats until the coast was clear. She didn't want further nudges and winks and confidences.

Carrie shook her head about the whole business. 'He's not a man I'd trust near me, ee, can you imagine it!' she said to Caz. 'Still, to each his own. I keep well out of the way, me. Serena's desperate, pet, desperate to talk.'

32

Serena growled and slammed the door. Knocking and running away, kids today, one day she'd get them and she'd get round to see their parents. As if she hadn't enough to do. Why couldn't things just be peaceful and nice like when she was little and the fields stretched forever to hills that kissed heaven and there was bread from the oven on the table. And a warm voice caressing her hair and tucking her in safe at night.

'Honest to God,' she told the pink-ribboned box of pot pourri, 'they never tell you growing up will be all work and people being nasty, aah, aah.'

She hit her cheek to drive the tears away and snarled at the kettle, so long boiling and all you want is a nice cup of tea. A nice cup of tea, yes, and a cigarette and to get straight.

Those quilt covers had to be somewhere, things don't just disappear, not when you've got your own home and you keep it clean and live decent.

Four days she'd hovered near the shop doorway, the bolts of cloth in the window daring her to come in. People like her didn't have material like that, it was too good for her sort, and they put up the prices like a barbed wire fence. Only she wouldn't be kept out, her money was as good as theirs. Anyway, there were remnants, she'd heard someone say in a café. She hadn't been too friendly, that one, you'd think she owned the remnants, people just didn't help each other and it wasn't right. But the mean-mouthed bastard had told her which shop and she was going to have the remnants and make patchwork quilts for her cousins. They'd pull them up at night and sleep tight, knowing she cared about them because she'd sewed the cloth together herself because she hadn't forgotten them and their dreams would be sweeter for it.

It had hit her when she was looking through photographs. There she was, seven, nine, eleven, thirteen, smiling at the funfair, laughing on the beach with her cousins, Mark and Matthew and Kathleen and Kerry. Somehow she'd lost them when she left home, never bothered to write, well how could you with a husband and a family that spoke no English to deal with, and what with the baby.

'Aaah, aah,' Serena wailed as she poured boiling water over a teabag and spooned in powdered milk, honestly there was war on in her life, and it was always money, she didn't like dried milk, but what could you do with no fridge and the flats were always too hot and the milk went lumpy and stinking in an afternoon. They didn't mind sticking you for heating you don't want, but as for a fridge, no, Mrs Parra, you're not entitled. No fresh milk.

'I don't want milk,' she snarled at the kettle. 'Do you hear me, always pulling bits of me away, I don't want milk. I'm looking for the quilt covers, make a nice parcel for Kathleen and Kerry, it'll be a nice surprise and maybe they'll ask me for a holiday, God knows I need one.'

Method, that was the thing. Start a job and finish it, start as you mean to go on, be thorough. Maybe the last time she'd moved, she'd packed them away against the time there was time to make it all nice. That time was now. So long as she remembered to get the dinner on. A clean house and a hot meal on the table, she mouthed.

She pushed her sleeves up to thin elbows – I've not let myself go like some I could name. Still got a figure. She put her hands on her hips and twirled. Yes. Start where you are. She slammed through the kitchen unit cupboards, tins of soup and sardines and scouring powder. A pile of ironed tea towels. 'Well, that's done. I've done that.'

She glared at the closed doors with white fists and a toe raised, daring them to lurch open. And if she looked later and the quilt covers were there, woe betide . . . woe betide.

'Aah, aaah,' she moaned, clutching her ribs, what had she eaten that had poisoned her. She crunched two aspirins and choked a little as she washed down the bitter powder. Pills? She knew about pills, Doctor Sylvester said she was good with pills. Doctor Sylvester had nice hands.

The quilt covers were so pretty. She'd stotted into the posh shop on the fifth morning, her mouth drawn in contempt as she dived at the remnant basket.

'Pretty, pretty,' she cooed, smoothing the cut squares with their bouquets and garlands of flowers. She'd need twenty and a lot of each pattern and set her shoulders to argue with the assistant suppose she said there were no more, people just couldn't be bothered to put themselves out even a little these days. But the basket was wide and deep and she piled up easily more than she could ever need. Plain Irish green that sang of ribbons and shamrocks and pixies, a cream lawn wreathed with emerald daisy chains. A bold pattern of milk-white lions dancing on their hind legs, tongues lolling and claws ready to box on a field as fresh as she'd seen from her cousin's window, the window of her bedroom when she was a little girl. They made a nice brown paper parcel and her sewing machine hummed them into alternate rows that filled the living room.

You don't lose something so precious. She opened the door of the walk-in cupboard by the kitchen sink. Her father glared at her from the darkness, sitting on the commode with his pyjamas wrinkled round his grey ankles in stripes of convict blue. His eyes were terrible, a flickering coal of hatred in the centre of their nicotined blue. Grey hair stuck up like a tattered wreath on his head and his thin lips sagged around his gums. She stared at him and screamed so she wouldn't hear the awful voice and its words blinding her like the air gun the day the boys had tied her up and shot her for collaborating with Hitler. Clumping, shuffling Uncle Iain, one-legged since Arnhem, was visiting and they were playing Resistance. Kerry was a spy and Kathleen was a nurse and she was a traitor.

'You boys go too far,' her aunt had said while Serena gibbered into her apron, terrified to open her eyes in case she was blind.

Now her father accused her while the stench of piss and shit filled her nose and had her gagging. '*You* make quilts? You couldn't even tie your shoelaces when you were a little girl or keep your man when you got one.'

She clawed at the light switch. With a click, the bare bulb dazzled her and her father vanished.

Good riddance, good riddance, she muttered, scanning the boxes for clues. SELL-BY CRISPS 10p. That was too square for folds of fabric, that would be sterilised jars for jams and pickles she was making this year, now she was better . . . FOR DINNERS AND TEAS USE MORTENSON'S PEAS, WE AIM TO PLEASE. A sturdy box, that, built to hold two layers of tins, she wouldn't have wasted its strength on material. OLD LEAKE GROWERS' ASSOCIATION. That would be lettuces and she'd discarded three for their slimy corners, mould on her clothes and ornaments, pooh, no thank you. It took two weeks to find the boxes she needed to move, scouring the supermarkets, begging and wheedling at off-licences and corner stores. It cost them nothing, nothing at all, you'd think it was gold dust she was asking for, a woman on her own has to be grateful for not being murdered or raped at a bus stop.

But Mortenson's Peas had sheaves of holiday brochures and photographs and she squatted on the floor to sort them. If you sort as you go, you know where you are.

People like her did go on holiday, there was no law against it. She had a right to take every brochure off the travel agent's shelf if she wanted to. It was all a question of money, but then she was careful.

'Don't want to go there again,' she told the cooling cup of tea, tearing a leaflet in half, 'we won't go where we're not wanted.'

She'd bought the ticket though it meant going short for a month and packed a little bag, more money. What a waste. She'd been down where the buses come in an hour early and had a cup of tea in the café, glaring her table empty, one hand gripping the handles of her bag. She'd asked the inspector about her bus and the peak-capped liar had said she was at the wrong station. Her plenty of time vanished as she ran along the streets, it was raining and her shoes slipped. Her bus had gone by the time she got there, gone by three minutes and her day shattered round her as she howled. The inspector there had talked to the desk clerk and tapped his head as if she was mad. Didn't he know that she'd scrimped and saved to buy a day out, she'd dreamed of the hills and the rivers and the seas. He gave her money back and she threw it at him with the bag. Money couldn't compensate.

Back in her flat she rang her MP. He was sly, never home. She told the social and the housing officer, she rang the bus company. She was still waiting for the solicitor on that one. They were all thieves.

'This won't buy the babby a new bonnet,' her mother shrilled at her, leaning on the edge of the sink.

'Excuse me,' she said from the floor, 'but you're ignorant. I am preparing a parcel for my cousins and that has my priority, Mother. I don't wish to know about your problems, dear, I have enough of my own to deal with.'

Her mother grumbled down the wastepipe. 'Bloody cow! Personal hygiene – you wouldn't know what the words mean!'

Now she had to mop the floor from her mother's footprints, wipe the sink clean from the grime of her hands, spray air freshener around.

Quilt covers. They must be somewhere. Look at the papers all over the cupboard floor – she'd never get straight. She crammed them back into OLD LEAKE GROWERS' ASSOCIATION. Let them rot with the scabby lettuce leaves, one day they'd know about it.

Someone at the door. Kids? The wind? She tore across the lino and wrenched it open.

'Mrs Parra? Mrs Serena Parra?' some smiling stranger come to waste her time.

'No lady of that name resides here,' she said. 'As you can see, I'm occupied and this is not a convenient time to call.'

She slammed the door and opened it again immediately. 'I shall be occupied for the rest of the day,' she said, closing her eyes in disdain. 'Don't come here wasting my time.'

The social worker sighed as the door slammed again and she heard locks and bolts rattling into place. Serena cursed her through the glass. She ticked her clipboard and walked back along the balcony, into the lift and down to her car.

Serena snapped out the kitchen cupboard light and closed the door on the evil smell of her father and his toothless sneer. Time to scrub her hands and scrub the potatoes for dinner. Scrub, not peel, to keep in the goodness. All the goodness of a potato was in the skin. Doctor Sylvester had told her.

'Doctor Sylvester, Doctor Sylvester,' she sang high and tuneless, 'we like Doctor Sylvester, don't we, he's a nice kind man.'

Potato.

'Oh God,' she sank against the cold metal edge of the sink, 'Lennie's coming back.'

She tried to stand up, to say aloud, my gentleman friend, to wink at the mirror, but her legs wouldn't have it. Lennie, Lennie everywhere, always coming back and never letting her alone, no, not for a minute.

'I said the bloody clock was broken and what's the point, Lennie!' she screamed, but it came out a whisper, 'and I've your dinner to get. What with, dear, the shops don't take bottle tops.'

There wasn't a chance he'd gone back to his flat? She slapped her face hard for a fool. He'd never be going back there, it wasn't his any more. This flat was theirs, she was his, they were husband and wife and he could do what he liked to her.

'We share,' she chanted, 'Mr and Mrs McCulla, we share, oh God, why did I marry him?'

Her mother lumbered out of the kitchen cupboard. 'Rather be a slut with no ring, a daughter of mine, is it?' she sneered.

'I am a decent woman,' she said, 'I've always been decent, your sort wouldn't know the meaning, dear, traipsing filth . . .'

She waved her fists at her mother until she disappeared. Lennie, oh, Lennie, just be kind, a bit kind, Lennie, like when we were courting. Till death us do part, oh Lennie, do you mean it? Nicely, Lennie . . .

She could clean the air from her mother and father, oh God, the smell. But there wasn't time. Not with the door about to burst open any moment and Lennie to be coming back, always coming back, and her never to have a moment's peace again, never, not for the rest of her days.

33

The next time she saw Serena, Caz was shocked. Her eyes burned as if she had fever, her cheekbones stuck out and her mouth sagged. Her hair was almost completely grey, dragged back into a tortoiseshell slide, and her hands had gone thin as plastic forks, clutching her flat shopping bag like a shield.

She was Mrs McCulla, a bride of six weeks.

'I've told them,' she confided in Caz, 'I had to, you don't like to, but Lennie's right, if you don't where are you? That's my point, I said, Mr Creased Shirt and the big desk, you could float a boat across it, the bastard, says he'll do something. They've all got bosses, and I'm giving it three days, long enough to see what's what. Ah hah!'

Who what when where why: Caz wondered which floodgate to open. 'Well, if something's bothering you,' she said.

'You know what I mean!' Serena laughed. 'See! You can come down to the offices, they'll listen to an educated person. I'm not ignorant but they take advantage of my nature. Then we'll be out of here! Not a word to a soul – you know what they're like round here. There's always your MP.'

It made as much sense as switching on the TV in the middle of a soap opera you never watched. No – less. Once, Caz had watched a five-hour Chinese epic on video. The invitation had been a great honour, while she'd been teaching art in Limehouse. Her Chinese student, Pu-Chieh Fu, asking her to meet his family, revered grandparents and all! She sat in the crowded Fu household, respectful and bemused. Pu-Chieh had tried to explain it to her.

This one – he's a bad man.

This is a good man who does bad things.

This is a bad man with a good heart.

This man is trouble.

Magnificently costumed warriors strode into a palace room. A man in blue sat beside the throne. One of the warriors raised a curved sword and beheaded him. Her student's family roared with laughter.

Samurai warriors rode over the plain and an old man in red stood watching them, arms folded, frowning. The leader of the warriors leapt from his horse and bowed. He snatched the scroll the old man was holding, then cut his head off with a sweep of his axe. The Fu clan hissed through their teeth, Pu-Chieh's father blotted his streaming eyes with a kleenex.

A baby was left in the shadow of a rock. Her friends nodded approval. A mother played with a chubby child in a silk padded jacket. Pu-Chieh laughed bitterly.

The epic rode on a whole set of codes and rules that she knew nothing about: second nature to her friends, too complicated to begin to grasp. Serena's world was as alien and complex, a jumble of broken mosaic scattered on shifting sands. She left the air itself fragmented, nothing could be relied on, none of her reality depended on what Caz already knew.

She went to see Carrie.

'The language, pet!' Carrie raised her hands helplessly. 'No one could say she was easy to live with, she'd drive anyone mad, but him shouting at her – and she showed me the bruises.'

'Yeah,' said Caz. She was now sleeping in her living room, she couldn't bear the 3 a.m. slam of the door, Lennie stomping downstairs, Serena twittering, the sound of fists and then an awful whimpering like a chained dog. Serena held her head high as she walked down the High Road, but every so often she'd let out a wail or a scream. More and more she'd stop a passer-by and pin them to the spot with tales of pain and persecution.

Sometimes Caz saw Lennie and he had changed. Always Jack the Lad in the way he walked, he moved like a monstrous android these days, planting his feet heel-first into the pavement, his mouth working over a jaw set like granite. He had become a thing of clay slapped over a steel frame. He was terrifying. As Serena had fretted into a pale shadow, he had swelled.

'It's awful, pet,' Carrie wiped a tear away, 'I know what she's going through. She's afraid to move for him. I cannot keep her out of my house these days. The other morning she was rolling on my floor laughing like a madwoman, pointing to here and her backside, he just wants her for one thing, poor woman, and she's got no escape.'

'It was better when they lived apart,' Caz said, 'at least she'd got her own front door.'

'That's her very words,' Carrie nodded slowly, 'but if you say owt against him, she's up in arms, says he's her man and there's women chasing him, even me. Did you ever? Chase that? I'd as like to be chasing cockroaches! My man was like that, you've no life at all if you're frightened in your own home. And ye see, I wouldn't say a word to anyone, I was so ashamed. Serena'll tell the world but she'll not leave him, she has to have a man, it's a sickness with her.'

Caz tried to imagine Carrie in thrall to a man like Lennie. It was hard, for now Carrie had a solid majesty and dignity that no one would challenge.

'I was daft, me,' Carrie said, frowning over that scared young self. 'Ye see, they all said he was a good man, he didn't gamble, he didn't drink, so they must have thought I was tight wi money. Pet, I had none. I didn't know what wage he earned, he'd have knocked me into next week if I'd asked him. I was fifteen when I wed him, I knew nowt. I think Lennie keeps her short, ye knaa.

He thought he was on to a good thing marrying her, with her on the social and the rent paid, he saw himself living like a king. But all her benefits is stopped wi being married and she hasn't a penny to call her own. I feel sorry for her. He'll have to give her money for her medicines and her food and all the bills now he's a married man.'

'I never thought of that,' Caz said, 'Jesus! And he doesn't.'

'Nah, not a bit of it,' Carrie said. 'She's borrowed off me for her cigarettes, mind, she always pays back. I've give her dinners, pet, she comes in like a starving waif and ye cannot refuse a body a bit of food. She eats it down like a caged animal, doesn't use a knife or fork to it, it's awful to watch, she keeps looking at the door in case he comes in. I've no peace with them.'

Serena told Caz that Carrie paces the floor all night and shits in the sink. She said that Carrie wees in milk bottles and throws them out of the window. Serena thought that if her house was clean and tidy then everything should be all right. She'd done the right thing: keeping house and getting married and nothing was right. Dirt disgusted her. The garden way below her window was a pauper's graveyard of shredded kitchen units, used condoms, piss-yellow newspaper, a grey doll's body with the head and arms ripped off.

'Carrie and her – that prostitute at seventy-one, they're mad,' she hissed at Caz, trapping her in the lift. 'They wait until it's dark and hoy everything out of the window. They're trying to drive me mad, I know it, they want to drive me away. I'd go tomorrow, yes I would, if it was convenient to me. I know my rights.'

34

By God, she knew her rights and now was the time to fight for them. Prison visitors, gaolers, torturers, extortionists, even Lennie was no friend still less a gentleman. Even Doctor Sylvester told her to take things more slowly and think before she spoke. The bloody cheek of it! As if she was to blame. It had always been the same. London, Tottenham, Darlington, Newcastle, Miston: full of spies and police.

She was finished with England.

She sat at her kitchen table with two packets of cigarettes, a plastic wallet of blue biros, a ruled notepad, a packet of envelopes and a sheet of stamps. The money she'd spent!

'No dinners for you this fortnight,' she said severely. Going hungry had never bothered her, she knew they could control you with food.

She folded back the notepad cover and started to write.

To whom it may concern.

I am writing to draw your attention to my situation, and if your hearts are not touched by decency and caring then don't waste your time by reading any further.

They have always known who I was and tried to keep it from me, but I know. Years of such cruelty as you wouldn't believe have made me sure of it. It's in their eyes when they look at me, it would make your flesh creep. I'm used to it, but I've HAD ENOUGH, do you understand me.

I'll start at the beginning.

Serena lit another cigarette and read what she'd written.

'I could go back years, dear!' she snarled, 'And maybe I will, nothing left to lose, oh the shame of it!'

She smoked swiftly, then a smile crept on to her lips and she picked up the biro.

Consider this, since if you've read this far, you'll understand. My course was set from the moment I was conceived. One cell split and that was my beginning. From that instant, I grew, learning everything that my parents' cells could tell me. As my flesh formed, I knew I would be dressed in soft silks and my tiny fingers stretched in the warm wet darkness, learning to touch and to hold. A gold sceptre would be mine. When my feet made toes, they wriggled, knowing velvet slippers and polished marble were their lot. My shoulders would carry cloaks and ermine would ruffle my chin. You've no eyes to speak of before you're born and nothing to see, but oh, you can dream. I dreamed pictures of rolling parkland, lofty turrets, grazing deer, liveried footmen opening every door, white gloved hands helping me into a golden coach. My empire would be vast, people of all races would line the streets and cheer me from East to West.

Even then, the dreams had shadows, as if it could all disappear any moment. There was shouting and anger behind closed doors for all the gold handles.

I was born early one cold misty morning and my flesh cringed at the dryness and cold of the world. How do I remember? Well, I do. I was blue and the doctor slapped me until I was pink. That was the first touch I felt. I drew away from the harsh cotton they wrapped me in, my ears longed for the dull pounding of my mother's heartbeat through the oceans of her body. The ceiling and the walls were dirty grey. There were dull green radiators with dribbles of rust and everywhere the harsh smell of blood and sweat and disinfectant. The light was darker than the womb, do

you see, I knew sunlight inside me and this was tubes behind
dusty glass. The walls had taken the light and this light was a
sham.

Something was wrong, dear, but what's a new born baby to do
but cry?

Serena cried now, tears slipping down her cheeks, cold and salt.
Poor baby, she crooned, poor little girl, I'll help you. She wiped
her cheeks and went on.

Born in wedlock, yes I was, but a bastard. My mother was
married to one man but my father was not the man she
was married to. It is a small detail and it has blighted my life.
If I had no knowledge of how things should have been then I would
have accepted the way they were. Ignorance they say is bliss,
although I can't see how anyone would have found bliss in the way
I was brought up. Dirt, poverty, anger, filth, punishment. The
part of me that was my mother longed to settle for this awful
life, the part of me that was my father was outraged and lost:
then there was me, the new person, who should have been a new
person. I was torn apart by them. His life tugged at me – leave,
go, these are not your people, her life said accept it, endure it,
forget.

What chance did I have of finding my own way, tethered to
my father's ways in memory and trapped in my mother's dingy
reality.

Then there was the man I called Father. Don't start me on
him! Think of nothing, halve it, take away decency and that
was 'Father'. Enough of him, his life was spent being cruel, his
words made my life a minefield. Remember I had been expecting
fields that were green and mine, a palace.

Serena stopped and lit a cigarette. She could see it now. Sitting
by dirty net curtains looking out over a back alley, waiting for the

slam of the door and her father's feet up the stairs. The stink of poverty and fear.

She snapped the biro in two, tossed it over her shoulder and took another one from its wallet.

I am a very clean person, which is part of my father's side. I never learnt that from my mother, I can tell you.

We lived in three rooms up seven flights of concrete stairs where the windows had been broken so many times they were boarded up and filthy words all over, piss and vomit like a carpet. When my 'father' worked he was drunk and we were frightened and hungry; when he didn't work, we were hungry and frightened. We? My mother, the 'father' and a child which came from both of them, Darryl, a boy, and me. Darryl came less than a year after me, it was as if my mother couldn't wait to clean all of me out from inside her. He was not happy, although I could see the way he found it all familiar, he ducked before the 'father's' fist reached him, he scavenged the cupboards and fed himself while I sat on the floor crying and dizzy with being hit and hungry. We lived in the three rooms, we went out only to collect benefit and buy drink and food.

This was until I was five.

You will know nothing of schools for five-year-olds in the 1950s. Lucky you!

By birth I should have had a governess, a music teacher, a singing teacher – everything I needed to educate me for my position. Instead, I got a wooden bench and a slate and forty other children to share the teacher. I was caned, I had to stand in the corner. I learnt to read and write very quickly and people noticed that I was nothing like my 'family'. There was talk and I had hopes that they would take me away and restore my birthright. But that class of person sees anything better than themselves as something to be jeered at. I learnt of the Crucifixion and realised that this was my Stations of the Cross. Like Jesus,

I fell several times and anyone who tried to help me was spat upon. Every day was a trial, and I had nightmares about what would become of me.

Of course it was jealousy.

'Darryl,' Serena said angrily, 'you did all right for yourself, didn't you, they kept you, didn't they.'

Years after, she'd seen him in the street and he pretended he didn't know her, said she was a loony and when she wouldn't leave him alone, asked her how much? He was his father's son, precious Darryl. Never mind, she'd show him. She sniffed and stuck her chin out. Oh, she'd tell them, all right.

There came a time when I was 'too much' for my 'family'. Too much, I ask you, well, they'd never been enough for me. Some stranger came and they asked me if I wanted to go. Now I know she was the first secret agent to start hounding me. I believed that I would be going where I belonged and said yes. I was a poor child, a poor child at the time. Since then I know justice here is a lie. That was when prison started. I knew they were out to break me. Why they didn't simply kill me was obvious: I was too important. I went into an institution with complete strangers who laughed at me, mocked me, beat me, abused me every way you can think of and I won't go into it. Jealousy again. But they got careless and took us on an outing one day. We went to Bowes, which you won't know. It is a castle in the French style and has more glass in one window than you'd find in an ordinary person's house. The walls were tapestried with big paintings in gold frames, the floors were polished like mirrors, the mirrors shone like diamonds. The chairs were solid gold, the beds were velvet with canopies as high as a bridge. It was wasted on all the other children. But I saw again as clear as day the pictures from before I was born. This was the sort of place I should be!

'Bowes,' Serena said. 'Yes, I know it well, they wouldn't even let me spend a night there. The cruel evil pigs, show you your birthright and put you back on a coach. Or a Black Maria, tie you up with wire, ah hah, I could talk. I've always known words.'

She lit another cigarette and ground her teeth. Her wrist was aching, but what was pain after all the pain she'd known in her life.

'Nothing to me, dear!'

I was clever. You don't let people know what you know because then they take advantage. If they'd found out that I was on to them, security would never have been relaxed. As it was, I put up with it all until I was sixteen and I escaped.

Why didn't I claim my birthright there and then? I knew they'd do anything to stop me. No, I was clever and went to London where you can be anonymous. I was biding my time. And then I met a man who fathered my child. Hajid. He was Egyptian and a decent man, or so he said. They say a woman calms down with a child and one night I saw in his face that he was a part of the plot. If I had accepted the life they'd given me, I would still be there. You see? Give the mad bitch a baby and make her forget her rights. I didn't fall for that!

I did love my baby but they damaged him in the hospital and he was never right.

As soon as Hajid knew I'd seen through him, there was hell on. He took my child and had me put in another institution where, heartbroken and crazed, I had nothing to lose and I told them who I was. They used drugs on me to make me forget, they shot my brain with electric guns, they tried to freeze my body. They have even made it impossible for me to have more children, think what a scandal that would cause and God alone knows where my son is. Nothing worked and I didn't give in.

This went on, they moved me back up to Newcastle into an institution and I stopped telling them the truth until they thought they'd killed my memory. My father's spirit was strong

*in me, I had seen his photograph in a magazine. His name I
won't reveal, apart from saying he is a duke and it's to do with
the capital of Scotland.*

*So when they thought they'd made me forget it all, I was let
out into open prison. A gaoler visits me every week and I'm
supposed to be her friend. Certainly she tries to make me
comfortable, guilt I suppose. I have been writing lots of letters
to put them off the scent before writing this one in the hopes that
it gets by the censors. Don't be surprised if most of this is crossed
out. Nobody here admits that they are in prison, you'd think it
was an ordinary housing estate, but I know. There are a lot of
old ladies, I don't know their crime, but they are so old they
couldn't do any harm. We are all political offenders, sealed
from the outside world.*

*There are some younger ladies and gentlemen and at last I
have a gentleman friend I can relax with. They managed to
clear his memory, he's quite simple sometimes, but he is clearly of
a better class or they wouldn't have put him here. But he
remembers enough to call me Princess and say that we deserve
better. He would also use his fists on anyone who tried to hurt
me and that's made me brave enough to be writing this.*

Serena read through the whole letter. That was more like it.
Now it was up to them what they would do, but someone
somewhere would have a conscience, surely to God the world
couldn't be filled with evil? She pursed her lips and wrote the last
paragraph very carefully.

*I have written to all the MPs in Parliament but they are in
the plot too and most of them didn't even answer my letters,
afraid I suppose and jealous of course, I've come to live with that.
I don't ask that my throne is returned to me, no, they can keep
it, but I deserve the respect and dignity they have spent so many
years throwing in my face. I want to leave England and live
out my days in a suitable style of life to my breeding. I ask for*

help and I don't expect it. There's never been any, but maybe you are different. I hope so.

I HAVE NO ONE ELSE TO TURN TO.

Yours sincerely

Serena Zachary.

c/o Miston Central Post Office,

Miston,

Newcastle-on-Tyne,

England.

The gaolers wouldn't get wind of this for a while. She knew they tampered with her letters, but this should fettle them! She tapped the sheets of paper into a neat stack and began again.

To whom it may concern . . .

It would be a long night. There were so many countries in the world, she decided to start with the hot ones. After all, it was high time she had a little sunshine in her life.

35

'You're looking tired, pet,' Carrie said, leaning on Caz's arm as they walked up to The Turk's Head.

Josie was walking behind them, Rose on her arm. She said she felt like Adopt-a-Granny on Saturday nights, but Caz said it was more like being adopted. She would have loved to take them up to The Turk's Head in a white Rolls Royce, only the fact that she didn't have one stopped her. Walking with Carrie and Rose made her feel gallant and privileged and she wore a white blazer with a carnation in the buttonhole. She'd splashed out on two garters for her favourite jaunt, bright pink for Josie, hers was a sequinned rainbow. In honour of Deaf Jimmy.

'Well, I guess I need a holiday,' she said. 'I'm good at holidays. Are you getting away this year?'

'Canada,' Carrie said. 'It's not a real holiday, I'm gannin to see me sons and grandbairns. I fancy a week in Scarborough for a real holiday, a bit song and a laugh. Me and Rose went there last year, no it was two years ago. Ee, we had fun. Stayed in a hotel and had our breakfast in a dining room looking right over the sea. There was a crowd of us, from me Thursday club like, but you could do what you wanted once you were there. Up all night, playing cards and having a bit drink. I'm not a lover of drink, but I like the company. Are you getting away, pet?'

Caz felt like she'd been on holiday ever since she wrenched herself away from London to Newcastle. Only a matter of years, but it was another life. Sure, she was broke, but she could organise her own time. The hills and lakes were a bus ride away, the sea was twenty minutes on the train. It was a gift.

'I dunno,' she said. 'Can't think where to go.'

'Well, ye're looking peaky,' Carrie said. 'You want to go on one of them cruises. I did once and it was the best time of my life. The sea air makes you feel lovely.'

'Me and Rockefeller,' Caz said. 'Although you can get over to Norway very cheap.'

'That's not a cruise,' Carrie was scornful. 'Nah. It's cold there, pet, I've seen it on the travel programmes. Ye're not on holiday if you need a cardigan, I say. Well, ye have to pack one here, but if ye're travelling abroad, ye want a bit sunshine like.'

'So what cruise do you recommend?' Caz said, smiling at how blasé Carrie sounded.

'Less of your lip!' Carrie dug her in the ribs. 'No, these days it's all aeroplanes, isn't it, pet? But when I was young, it was cruises. That was where the film stars went, ye'd see them in the pictures. And royalty. Ye'd see photos of them in their furs going up the gangway of the Queen Elizabeth at Southampton, waving and smiling and everyone had it as a dream. We were poor, Caz, dirt poor and everyone needs a dream.'

'True enough,' Caz said. For her generation, there had been many dreams of travel. Buying a double decker bus and going overland to India. Hitch-hiking almost anywhere. Getting a ticket for the Magic Bus that couldn't guarantee you'd get where you wanted always, certainly not when you wanted, but man, oh man, what a trip you'd have not getting there.

'Let's have a bit seat,' Carrie said, 'the slope takes all me puff. Aye. I've not told ye about me cruise, have I?'

'Go on,' Caz said, loving the way Carrie twinkled with pleasure at the start of a story.

'Well, it was after he died, happy face, me husband,' she said scornfully. 'The money we found hidden in the house, pet, ye'd not credit it! Me without a pair of shoes on me feet! He was a mean man, pet, never bothered wi the bairns or wi me – and he had nobody else! And the best bit was a leather pouch he'd sewn inside me cushion. I knew the thread was different, but I daresn't look while he was alive. All his redundancy money, pet, and the insurances, all of it hidden and me selling me few bits of ornaments to feed his miserable face!'

'You must have felt awful,' Caz said.

'I felt like a fool, pet, tell the truth. All those years when the bairns were walking round like tinkers, the truant man coming to get them to school when they took it in turns for we'd only one pair of shoes! All those years of feeding them barley broth and bread and them crying wi hunger: I thought I'd done me best, but here, all the time, we could have been comfortable. Never mind. Me daughter opened the desk and the five pund notes was dropping on the floor. Notes from before the war, notes from Scotland – he'd worked there after the war for a year. When we counted it all up, we had three thousand, seven hundred and eighty-four pounds. We just sat and looked at it. I couldn't even cry and me daughter was raging.'

'And that would be worth – oh – a hundred thousand now,' Caz said.

'Easy,' Carrie said and her mouth went hard.

Rose and Josie came up to the bench. Caz stubbed out her fag. 'I'm just telling her me life story,' Carrie said, rising and taking Caz's arm again.

'You've got a book there,' Rose said. 'Never lived anywhere but Miston, have we pet, but we've seen life.'

'Never a truer word,' Carrie said. 'Aye. Well, me daughter says, Mam, blow the lot. Ye've given yer life blood for it. I says no, we all suffered for him. I was reckoning up. I says here, I'm giving all four of ye seven hundred and fifty-six pound sixteen shillings. Ye've had nowt from him all yer lives and it's only right. Me daughter said she wouldn't take hers, she didn't need it, but I says just for once madam, ye'll do as you're told. Seven hundred and fifty-six pound sixteen shillings. Me lads in Canada was just setting up a business and it helped them. Terry, me youngest lad, he was down in London training to be a chef and it got him started in his own caffy. But me daughter – she's a bugger.

'I went in the travel agents and I says to him, have ye got a Christmas cruise. I did! I paid for it cash and there was still money. It was lovely. I went out and bought me costumes, all new, me shoes – I had five pair. All new. I went in shops in town I'd never even known was there. I bought all me luggage matching and took a taxi home. Aye. So off I went. Ee, I'll never forget it. Me, on the deck of the Empress of Britain, crossing the equator on Christmas Day! I never went to bed for three days, I had to see the sun rise and set and moon come up. The moon and sun are bigger down there, ye hardly recognise them.'

Carrie squeezed Caz's arm and smiled beatifically.

'That was the best thing ever happened in me life, pet. The Empress of Britain. It was a ship bigger than the High Street, mind, ye could spend a day walking round it. Swimming pools and tennis and everything. We went past the islands, I cannot remember the names of them, it was all sunshine and trees you'd think they'd made up. Ye see it on television now, but I'd never seen owt like it. We were eating fruit I'd never heard of fresh every day. There was an orchestra playing every night and they asked me for a request one night. I said, play 'The Blaydon Races' and I'll sing, mind, I had to speak slow, for I was the only Geordie on board and I was afraid they'd not understand me. I had to talk all posh, you know! But they got me meaning, and after that it was hello, Geordie, good morning, Geordie, good afternoon, Geordie. I felt like a princess. I even had me dinner at the captain's table more than once. And when I come back, there was a pile of welcome home cards from me children and a brown envelope. Me daughter had opened me a savings book and they'd all chipped in: she'd give me all of hers except what she needed for a cot for the bairn. The other three had turned up fifty pund each. She said in her card, Mam, we never want you to be short again. Bless her, she's a kind heart.'

They were at the door of The Turk's Head.

'Will you sing "The Blaydon Races" tonight, Carrie?' Caz asked.

'Well, I might,' said Carrie, 'only the stairs takes all me breath. We'll see.'

A Christmas cruise! Caz smiled. How many times had she and Ben dreamed of a cruise – the Caribbean, the Galapagos, the world . . . Sailing together, flying together – all her dreams ended the moment she knew for sure that Ben could never dream with her again.

But listening to Carrie's bright memories, she wondered. Maybe one day she would take a cruise, a balloon flight, a raft along the Amazon. Maybe it was time to start dreaming again.

36

Deaf Jimmy was thrilled when Caz and Josie flourished their garters at him. He blew kisses and waltzed stiffly with thin air. Emily giggled and insisted on buying them both a drink. Rose sang 'I'm Hurt' and everything was just the way it always was in The Turk's Head on a Saturday night.

There was a woman as tiny as Edith Piaf, with the same bubbles of thin dyed hair, the same huge bright eyes. Laura Anderson called for a hush, pointing at her.

'That's the lady who had us all singing "Happy Birthday" in here the other week. Aah! isn't that nice? Only now we find oot she's thinking she's royalty. This was an unofficial birthday, wasn't it, hinney? Her birthday's in February. Can you beat it for cheek? Good evening February – did you not know they've had people in St Zach's for less? They have! Happy Birthday! You owe us a song, madam, so get up here and sing it and we'll have no arguments!'

Blushing February made her way to the mike. 'Anyone can get confused,' she said. 'I like the tune for "Happy Birthday", me, it was all a misunderstanding. Ee! What'll I sing?'

' "Who's Sorry Now?" ' Laura shouted.

'That's Mary's song,' said February, giggling. 'No, I'll do ye "Sweet Sixteen". Cuz that's how old I am.'

'Would you credit the face on it?' called Laura. 'God help us, Marcia, you're involved in fraud tonight!'

Marcia smiled and rippled her fingers along the keys.

'Ye'll have to help us wi the chorus mind,' said February.

When she came to it, she stuck the microphone out for the whole bar to join her.

'*How old am I?*'

'*You're sixteen!*' they told her.

'*And what am I?*'

'*You're beautiful!*' they howled.

'*And whose am I?*'

'*And you're mine!*' they finished.

The applause was long and enthusiastic. Deaf Jimmy whooped and it caught on. The room erupted with owl cries and Indian war whoops until February was laughing helplessly, trying to hand back the mike. Laura would have none of it.

'This is your punishment, ye cheeky wench!' she said.

'Well, I'll go on,' February said, 'I'll do ye that Eartha Kitt one – "Old Fashioned Girl". The one wi the millionaire in it.'

'Aye, and the day ye get a millionaire, lass, they'll be giving gold bars away wi the pension!' Mary bellowed.

The end of another good night, and since Josie was going to see George and Michael the next day, dragging Caz along for a business lunch, Caz insisted on staying in Miston.

'I need me roots around me tonight for the onslaught of poserism,' she said.

She saw Carrie to her door, and they both stopped at the sound of raised voices and smashing china down the balcony.

'Lennie and Serena,' Carrie said, 'I'm thankful me bedroom's not next to them. Will ye sleep, pet?'

'I've shifted into the living room,' Caz said, 'I can't stand it.'

'I'm frightened for Serena,' Carrie said. 'She's got no family to stick up for her and I knaa what that's like, seeing as mine was driven away by him. Ye get scared and it's no way to live. At least she hasn't got bairns. I always thought that was the worst of it, I knew the bairns would be hiding under their blankets, just hoping he'd stop. They never said nowt, but in the morning, they couldn't wait to get out of the house for school. Not Jessie, she'd stay with me till he was gone to work. She'd look at him, ye knaa, like he was dirt and she'd be all lovely to me – bold, she was. I said she was me little knight in shining armour, but it's me should have been standing up for meself and her too. Mind, I'd stand between him and the bairns. He was a cruel man.'

Serena screamed and there was silence for a moment.

Caz looked at Carrie. Their eyes said the same thing.

'One of these nights, there'll be the police and an ambulance,' Carrie said, 'and we'll all feel bad about it, but ye knaa and I knaa, there's not a thing can be done to halt it.'

'I suppose,' Caz said. 'Wish I was eight foot tall sometimes.'

Carrie laughed, sadly. 'Get yersel to bed, pet. Fretting yerself all night won't do a bit of good.'

'It was a bad day when I got tied up with your family!' Serena shrieked.

Lennie started shouting again.

'Aye,' Carrie said, 'the lass never spoke a truer word. Goodnight, pet. God bless.'

'Goodnight, God bless, Carrie,' Caz said, and went into her flat.

Her bedroom was a no go area, but she still had to pee and through the back wall of the bathroom she heard two sets of feet thundering up and down the stairs, the noise of a flat palm hard on a face, a shriek, a whimper, cursing.

She closed the bedroom door and the living room door. She couldn't hear it now, just felt a flashfire of rage that it was happening and there was nothing she could do. The Turk's Head had been wonderful, and now she was deflated, grey, sure of, at best, broken sleep.

She put on Phoebe Snow.

'*I started seein' double, got myself concerned . . .*'

A glass of brandy.

'Headin' straight for trouble
and I got no place to turn . . . '

Maybe the heartache strumming through the air would wrap her in its wild and wistful heartbeat and the brandy would rock her into dreamland.

From where she lay on the floor, her eyes were drawn to the Japanese dragon's head swirling over the corner panels, breathing fire. There was a crash and a wail through the wall and both closed doors. Her flat felt dangerous.

'If I can just get through the night . . . '

She concentrated on the golden eyes and scarlet flight of eyebrows and scales flowing to the ceiling. It was a map, perfect rounded hills and paths and rivers of white carrying her away. She forced herself back to the golden all-seeing pool until the rest was a blur.

'Hold me, hold me tight . . .
gonna be alright . . . '

She was a tiny winged creature creeping along the dragon's spine, slipping into the white seam of wood, flying blind through darkness with the scent of dark metal all round her. Way below, she could hear Phoebe Snow's angel voice singing *soothing, it's soothing to know you're somewhere in my world*. So tender. And then there was wood against her fingertips . . .

37

She pushed at the wood and it flew up as if someone on the other side had torn it free. A clean sweep of wind corkscrewed down the shaft and whistled her upright on to the grass, blowing her fringe clear from her brow. From absolute dark to clear light and air. It was night-time, the same as Galleon Heights, and a half moon rode on silver breakers of cloud caught in a spray of stars.

Once she was sleeping outside with Ben in Corsica, and they lay looking at the sky. They dreamed back to a time when stars made bright patterns with no names; they dreamed that they'd just sprung from the earth like desert flowers and everything was new.

'Say it's the first time we've ever seen stars,' Ben said, 'what would we call them?'

Caz smiled, remembering. Long-tailed Tiger, Silver Peacock's Tail, Arrow-head, Flying Spear, Amazon's Belt – oh, they were very righteous young women, lying on Mother Earth and making their own sense of it all. Wherever she was now, in this land of the lake and mountains, the stars were in place. Only these days she was neither so righteous nor so young. Amazon's Belt, spears and arrows, outrageous fortune? She looked up and it was Carrie's sparkly brooch she saw twinkling from a million miles away, Rose's shimmery necklace was the galaxies, Carrie's diamond chip eternity ring hung on the dark sky.

She could hear the wind playing with leaves and branches. Something very faint like bells from over the rise. An owl cry.

Shades of grey took form: blades of grass sparking with dew and moonlight, tight daisy heads were a Hansel and Gretel trail of bright scattered crumbs. At the top of the rise she was dazzled again and blinked until she could pick out water, grass, trees: black, grey, dashes of white by the shore, stippled silver across to the mountain shadows.

She crouched suddenly – there was a fire down near the lake, and its orange aura silhouetted solid shapes and sharp lines and smoke. Huts? Tents? She couldn't be sure. She felt vulnerable on the skyline. Things were moving: animals? people? Her heart raced. There was no cover between her and the fire: she could crawl, but creatures of the night would spot that before she'd gone fifty yards. She could saunter over, tough it out. Equally, she could walk to the shore and bathe her hands and face the way she'd planned and let them approach her if they so wished. Or not.

She settled for a saunter, hands in pockets, clutching her crystal, aware that she was tense and angry that anyone else could be here. But why not? No one owned this place. Reason didn't stop the gut reaction, it never did, it just made her act like a civilised being, while inside her a she-wolf snarled.

She felt less ruffled as she drew nearer the fire and its makers: there was the sound of voices, but they were quiet; people were moving around with a serenity that comes from being totally involved in your own business. For them she would be the intruder and she made her way to the water's edge some distance apart. Her hands thrilled at the feel of cold water and she rubbed them into her ears and brow to wash away the jagged echoes of Lennie and Serena.

Someone glided across the lake in a boat, stowed the oars and waded ashore. They tied the mooring rope at their waist and banged in a stake. The boat was a slender craft, with a wide padded seat at the back, like a gondola made purely for pleasure. The rower was a man who lashed the rope tight and squatted to fill a jug. She looked directly at him and nodded. He nodded back and strolled over to the fire.

She picked out three caravans in the hazy orange light, old fashioned gypsy caravans with brightly painted wooden curved tops and custard yellow wheels patterned with scarlet. In the shadows, three big horses cropped the grass with a rasping sound like crunching apples. The softly ringing bells came from the sleeves and skirt of a woman dancing, while someone sat tapping a rhythm on a tambourine.

Four other people were setting up a cat's cradle of ropes from the trees to poles tethered in the ground. She could see a harlequin tossing up shiny clubs. Firelight caught the smooth forms and turned them into flyaway tatters of flame. Another harlequin flipped over backwards and crab-walked towards her, his painted mouth grinning in upside-down tragedy. As he circled away, the dancer eased into the splits, flexing her thighs like green wood. The black and white crab leapt to his feet and on to a monocycle, zig-zagging through the acrobats, ducking the juggler's neon blur.

The ripples of the lake picked up all the colours and made mosaic fragments. Woodsmoke drifted past Caz and she had a cigarette rolled and lit without noticing. A circus. Travellers. She'd always wanted to run away with the circus as a child, just to get over the hills and far away and never be settled in one place again. The wish was still there strong as ever. Pick up and go? She had no ties.

It was a child who came up to her. She didn't hear any steps: one minute she was alone and then the child was just standing there looking at her.

'Ma says you can come and get warm if you want.'

'Well, OK, thank you,' Caz said, 'maybe in a minute.'

The child sat down.

He wasn't a child like the trainee Mafia raging round the green at Galleon Heights. He had a stillness like the little Chinese girl but with none of her fears and tears. He was just a small person who appeared completely at ease. Composed. Caz felt that if she got up and walked away, the child would follow – at a distance. He was keeping an eye on her.

'Circus?' she asked.

'Yes,' he said, 'you come to watch?'

'Maybe,' Caz said, 'I didn't know you were here.'

'Where are you from then?'

'Oh, over there a way,' Caz said vaguely, waving behind her.

He stared at her, then to where she had pointed.

'Yeah?' he challenged.

'Yeah,' Caz drew the word out.

'You come from the Hole?' he clicked his tongue scornfully.

'Maybe,' Caz said.

'Nah,' he said, 'no one comes from the Hole.'

He looked closely at her. '*Do* you?'

'Yeah,' Caz said. 'A hole. Unless there's more than one.'

'There's only one Hole,' he said. 'Hang on.'

Now he sounded wary and scrambled to his feet to pelt back to the fire. A few minutes later he was back, hands in pockets, whistling. 'The circus'll be a while,' he said. 'Do you want to go on the boat? I can do the boat.'

'Yeah,' said Caz, 'that'd be really nice.'

'Come on then,' he said. 'I'm Tom. You'd better take off your shoes.'

'I'm Caz.'

She paddled barefoot in the icy water to the bobbing side and sat on the wide seat, feeling like a grand duchess, for the arms curved around her in padded elegance and the back rose over her head like a canopy. She must be all right for them to let him take her on board. The boy cast off and rowed expertly into the darkness.

From the lake, the campfire cast huge shadows back against the grass. The acrobats seemed to be dancing, the dancer weaving a frame with every gesture. The whole scene telescoped away and all she could hear was water against the blades of the oars, the weight of the boat pushing through waves. Now and then a bird skimmed the water although it was night.

Tom rowed without a pause until the mountains loomed over them and he glanced over his shoulder. 'Right,' he said, 'I'll light the light.'

Caz hadn't noticed this, a glass lantern caged in wire, hanging from a pole. The beams landed on the water and slid like huge fish scales on the surface. And then they were going into a narrow creek and the boy lay on his stomach, paddling with both hands. Sandy banks almost touched the sides of the boat, until they became rock and the water flowed deeper. The boy was pushing them off right and left with his palm as the wooden prow creaked, bumping gently. A frog jumped into the boat and out the other side, startled at the light. She could see velvet moss and dank cracks as the rocks rose higher around them. Tom reached up and tugged aside a curtain of ivy. Suddenly the stars went out, the moon vanished and there was a golden roof of stone hollowed above them. The boy looked over his shoulder and grinned.

The current drew them down the tunnel, the lantern picked out hints of pale blind fish in the ripples ahead. The roof glittered with scabs of sharp crystal. The boy turned on his back and made the boat pause with the bare soles of his feet.

'As you come into the tunnel of the Great Ones, let us stop and wonder for a moment,' he chanted. 'All around you can see priceless diamonds, sapphires, emeralds, amethysts and rubies, lapis lazuli and turquoise, the jewels of kings and queens. Who were the Great Ones that they could afford to stick a king's ransom on the rocks like chewing gum? We shall now move on.'

He rolled over again, winking at Caz as they bumped along the twisting waterway. The beam made a golden arch ahead of them and suddenly, the top of the arch stretched into sallow ripples as the roof rose in curves. The water sprawled into a lake and the boy grabbed a rock jutting beside them.

'This is the first cave of the Great Ones,' he intoned. 'It is higher than any cathedral and its roof is more beautiful and delicate than anyone could carve. This lake is turquoise and no one has ever swum to the bottom, not even Prince Neptune who can dive for fifteen minutes without breathing. Look around at this cave, consider who the Great Ones might be that this is just like a front porch to them.'

Caz had been into the Blue John Caves near Sheffield. She'd winced at the holographic wonderland of the caves at Cheddar Gorge, and the commercial disaster of Mother Shipton's Cave. But here, no tourist board or millionaire magician had left their mark. This cave was just the way it would have been when the Ice Age crunched great tracts of rock upwards until they made mountains, a stream-fed pocket of air sealed in stone. Reefs of stone split the lake surface and as far as the light went, Caz could see pools, ice-blue, white, robin's egg blue. Her face was damp with still swathes of mist lying everywhere. Rock rippled down in stiff folds like faded tapestry hung at the windows of an empty mansion.

Above every pinnacle of stone thrusting up through the icy calm of the pools there was a needle-sharp tip rising to a solid base hidden by shadows in the roof. Each reflection was a perfect elongated O, archway upon archway of darkness drawing her eye to a blackness so deep that no beam could reach it. The cave was full of mystery and danger.

Tom let go of the rock and the current drew the boat through the frozen cavern, casting forest shadows all around it. Gradually the lake shrank to boat width and the prow nudged into the next tunnel. Here, the rock shifted to charcoal black slashed with shiny veins of grey.

'Close your eyes a minute, Caz,' Tom said urgently.

She felt the boat stop and heard his bare feet on stone and the sound of flint striking. The sound went further away and came back on her other side, like an echo. She could smell singeing.

'Open,' he said.

Her eyes were met with dozens of firefly sparks and the lush greenery of a jungle. Two scarlet parrots sat on a branch ahead of her, turning their heads stiffly, carefully raising their rainbow wings. A monkey swung from the trees; the solid comical head of a hippopotamus raised from the water ahead of them and blew bubbles. Tom untied the rope and steered them along slowly. The jewelled scales of a snake slipped around a tree trunk and the huge head flickered fangs, blinked and was still.

'Is this Atlantis?' cried Tom. 'What has lured these exotic creatures out of the blazing sunshine down into the bowels of the earth? The Great Ones were magical beings and when they chose to live underground, they brought all of Creation with them. This is the world's only subterranean ark and we can only marvel.'

Now they were near the swinging monkey, Caz saw that its fur was rubbed in places and its eyes were glassy. It didn't leap and land and preen, just swung rhythmically to and fro. There was an elephant beyond the trees and it raised its trumpet and squirted water. Just a fraction too regularly and slowly to be . . . real?

Blink and believe, or think and question and doubt – Caz blinked and heard the macaw screech, the distant luxury of a waterfall. Pink flamingos preened in the primrose light, and a giant turtle lumbered to the edge of a pool. She noticed Tom's bright eyes searching her face and she grinned.

'Magic,' she said.

'It is,' he twinkled, 'and ladies and gents, you haven't seen the half of it. Riding through the jungle which would be the front hall of the home of the Great Ones, we come to a waterfall higher than Niagara. Only the Queen of all Acrobats, Lady Eagle herself, has ever crossed the dizzy heights of this natural wonder.'

The sound grew louder as the boat took another bend and Tom

jammed it still. Caz couldn't even see the top of the water: it fell in a sheet of silver exploding bubbles the size of footballs and golf balls and marbles and beads into a deep lake. He kept the boat there for a few minutes and then, shouting *Hold tight!*, he ducked down and the boat shot straight for the heart of the falls. The lantern was doused and Caz was soaked in seconds, chilled through, plunged into darkness with Tom's laughter echoing round her. She whooped with joy.

It felt as if they were hurtling downwards for the wind stung her cheeks and she had to grip the arm-rests to stay sitting. With a lurch they stopped and she could hear Tom moving: suddenly the lantern glowed again and flared into life. They floated onwards.

'You have wondered and marvelled, ladies and gents,' Tom was breathless. 'What can I tell you about the mysteries you are about to witness? We call this the Hall of the Great Ones. Is it a shrine? A ballroom? A dining room? Who can tell? All around are statues of magnificent proportions and the beautifully carved faces express a wisdom and serenity unsurpassed.'

As he finished, the boat moved through another tunnel which led to a cave so big neither the roof nor the sides nor the end could be seen. Tom grasped the smallest toe of a gold stone foot the size of a car and Caz looked upwards. The statue would have dwarfed the enigmatic figures on Easter Island, the impression of god-like power glowed from the great calves and thighs, the chest and chin towered over her.

There was a forest of these statues and she gazed at all the different faces. Buddha-like in mirth, Sphinx-like in supreme indifference, delicately carved like the face of Krishna in a temple frieze. Columns rose out of sight, carved with hieroglyphs, messages and maps that no one can remember how to read.

As they moved off, she noticed a gigantic fallen head, its broken lips lying in a sardonic smile, eyes quizzical below cracked brows. Its great hand curved on the sand, a fallen sceptre shattered out of its reach. The water twisted through pillars and made islands for the statues and, though they were inching along, she knew she was missing so many things: she wanted to go back and look again and again.

'Perhaps there are other caves where the Great Ones lived,' Tom intoned, 'perhaps they are living still and have merely withdrawn deeper into the heart of the earth. One day we may discover them and all these mysteries will be unravelled. Until that day all we can do is look in amazement at their works.'

The stream broadened and bore the boat quickly into pitch blackness, almost racing them away. Tom extinguished the lantern and all at once night air filled Caz's head, a million stars twinkled once more and the moon floodlit the lake.

'Well,' said Tom, 'what do you think?'

'Gob-smacked,' Caz said. 'Wonderful. Astonishing. Unbelievable. I just want to go through again.'

'Everyone does,' he said, 'but that'll be another night. It's about time for the performance. We've got to go.'

He unfastened the oars and rowed steadily towards the distant glow of the campfire.

38

Caz was sitting drinking smoky coffee and watching the final workings of ropes and drums and ladders when the woman who'd been dancing came and sat down beside her. She lit a pipe and stared into the fire, yet there was a welcome in her every gesture stronger than hello or an exchange of names.

'Tom says you come from the Hole,' she stated.

'Well, *a* hole,' Caz said. 'He said there couldn't be more than one.'

'There isn't,' the woman said. 'We know these parts very well and believe me, there's only one Hole. What's down there?'

'Well,' Caz said, 'I live down there. The thing is – it wouldn't make any sense to the others living down there. Me being up here. Because it should just be sky.'

'There's the sky up above us. Tell me about this Hole – what do you have for sky down there?'

'Same thing for sky,' Caz said, 'and then there's flats, houses, streets, people, lots of people – a city, the ocean.'

'Oh, is it,' the woman said, 'well now. Where's the ocean?' She looked straight at Caz.

'East,' Caz said.

The woman pointed to where the mountains met. 'Our nearest is a good way over there.'

'Same direction – I think,' Caz said, 'east.'

'And west too, if you go far enough. And north and south'll take you to the ocean as well,' the woman smiled. 'Never mind.'

There was a silence.

'And you live down the Hole?'

'Yes.'

'None of us have been down there. We lost one of ours – oh, years ago – and they say she went down the Hole. We stay here for a couple of weeks about this time of the year, just to rest a bit, it gets really busy in the summer. Gives the horses a chance to get their strength. The summer she disappeared, we stayed on nearly two months, waiting for her to come back, looking all over. Not a sign. Just the Hole.'

'She never came back,' Caz said.

'That's what I'm telling you,' the woman said, 'I was a child at the time. She was my great-grandmother and I sort of remember her, but then she's been talked about so much it's all got blurred. I think two of the men went down but they said there was nothing there. And now you say there's a city and people and flats and the ocean.'

'There is,' Caz said.

'Ah hah,' the woman said, banging her pipe on one of the hot stones holding the fire, 'that'll all be new. I'm talking years back. Never mind. Tom says you'd like to see the circus.'

'If that's all right,' Caz said.

The woman laughed out loud. 'You've got to say what you want,' she said, 'there's no room for polite round here. Manners, aye, but polite – can't be doing with it!'

'I want to see the circus,' Caz said.

'Then you will. But remember, you must always say what you want.'

Caz smiled. 'Sometimes,' she said lightly, 'there's no point. When you can't have it.'

'Like my great-grandmother,' the woman nodded. 'I don't feel she's dead, but she probably is, she might as well be. It's not knowing.'

'Well now,' Caz said, 'at least you've still got hope.'

'True,' the woman said. 'You've lost someone yourself, haven't you? I know. Only this one's dead, no doubt about it. She's been dead for a few years, Ben, hasn't she?'

'True enough,' Caz said, her heart racing. She tried to keep her voice normal. Talk normal. But what was the point with the woman's all-seeing eyes looking straight into her soul?

'It was going through the caves that made it all come back – Ben would have loved that.'

Ben. It was the first time she'd said her name out loud in years.

'She's got your eyes to see it with,' the woman said. 'Did she like the circus?'

'She loved it,' Caz said. 'Circuses, fairs, anything like that. She said it was magic . . . she made everything magic.'

'Then that's why you're here. To enjoy it for both of you,' the woman said. 'There's been tears enough for Ben's death. I know. It's time for enjoying all the things she loved, time for joy that you knew her – am I right?'

Caz was crying but she nodded.

'Then let the circus begin!' the woman called.

39

Caz was stunned. All her carefully constructed walls had come tumbling to dust at the woman's words. She knew: she had spoken Ben's name and knew that she was dead. She knew everything and it was all right. She sat by the lake, her soul naked, her loss a painful fact of life. The dancer even knew that Ben was a woman, and for the first time since her death, here was someone who had no reactions for Caz to deal with. Just the outrageously simple statements: *there's been enough tears*, and *it's time for enjoying all the things she loved*.

All her feelings had been frozen and buried deep in a time capsule. At first she'd felt numb, the reality of no more Ben was too much to take on board. But time had taken care of that, minutes and weeks without Ben turning into years. Knowing for sure she'd never see her face again, never hear her voice again, apart from five answerphone messages she'd saved from the heady honeymoon of their first year together.

I hope this bloody thing's working, Caz. I'm going to be back at eight. Love you to bits. It's ME! Did I say that already?

She knew them by heart.

Caz, it's me. Are you there? Pick this up if you are? No? Are you there? Well, obviously not. I'll see you soon. Love you.

The other three were just 'Hello, are you there? It's . . .' and the crash as she grabbed the receiver and cradled it by her ear. Home soon, d'you want a pizza? See you in The Dirty Duck in half an hour. See you, see you soon, see you later.

All the things they enjoyed . . .

Ben was a whizz with lights and even their kitchen could be turned from sunset to starlight to blazing Mediterranean noon at the flick of a switch. Their bedroom was the stateroom of a galleon – how they both loved ships! – and Ben had contrived portholes. Caz painted exquisite miniatures of South Sea islands, arctic floes, tropical shores and they lay making love, with all the joys of creation drifting by on silent cogs and wheels. Just before the fire, the project had been to add music and moving figures. Maybe that was why the boat ride through the caves with Tom had been more than magical: his enthusiasm was a mirror to Ben's bright eyes when she devised a new piece of wizardry.

There was something about time here, as well, the same sort of feeling she'd had years ago when they all moved into Trimdon House. Anything they did had to be right: it was no good just painting doors and windows and walls, the colours and textures were vital. It was worth making minutely detailed stencils for days to get them perfect. Everything had to be pleasing, since this was their home. Time stretched ahead of them like a river in a medieval landscape, its silver flow tantalising and endless.

These circus people had painted their caravans with love and laughter: it was in their eyes and movements, a way of enjoying everything that needed to be done. The meticulous knotting of tightropes, the tamping down of earth for tumblers and acrobats. The dancing woman had practised the same movements over and over until she and the beat were one, veiled arms painting a story in the air.

The moon sailed from behind a cloud to complement a perfect performance.

It started high in the trees, and the acrobats had black costumes picked out with luminous paint so that it was anything but people dancing in the dark. There were dragonflies and seagulls, snakes and high-stepping deer. Night made the trees and ropes invisible:

all she could see were fantastic creatures leaping and turning cartwheels.

Their finale was a pyramid turned upside down, flashing along on the monocycle, the wheel a glowing blur, as if a chill fireball blazed the trail below them. She clapped loudly and whooped. Tom was at her side and grinned at her. 'Sound effects,' he said.

Everything changed from eerie austerity as the clearing exploded into the carnival panache of clowns. Their genius turned everything haphazard with breathtaking timing where everything verged on chaos. Disaster threatened to the last second and righted itself, teetered again to sprawl in a mêlée of outsize feet and jets of water. Finally – sheer panic as the drums and tambourines slowed and rattled and they rushed out of sight, feigning terror.

Caz felt a prickle of danger, for the next figure was awesome, twenty feet tall, walking deliberately slow, menacing the air with huge hands and a grotesque death's head turning slowly. Ben would have clutched her arm at this point and shrieked. It stood stock still and a clown ran back with a ladder, egged on by a clutch of comical faces peering round a tree trunk. The clown propped the ladder on one high black shoulder and climbed up like a cartoon mouse chased by a cat. He slipped and clutched one of the massive buttons, then another: there was a sound of ripping cloth and the black coat slid to the ground. Inside, the figure was three more clowns, the bottom one teetering on stilts until all four tumbled down and bowed.

They made a great business of sweeping the ground and every clown flourished a trumpet to blow a brassy fanfare as the dancing woman drifted into view.

Her dance was hypnotic, all her veils shimmered silver and gold and the bells were sweet and sharp as cowbells on a distant hillside. Caz and Ben had heard this in Switzerland; in Corsica they'd heard the same and it had turned out to be a herd of half-wild goats lolloping downhill through dry spiky bushes. Their hooves thundered, raising a pink cloud of dust on their way to be milked and watered at a tiny farm well off any beaten track. She had a photo of Ben squinting against the sun, feeding a sassy kid from a bottle. They'd dreamed of a smallholding, goats and chickens and dogs and babies . . .

The woman danced and her hands were compelling. Her liquid fingers told stories: she was spinning and weaving, she was planting and harvesting, she was playing with children, every dance was a tale of love and living. Stories of loss and longing unfurled. Caz was filled with glee, moved to tears, it was as if the woman had reached inside her and seized her heart, milking her of every emotion, probing deep beneath the skin and the bones to waken memories.

When she vanished, Caz was drained, she closed her eyes with the dazzle of it all. She could feel Ben's warm arms round her. When she looked again, all the circus was there, dozens of eyes asking her – well?

She stood and bowed and clapped them all.

'Like it?' the dancer said.

'Love it,' Caz said, 'magnificent.'

'Good,' the woman said. 'And were you laughing? And are you crying?'

'Maybe,' Caz said. 'I could feel her – Ben – you know? You're right, she would have adored it.'

'Oh, I'm right,' the woman said. 'And here comes a new day, Caz. I wonder if it will be dawn down the Hole?'

The sky was melting into pale shades of blue and the ripples of the lake shuddered like cherished antique silver, picking up a pale glow as the sun crept towards the horizon.

'I wonder,' Caz said, 'we'll see.'

The woman took her arm and walked with her to the Hole. 'You don't have to go,' she said, 'but you can come back. Just – if you find a very old lady, remember she might be my great-grandmother, Tom's great-great-grandmother, and we'd love to see her again . . .'

'I'll remember,' Caz said. 'Maybe I'll see you again?'

'Maybe,' the woman said. 'And – remember Joy. For me, for Ben, for my great-grandmother. It's my name, but it's also as important as breathing. Joy to you on this new day.'

'As important as breathing,' Caz said, 'yes.'

Joy kissed her cheek lightly and walked back to the shores of the lake.

Caz woke to a song.

'*This time when I reach out, it may be my last try . . .*'

It was one Ben would have loved and amazingly, she listened without tears. The sun had risen and she made coffee to take out on to the balcony. She rewound the song and sat beside the riot of nasturtiums, enjoying the view. Dawn over Newcastle, street lights glimmering in the mist, pigeons nudging and scrabbling over head.

> '*I want something real,*
> *something I don't have to conceal,*
> *I want something real one time before I die . . .*'

She decided to write to Charlotte, she owed her a letter, hadn't even thanked her for the wonderful flowers. Of all people, Charlotte would understand. She'd been there all those years ago and knew everything about Ben and Caz and the last night they would ever be together.

Part three

40

Serena rose early and slipped out of bed. She looked down at Lennie, sprawled on his back, mouth open, his sharp yellow teeth flecked with spit. It was like having an animal in the house sometimes, it was, honest to God, only animals were cleaner and didn't shout and do dirty things to you all the time. Well, this was one day he wouldn't ruin. She crept upstairs and dressed, hands shaking, she was going to be out of the house before he woke. She slipped on her shoes and tiptoed to the cupboard.

A bowl, cornflakes. She wrote a note.

Dear Lennie, I have taken myself out to get some fresh milk for your breakfast as I know you like it and the powdered isn't fit for a pig to use made up. I may be gone some time but do not worry yourself or come after me, have a nice bath and I will see you soon. I will be back, I know what I'm doing. Serena.

That should keep him tethered. It seemed to take forever to ease the door open and closed and locked without making a noise, but she did it and scurried along to the lift, clutching her purse.

The post office wasn't yet open, there was a good forty minutes to wait for that, always waiting she was. The people at the bus stop were staring at her and talking but she stopped herself shrieking at them.

Pretend they don't exist, they know nothing about you, they're not interested. They don't know that they're yesterday's news once I get away. She saw her reflection in a plate glass window: she was hunched and her face had twisted again with the effort of losing those nosy prying bastards acting as if they had somewhere to go, flaunting that they could get on a bus and no one would stop them.

She swept herself upright and smoothed her jacket. Walk slow, she told herself, window-shop. And don't forget the milk or there'll be hell to pay.

Not that she couldn't cope with it. He put the pain on her with his fists, she let it out with a scream and there were bruises all over but she didn't feel it, unless he caught her when she relaxed. She'd learnt to catnap, instantly awake if he stirred, ready.

There was a café open and she smelt bacon and coffee and toast. That would be nice but he'd want to know what she'd done with the money, he'd rather she starved or died of thirst than enjoyed herself. There was a shop open and she swept in regally, smiling at the woman behind the counter. She was about to tell her it was a good morning and Lennie didn't even notice but that was men for you, then she stopped, gripped her jaws together. They didn't need to know her business, she was too open and that's how people could take advantage.

When you're in a paper shop, buy a paper. Doctor Sylvester was so patient, he didn't know that she already knew everything he told her, he didn't know anything except being kind. She took his words as gospel, ran his sayings through her mind for comfort. A kind man, not one of the gaolers and plotters. He said he wanted to see her out in the community, poor man, his hands were tied by their rules but he meant well. His hands were clean and he kept them to himself. He was a prince among men, one of her own kind. Doctor Sylvester.

Buy a paper.

There were the dailies, but Serena had her suspicions. One week they'd say the hospitals were closing and she'd walk all the way to St Zachary's and it would be open and she'd hang around until she saw Doctor Sylvester's car and breathe again. The next week they'd say the Queen was going to abdicate, a day later they'd come to their senses and say God Bless You Ma'am as was only right and proper. She wasn't about to pay good money for lies.

Her eyes raked the lower shelves, until she saw the title 'Monthly News of The Planet: The Paper That Cares For All Of Human Life and Shares It With *YOU*'. There was a page-size photo of a strange child under the words, a child with pointed ears and sharp teeth and eyes huge and luminous as giant marbles. The caption was 'BAT OR BOY: BROUGHT UP IN A CAVE TWO MILES DEEP, HE SEES IN THE DARK AND HIS EARS ARE BETTER THAN RADAR, SAY SCIENTISTS. World Exclusive Full Story, page 53.' That was more like it, you should take an interest and God only knew which part of the planet she would be living on before this wicked year was out. She picked up the paper: there was something familiar about the mouth stretched into a silent scream and the way the child stared straight at her.

'I'll take this and twenty Gold,' she said, raking coins from her purse.

The post office was still closed and the spies at the bus stop had vanished. Lennie was nowhere to be seen: he must still be sleeping. She went into Koffee 'n Kreme and treated herself to a cup of coffee. He couldn't grudge her that and be damned to him if he did. *If you go into a café you must buy something to eat or drink or both and sit at a table.*

She sat round the corner away from the windows and scrabbled the cellophane from her cigarettes.

Page 53 had more photos of the Bat Boy and the caves where he had been found, fighting tooth and tail not to be caught.

'Poor Bat Boy,' crooned Serena, 'I'd take you back there and leave you be, poor baby.'

Don't talk out loud unless you're having a conversation. She gnashed her teeth, that was the hardest, sometimes you didn't know if you'd said it out loud. And very often when you were sure you had spoken out loud, people just walked past and you shouted so you could be sure and still they didn't hear. But the café was empty and if she concentrated on keeping her lips together apart from the coffee and the cigarette, it would be all right. Because they didn't like you talking, they asked you to leave, even dragged you out, she knew.

As she read, her eyes kept flicking back to the picture.

'The boy is completely wild and communicates in squeaks, occasionally roaring if frustrated. He will not wear clothes. He cannot tolerate daylight and is active only in the hours of darkness.'

His eyes glared at her.

'He will eat no human food, but if insects and flies are released in the room, he moves like lightning to catch them.'

She looked at his spread hands and their sharp nails, clawing at the air.

'He consumes his own weight in insects every day and will drink milk if a little animal blood is mixed into it.'

Her hand shook and her head swam.

Lennie roared all the time and said he was frustrated.

He slept all day, just filled the flat with his anger, strutting around without a stitch, disgusting. Only putting on his clothes to go to his bloody beer and his working all through the night. She had her suspicions.

And eating! Lennie ate with his fork held like a dagger, his face lowered over his plate, stuffing and chewing and swilling it down with beer, stuffing and making noises and wanting more, always wanting more.

Flies drove him mad, they drifted in through the window and he ran around the room, his thing dangling, grabbing at them and swearing. If she kept the windows shut, the flat stank of his body, every room had a bitter edge of sweat to it.

She looked at Bat Boy and nodded. Even the ears were like Lennie's.

Lennie should be in a cave two miles below the ground, he should. Doubt stirred in her: she'd never actually seen him eat a fly, he stomped to the window and tossed them out when he caught them . . . or did he?

Well, this would never do! Milk.

She scalded her mouth with the rest of the coffee and rushed out. The post office was open.

'Are there any letters for me? Serena Zachary, in care of yourselves?'

'Not today, pet,' said the counter clerk. 'Try again tomorrow.'

'I shall,' she threatened, 'I shall be back, thank you.'

Milk. Lennie's breakfast. And she'd just try something today, just to find out. Her eyes gleaned the pavements and balcony, now and then she dipped down and picked something up.

God was good to her: he was still sleeping. She shredded her note.

'Breakfast in bed, Lennie,' she said and watched him like a hawk as he guzzled until the bowl was empty. He drank a mug of tea.

'What are you smiling at?'

'Nothing,' she said.

He flicked the television on, had sex with her and fell asleep again. She waited two hours, watching him. That was long enough. She shook him awake. 'Did you like your breakfast, did you, Lennie?'

'All right,' he grumbled, 'let me sleep.'

'I thought I should inform you,' she said, 'you ate your cornflakes and drank your tea, but you've also eaten seven flies, and you liked them, Lennie, I know you did, my precious.'

There was something in her eyes that stopped his fist.

'You're bloody mental!' he exploded. 'You've done it now! Flies!'

'And spiders,' she chanted. 'Spiders and flies in my parlour, poor little bat man.'

Lennie rushed to the bathroom and made himself violently sick.

'Too late,' she shrieked, 'two hours too late. You've eaten flies and digested them now, Lennie, and it just goes to show. Go back to your cave and be happy there. Go on, two miles deep and be happy. I'll divorce you, go back, I'll divorce you.'

Lennie threw his clothes on and she followed him around the flat, humming, with a serene smile. He was packing his bags, she knew he would, he knew she had found out about him, she had found him out.

'O-U-T spells out and out he must go.'

The flat was beautifully quiet when he'd gone. His keys lay on the floor, she had opened the windows wide. She sat at the table, reading *Monthly News Of The Planet*.

'Heir To Cannibal Throne Found In Vegetarian Restaurant!'

Imagine!

Her day would come, she was sure of it. And now there was an end to waiting in sight, she could wait for as long as it took. She mustn't be too hasty, although she longed to run down the balcony screaming that he'd gone and would never be back and she was free. No, no, let him be a Missing Person, that was best.

41

The minute she saw Caz, Serena's mouth opened and words gushed like brown water flooding a drain.

'It's not right,' she said, 'it's disgusting, he's mental, you know, drinking and gambling. He wants fifty pound a week for beer and gambling, fifty pound, it's just not right. Mental, who's mental, there's an amount required by law to live on, God knows it's not enough and he doesn't care, he's got to have his dogs and horses, I'll dog and horse him with his pints and a hot dinner on the money he gives me. Gives me? I'm supporting him and with my health, well it's plain as your bloody backside excuse my language . . .'

Caz walked past her in mid-flow, right now she just couldn't handle forty minutes of Serena babbling and raging. When she'd heard a barrage of blows and curses through the breezeblocks, Lennie screaming every bastard under the sun and the inevitable wailing of defeat, she'd stop and look Serena in the eye while she raved. She'd listen for twisted cryptic clues to the tortuous reality. She'd tell Serena to take care of herself and mean it, she'd ask her if she was feeling better. Days that Serena roamed the balcony in her thin dressing gown and flapping gold sandals she'd tell her to go and get dressed and get warm.

But things had been very quiet for the past few days. And here was Serena careering down the surreal highways of paranoia and abuse, howling at the demons riding and driving her. It made no difference if you listened to her and times like today Caz had more than enough on her own mind. Serena would already be complaining to thin air before you appeared and the tortured words whined savagely on past you, rattling like slaves chained together and flung overboard in a storm.

Serena's eyes terrified Caz the first time she'd stopped her, barring the narrowest part of the balcony. One arm raised like Macbeth's witches, she scattered pestilence and ruin over the green. She came too close the way drunks and other dangerous people do. Space invaders. Caz stood her ground as waving nails gouged the air an inch from her eyes, and Serena thrust her chin into her face with the awful gapped and jagged teeth snarling her furious misery. Twenty-five minutes later, she edged past and backed along to her porch, nodding, saying yeah, shaking inside.

Caz made detours to her front door after that, tense and tiptoeing, dashing for a lift, looking both ways before leaving her flat. Serena cornered her once when Josie came to visit: she was there beside her, nose thrust through the doorway, cackling that They had been told good and proper and not before time. Caz wanted to scream go away and slam her out, but she couldn't. She used the I-will-not-be-ruffled tone she'd learned when she was teaching inner-city teenagers and Serena was happy with that and took herself home.

'A method,' said Caz to Josie. 'Christ, I'm shaking. I just suddenly thought of that kid with the knife, years ago. Hence the Joyce Grenfell.'

'Well done,' Josie said, 'I think you've cracked it.'

'Yeah? I hope so. I can't shut the door in her face – I try just to make sure the door never opens on her face,' said Caz. 'It's worst when she gets you by the lift, you're trapped. She keeps her finger on the button so the doors won't close and you're there for hours.'

But then there were times when she just couldn't take it, like today, when she didn't even slow down to pass Serena, just left her ranting at the drizzly sky and double locked her door.

She felt shaky after one of Serena's rants: shaky and enraged. Not with Serena, as Carrie said, you can't blame her, she can't help it. Enraged with Lennie for a start, since he was driving Serena closer and closer to the edge of the cliffs of madness. Before, she'd been in a Dali-esque landscape where clocks melted and furniture grew feet and faces. Now she was in a blood-red Max Ernst nightmare where the feet of chairs had claws that ripped her entrails and the air materialised into bulls-head masks with savage beaks that stabbed at her heart. Look, she'd never function the way people were supposed to, people like Serena had a thin time of it. She had fluttered through her bizarre world, tripwired by reality, but Lennie's reign of terror had her crazed and panic-stricken from dawn to dusk. He worked nights so her days were upside down, cleaning the flat when he left at eleven, cooking his dinner at seven in the morning: wives look after the house when their husbands are out at work and always, the dinner on the table when they come home.

Even if they throw it up the wall, punch you to the ground, rape you, piss on you, you must have provoked it. Serena whimpered to the carpet *I'll do better, I pleased him once, I'll do better then all this will stop and we'll be nice again*. His eyes made her blood run cold.

Serena and Lennie laughed together in the beginning, went shopping like married people do, shared their food and their time. There was always him wanting to put one in, but that's what men were like and he laughed in those days and it was all over so fast she didn't mind.

Now he didn't ask her or kiss her, just knocked her to the ground and took her flat on her back or flat on her face, he didn't care. Five minutes later he'd do it again, or drag her hair and push her face against him, slapping her until she opened her mouth and had his thing inside it, shoving and shoving until she was sick and then he slapped her senseless and stood over her while she cleaned it all up. He said if she was a proper wife he wouldn't have to, she made him.

And he always said she was lucky to have him, he could just walk out and there'd be hundreds begging for it out there, hundreds. He stayed with her because he was sorry for her and she couldn't manage alone.

If he walked out in the daytime she'd just lie on the floor where he'd left her and feel like she was dying. If he stayed in, he'd hurt her until she felt she was dying.

She became dangerously thin: her skin wasn't young enough to be gaunt, but her cheeks were a waxy grey, the skin looked sickly and soft as if some infection lurked between her bones and the surface. Her hands were ivory, the bruise-coloured veins a startling map below her fingers where the joints looked swollen, gathered into bloodless nails. The shadows under her glittering eyes were meat hammered until it was dead.

Caz wanted to talk to Lennie.

She wanted to tell him she knew what was going on and it had to stop.

She wanted to be part of an over-muscled Mafia family and send her bouncer brothers round to tower over Lennie and scare his raw fists away from Serena's skin and bone terror.

She'd rung social services one day when there was thumping in the bathroom and Serena was crying thin high wails while he roared. They said they 'know the situation' and 'want to build up a relationship of trust' with Serena. 'We visit her every week.' She wouldn't speak a word against him even if she was black and blue and she'd claw the eyes out of anyone who suggested that there was something even slightly wrong with her man.

Another time, Serena came running along the balcony, screaming no, that's enough, just stop it and Lennie roared after her and dragged her back into the flat bellowing.

'Let's finish it once and for all you cunt, that's it.'

Caz rang 999 emergency, and she bit through her tongue while she talked to the police. They said they'd be round, but Caz knew they'd ring the local station and the duty officer would say, hold on, not number seventy-four again, we know the situation and there's piss all we can do.

So everyone knew all about it and no one could do anything.

Caz felt like Serena had been born somewhere with her victim's destiny mapped out and Lennie had been born somewhere else with his blueprint of cruelty and now they'd met and all the lines joined seamlessly and they were locked in it. A hundred years before, Serena would have been ranting and raving in an asylum and Lennie would have been standing over her with a bunch of heavy keys, a raised fist and a look of loathing and triumph burning in his wicked eyes.

42

*Elm Villa, sheltered accommodation. Like you've
never known it!*

Summertime and the living is . . . getting easier.

Dear Caz,

*It is strange, feeling happy, and you sound so happy too. I
didn't think any of us would ever be happy again you see. It
seemed as if we'd forfeited that somehow, you and I especially.
I'm glad you're happy. I was thinking of you only the other day
and wondering how Galleon Heights suited you. Bugger the
landlady: your 'revenge' is only marred by not being able to
witness it. Never mind! Having done that massive upheaval Up
North, three years in one place was too long without it being
your own. Given the circumstances of your deviant fame and
all. Given the circs, as Ben used to say, do you remember?
Anything from food to fornication: given the circs it's spaghetti
à la maison. Given the circs I shall postpone my desire. That
was the time you passed out on that awful sloe gin Andy and
Alex got in Corfu.*

*I miss that shorthand we all had, you're the only one worth
writing to because you write back. I never expected that we'd
still be in touch: what is it, six years since we were all together?
Given the bloody awful circs I least expected it of you. But you
seem to be making something of it in Newcastle and I like the
sound of your friend Josie, she must be good for you, what's
really going on, my lady, you're protesting so much when I*

*haven't cast a single nasturtium on the circs. By the way, your
nasturtiums sound marvellous.*

*I have to confess that these institution corridors have become
– somehow – sexy, since Daisy arrived. She says 'Just cuz you're not
doing it doesn't mean you can't think about it.' We've started
renting adult videos, do you know, the nurses used to pick stuff
like 'Watership Down' and 'Back to the Future', as if disability
somehow suspends you between childhood and adolescence. Most
of the staff are embarrassed when we cheer the rude bits, you know
that awful patronising matronly tone? Daisy tells them to stuff
it. I think I've always been too polite.*

*So you've finally met someone who knows about Ben! It must
be a relief even in a dream. I haven't heard from David –
surprise, surprise – and I can't let go of it. I feel I am still the I
that is I, and while I rationalise that there are few who would
want a deep meaningful etc. with a crip, I am still bloody angry.
They say time is a great healer, but I can't see it healing me. I
don't think I would have cut myself off from him totally if it had
been the other way round, but that's easy to say.*

*I haven't been able to mention him until now. It's a bit like
you and Ben, except that he COULD be in touch and isn't. If
I didn't know you so well, I'd suspect that the land in the sky was
due to illegal substances, but you never went in for that. Ben said
you were both so high on living, it'd send you into orbit. Given
the circs of eternal love. But you need to start carrying and
owning it, not wearing a suit of armour, a ball and chain. If
you see your sky lady again – see if she knows about me!*

*Of course I want you to come and stay with me for a long time,
but you won't, so even a weekend would do. Given the circs I
shan't be doing a lot of travelling in the foreseeable.*

*Did you see The Dong on the telly? I was foaming as much as
circs permit – he's now Mr Ecology and came third in Hereford
and Worcester, he's teetering to right and left, he has a
parliamentarian gleam in those dodgy little eyes. Sometimes I*

wish I had the balls to ring the News of The Screws and make a bloody fortune – do you remember the way he used to pick off third year blonde students to nurture his revolting libido – but maybe I'll wait until he's elected.

But in the ongoing no ball situation in which I find myself at the present time, what good would money do? I suppose I could try and contact the remnants and split it. Or maybe just you and me, Caz, sixty: forty, right down the middle.

Daisy's still here and we go swimming and play cards and go to the theatre. Big Mick has Fallen In Love with Daisy and talks to me endlessly, because she just laughs at him. She says somewhere like here makes you forget what life's like on the outside.

'It's so bloody cosy, Legless,' she says, 'handrails and ramps everywhere. Just imagine going up the pub with no one to lift your chair.'

I too have some secret news. Not that you see anyone who knows me, but I'm scared in case it doesn't work. It was watching Telethon that did it. There was a gutsy little kid there, running round and he said 'I don't know what it's like without plastic legs, really.' Cue kleenex, we clapped and stomped as only we know how.

I'm going to try plastic legs. It's weird to see that written down. They say I can, but the spinal injury means the best I can hope for is a drunken sailor roll. I took Daisy with me and she said, 'Well, Legless, that'll cover up your secret boozing.' She's going for a bionic arm, scared in case it's no good, but, she says 'I'll be buggered if I don't try.' Mick says 'Any time, Daze, you know where to get hold of me.' The nurses say, now then, Mick, now then, Daisy. Daisy just laughs at it all.

Excuse the note of mild hysteria, I have an interview with the leg man after 'Neighbours'. Do you know, I used to live for 'Neighbours', it made my life seem action-packed by comparison. But tonight it's 'Neighbours', the leg man and 'The Virgin

and The Gypsy'. From Ramsey Street to rampant Lawrentian
lust via a giant step for me!
  Keep your fingers crossed!
  Yours until hell freezes over
  Charlotte

Caz read the letter through again, and when she'd finished, she shot her fist into the air as a salute.

'Yo, Charlotte!' she said softly, between laughter and tears. She'd always assumed that Charlotte's injuries ruled out artificial limbs. Over the years, Charlotte had joked that she was auditioning for Joan Crawford's part in a remake of *Whatever Happened to Baby Jane?* That was when one of the nurses had suggested she keep a pet canary. There had been other jokes, maybe someone would do *Freaks II*, maybe she could be the person inside a Dalek. Cruel jokes barbed with self-loathing.

And she'd never mentioned David, apart from bitter asides about people who couldn't see beyond their own pain. Her tone was sometimes resigned, self-pitying, grey and flat. Then she would rally to self-mockery. Caz knew she was devastated: she'd been pregnant and the accident had taken her baby and her legs in one fell swoop. When David stopped visiting, it was the end of her world.

Couples. Caz and Ben, David and Charlotte. Love written in the stars, affirmed in every glance and action. After Trimdon House was gone, Caz had thought, from her living coma, 'Oh, well, at least she's got David. He'll work something out.'

This letter and the one before spoke of real change. There had been sparky people like Daisy before, bright and full of fight. Charlotte had watched them come and go. But this time, she'd grabbed hold, she'd said, 'Hey, I want a piece of that. I'm Charlotte. I deserve it and I'm going for it.'

Something real.

43

'Well, I've not seen hide nor hair of him for these past weeks,' Carrie told Caz, jerking her head at the closed door of Serena's flat. 'Good riddance, I say, but then bad pennies as well, mind.'

'Uh huh,' Caz said, 'it'll be quieter without him.'

'Well, pet, she's not the type to live alone,' Carrie said, pursing her lips, 'she'll have another fella in there as soon as she's sure he's not coming back. It'll be all change, mark my words, I've seen it all before.'

'On with the new,' Caz said, 'well, she couldn't get much worse than him.'

'A couple of years back she had three on the go!' Carrie chuckled. 'All from St Zachary's. One on a Monday, one on a Tuesday, the last on a Wednesday. And then the first one back for Thursday and so on. She was making her mouth go about what it cost to feed a man, and her next door was laughing and carrying on, she said, feed 'em, Serena, is that what you do? Ee, Serena was wild. That's not her who's next door now, Serena moved. She can get a move just like that, wi her history. If he's out of the picture, she'll be moving again soon.'

'Be hoped she moves out of here,' Caz said.

'Ah, she'll not do that,' Carrie shook her head. 'She's known here, she knows what she can get away with, all the ways ye can twist the rules. Ye'll hear her say she hates it, but I'm telling you, she'll never leave Miston. Nah. And there's empty flats all over.

Maybe God'll be good to us and shift her to another balcony. I doubt it mind. This is one of the nicest ones and she knaas it. Aye, there's times I think she puts it on.'

'Act daft and you get,' Caz said.

'That's it,' Carrie said. 'Mebbes we should all go doolally tap and get ourselves a social worker! Serena will have told you I'm senile? I thought so. She's after me crystal, see, I saw her eyes when she come in last. Aye, aye, I thinks to meself. I've had a change around and there's none of the chairs is near me bits now. Ye have to watch her. But she'll be calmer now she's shot of him.'

44

Serena was better off. She had her own money again for a start, no more begging him for coppers for cigarettes. And no one turning their key in her lock any time of the day or night. But she still woke with nightmares of him creeping back, appearing beside her with his fists and his thing and the evil bat smell of him. She demanded a new flat and sat there until they gave her a key for two doors down.

She liked it at once: there was no shadow of Lennie anywhere and her eyes lit up when she saw the telephone lying by the stairs. A telephone – they were getting very careless indeed.

She was better off.

She was also more determined than ever before. They had sent Lennie from his deep hellhole to torment her and probably to kill her. If she hadn't been smart, they'd have got their way as well. This time there was no room for mistakes.

'When I find another gentleman friend,' she told the mirror, 'I shall be sure to go through the *Monthly News* with a magnifying glass before I permit any intimacy. You won't get my key, no my love, I'm sorry to say it but I know what they're about.'

She brushed and dusted and swept and howled until they promised to redecorate for her. No one from the past would be able to find her, not her mother, not her so-called father, none of the bastards who'd tried to kill her or drive her insane. Not Hajid or his mother or his father, not Lennie. Especially not Lennie. She wouldn't be here for long anyway. One day she'd walk into the post office and there would be a dozen thick white envelopes with golden seals and stamps from all over the world and she would be saved.

'I shall have my pick, dear!' she told the window.

She moved her things in, settled them in place and stopped for a cup of tea and a cigarette over the *Monthly News Of The Planet*. They had found a giant snowball in the Arizona Desert, which just goes to show.

'I could tell them things,' she said, 'ah, I could talk!'

She looked around the room, and sank to the floor with a howl. They had stolen her telephone.

Cruel, cruel, cruel! They'd left the socket to mock her, to drive her insane, but she hadn't cracked yet for all the wicked things they'd done. She wouldn't crack this time. The bloody prison officer could sort this out, she had rights as a political prisoner even if they wouldn't admit that's what she was.

Tuesday was when the prison visitor knocked on the door – 'Call yourself a social worker, but I'm no fool. Let her work for her traitor's thirty pieces of silver,' Serena growled.

Most often, she ignored the knock, the cheek of it, rattling away like she had a right to come in. Sometimes she opened the door and kept Mrs Nosy Boots standing outside. Then again, she might hurl abuse through the letterbox.

'Don't I have enough to do? You effing blinding effing eff!'

Her mother's bulk sagged on the edge of the sink, jeering and tossing cigarette ash on her clean floor. 'My little crackerjack, got a social worker, have you, pet? Got a woman coming in once a week, you dirty bent cow!'

She'd disappear the minute the social worker came in. Mrs Bossy Parker with the power of life and death in her briefcase. So many questions and writing down answers bold as brass, not pretending even, calling herself a friend, well, what friends ever wrote down conversations, she would like to know.

'It's just so I remember, Serena. I see so many people.'

Well, that was fine, wasn't it? A social worker with no memory, just her luck to get a dud. A social worker who saw so many people who's to say she'd remember to look at her notes? What if she looked at the wrong notes? Her down on the green with three children and God knows how many fathers between them, for example. No doubt Serena would be getting nappies and bunk beds delivered to mock her even further.

'I'll throw them over the balcony,' she muttered, 'and all the trays of baby food, ah ha ha. Now they're putting glass splinters in the food! I'll make sure no poor little baby has to eat them, they'll all be smashed on the path and I'll laugh. It's only right. Dogs. The poor dogs would eat anything round here it's a nasty area, the poor dogs will have their tongues cut to ribbons, no, I'll put them on the bench outside and we'll see who helps themselves, I'll tell the social worker who needs handouts suitable to their situation.'

But there'd be none of that when this Tuesday came around. Maybe it was today, if it was daylight. Tonight and too late if it was dark. Everything was still packed, how was she to know without a calendar.

'Calendar,' Serena crooned, 'calendar, calendar, I love you, my little calendar girl, calendar girl. Calendar.'

She stood stock still halfway up the stairs, hands stretched like claws. The rest of the words were a blank. Lost.

'Calendar girl,' she whispered, imploring the empty air.

Every day, every day of the year. Someone had bought that record for her.

Her mother stood at the top of the stairs in her coat and hat, one hand scrabbling through her handbag. 'Keys,' she shouted, 'keys, where are my keys, you've hidden them.'

'He bought it for me, "Calendar Girl", it was a present, actually if it's any of your mind your own business,' she said, sticking her chin out.

'Bought it for you? Who?' Her mother was seven feet tall now, her voice echoed like a foghorn. 'And if he did, you slut, what for? Presents cost money and you've no money. Where did you put it, my little fool?'

'Don't say that,' Serena collapsed on the stairs, 'I've other things to do today, Tuesday, I've other things that are most pressing and urgent. I can't be looking for a record all day.'

'Who gave it to you? What for?' Her mother's voice rained down the stairs like a rubbish truck emptying on the tip.

'I'll give you what for!' Serena sprinted up the stairs and head-butted her mother's coat. 'Get out of my house, prying and making me forget things. And how did you know where I live? I've moved, I've moved.'

Her mother pulled on gloves ominously. 'God save me from an ungrateful child,' she intoned the way the priest said Mass. 'Your mother will always know where you are. You're my flesh and blood, mothers know these things. Tuesday is it, today, you – *inmate*! I'll Tuesday you. You need medicine, you, you're sick, Serena, it's your father's bad blood.'

She slammed the door. Serena lay on the floor. This place was supposed to be safe, a little home. Her father couldn't come here, surely she'd seen the stone with his name on. But where. Where was anyone when you needed to know?

'Oh, God help me,' she moaned, beating her head on the cupboard, 'Tuesday, Tuesday, if I could find my calendar. Aaah, aaah, "Calendar Girl". She's taken that record, I know her. Where did they bury him? I said burn him, throw away his dirty ashes, but who cares these days.'

She made a cup of tea and drank it though the milk was sour. It was a penance, the wispy white lumps, it tasted awful, but better than medicines. You could make people leave you alone, even your family, it just took an injunction. She'd phone the police. Her face went crafty and knowing. Yes, that was it. Tuesday and the social worker. Mrs Sly Boots, she'd show her how to make herself useful. A woman abandoned by her cruel husband although she loved him dearly and doted on his every need. How was a woman to manage without a telephone with everything so dangerous these days, you needed the emergency services, it was a lifeline.

'You tell me I'm not allowed one, Mrs Lazy Boots!'

She waved her bony fist at the empty chair where she'd give Mrs Life and Death a cup of tea. Missus? Anyone can wear a ring, thought she'd be fooled, did she? A cup of tea when she came. Tuesday. She felt her legs waver into grey indecision. Upstairs downstairs . . . she bolted for the door as she heard footsteps and fluted her politest tones at the postman.

'Lovely weather for the time . . .'

'It is.' He was wary. He'd met Serena before.

'I am expecting a letter,' she said, 'they said it would be posted on Friday. From London. Business.'

'Well, it should be here now, what are we, Tuesday? Nothing here, I'm afraid. Give it 'til tomorrow, shall we? Before you bother with a missing form.'

'Oh, I wouldn't waste my time,' said Serena, 'I shall telephone them, you see, and they'll send it record delivery. Then you can be sure.'

'Always worth it,' the postman agreed, relieved. He'd got off lightly this morning, sometimes she accused him of posting threatening letters to her and once even a bomb. She never got letters to speak of. Just her giro, and brown window jobs. Nothing personal.

Serena closed the door. It was Tuesday. It was morning, time to get fresh milk for the afternoon.

45

If you walk on a crack in the pavement, a nasty man gets you and drags you two miles deep under the paving stones and you'll never be seen alive again. Two miles deep to a cave where the sun never shines and leathery wings fly round your face in the darkness. Serena stepped carefully over every line joining the paving stones. A scuttling figure in black robes appeared at her side, sandals slapping carelessly on every crack with nothing to be afraid of. Well, she would come now, Hajid's mother, come to crow that another man had left her, no one would have her.

'You're wrong,' she said, 'he was a better man than your son Hajid, a decent man was Lennie. He married me, made me Mrs McCulla and it was I who got him to leave. Mind out now, he could get you yet!'

The black figure shrugged and muttered, sandals slapping carelessly on every crack she came to.

'Oh, of course, I forgot, yes,' she told Hajid's mother, 'you must be immune with your black robes, you old crow, you've the mark of sin on your brow and even the monsters won't touch you.'

The dark eyes glittered at her.

'Oh, you can't scare me,' she said haughtily, 'I am a good Christian woman and attend the church regularly. I've sent him back to his poor cave, the mutant. He's got no way to touch me and none of your spells can harm me. I don't want you walking beside me, people will stare and think I'm cursed too.'

But the black figure kept up with her, a rogue breeze whipping her veils to catch on Serena's legs.

'Get away from me!'

Oh, that was charming, wasn't it, now the children had seen her and started jeering and laughing. Five teenage girls, flashy in silky pastel shellsuits, hanging over the bridge over the motorway, chewing gum and showing their fillings, didn't they know the wind can poison your teeth, you should keep your mouth closed unless you've something sensible to say. There'd be no sense from this gang of hussies. Serena clutched her handbag and shopping bag and stormed past them. Jesus! She'd almost forgotten about the cracks. But it must be all right on a bridge, the nasty man lived underground, although maybe he could make the bridge split and drop her a hundred feet on to the five lanes of busy traffic.

'And that would suit you very well, wouldn't it, *wouldn't it*?' she snarled at Hajid's mother.

She went into the bakery. Oh, the shame of it, the silent black figure flitted in beside her, you couldn't scream at her to leave you alone in a public place like a shop, she looked as if she belonged with you.

'I'm not with her,' she told the girl behind the counter. 'She just comes along to make a nuisance, doesn't come from round here, she should be in Tottenham. Tottenham. Not Miston.'

'Can I get you something?' said the girl, swallowing a giggle. You got some right ones round here.

'I want a nice loaf,' said Serena, 'for the sandwiches, you see. For tea. I don't know why I should tell you what for. I want a loaf.'

'White, brown, wholemeal, country grain, bloomer,' the girl yawned.

'White, I believe it's considered the right thing,' Serena told her.

'Sliced?'

'I have a bread knife!' Serena shouted, 'just give me a loaf.'

'Ee!' The girl was indignant as she wrapped the loaf. 'Fifty-eight pence.'

Serena counted coins from her purse and made little piles of pennies and fivepences. Her sort wasn't to be trusted to give the right change and with the price of things these days, it was hard enough without being robbed.

Hajid's mother shuffled out beside her.

'Did you ever!' said the next customer.

'Ah, she cannot help it, love, poor soul,' the girl behind the counter shook her head. 'She's got a tile off, that one, you cannot blame her.'

'There was a time when they took care of her sort at St Zachary's. They say it was a bad thing to lock people up, but just look at her, poor soul, she doesn't know where she is half the time.' Another customer, Carrie, sighing, shaking her head.

'Aye, she'd be better off at St Zack's,' the assistant said. 'They do take them in still, but only for a few weeks. That's when we don't see her, she's away on the zig-zag and always comes back better for it.'

'It'd take more than a few weeks on the zig-zag for her, pet,' Carrie leaned on the counter. 'I live a few doors from her, it's awful. Me neighbour says she's man mad. Man mad, well, that's part of it, but she cannot help herself, it can't be cured. She got married and now he's left her, mind, he was a bad lot. Only wanted her for his bed. Now he's gone she's moved again. She was moving yesterday, God help me, two doors nearer. She can't be still, Serena. I just hope me neighbour lasts out her natural puff, I'm telling you, as soon as her flat's empty, Serena'll be after it. I cannot be cruel to her, but ee, I couldn't stand her right next door to me.'

Serena speeded up, knocking into clusters of shoppers. Hajid's mother stuck to her side like glue.

'I'll get rid of you,' she shrieked and dived into the butcher's. That was an unholy place, according to Hajid's mother. She thought animals should bleed slowly to death: if that was religion, then it was evil. When she lived with Hajid, she cooked him pork chops and bacon, chicken and lamb chops, he always had a good dinner. His mother wept and said it was unclean. The evil cow! Serena's kitchen was topped and bottomed every day. No one could call her dirty.

'Hygiene,' she muttered at the sawdust on the butcher shop floor, sneaking a glance at the doorway where the black robed figure stood like the Angel of Death waiting for her. She closed her eyes and wished her to be gone, before it was her turn to be served. She had no business in the butcher's, she hadn't the money even for a half-pound of bacon. But she made a great pantomime of peering at the unholy rashers and the raw pink pork links.

The woman ahead of her moved sharply away, the woman behind her kept a distance. You could never tell if they were harmless or would suddenly turn, and if you got talking to them, well, that was you gone for the day.

'Yes, pet?'

'I'm just deciding,' Serena shouted, 'between pork chops and a ham shank, I never can decide which, please serve your next customer, while I think.'

She bared her teeth in triumph: the figure had vanished. So she gave the butcher a fierce grin. 'I'll have to call back,' she told him and sailed out into the street.

'I'll not hold my breath, like,' he said to her back. 'Pound of mince is it, madam?'

She'd won! Hajid's mother had only come to spoil her day and put her off her shopping. She'd have sat in the kitchen muttering into her black veil while Serena made tea for Mrs Know It All, then laughing aloud at the milk gone sour and none fresh. Lady Bountiful would have made her spy's report and there would be an end to having a telephone. Hajid's mother wanted her locked up away from the world with no friends and no way of finding her son. Well, that wasn't going to happen. Soft in the head, was she? She'd outwitted her this time.

She walked down the street chirpily. To the newsagent's for milk and a newspaper. One of the dailies that told lies: didn't anyone else notice this? Or were they waiting for her to go along with it all? Today she'd pretend she did. She bought the *Mirror* and the *Monthly News Of The Planet*, rolling it tight and hiding it in her bag. No one must know about that or maybe they'd discover her plans for getting out of Miston one day very soon.

She went into the post office. 'Have you received any correspondence for me?' she said icily. 'Serena Zachary in care of yourselves?'

'Whey no, pet,' said the counter clerk. 'Maybe tomorrow.'

She glared at him – surely not! Another plotter stealing her only hope of escape? She should never have trusted the Royal Mail, not since all those divorces. Never mind, soon she wouldn't need it.

She had her milk and her Daily Liar and she would read every word. Mrs Interfering Busybody would see that she was taking an interest in everyday things and keeping up to date. Her sort thought that was important and if she'd learnt nothing else, Serena knew you had to play by their rules when it came to getting your rights.

'Telephone, telephone, telephone,' she chanted all the way back to the flat, 'I'll give you a ring, my love, a ring for your finger and bells for your toes.'

46

Caroline Birch, the social worker, was resigned to ticking the No Access box every time she visited Serena. She was supposed to put in a report for each visit, failed or successful, and she did. The language had to be such that files could be read by clients with no fear of litigation, and her department had developed a coded sub-text for all such reports.

Client refused me entry and became volubly distressed.

Client asserts that I am persecuting her, unable to open door.

Client continues to be wary, v. concerned about sup. ben, which she feels is being withheld. Visibly distressed.

Client h. complained to MP, housing office, city hall (see telephone logbook). Nature of complaint uncertain. Client unwilling to discuss.

And so on through Serena's three-inch-thick file. In four years, Caroline Birch had sat and talked to her seven times apart from the initial interview in St Zachary's day lounge while Serena was being prepared for independent life in the wider community. She was able to wash herself, dress herself, cook and clean and manage money. But Caroline Birch and every member of staff knew Serena was no more prepared to cope with life on the outside than the day she'd been picked up wandering down the central reservation of the A1(M) four miles north of Darlington.

She said she'd been driven from London by people who'd stolen her son and threatened to have her murdered. Her mother lived in Newcastle, she said, and would give her a home. Enquiries revealed that she had a son who was mentally retarded and lived in one of the Victorian institutions on the outskirts of London, originally built for the morally insane. Her parents had lived in Newcastle, but both were dead and she'd spent most of her childhood years in care. And out of care when one parent had left the other and needed to produce a child to get a new flat. Then they would get back together and dump her back with social services: beyond parental control. She had almost certainly been sexually abused, although such things weren't noticed or discussed when she was a child.

When she was sixteen, social services washed their hands of her, and she'd drifted around London, relying on a series of boy-friends, more or less on the game, but never taking hard cash. Until she met Hajid, who set her up in a bedsit and promised to divorce his wife and marry her.

But there was no divorce and Hajid disowned her after the birth of the child, his religion pronouncing his whole family shamed that he had been an adulterer. The idiot son was clearly a sign of judgement from God.

Serena was sleeping rough, running away from a hostel place-ment because the people there were dirty alcoholics. She'd been hitch-hiking, getting laid by long-distance lorry drivers and cruis-ing commuters and the only wonder was that she was still alive, not just another nameless discarded lay-by corpse.

In need of care and protection, like she'd been all her life, they managed to place her in St Zachary's. She'd been there for two years, more or less happy. She had several gentleman friends on the same ward and she'd been sterilised without knowing it. Only now that the policy was to clear as many wards as possible, anyone who could stand on their own feet was to do so – with support. It was called community care. If that was economy, then it was a false one: Caroline Birch made a weekly visit, the police were called out from time to time when Serena went wandering and harassed housing officials fielded complaints about her every week. Multi-agency involvement, the jargon said. It cost dear.

Maybe once a year they took her back into A ward, three weeks of regular medication and people to talk to. Twenty-one days on the zig-zag and she was out again, careering along the tracks of her days. A tile off, a screw loose, lost whatever marbles she might have had in a game of life where the rules didn't fit the world as she knew it.

Today Caroline reckoned she'd be let in and get the full performance: Serena the gracious hostess presiding over her best china and holding a conversation that would pass as normal. She'd just moved and would want every grant going for her new home. Which was fine by Caroline: when you're convinced the world is booby-trapped and plotting against you, the last thing you need is money troubles.

And Serena managed very well. She swore down she never took money from her series of gentleman friends and certainly her flat showed no signs of extra earnings, immoral or otherwise. It was always immaculate – Serena polished and scoured furiously – but spartan. She had a few treasures and a display cabinet of gilt and mirrored splendour to house them. One of her admirers in St Zachary's had presented it to her: it was the first thing that she'd owned since the bedsit and Hajid. She took enormous care of her possessions.

The top shelf of the cabinet held six glasses with pink checkerboard rims under a line of gold. There was a stopped china clock on the lower shelf, white with curls of blue and gold and a pink-cheeked cherub either side of the still face. The top of the cabinet had two icons either side of a cellophane-wrapped box of pot pourri: the Madonna and Child and Christ Crucified. The cabinet had always looked like this, in her room at St Zachary's and at each of the five addresses she'd had since. Caroline Birch felt that it was one of the main reasons Serena bothered with a place to live: you can't wander the highways with a large piece of furniture on your back.

She rattled the letterbox and stood back. She hadn't forgotten the bowl of soapy water Serena had dowsed her with once before slamming the door again. Mind, it was better than a pit-bull, a knife, a Rottweiler, a volley of empty Special Brew cans: the daily debris of a social worker's life. She and her team met on Friday afternoons to share the horror stories, debrief for an attempt at a relaxing weekend. They felt that they barely grazed the tip of the iceberg.

'I feel like a bit of used sticking plaster sometimes,' one of her colleagues said, 'and the clients have got gaping wounds.'

'Gangrene,' said Caroline, 'I'm aspirin where they need penicillin. I feel like a pocket knife being asked to perform major surgery.'

'I'm just a matchstick being asked to dam a river, and strike a light at the same time!' Toby declaimed, the campest member of the team.

'Put me down as a plastic seaside bucket trying to empty the ocean!' Della, the team leader.

Then they would all go to the pub, slightly hysterical, racked by guilt, laughter and lager the only way to diffuse and deal with it all.

On paper Serena was a success story, but how could you measure the Siberian chill of terror in her eyes, the fear that flickered from her angry tongue?

Caroline shifted her bag to her hip and rattled the letterbox again.

47

'Oh, Mrs Birch, how kind of you to call,' Serena flung the door wide. 'Do come in, I've just finished reading today's paper, Tuesdays are most interesting, don't you find?'

'Thank you,' said Caroline. She was always Ms if she had to be anything, but when a client assumed her to be Mrs, she found it was best to let it ride. Probably it made them feel more comfortable, and after all, her politics were not the point of discussion. She wore a white gold wedding ring on the third finger of the left hand, after all. But the ring had belonged to her grandmother and that was the only finger it would fit.

'Take a seat, Mrs Birch, I have the kettle on, a cup of tea, would you like a cup of tea, nice tea, do you think?'

'That'd be lovely,' said Caroline. There were houses where she had to find ways of disposing of her cups of tea, purely for health reasons. You couldn't fault Serena on cleanliness.

Serena twisted her face at the kitchen window. The kettle had been boiling furiously ever since she got in from the shops. No one was going to find her unprepared, especially Mrs Do Goody Two Shoes Silver Birch with her nasty cheap silver wedding ring. Today she had silver spider webs as earrings, and Serena shuddered, insects! Enough to make you scream like when she was a child and those boys threw things in her hair, sometimes just pretending for the fun of seeing her dance up and down, shrieking and getting told off. Tell-tale tit, your tongue shall be bit. She clamped her jaws closed. No, no, she knew their game. Nasty nasty boys.

She swilled the teapot out savagely. It had taken an age to find it, time wasted that would never come again. The spout clashed on the stainless steel sink. Didn't even chip, see, that's buying carefully, a few pennies more means quality. It was the same with tea. Cheap tea was sweepings off the floor, and there was a Food Weighhouse on Miston High Road, where they had all the better brands, but loose so you weren't paying for their packets, no, you scooped out just what you needed into a plastic bag and they weighed it and took your money.

'I have matching canisters,' she told Caroline Birch. 'They make a vacuum because it's the air that brings staleness. Tea, sugar, coffee. Only I don't drink coffee, it's bad for your nerves, so that's where I keep the dried milk, because I am not in possession of a refrigerator at the present time. It's not necessary, I'm told, they told me at the office it isn't necessary. But today I have indulged in fresh milk for my teeth.'

'Don't you get fed up with dried, Mrs McCulla?' said Caroline, while Serena rattled the cups on to the table.

'Don't start me, dear,' said Serena, cackling. 'Fed up? To the bloody teeth with it, excuse my language.'

'I'm sure we could sort you out a fridge,' Caroline said, making a note.

Serena paused with the teapot in mid-air. Nosy imposter! A fridge would be handy, handy dandy, but was there any need to write a letter about it, who would be reading it and sniggering about a woman who had no child and no fridge? She cleared her throat. 'Oh, there must be other people more in need than I, what with kiddies, you see, my kiddy's not with me at the present time. And there's only one bedroom.'

So it wasn't a fridge she was after. Mind, she should have a fridge and Caroline would see to it. But obviously, there was something else Serena had in mind, the purpose of this tea party.

Only one bedroom? Surely Serena had given up on having the boy back, after the tortuous legal battles? The boy was a ward of court for life. Serena had raged at the judge when he declared her an unfit mother: *And are you a fit mother, this court, is this justice, I'll see my lawyer* . . . They didn't even charge her with contempt. Just treated her with it. And surely she wasn't wanting a two-bedroomed flat? They'd been through that one for the third time only months ago. Caroline sat back and waited.

'Do you think you'll like being in this flat, Mrs McCulla?' she asked. 'You've already made it look nice, what, in only two weeks.'

'I'm always happy to roll up my sleeves,' Serena said, *you patronising cow*. 'I shall be glad to be away from that filthy slut down there. I have standards. My gentleman friend will be decorating for me as soon as he's back and they get my money sorted. Of course, I'm used to better, dear. My family would be shocked to find me in such a place, I can tell you, we were always very careful about the area. But beggars can't be choosers.'

'Now, Mrs McCulla,' Caroline said, 'we did offer you other places but you said you wanted to stay in Miston. Do you remember?'

Serena remembered, all right. They'd locked her in a room with Mrs Two-Faced Thief and a prison officer and wouldn't let her out until *the matter was resolved to everyone's satisfaction*. Everyone didn't include her, of course. Prison officer who said he was a housing officer, smiling with a suntan, they went abroad on her money and came back with diseases so they could infect her and she'd die and that would be an end to the embarrassment of keeping her locked away from her rights. But I'm fit as a lop, thought Serena, I take my medicines and their dirty germs come nowhere near me.

Offer was it now? They'd mentioned Copperfield, Clay Bank where all the criminals were kept, they'd even suggested Paris, but she wasn't going to be deported. They just wanted rid of her. When they talked about Gaelwood, over in the wicked west end of Newcastle, she knew they were serious. They'd do anything to be shot of her, send her papers over to another office so they could be lost on the way and she'd have to start again, walking miles from office to office, building up her case again from scratch, treating her like dirt. They must know who she was or they wouldn't be so keen to get her shifted. She decided to stay in Miston, even if it was just an open-air prison. Her day would come. Justice would be done and seen to be done.

'Naturally, I don't wish to live among strangers, Mrs Birch,' she said, grinning frantically. 'That is natural, is it not, Mrs Birch? Natural and normal to belong here.'

Even though I don't.

'Of course,' Caroline said, 'you seemed to be saying that you aren't happy with the area.'

How much does she know?

'It will do for the time being,' she said ominously.

'Well, that's good,' Caroline said.

Serena lit a cigarette and flicked the burning end at the ashtray. *Do you smoke, Mrs Birch? Then buy your own, dear!*

'Perhaps you'd like to see around the flat?' she said.

'If you'd like to show me, I'd be very happy.'

That would make one of us.

Serena darted down the stairs. 'As you see, I have a bathroom containing a bath, a sink and a lavatory. A bedroom with a balcony door and windows with locks which is necessary for a woman living alone these days, you must agree.'

'It's lovely,' Caroline said.

'I shall do the bathroom with contour as soon as the money comes,' Serena said. 'White is for prisons and hospitals. This is the sitting room. Unfortunately we can't sit here, since my furniture hasn't arrived yet. It's in storage.'

Caroline made a mental note: Serena would never ask for a suite, but would gabble out storage fees that matched the price of a new one to the penny. If it made her feel better . . . Caroline believed that everyone had to have their dignity and treated her clients with respect. Serena would never see the paperwork, a marvel of fiction concocted to suit the system she worked for. She had no respect for the rules and sub-clauses, they were to be manipulated. The result would be a tidy file with no questions asked and Serena would get her flat furnished without losing face.

'Have you noticed what's missing, apart from my good furniture?' Serena said, pouring more tea.

'Well, you haven't had time to put up your photos,' said Caroline, 'and you'll be needing carpets – will you?'

'It is the custom,' Serena glared, *the cheeky bitch!* 'I understand that most dwellings these days are carpeted, unless something's changed? Unless I was supposed to take up the second-hand rubbish from the last flat and install it here at great personal expense? I accepted the last flat with carpets that you wouldn't put a dog on since I was desperate but I didn't think another person's second-hand, third-hand leavings were to be considered as I was packing, excuse me.'

'Of course not,' Caroline wrote some more. 'We can give you vouchers and you can go shopping and pick your carpets.'

Oh, the shame of it. Vouchers. Wartime, prison shops that sold cheap and chatty goods, that was all she was allowed. Never mind, that was a fridge, a suite and carpets without so much as a frown. Mrs Community Purse must have killed someone off to find all this money so easily.

'That is by the by,' Serena said, 'I viewed this property and accepted it on the understanding of a telephone.'

So that was it. Caroline groaned inwardly. There were thirty or so pages in the file documenting Serena's last attempt to get a phone, claiming her aged mother was ill and her father needing emergency visits. She'd blown it, since the file also recorded their death.

Nothing to say, you lackey? Am I not allowed to communicate with the outside world, has that privilege been taken from me as well?

'As a woman living alone,' she said, 'in an area which is dangerous. Not allowed a dog, they took that away. Abandoned by my dear husband, the bastard, excuse me. As a defenceless single woman. I need to telephone Doctor Sylvester in emergencies and the nearest phone box is vandalised. If I could walk the two miles. On your head be it. Would you care for a biscuit?'

'No, thank you,' Caroline said automatically.

'They're not poisoned!' Serena was shrill.

A mistake, a mistake. She stabbed her cigarette out in the ashtray and lit another. Just say nothing now, wait for the words to vanish, Mrs Birch Rod probably didn't even notice.

It was possible to get a phone. Caroline dreaded not so much the paperwork as the inquisition and the implication that she was being conned. From her boss's point of view, she was; from her point of view, she was just doing her best to paper over the cracks. If Serena could work, she would, and she'd pay for it herself. But there wasn't a job anywhere that could contain Serena. She just hated the way Serena made her the enemy, understanding that she was, she had the power to authorise the basics in life and you can't have an ally who decides the necessities of your way of living.

'Well, I'll have to get back to you on that,' she said. 'Is there a socket here?'

Sneaky bitch! You know there is, you were here snooping when I viewed this awful place!

Caroline caught the awful force of her glare.

'Just that it costs less than having to put a line in, Mrs McCulla,' she said wearily. 'We do have a budget, you see, and I can juggle it, but no one can work miracles.'

'I was not aware that a single woman on her own requiring contact with the outside world was regarded as a miracle, these days, but then who am I?'

Caroline sat in her car and smoked a joint. Bugger it, she'd ask for everything twice. That was almost sure to work. The accountants would pare it down to slightly less than half, and they and she would feel they'd gained a victory.

And Serena would pace her newly carpeted floors, maybe happier for maybe a few weeks. She could sit on her new sofa and dial any number she liked. MPs, doctors, housing officers, the dole, the health authorities. No doubt she'd jam the switchboard at the office: must remember to warn them, thought Caroline. Was it the right thing to do? Was there a right thing to do? Did anyone know?

She wondered if this was the beginning of job burn-out, or the middle, or if she'd been working so long with people like Serena that she wouldn't recognise burn-out if it scorched her weary face.

48

One week The Angry Man came walking into Miston. He was walking from Land's End to John O'Groats for no reason other than that he bloody well wanted to and whose business was it anyway. He'd been on the road for five years, walking jagged zig-zags from coast to coast. His paths were seemingly arbitrary: curved, straight, forked lightning – he frequently doubled back. He carried armfuls of odd objects like a *Crackerjack* contestant, and Father Christmas sacks of bulky things as well. He would make a pile of things and move on with what he could carry, make another pile and go back for the rest. He said, what's the hurry, life's too fast nowadays.

He said that cars and trains and aeroplanes made a mockery of contoured landscape and old paths. Bicycles were all right. Gliders were all right, clumsy copies of birds, but quiet. Maybe seeing the land from a bird's eye view might teach the pilot something, if only that there were other points of view.

He said it was evil to blast a hole through a mountain that had been there since mammoths grazed the earth just to hasten commuters from their homes to their offices. Hills were to climb or take the easier path around. Bridges he allowed, old, stone, arched, single track. Any metal structures demanded the electric wrath of heaven: pylons were lightning rods inviting blight into the soil.

'Do you ever see sheep huddling round a pylon? Or cows? Think about it, use your bloody mind!'

Skyscrapers were Towers of Babel, and lest the Christians had the illusion he belonged to them, so were cathedral spires. Old stone church towers he allowed.

Mainly he was angry that nobody seemed to think any more.

Caz had seen him on the six o'clock news once, haranguing reporters who imagined they had a scoop. The Sunday scandal sheets had run a centre page on him, sandwiched between adverts for hot stuff, big boy, tie me up and so on phone lines, adverts for exotic lingerie and marital aids. Apparently his only base was a tied cottage in Waternewton, Lincolnshire where his brother lived and refused to comment in whorls and questions marks and stars meaning swearing.

The WORLD EXCLUSIVE revealed only that his name was Angus Mannfred, and with the usual tabloid confusion between journalism and alliteration, started a chain of nicknames. Angry Angus, Mad Mannfred, The Waternewton Wanderer, Angus the Angry Man, The Lincolnshire Loony, Fierce King Freddy. Within a week, he was on the news simply as The Angry Man. In another week he was yesterday's news apart from fleeting foul-mouthed brushes with local TV stations as he stalked across county boundaries, a flurry of disgusted and more-to-be-pitied letters batting around in his wake on the correspondence pages of rural Arguses and Mercuries and Heralds.

He was exciting. He was mad, bad, dangerous and impossible to know. He didn't care what anyone thought: often he was quoted as saying that most people would die rather than think and most people do just that. They asked him what he thought of his nickname and he shouted: '*Angry*? You bloody fools!'

The Angry Man arrived at the forked tail of Miston High Road in the middle of one night and dumped one of his bulky packages in a boarded-up doorway. He climbed back over the railings of The Drop to collect the rest of his goods: he'd refused to walk along the tarmacked girdered height, preferring to slip and slide through brambles and allotments and scrap yards and rusty barbed wire craters. He left his things at the bottom of The Drop and crossed the crumbling gully where the river once flowed. Up the mud-slide chicken-wired bank to the railings and the doorway where he'd camp until he chose to move.

It took him seven scrambles to assemble everything and he unfolded a greasy sleeping bag and slept, his lumpy parcels half barrier, half bed. Dawn and the milkman passed him by. Shop-keepers asked each other was it or wasn't it and once they'd decided it was, got on with the business of their day, something new to spice it up a bit. He was a celebrity, been on the TV and if he was an awkward bugger, then who wasn't at some time or another.

'I'd like to give him a cup of tea, ye knaa, a meal,' said Dora in The Ritz.

'Are ye right in the head?' Lilian shouted. 'Roast and mash twice, Betty. Ye've polished that front window all morning looking at him. He's just a dosser, man, ye start that give him a cuppa malarkey and we'll have a queue come teatime, turn the place into a friggin' soup kitchen. There's tables need doing, Dora, wake yersel up, man.'

'What's this?' Betty peered over the road.

'It's that fella they call The Angry Man, set up home in Long's Butcher's doorway, you know Long's, closed these eighteen months. Our Dora thinks we should give him a cuppa.'

'Well, he doesn't bother anyone,' Dora said.

'Bothers me, pet,' said Lilian. 'It's disgusting, living on the streets and in ditches. They say he's an educated man.'

'They can be the worst,' said Mrs Anderson knowingly. 'Look at Stewart that married our Rachel. Teacher? I wouldn't trust him wi' hot water and a teabag.'

'We cannot stand here all day,' Lilian said, 'this'll not pay the tally man.'

'I think ye're wrong,' Dora said.

'You'll learn,' Betty said, ambling back into the kitchen.

49

az was vaguely aware of The Angry Man, there had been such a flurry of silly season stories about him that even she had noticed. Good on you, she'd thought, do what you want and let them puzzle you out. It was Carrie talking that reminded her.

'He just sits, ye knaa, pet,' Carrie said, 'doesn't seem to bother anyone and he's not like the tramps you see all over, never a bottle or a can in his hand. I cannot abide that, roaring drunk at ten in the morning, lying in their own mess all day, it's disgusting. Rose says they're to be pitied, but I cannot.'

Her eyebrows bristled and she shook her head like Solomon. 'Naa,' she pronounced, 'it's them that have chosen to get theirselves drunk, isn't it. No one's stood over them saying, here man, ye hev to drink this doon until ye're sick wi it. Soup kitchens and free beds – I cannot see that it's right unless they're going to stop drinking. They get theirselves in a state that they cannot look after theirselves, and then some do-good types comes along and says I blame the government? They're daft, that lot. I'm not saying they shouldn't be helped, God love them, we're all human beings. But help them if they've took the pledge, since they're sick with the drink. Ye should learn what ye can enjoy and stick to it, I say.'

Caz nodded. So much for winos. Carrie had spoken.

'What I understand wi this fellow – Angry Man, isn't it? – he just wants to walk all over and take a canny good look at it all. I'd not choose it meself, but then he'd not choose to sit in this flat knitting, so who am I? I've got to be busy, me. I cannot understand me son in Canada, he's bought a geet big house in the middle of nowhere. Nothing but trees, pet! Ye hev to hev a car to get to any shops. I couldn't stick it if they weren't me relatives.'

'I always dreamed of living in the middle of the country,' Caz said.

'Aye, pet, but what would ye do all day? Tell me that!'

'I'd paint – go for walks, enjoy the fresh air. I think it would be peaceful.'

'And what do ye do all day now?' Carrie was twinkling.

'I paint, go for walks, take the train to the seaside . . .'

'And are ye telling me it's not peaceful?' Carrie teased. 'In yer beautiful countryside, ye'd hev no shops for yer tabs and coffee and papers. Naa! Ye'd hev to come into town for that! Ye'd never see a soul from morning to night!'

'OK,' Caz laughed, 'maybe I just need places like that to visit, have holidays.'

'And have ye fixed yersel a holiday this year? Ye hevn't, hev ye? Caz, ye're young, ye should get yersel sorted wi holidays, it gives ye a dream to go on. Me and Rose is off to Blackpool next month, wi the pension club. Ye should gan there, or Scarborough wi yer friend, have a bit laugh, lass.'

'Well, when we've seen this project off,' Caz said. 'Oh, Carrie, I've got such a lot to do.'

'Get away,' Carrie poked her, 'ye could get it all done in a week, only then what would the buggers pay ye? I did the same at the factory. Ye hev to look busy, I knaa. Where are ye off today?'

'We're going to look at this site,' Caz said.

'Gardens, isn't it? Mind I want to see this project when yez're done!'

'You'll be an honoured guest,' Caz said.

The festival site was four acres of wasteland sliding along the south bank of the Tyne. Great yellow diggers stood silent like dinosaurs, iron teeth marks all over the mud and grit. The part they were bidding for was a quarter acre, thick with nettles and fireweed. Mossy heaps of old bricks made walking tricky, for at some time people had lived here. At first, they thought they had a mound to play with, but dragging the brambles aside showed the shattered shell of a house, its red bricks charred, the first seven steps of an old staircase a sooty silhouette on the wall.

'Blimey,' Josie said, 'it looks like there was a fire.'

'Yeah,' Caz said, 'I'm going to have a wander.'

'Artists,' thought Josie, watching Caz stump away, 'if you didn't know them, you'd have them all certified.'

Caz knew Josie was watching her and she just wanted to get out of sight – right out of sight and away. She found a thick veil of bindweed dragging a wall into the ground and wriggled behind it. It was dank, ridden with woodlice and spiders and snails, but she crouched down, perfectly still. This would do.

She'd been back to Trimdon House although she didn't want to: Charlotte had begged her to go. Just to see it one more time and come and tell her all about it. She said it would help, it would make it real. As if the ghosts of her own legs and her forever empty womb weren't enough: what did she want, Charlotte?

Caz had thought about lying to her, saying she'd been back and there was nothing to see. She fought the trip for months, and it was only Charlotte crying on the phone that finally got her there.

'Don't you see, Caz, I can't go. Probably never. Please help me.'

She'd taken the number 15 bus, and made herself sit on the top at the front, just like she always used to. But the bus was a new one, with hissing central doors and sharp corners. Nothing stays the same. The chip shop was a hairdresser's when she got off the bus, the chemist's was boarded up. The grocer's was a video-hire cum off-licence. She crossed the road to the three black bollards at the mouth of Java Lane. Dogshit Alley, as they called it. Trimdon House was round the corner at the bottom.

She walked down the alley with her eyes on the fouled uneven paving blocks. Her feet knew the way and she only looked up when she was standing in front of the fenced-off site.

Trimdon House, gaping black bricks. DANGER, written on three red and white signs. Smoke-charred glass littered the ground. Alex and Andy's shattered Tiffany shade lay as if thrown in anger. She thought of picking her way through the wire fencing and up the stairs – for what?

DANGER. KEEP OUT.

David's pile of blue roof tiles was ashy rubble. The shape of the stairs was etched like fallout, a bath hung from pipes, melted like candlewax. Her bath, Ben's bath. Downstairs, the debris of all the storeys above, the brand of a chair back white on carbonised plaster.

What could she say to Charlotte?

'I went back. It's – finished.'

'Thank you, Caz. I just had to know.'

A whisper over the wires.

And now she'd be working on a site where fire had swept away more lives. She found she was crying: the land in the sky, Charlotte's letter and now this. Her hands were shaking too much even to roll a cigarette. It was the dark outline of the stairs that had finished her. Stairs meant people climbing up to the bathroom, up to bed, stairs were somewhere for living feet. Stairs had become a trap, filled with oily smoke, heat that blisters and blinds.

She still wondered about that, could she have got up the stairs if they hadn't pinned her down? The last time she'd ever see Ben, a terrified face at the window, hands smashing glass. Too much smoke to be certain. Glass cracking in the heat and Ben screaming. And then not even silence. No, so loud it fills your head, the deafening carnage of flames, roaring, crashing, fire engines wailing and great fat hoses gushing the scarlet flames into more smoke, more smoke – and all too late.

'Ben,' she forced the name through every cell, though her mind had fought the cry for years, 'Ben, Ben, I love you. Ben?'

There was only silence, silence like the wind.

'Oh, Jesus,' Caz thought, 'Ben? Help me? I miss you.'

50

This would never do. Somehow she had to get on her feet again and act normal with Josie. Talk Normal, as her badge said. Otherwise she'd have to explain everything and then deal with Josie's responses. Caz had winced at how careful people were with her after the fire, expecting tears or other equally embarrassing displays of grief. She was renting a bedsit in Plaistow and when she was alone there, in her own four walls, she cried all the time. She had to force herself to go out.

She and Ben used to go into Diva's and The Roost, Tilley's and The Dirty Duck: all in the East End, tough and friendly and within walking distance of East India Dock Road and Mile End. They played pool and filled the juke-box with Liza Minnelli and Ella Fitzgerald while the queens tisked and giggled. They drank pints and smoked roll-ups while the boys were strictly g and t and cocktail Sobranies. Nice places, scruffy, soaked in beer and smoke and sweat, tolerant of the three local crimplened transvestites, their sixties chiffon scarves tied at the neck with an imitation pearl brooch, the clumping elegance of their size 12 stilettos. The girls chalking their cues, the boys preening and swooning. Call it fun.

After the fire, she had to have a few drinks before she went out, to fix the mask in place for the evening. The mask could smile and chat and camp it up, while she stood frozen in her don't give a damn survival suit. But at some point, someone would came over, draw her to one side and murmur, *Oh, Caz, I was so sorry to hear* . . . or words to that effect. And what could the mask say to that? It was programmed only to go through the motions of appearing to be happy. If she let it slip, she'd be naked and weeping and who could keep their feet in the flood of total loss?

So she trawled the depths of her being through the haze of smoke and drink and the mask managed a cackle and a savage, 'Well, it's just one of those things, isn't it?'

That horrified them, how could she be so callous? What they wanted and all they could deal with was a nod, a muttered thank you. Civilised grief. It made her mad, why should she hold back so that they had no pieces to pick up? It was best if they said nothing, but then again, how could they? No doubt they thought silence would make them seem heartless and uncaring.

There were no right words to express sympathy.

There was no right reaction to the words offered.

She bought an answerphone so that no voice could surprise her. Every call was monitored and most she didn't answer. After a while, the phone was virtually silent.

Now she would only go to places where no one knew her. All the way to Camden Town and the cheerful anarchy of The Black Cap, where you could chat without chatting up and vice versa. Once she was so drunk she found herself going home with a young black woman, a complete stranger who danced like an angel and said her name was Danny. She sobered up in the cab and thought, Oh Jesus, what am I doing.

'Case you're wondering, babes,' said Danny, making coffee, 'this ain't a pick up. You got tears all over your heart and there's something dead in your eyes. But you can't afford a cab back to Plaistow. This is a crash, girl, get some sleep.'

'Didn't know it showed,' Caz said.

'It don't. But you can't hide nothing from Desperate Danny. I've been there, broken heart and everything. Forget the bitch, she ain't worth it. You want to eat cow pie, like me.'

'It wasn't like that,' Caz said. She wanted Danny to just shut up.

'It never is,' Danny rolled a joint. 'You're soft, you're thinking, well, maybe there's a chance.'

'Fuck,' Caz said. 'Leave it, will you.'

'Nah,' Danny grinned. 'You just want to wallow, your sort, well, that's up to you. But you want to get up, get fine and get down, girl.'

'Fuck,' Caz said. 'Danny, knock it off, will you.'

'All right, babes,' Danny said. 'Only you know I'm right.'

Caz stared at her. They'd never meet again.

'Listen,' she said. 'She wasn't a bitch, right? She's dead, Danny, burned to death.'

'Ooh,' Danny said. 'Well, punch me in the mouth, shit, I'm sorry. I didn't know her – I don't know you, but I'm sorry. Here.'

Caz smoked the joint for a while.

'At least I've said it,' she said. 'I kept thinking no, it's a mistake, sometimes I wake up and then I remember. No mistake. Nothing.'

'Sleep in with me if you want,' Danny said after a while.

'No shit, babes.'

'Thanks,' Caz said, 'but I'll use the couch, if you don't mind.'

'Course not,' Danny stood up. 'I'm next door if you want to talk or anything. Night, babes.'

She squeezed Caz's shoulder and went to bed.

That night, lying dry-eyed and awake on Danny's couch under a duvet and sheets pilfered from the Royal Free Hospital, Caz decided to move out of London. Sooner or later every place would know and its blanket sympathy would drive her away. Although any time she was out after that, Danny was around, her self-appointed guardian angel. She never said anything about Ben, just bristled if anyone got too close.

The residency came up in Newcastle and Caz applied. Newcastle would do. She didn't know anyone who lived there and she'd never even driven through it. Danny saw her on to the coach and didn't waste time promising to write or keep in touch. She often thought of Danny.

Four years later and she was crying under a blanket of bindweed, her best friend wandering round outside somewhere. A best friend who didn't know about Ben or Charlotte or David or Alex or Andy or Jay.

Ho hum.

Caz crawled out of the dank green tunnel.

51

Josie was standing by one of the diggers, making notes.

'I thought I'd lost you,' she said. 'What do you think – oh, Caz, you've scratched your face.'

'A flesh wound,' Caz said, she hadn't even noticed, 'but now you mention it, it stings. It's nothing. Just how free can we be with this little patch of paradise?'

'As free as we want. I think we should get it cleared, it's impossible to work out with all this rubbish everywhere.'

'Well hang on, New Broom,' Caz said, 'you're the seeds gopher, ain't you? I fancy working around it, incorporating what's here. Like that burnt-out cottage.'

'Oh gawd, Caz,' Josie groaned, 'I knew that had given you ideas. Artists! What do you want to do with it?'

'I want it to be alive with flowers,' Caz said. 'Listen. I want to do shadow people on the walls and make old street signs – we can get the right names from the library. And I want fire flowers all round it. Red hot pokers, scarlet lilies, runner beans, nasturtiums – shaddap you face – they go on for ages, and they're orange and crimson and gold. Marigolds. A very neat little old fashioned cottage garden and then this blazing bloody anarchy behind it. Look!'

'I see,' Josie said, 'find out what exactly was here before and –'

'Say it with flowers!' Caz spread her arms and sang out loud. 'That's me, Dorothy Squires. I love her. The whole thing – say it with flowers and *trompe-l'oeil* paintings and sculpture. Cheap and cheerful, like a street party.'

'Yes,' Josie said. 'That's brilliant. And beautiful. That'll do George – what about Michael and his future future fixation?'

'A space ship,' said Caz. 'Only it'll be a sort of surreal conservatory, a glass house with silver wings, sort of futuristic birds and insects hovering over it all.'

'I'm a bit relieved,' Josie said. 'I had a distinct feeling that you were losing interest in this project and it would be down to me. I hope you don't think I'm rude, but you do have a way of just disappearing, Caz.'

'Do I?' Caz feigned surprise. 'Yes, I suppose I do. Just that I work so much on my own, Josie. Like always. The few times I've worked with anyone else recently, it's been awful.'

'Well, you can do it,' Josie said. 'Didn't you say you had a partner in London years ago, that you used to do wild and wonderful things with? A psychedelic squat?'

Caz's skin prickled. 'Did I say that? Well, I suppose I did. Was I pissed?'

'You were a bit, you were very lyrical. Remember? It was the night I got that Greek brandy. You said it brought it all back.'

'Tears before bedtime?' Caz said, fishing. Just how much had she told Josie?

'No,' Josie sounded surprised. 'You were deliriously happy all night. You went off at dawn to swim in the ocean.'

'Christ, yes,' Caz said. 'I did it too, you know. It was bloody freezing. Oh, that's another thing. I want water pumps, or a water pump at least, dragon's head, wrought iron, always gushing. That might help with keeping everything going as well: it's going to be a scorcher next spring and summer.'

'Practical, eh?' Josie took her arm. 'I've drawn a rough plan of what's here, shall we go and sketch it in? Just to get a clearer idea of what's what?'

'OK,' Caz said. 'Isn't that bar on the boat open all day? I fancy water with the wine.'

She wanted to tell Josie about the land in the sky. She even wanted to tell her about Ben, now that it was all welling up and none of it seemed so dreadful since she'd seen the circus. One day she would.

They walked the gangplank and ducked into the bar to sit over lager in the gently shifting low-ceilinged room.

'Flags,' Caz said, 'Newcastle is so much tied in with the sea – hang out more flags. I've got a friend down south who makes beautiful flags. Charlotte. Could we use her? And fairy lights, Josie, we must have fairy lights – just to twinkle at dusk and in the darkest nooks and corners. What do you think?'

'You'll have to scratch your face more often, my girly,' Josie said, laughing, 'it does wonders for your imagination.'

52

Caz was trawling Miston High Road for bits, an excuse for mooching. Actively mooching. She knew she wouldn't find anything much. Trawling was a way of keeping her feet on the ground when all she wanted to do was skip and sing, improvise songs in cod French, vamp everyone – even the newspaper lady – with a deep Eastern European growl.

The bits were for the scale model she and Josie were making. The burnt-out house had become a focus, and where a few years ago, she would have thrown the whole thing in at the sight of it, now felt like the right time to move on. With joy, with celebration: they'd decided to get some archive tapes from the BBC for the twenties and thirties and have them playing as background. They'd found out that the wasteland had been called Dreamchare in the days when it needed a name. The people there worked mainly on the Tyne, unloading goods from small river craft to fill the holds of ocean-going merchant ships.

Caz looked up the name. As well as the obvious, *dream* meant joy, jubilation, music, minstrelsy. The word *chare* held every meaning from turning out a piece of work to turning your hand to anything.

They would have been a make-do-and-mend, odd-jobbing people, the inhabitants of Dreamchare, making good torn nets and wind-ripped sails, splintered hulls and rusted anchors. There was a huge smithy where chains were forged and links welded. Whatever needed to be done in the business of boats, someone in

Dreamchare could be found busy doing it. And she saw them as dreamers, whistle while you work, sing a song of the open sea, dream of faraway lands brought alive by the sailors and their wild tales.

In its heyday, Dreamchare had a larger than life cast of saints, scoundrels, drunkards and whores. There was a story about Jack Murphy, Newcastle's Dick Whittington, who'd made a fortune breeding terriers and sending them off into the brave new lands miles across the sea. One old book had an etching of Riverbank Sally, who lured many a young hopeful down the primrose path and eventually married a duke and got presented to the king. Mother Whelton had healing hands and was revered more than any physician. Even lords and ladies drove their fine carriages to her door. There was a ballad about Tugboat Henry who could drink the Tyne dry and be roaring for more – and he was matched only by Scarlet Nell, his six foot wife whose flailing fists and flaming hair were the stuff of legend.

Under the predatory thistles and ankle-wrenching clumps of grass, they'd stumbled on the bones of cobbled streets and decided to have them cleared.

'Even if they're broken,' Josie said, 'it'll give paths and if they're too bad, madam, you can go all mosaic with a small m.'

At once, Caz pictured turquoise boats with golden sails and dolphins with mirror eyes floating beneath her feet.

Most of the models would be papier mâché and card, but she hoped for a few doll's house people and tiny artefacts: making a beautifully detailed pump barely two inches high would be very fiddly, and it would have to be perfect to give Michael and George no choice but to love the idea.

She was looking in the window of Toys 4 Boyz N Gurlz when she heard her name.

'Caz Hewson?'

And again, like an echo.

'Caz Hewson.'

She turned: it was The Angry Man, sitting in the middle of his things by the boarded-up window of Madame Raphael's Milliner's. Years in London had trained Caz to avoid and ignore loonies, but here she was in Miston and he was looking straight at her.

'Could be,' she said warily.

'You don't recognise me.'

'No,' Caz said, aware that passers-by were slowing down and watching them. *Ee, pet, I heard that fella The Angry Man talking the day, he was talking to a lassie, she's not from round here, but I've seen her on the High Road the last few month.* By the time she hit The Turk's Head on Saturday night, they'd already have her down as engaged, or at least, a relative. No one would ask the question direct, but they'd all be hinting and pressing her for details. What the hell, in for a penny, in for an ear-pounding. She sat on the pavement.

'Have we met?'

'It's David.'

Jesus! With the beard and moustache, she'd never have known him. She must have walked past . . .

'. . . me about half a dozen times. I wondered if you were ignoring me, then I saw a mirror this morning and thought, no, you wouldn't know me. Or want to know me?'

She looked at him. David who'd run out on Charlotte – also David who'd shared all their lives for nearly nine years.

'They say you meet the whole world on Miston High Road,' she said. 'Wow. I came here to get away.'

'Well, you can,' he said, 'I'd understand.'

'No,' she said, 'no, David. I've heard bits about The Angry Man, but I never associated it with you. Don't they call you Angus?'

'They do,' he said. 'It's a family name. I was staying with my brother for a long time and they wouldn't leave him alone until he told them my name. I'm Angus David, he's Angus Peter. Even my sister's Angus Jane. You know, we just called each other Angus, me and Peter. He drinks a lot and it's easy to be with your family, you know, after what happened. Then I thought, sod it, I've lost enough time with all the beer so I hit the road.'

'And the headlines,' Caz said.

'I didn't want that,' David said, 'I thought telling them to piss off would make them go, but it only encourages them.'

Caz nodded.

Times like now it seemed that her life was a jigsaw puzzle. Going to art college and meeting Ben and Andy and Alex and Jay and Charlotte and David, she felt she'd been incredibly lucky. In one fell swoop, she'd been given all the pieces and her life would be simply a process of fitting them in place. But the fire had blown it all away, leaving her with a handful of pieces that didn't fit and no way of making a picture ever again. In the years since then, she realised that some of the pieces were double-sided, some were scorched beyond recognition or redemption, some were blank. Since then, she'd met people who gave her a fragment she recognised as belonging somewhere: it was rare and to be treasured.

And now in this year of wonders, a whole new set of pieces had come her way, with the promise of making a real picture all over again. She'd met Carrie and the gift of her timeless wisdom; she'd seen the charred house and had the chance to make of it something gloriously new. This year there was the flat no one could throw her out of, the magic land in the sky: places where she belonged. And there was Joy in the magic land in the sky, Joy who knew about Ben and probably everything else as well. Charlotte's letter had dropped through her door, weaving the past into the present and she was determined to bring her up to Newcastle somehow to be part of it, to make her wonderful flags again.

And now here was David.

The Angry Man.

53

'Well, Caz,' David said, 'thanks for asking me up.'

He stood awkwardly beside the door, just the way he had when she and Ben asked him in to show off their flat. Somewhere he'd got the idea that all lesbians were separatists and, being a new man before the high-priced tabloid glossies got hold of the term, he didn't want to intrude. He thought they were going to soapbox him, he was waiting for a lecture.

'I'm not just being polite,' Caz said, the way she had then, 'you're welcome. You want a coffee? Tea? Beer?'

'Beer,' he said. 'This high summer brings a hell of a thirst. I don't drink in the street – what would people say! – and pubs aren't exactly keen on me.'

'No,' Caz smiled. 'Do you want a bath? You don't stink or anything, David, but living outside . . .?'

'I'd really like that,' David said. 'When I was first on the road, I was itching for a bath and a shave, but now, I wash where I can, comb the face fungus every day and hope for the best. Hot deep water and bubbles! It's been a long time.'

'Have a shave,' Caz said, 'if you want.'

David shook his head. 'No. That'd have all the bloody media out again, can you imagine? WORLD EXCLUSIVE: First Pictures of The Angry Man Sans Beard, Moustache and Everything! Has the Samson of the Roads lost his strength? Turn to Centre Pages.'

'Well, whatever. Help yourself,' Caz said, amused at his self-importance. 'I'll be on the balcony.'

'The windy old baloney,' David said. 'Do you remember, Alex and Andy used to say that. "Cosa Nostra, our little pied à terre is festooned with many an old baloney." Do you ever hear from them?'

'Occasionally,' Caz said. 'They send a Christmas card, all tinselly camp from San Francisco. They're still virgins, they say there's so much death in the community, sex has become repulsive. The little death: it's not even part of a bad joke any more.'

'I wondered if they'd fall in love,' David said. 'They were like – two halves of a whole?'

'Weren't we all, dear,' Caz said with an edge in her voice. David looked down.

'I'll take that bath,' he said.

Caz sat on the balcony with her coffee. Serena appeared, smiling like a Cheshire cat.

'Hi, Serena.'

'Hello, Caz, isn't the weather lovely for the time of year?' The royal garden party voice.

'It is,' Caz said.

Serena sat down and crossed her legs. She lit a cigarette. 'Visitors?' she asked, blinking rapidly.

So that's what it was about. Serena had seen David come in with her. She was just bursting with curiosity.

'Yeah,' Caz said, 'visitor, anyway. He's having a bath.'

Serena dug her knee and winked. 'Men are filthy,' she hissed. 'My late husband, excuse me, my husband at least until my solicitor can sort it out I shall have to use that name, he was a dirty pig. More used to living in a cave, dear.'

'Uh huh,' Caz said.

'I know who he is,' Serena whispered, 'your friend. I shan't say a word, dear. Just I would like to ask you a favour if it's not too much trouble. It will be returned. I never forget a face or a favour, you understand?'

'Go ahead,' Caz said, 'only I can say yes or no?'

'Naturally, if that's your attitude,' Serena clenched her teeth.

'No, it's just that – oh, go ahead, ask me. Just I don't want you being upset if I can't do it.'

'Nothing could upset me after the life I've had,' Serena said. 'If I told you half! I realise my nerves have been a bit bad lately but now that that effing pig has gone! All I wanted to ask you is if I could have a little word with your friend.'

'You'll have to ask him,' Caz said, 'I don't mind.'

'I'm not after him,' Serena winked. 'No. Although I would have thought a nice well-brought-up girl like yourself could have done better, but it's none of my business.'

'He's a friend,' Caz said.

'I can call back later if it's inconvenient,' Serena shouted. 'Excuse me, I know where my nose isn't wanted.'

'It's fine, it's just fine,' Caz said. 'Wait till he gets out of the bath.'

'Have you travelled in foreign parts?' Serena said suddenly. 'You have the look of a person who might have been abroad at some time. It could have been a holiday or even a position of employment. Have you been abroad?'

'A bit,' Caz said.

'It's useful to know,' Serena said, 'I may be needing information about a foreign country in the near future.'

'If I can help, I will,' Caz said.

Serena tapped her heels and laughed to herself.

'Christ, that's better!' David came out on the balcony, his hair and beard sleek with water.

'Angus,' Caz said – why Angus? well, why not? – 'this is Serena. She's a neighbour of mine and wants to have a word with you.'

'If that would be convenient,' Serena said, eyes glued to David.

'Sure,' he said.

'I'll get that beer,' Caz said.

In the kitchen she wondered what Serena would be 'having a word' about. She leant on the doorway out of sight and listened.

'I was wanting, em, excuse me, this may seem familiar,' Serena said.

'No, go on.'

'I've read about you, I've seen you, you're The Angry Man,' Serena almost whispered. 'You use terrible language and you say things they don't like. We've got a lot in common, you and I, Angus, yes we have.'

'Well now.'

'Why haven't they locked you up?' Serena demanded. 'Why do they let you go anywhere you want with your dirty mouth, excuse me but it's true, and you don't have a house or anything and they leave you alone. They won't leave me be, you see, questions, questions until I could scream. Then when I do, dear, it's lock up time. I've had it to the back teeth, dear.'

'That's hard,' David said slowly. Caz could feel him willing her to come back and dilute the atmosphere. She lounged against the wall, biding her time.

'I suppose I don't care what anyone says,' David said after a while. 'Maybe being a man they leave me be. They probably want to scream and shout too, but they're frightened so they behave themselves. I can't be bothered any more. Does that help?'

'Can't be bothered. Don't care what they say. Scream if you want. I knew you'd help, you're like Doctor Sylvester.' Serena gabbled.

'No,' David said, 'I didn't say scream when you want. People think screaming means you want help. If you want them to leave you alone, you have to just go about your business very quietly so that by the time they notice you, you're no threat. You're just a daft fellow who's tramping all the old roads and there's nothing they can do with you. I keep moving.'

'I can't, dear,' Serena laughed bitterly, 'this place is an open-air prison. I can't leave.'

'Oh,' David said, 'you want to leave?'

'Most certainly I do!'

'If you really want it, you'll find a way,' David said.

'That's true, very true. Ah, dear Angus, you're balm to my spirit,' Serena crooned. 'Yes, dear, I shall send you a postcard.'

Caz coughed and came out. Serena was half-standing, smiling beatifically. 'I shall leave you to your company, he's a very nice visitor. Visitor,' she said. 'Not a word, Angus, everyone's got ears these days.'

'Mum's the word,' he agreed.

Serena sailed down the balcony singing 'If I Ruled The World' in a high cracked voice.

'Well now,' Caz said, 'meet the neighbours.'

David grinned and opened his beer.

'A dropped stitch in the tapestry of life, Caz,' he said, snorting with laughter. 'I assume that's the world famous community care programme? I thought so. It's so effective, isn't it. Christ!'

54

Three beers into the afternoon and do you remember had taken them through Andy and Alex with ease. San Francisco was far enough away to speculate about.

'I might go there some time,' David said. 'I know I can live with nothing now. God, I always used to make such detailed plans.'

'I wondered about it,' Caz said, 'only I love living here.'

'You do, don't you?' David waved at the forest of nasturtiums. 'These are amazing. You were the plastic flower fiend back then. Miss Fake Fuchsia, Alex said.'

'Scarlet tulips in the window-boxes,' Caz said. 'Yes. They only need a wash every few months. Blue roses on the balcony, and I mean blue! I never wanted anything to tie us – *me* – to a particular place. Now, I think it's better to act as if you live somewhere properly. You know. Like other people do, just everyday living. I might even get a dog. Why did we have to agonise about everything, David?'

'Everything mattered,' he said. 'Every action had a ripple effect and we knew it. I think we were so scared of doing the wrong thing, taking the wrong road and finding out later. I had a fear of "if only". I mean, college, well, *college*. Then we were all at a crossroads. So we built a house there rather than have to go our separate ways. That's what I think, anyway.'

The lamp on the green fizzed and became pink.

Caz felt more words hovering in the air: words that she didn't want to give breath to. Ben. Fire. Charlotte. Baby. Why? Was this another crossroads with her stubbornly sitting still for fear of taking the sinister path? Whole sentences ran through her mind but her mouth stayed shut.

'Do you ever hear from Jay?' David sounded like he was making conversation. Neutral ground. Maybe he was feeling the same ghosts nagging for acknowledgement.

'Again, sometimes,' Caz said. 'Usually 3 a.m. phonecalls when she's incredibly drunk. She's so articulate I don't even realise until she starts repeating herself, or crying. Her work's admired, but she just takes the piss out of it, it doesn't matter to her.'

'What's she doing these days? Apart from being pissed off and getting pissed.'

'Falling in love,' Caz said. 'She has a talent for that, verging on addiction. Always with the wrong people, always unrequited. I think if you put Jay in a room with a hundred people, ninety-nine nice people and one neurotic egomaniac bastard, she'd find the bastard and go head over heels.'

'She never seemed to want a relationship,' David said.

'She didn't,' Caz sighed, 'we were her family, her necessary baggage, all of us. She said her happiest times were when we were all sitting round late at night talking. She said if it wasn't for sex, she wouldn't bother with anyone else. She said she felt like the cat with the cream, the six most special people in the world and her belonging with them.'

The ghosts pressed closer.

'Maybe she'll meet Ms Right, if only by the law of averages,' David sounded light.

'Don't,' Caz said, 'just don't. This isn't a cocktail party. Jay's whole world went up in flames, David, that's why she gets smashed every day, that's why she has £500 phone bills and a heart in smithereens. She's a walking casualty. We all are.'

For the first time since he'd spoken her name on the High Road, their eyes met.

'I know,' he said. 'Fuck it, it's not a cocktail party. Tell me about Charlotte.'

'Are you sure?' Caz said. When he said yes she went inside and got Charlotte's latest letter.

As he read it, he started crying without a sound, tears just washing out of his eyes and down his cheeks.

'I'm not making excuses,' he said, 'there are none. After the fire, we were both in hospital. You'd vanished, so had Jay and everyone. Mine was nothing compared to hers, so I was walking after a week or so. I went to see her – Charlotte – and she was in a coma. They said she'd lost the baby and might lose her legs. I sat by her bed for hours, talking to her. It was like that for weeks and then they discharged me. I went to my brother's and visited every day. I kept thinking, please, please let me trade my legs for her life, take one of my eyes, anything. Once the burns healed, you see, I'd got off lightly. Then they took her legs off and she was still in this coma. They said she wasn't likely to pull through and I just couldn't stand it any more. Stand it! Jesus, even the words hurt. So I didn't see her for a week, then a month and then it seemed too late.'

'I don't have a judgement,' Caz said. 'This is the first time – no, there was Danny – the second time I've talked about it.' She thought: no, the third. There's Joy.

'So I pissed off,' David said bitterly, 'and once I'd done that, I didn't go back. What should I do, Caz, I'm not asking you. I am asking you, but you don't have to work it out for me.'

By now the lamp on the green was orange.

'You have to do what you want,' Caz said. 'I don't think any of us are in line for medals.'

'I'll get some more beer,' David said.

'What about your things?' Caz said. 'Miston isn't Clay Bank, but even here, piles of things lying around are fair game.'

'It'll be less for me to carry.'

She watched him walk away and wondered if this time he'd come back or whether next week's news would be a sighting of The Angry Man well over the city limits, striding purposefully to yet another nowhere.

Part four

55

Carrie came along from the lift and her face lit up with a smile when she saw Caz.

'I'll have a seat,' she said, putting her shopping bag and handbag down. 'Visitors?' she winked and twinkled.

'Just a friend,' Caz said.

'I saw ye talking on the High Road,' Carrie nodded, 'I wondered if he was bothering ye. Then I thought, Caz knaas what she's about. He's a friend of yours?'

'It's weird,' Caz said, 'I knew him years ago.'

'Never in God's world!' Carrie took her hand. 'It's a wonderful thing when ye meet up with an old friend by chance. Take me and Rose, hadn't spoken for twenty-three years, ye knaa, with my man being the sort he was. Then I was shopping one day, singing me heart out. That morning I'd taken off me wedding ring and hoyed it down the chute, I was getting me shoes for the Christmas cruise and I heard her voice. Carrie Ives? she says, and I turned round. Rose Easton, I says. I'll call ye the merry widow, Carrie Ives, she says, it's lovely to see ye smile. We went and had a coffee. Hardly a day's gone by since that we've not seen each other. It's never too late to pick up and start again wi an old friend. Ye must be ower the moon.'

'I suppose I am,' Caz said, 'I'm still stunned.'

'Aye, it'll be d'ye remember when all night, I can tell,' Carrie stood up. 'If ye fancy a bit company, come in later. I divent like being with old people all the time, I like the young uns, me. Bring yer young man wi ye. I expect there's a nice face under all that beard.'

'I'll take your shopping along,' Caz said.

'There's nae word from *hor*,' Carrie jerked her head towards Serena's flat. 'No sign of Lennie nor any other gentleman friend. It'll not be long unless leopards has took to changing their spots. Let's enjoy the bit peace while it's here.'

'I saw her this afternoon,' Caz said, 'she wanted to talk to my friend.'

'Well, it's a bit excitement for her,' Carrie said smoothly, 'him being a fella and all. Mind, ye'll hev to watch her, she'd pinch owt if she felt the urge. Especially men. I've not seen ye for days, Caz, you nor Josie either. How's yer project? Ye were off to look at the site, last time.'

'We're doing a model,' Caz said. 'I'll have to show it to you. It's over at Dreamchare – what used to be Dreamchare. I've been reading about it.'

'Well now,' Carrie sat down, 'do ye want to know about Dreamchare? It was a place I went when I was a bairn, before the bombers came up the Tyne and put an end to it. Terrible days, pet, they bombed the shipyards and be buggered to the poor souls living beside. When I was a bairn, they had a carnival there every year, at Eastertide. Pet, it was like fairyland – for bairns especially, ye knaa. When ye've been born and raised in Miston, ye daen't need a lot to make ye feel special. We couldn't pay for all the rides, but me mam would always find us the coppers for one. I always went on the same one. It was a geet roundabout, horses wi golden manes and eyes like diamonds. Do ye knaa, I can see it now! Ye had to let the man lift ye, the horses was so high up and I always rode a horse called Merrilegs, me.'

'I've got a horse called Merrilegs,' Caz said, 'a roundabout horse.'

'Hev ye now?' Carrie leant forwards. 'Well, I shouldn't be surprised, not after Gladys the dragon. Ye've got some lovely bits.

Mind, your Merrilegs'll not be the same one. We're going back, what, sixty year or more.'

'It could be,' Caz said. 'Come and see.'

'I will! Where did ye get yer horse?'

'We were doing a play,' Caz said. 'It was about a travelling fair that just got poorer and poorer until there was only the roundabout left.'

'Is it,' Carrie said. 'And then what happened?'

'Well, it just sort of ended,' Caz said, 'with the woman who owned the roundabout sitting beside the horses, saying "I don't know what to do . . ."'

'That's no ending!' Carrie was scornful. 'They do that a lot these days. They daen't seem to have the knack of making a proper end. I've seen it on the television. Ye think ye're halfway through, it's all so complicated, and suddenly it's the end. Nothing's happened, the people is just left. I should write plays, me, I'd give them a proper ending. Ye cannot leave folk hanging in mid-air! Ye should have had the roundabout saved, pet. Summat cheerful – God knows there's enough sadness in the world.'

The playwright had said the ending was like life, unresolved and anxious. But everyone wants happily ever after, and against all experience and reason, strives for it, clings to hopes and dreams. Caz pictured the roundabout newly painted and turning, the gilt horses riding up and down with music like bubbles cheering it on. She would have scorned any such Pollyanna solution years ago, delighted by the careful illusion of ageing and decay she'd painted into the set. Now she thought maybe Carrie was right. Angst is the privilege of youth, when there's all of time ahead to make mistakes and start again.

'Merrilegs is downstairs,' she said, leading the way. She'd never asked Carrie downstairs before, it was such a mess. But now she knew Carrie she didn't care.

Her plan was to find or make a wooden pole twisted like barley sugar and fix it to the floor and ceiling so that the glossy horse could stand proud in mid-air, turning to face the room or look out of the window over the valley. For the moment, Merrilegs was propped against steel shelving, a pile of books holding her unsteadily upright.

'Here she is,' Caz said.

Carrie stroked the cowlick of glossy gold between her pointed ears. Merrilegs's mane was swirls and waves of yellow and orange, rich with layers of yacht varnish, and Carrie ran her hand over them. She bent to look into the chocolate brown eye and took hold of the reins, jingling with golden bells from Marrakesh.

'Aye, she's a beauty,' Carrie said. 'Are you Merrilegs from Dreamchare, I wonder? Hev ye changed her, wi painting, like?'

'Well, she was very faded and chipped when I found her,' Caz said. 'I filled in the deep scratches and made her a new leg: the old one was splinters. There was a bit of paint left on her and I tried to match it as best I could.'

'Now, that's you,' Carrie pronounced, patting the padded velvet seat. 'My Merrilegs had a wooden saddle, worn smooth wi riding. Ee, ye knew ye'd been galloping after ye got doon! And them reins is different. In them days, she hadn't but a strip of leather, worn smooth wi all the bairns's hands hanging on for dear life! I knaa they didn't gan fast, but for a bairn, well, ye felt ye were flying.'

Caz nodded. She had thought of making wings for Merrilegs, even papier mâché-ed a prototype, but they looked wrong. They had turned into Demelza the flying pig whose sly come-hither snout nudged the lampshade in the hall.

'Aye, that's her name, Merrilegs,' Carrie traced the letters on the swallowtail flourish at her neck. 'That's the way they looked, pet. Mebbes this is my Merrilegs. It doesn't matter, does it, she might as well be. Was her name on when ye got her? Where did ye find her?'

'I found her in a skip,' Caz said, 'over at South Pendleton, you know, where I lived before here. There was an E and an R and a bit of an S. I think I got her name from a story I had when I was little, *The Discontented Pony.* A live pony who wanted to be a roundabout horse, then found they weren't real and went home again and lived happily ever after.'

'That's more like a story,' Carrie said. 'There was a Merrilegs in *Black Beauty* and all, ye knaa. Black Beauty, Ginger and Merrilegs. She was a spirited thing, Merrilegs, then someone bought her and used her badly. Broke her spirit, like. I cannot mind what happened after that, only I think it all came out right for her. What are ye gan to do wi this un here?'

Caz showed her a sketch of the twisted pole. Carrie looked at the ceiling.

'Ye could dae that here, pet,' she said. 'The ceilings and floors is all concrete and ye could make her firm. When she's fixed, I'll come visiting and have a ride. If she can take my weight, she'll do! Not that I mind me weight.'

'No,' Caz said, 'I can't be bothered with all that thin is beautiful number.'

'Daen't bother yer head wi it,' Carrie said, patting her stomach. 'I've known thin, I've known years when I could count me bones. Rose says to us, Carrie, yer gettin fat. I says, I knaa, lovely isn't it? Never mind thin, pet, this geet belly of mine means money!'

56

'**C**az?'

'That's yer young man back, pet,' Carrie stroked Merrilegs's head again. 'I'd best get back and get me tea on. Mebbe see yez later.'

David stood in the doorway of the flat with a wine shop carrier and a dustbin bag bulging with parcel tape and twine.

'This is Carrie, David,' said Caz, 'David, Carrie.'

'Ah hah,' Carrie said, nodding, 'mind yez divent bevvy all night, now, our Caz has got work to do, ye knaa! Daen't forget to call by, now.' She smiled serenely and walked back to her flat.

'She seems nice,' David said. 'I've shifted the rest of my things – one of the women in The Ritz said I could leave them out the back there, the yard's locked. Dora. They're so – nice, here.'

'They are,' Caz said. 'Feels like home to me, at last.'

'I've got something for you,' David said. 'Consider it a house-warming present. It's in here.'

Carefully, he untied the string on one of the black dustbin bags, and took out a Harrod's carrier bag, lumpy with a coat and a shirt and a jumper wrapped round another carrier bag inside it.

'Sorry about the vagrant packing,' he said, 'it's the only way to keep the rain out.'

'It's like pass the parcel,' Caz said, as he unwrapped the plastic from layers of newspaper, 'Jesus.'

The last layer was the front page of the *News Of The World*:

PRINCESS'S PAL IN PALACE POT PARTY! He took out a bottle and put it sideways on the table.

'Ben made it,' he said. 'I'd got it in the van the night of the fire. It was going to be a surprise for you. You should have it.'

Caz crouched to look close. There was a ship inside the bottle, CAZ VII, and her body lurched with recognition. She remembered when Ben had decided to mistress the art of putting ships in bottles. They'd met an old chap in a pub who used to do it and Ben had combed the libraries of Stepney and Mile End, finally finding a wartime *How To* paperback in Whitechapel. The first one had taken weeks of fiddling and cursing and false starts; glue that wouldn't hold and glue that set too fast. Once Ben had a project she lived it and she'd done nothing else for weeks. Finally, she'd woken Caz at four in the morning, with the first ship-in-a-bottle and a bottle of champagne to launch it. Well, they called it champagne. Finances dictated that they become connoisseurs of fake champagne and this was pink and fizzy so who gave a damn about labels.

The first ship rode on curls of snowy foam and stylised waves of butterfly turquoise.

'Look,' Ben said, her voice welling with pride and excitement.

On the prow the size of a match-head were the golden letters: *CAZ I*.

'Your boat,' Ben said, 'the first of an argosy! I've got the hang of it now. This is the sort Columbus would have sailed in. I'm going for the Francis Drake look next time. Do you like it?'

'No,' Caz said, 'I love it. It's perfect. You're perfect. It's brilliant.'

Ben set the bottle in an oval of white diodes on a glass shelf and pointed out the whale and the dolphin and the octopus and starfish she'd painted under the ship. It was sheer magic. After the fire, Caz wondered what she'd gone back for – was it the ship, had she gone back and been trapped, or just been trapped? She'd never know. One minute she had hold of her hand in the blinding smoke and heat, the next, she was alone. Forever.

Here and now in Galleon Heights, she gazed at *CAZ VII*, Ben's ornate rendering of Noah's Ark. People had said she should sell them, but Ben had only laughed.

'Three hundred quid to some mindless Covent Garden yuppie? Balls! I'd do a commission for seven thousand to take us on a cruise – not a penny less! They're all for Caz – and I guess I'll do ones for Charlotte and David and Andy and Alex and Jay.' That was Ben.

There had been *CAZ II*, a pirate ship, *CAZ III*, a sampan, *CAZ-RA*, a reed raft, then a dhow, and a barge. She had plans for a wrecked fishing boat and a rock alive with mermaids, a felucca gleaming with pirate gold. But this ark was the last one she'd made. Ben's last secret . . . Everything about it said Caz and Ben: the window-boxes trailed roses, there were minute portholes where tigers and zebras and leopards smiled. One tiny Mrs Noah wore a kimono, the other had overalls and they stood on the deck holding hands with an elephant squirting a silver jet of water over their heads. And all the waves were alive with starfish and flying fish . . . pure benthos. And then she saw her own eyes made huge, as if in a curved ghostly mirror. That long ago 4 a.m., they had knelt on either side of *CAZ I* and their eyes had met through the glass . . .

David opened a can of lager and the sound cracked her alert. She stood up, her feet and legs fizzing with pins and needles.

'Yes,' she said, unable to look at him direct. She'd almost seen Ben's face again through the curved glass, the shadow of her smile. That was the first clear thought that had come to her through the numbness after the fire. *I'll never see you smile again.*

'I'm sorry,' David said, 'I didn't think, it's just, it's been so long . . .'

'Nothing to be sorry about,' Caz said, 'I'm glad to have it. Glad? I'm really pleased. More than words come near to. It's just that I never thought there was anything left, you know. She was wonderful, wasn't she?'

'Oh yes,' David said, 'and then some. She just made things – fairyland? And it was all you, Caz, you and her. Even down to the roses in the window-boxes. Rosa Mundi, your one horticultural success. Triumph.'

Caz opened her lager and sat down. 'Yes,' she said, 'we did it with grow bags, didn't we? All that summer, Christ, I can smell that perfume even now. A rose for my rose. I'll make *CAZ VII* a glass shelf and give her spotlights – do you remember? Of course you do.'

And it seemed to her that she could cry, for all the hollow years since Trimdon House, all the soulless rooms where she'd eaten and slept and woken alone. As if she was the ghost, drifting from London E15 to London NW6 to South Pendleton, all the places where she'd never bothered or cared enough to make a mark. And now she was somewhere like home and the walls and ceilings were wild and alive. Sea-horses and dolphins arching over the stairs, dragons guarding the entrance to the Hole that reached to the sky, Merrilegs in all her glossy silence: Ben's ark, *CAZ VII*, had been all over England wrapped in cloth and plastic and crumpled tabloids and now it had landed and drew all of 77, Galleon Heights around its miniature brilliance.

57

Caz set the bottle on a shelf for the time being, until she created its new Ararat. For now, she angled a spotlight to bathe the ark like sunrise. She dug through the tape box and found 'A Night In The Tropics'. She'd bought this copy in Newcastle, but she'd never been able to play more than the first few bars. She and Ben had bought it blind – rather, deaf – arrested by the composer's name, Louis Moreau Gottschalk.

'There's a double barrel to conjure with!' Ben said.

When they'd played it for the first time, her spine had tingled with delight. It wasn't jazz or blues or straight classical precision, but a rich tapestry woven with all of these. The music rang around their ocean-bound bedroom, a clarion call of parrots and palm wine and waves that break over conch shells and fill their rosy hearts with foam.

'I always pictured the Ark on grey seas,' Ben said, 'until I thought about it. Of course, the seas would be postcard blue and hot – Mediterranean sizzling! You know, if they'd played music on the Ark – and they must have done, it would have sounded this way. Darling – it's our song! I want to make things that make people feel how I do when I'm listening to this!'

She'd sounded gutsy and fierce, her grey eyes almost black in the candlelight. Always driving herself, *my dear, when they come to interview me, I'll just say I hone myself to the bone to create three-dimensional cartoons. Summat to laff at.*

She did.

Caz considered telling all this to David, then decided no. He was David, but the years lay between them like the beard and moustache covering his mouth. Time had painted shadows into his eyes, shadows of people and places she knew nothing about. Lines sketched on his brow by frowns she'd never seen the beginning of, and worries she'd never heard about. Mainly it was his unresolved business with Charlotte that made her wary. She knew in her guts that if Ben had survived, no matter how damaged, she would have been there. If she'd been broken by falling masonry or timber, Ben's hand would have held hers through the coma, her face would have been the first thing she saw as she swam back into the world. And vice versa. It was difficult not to judge.

You must walk a mile in another person's moccasins to begin to know their life, as the saying goes. She tried it out and still felt uneasy. Caz was sure that hers was the greatest loss in the fire. Where there's life, no matter how crippled, there would be love and hope. David had run away and got stoned and drunk and let shame and fear keep him on the road, any road apart from the one that led to Charlotte's door. She told herself to leave it, be patient. Listen.

David drew on a cigarette and drank some lager. 'Yes,' he said, 'Ben was something else. God, wasn't it all a long time ago? Who are you seeing now?'

Caz couldn't believe he'd said that. Her face stung. Time and the circs – always the bloody circs! – had made a stranger of David yet here he was, sprawled in her sacred space as if he belonged, as relaxed as if he owned it, and throwing his questions at her as if he had a perfect right. She focused on the bright-lit ark in its dimpled bottle. She did not give herself permission to scream at him, but she had to make him back off.

'Oh, you know,' she said, as lightly as she might in the Lovenest or at some Chianti and canapéed preview party, 'I live for Art.'

'Come on,' he said, 'that was always a bit of a joke, Caz. Not your art, before you go off it, but that whole ethos. Art is a part of life, no more, no less.'

'As you said,' she spoke carefully, 'it was all a long time ago.'

'Oh, subject closed?' he mocked. 'Hey, life goes on, you know. I want to know, Caz, know how you get through your days. You seem to be managing a hell of a lot better than me. Maybe I'm looking for answers? Help?'

I know, thought Caz, floundering in her mind for ways to shift him. Help? David had a hardness now and it was distasteful to her. She'd heard it when he was talking about Charlotte and taken it as his way of dealing with guilt and grief. Sarcasm adds a sparkle to playing with ideas, self-mockery is safe. But this wasn't toying with words and concepts. David was playing with people – her – and his sarcasm turned on a whiplash of cruelty. She felt that if she opened her heart to him as he clearly wanted, it would be just so that he could observe the raw pulse of her life.

Emotional vivisection.

'Work,' she said severely, holding her knees, 'just that.'

'And I suppose you think I've copped out?' He drank more lager. 'I didn't think I'd ever hear you sounding so dedicated. Apart from love, of course.'

Goddammit! A picture of Joy by the lake snapped into clear focus in her mind. *You've got to say what you want, Caz.* She creased her eyes to see Mrs Noah in her pomegranate kimono. The ark that Ben made.

If she carried out Joy's advice to the letter, she would now be saying: *I'd like you to leave.* For if David started asking about any area of her life, she would still feel like clamming up. The music finished and she put on her Gipsy Kings tape: safe and familiar sounds.

'Like, I did drugs,' David said, 'I started reading Castaneda and Tim Leary and I thought, maybe they know something. Drugs take you somewhere else, you know, Caz.'

Caz thought drugs were like getting a madman to blindfold

you and take you on a fairground ride with no safety bars. Could be the ghost train, could be the rollercoaster, you'd never know until a rush of wind ripped the cover from your eyes. Then you could go *oh wow look at the amazing lights, man*, or fall screaming, and lie broken a thousand feet below.

'Yeah,' David said, 'I loved cocaine. It's the champagne drug. I did some speed: whoo! Left my body stretched and shaking for weeks. Too much. I did smack once.'

'Once?' Caz said. She didn't believe him.

'Once,' David nodded. 'It was wonderful. Everything was so intense, just so intense. I walked round the next day and realised I had a choice. You know, everything looked so grey and ordinary! It was a beautiful summer's day and the sun was pale. The grass was like faded rags. That's when I decided to hit the road. Smack could make everything so brilliant and I was scared of the feeling when you come down. Nothing matters, nothing looks any good. Your feet feel like lumps of dirty mud, your skin feels like sailcloth. Yeah, it was a choice: dreamland at needle-point or try and accept that daylight's as bright as it's going to get. You know?'

'I think so,' Caz said.

That was the way she felt for years after Ben died. Sunshine so what. Daffodils who cares. Paint a picture, Caz, yeah and what the hell for? Knowing that each hollow day was as good as it was ever going to be without Ben. She'd even seen a therapist who was sold on loving yourself. When she looked in the mirror, she could see a nose, mouth, cheeks, forehead, eyebrows, hair. Her eyes were dead: there was not a spark of anything to love.

Oh, her head could do it: I am worth loving, I am a nice person, since I've rejected suicide as an option, I will find a reason for living again. But her heartbeat was tired and every part of her body ached as much as her spirit. Lifting a brush towards a canvas was sheer pain. Until the night she spent on Danny's broken couch under her pilfered bedclothes, the night she cried, she was a walking corpse. Maybe Ben had been her drug: Ben's love was all she'd ever dreamed of, after all.

The phone rang.

'Caz? It's Josie. I was – sort of expecting you? Have I got the night wrong?'

'No,' Caz said, 'I'm so sorry. I've got a – friend – here. I just forgot.'

'We're supposed to be doing the model,' Josie said stiffly.

'I know,' Caz said. 'It's David, you see – he – well, I haven't seen him for years, Josie. I really am sorry. Listen. Could you bear to come over here? I swear I'll do nothing but the model from tomorrow morning.'

'Charlotte's David?'

'As was,' Caz said. 'You've got every right to be furious with me, Josie. Shit.'

Josie pursed her lips. It felt like yet another Caz-goes-missing, and she tried to reason with her frustration. 'I'll come over,' she said, 'if you want me to.'

'I wouldn't ask,' Caz said, 'I'm so sorry.'

'I'm on the way,' Josie said.

'Female trouble?' David's eyes danced.

Caz looked at him – damn him! she was just beginning to feel easy! – then started to laugh.

'Give it up, Mister Guru,' she said. 'My friend Josie's coming over, that's all. I should have been there, only it's not every day I pick a man up, out of the gutter or otherwise.'

'I'll behave,' David said.

'She doesn't know about Ben,' Caz said. 'No one up here does. That's how I want it. She's heard about Trimdon House – as far as she knows, it was a sort of hippy arty commune that folded after a while. Charlotte had an accident, that's all, you just went your separate ways. I've never gone into details with Josie – or anyone else. I tried to start again when I came up here.'

'Present tense?' David nodded. 'I see. Past imperfect – Christ, there's an understatement! Present tense and future perfect.'

'We live in hope,' Caz said softly, gazing at the magical ark glinting in its bottle. She switched off the spotlight.

58

'Well,' Josie told the sleeping cat, 'it looks like we're not having an evening in after all.'

She stood and reordered her thoughts. Coat, scarf and bike elbowed fire, wine and work to one side. Fireguard. Lock windows, lock doors. Leave a light.

Josie had spent her childhood with her grandparents in a house where everything was regular and slow. At around four o'clock, for example, her grandfather would check his watch and say: 'Isn't it about time for a cup of tea?'

Her grandmother and she would go into the kitchen. Tea. You polished the tray and put out a crisp traycloth from the second dresser drawer. You hotted the pot and fetched the milk jug with its beaded muslin from the stone pantry; you took biscuits from a tin and arranged them on a plate, set out cups and saucers and teaspoons, a tea strainer and a sugar basin. You measured the tea in a crested Coronation spoon, one for each person and one for the pot. Then you took the laden tray into the lounge and put it on the table. Granny poured and milked and sugared. That was how you had a cup of tea.

When she grew up and visited a friend's house, she was amazed. Her friend's mother threw a teabag in a mug and drank it as she dashed from room to room on the way out. 'You'll find something for tea, won't you? I'm late!'

But she'd been Invited! Josie watched her friend open spaghetti and leave the empty can on the table. She watched her make toast and take out two odd plates to eat it from. She didn't say a word, fully expecting some Adult to come in and tell them off. In her house, Proper Tea involved a tablecloth and tea plates, sandwiches and evenly cut slices of cake. She felt daring, drinking pop from glasses with the radio on, leaving dirty plates beside the sink. It was exhausting, she decided, but such fun. She didn't invite her friend to tea, however: she was unsure, embarrassed by how different her home was. She was shy and ashamed and wholly protective of the two slow old people who ordered her world.

She was a teenager before she started to giggle at them.

'Would you like a cup of tea now, dear?'

Her grandmother, grown restless. The response never varied: her grandfather folding his paper, changing his glasses and looking at his watch. 'Good Lord, yes, it's ten past!'

His watch told him when it was time to go to bed, time to get up, time to switch on the heating, switch on the lights, mention lunch. Would you *like*? Only if the time was right. Once his watch stopped and they sat helplessly until dark. The next day, he took his watch to be mended and bought a clock. 'We can't be caught like that again, eh, Josie?'

Josie couldn't wear watches: she'd been scolded for the suspected sins of overwinding and underwinding, but the truth was that watches just stopped after two days on her wrist.

Her grandfather's clock now sat in the centre of her mantelpiece. Caz had been due at eight: she'd waited until half past to ring her; half an hour was time enough to get lost or be delayed. Punctuality matters when you live alone and Caz knew that.

Keys, purse, gloves.

Tonight, she'd bought wine for Caz coming and put out two polished glasses. She was soothed by the comforting sound of the tray rattling gently as she walked down the passage. She looked at the firelight glinting off the bottle and the crystal, dancing on the polished silver of the tray. The huge table in the living room was laid out for model-making: she'd tacked card to a board and set up card tables with all the equipment she'd been gathering for weeks.

And now it wasn't happening: some old friend of Caz's had blown her cherished evening away – no, aside. Aside for less than twenty-four hours. Josie sighed. She'd found that, with living alone: a last minute change of plan left an uncomfortable gap. It wasn't reasonable to be angry about it: things happened, life did not run in the silent clockwork manner of her childhood home. Older people were utterly reliable, Josie had found, but now that she was in her thirties, her friends around the same age, she wondered if anyone would ever think that of them. She'd found that life is haphazard in a way she'd never imagined: you could see last minute change as a disappointment and fret about it, or welcome it as a surprise and enjoy.

It wasn't as if Caz had left her high and dry after all: she was going to have an evening involving company, but her tidy mind fretted. She wished she could have said *damn* or snapped at Caz, but it just wasn't in her. Since Josie was extremely patient, she considered it the most overrated virtue of all. You never value things which are as natural to you as breathing. No matter: she put the wine back in the kitchen, the glasses back in the cupboard and the tray slid between the stove and the dresser with the other trays. She closed the damper and put up the fireguard and locked the cottage.

She wheeled her bike to the gate and looked back and closed her eyes. Then opened them and smiled. Angels with silver hair had always taken care of Josie. The cottage was a legacy and the only place she'd known as home since her grandparents had died.

Thank you, Miss Rainier, she thought, you'll never know how much I thank you.

She cycled along the muddy path leading to the moonlit drive winding through the estate. It was three miles to the sprawling outskirts of Newcastle, two miles further brought her to Miston and on a good day she could do it in twenty minutes. Tonight, she would dawdle a bit: maybe get there at nine fifteen. Caz didn't have a bedtime after all, and neither did she. Bed happened when the conversation dried up and all the bottles were empty. She might be up all night.

It was at times like this that she was grateful for the fixed routines of her childhood: everything spontaneous held the thrill of adventure. Evenings with Caz were like pass the parcel: time was layers of tissue, every layer held a prize and you never knew what it would be.

59

It was the sort of night where the moon rides over clouds soft and curved like the inner-wing feathers of a swan. It isn't midnight, but the sky is midnight blue and the stars are scattered like a broken diamond necklace on deep velvet.

'That,' thought Josie, freewheeling down the Fossway, 'is the sort of night it is. What was Caz's nature poem?

I watched the clouds a-billow
Atop the cliché trees,
My heart went cliché cliché
And brought me to my knees.

'Stick to the day job, girl,' she said, riding through the red light next to the Lazer Sensarium, a dark converted garage where young men and boys could play at blasting each other's guts out with bands of light like skipping ropes on acid for £2.75 an hour.

Living dangerously already! She flashbacked to the red light: she hadn't even paused. It was a first and she was delighted with herself. Josie was the one who'd sat at a red light on an empty street for twenty-five minutes one cold rainy 2 a.m. Finally, she'd dismounted and wheeled her bike to the next corner before riding off again, and every police siren had her heart beating too fast, her mind gabbling excuses for her Unlawful Deed. Fear was a bad bedfellow and her fears went everywhere with her, clinging like wan and sickly infants: since she'd met Caz, she was getting better at laughing them away.

You gotta laugh else you cry, innit love?

Caz's slogan beat the pants off 'look before you leap' or 'better be safe than sorry' for a motto. Those were her grandmother's catchwords. She'd cornered the market on sayings laden with suburban standards and old testament gloom. *All fur coat and no knickers* – that was for the peroxide assisted blonde who moved in over the street. *You can't touch pitch and not be defiled*, ditto when a boyfriend of Afro-Caribbean extraction moved in. *The road to hell is paved with good intentions*: rolled out *à propos* the blonde's neighbour when seen going in for a coffee. *There's many a slip twixt the cup and the lip*: the blonde was wearing a flashy engagement ring which Josie privately thought was the most beautiful thing she'd ever seen.

Her grandmother had watched the wedding party leave and return and her comment was: *Well, she's made her bed and there she must lie.* Josie was convinced that she was disappointed when the blonde and her dark beau were openly and unashamedly blissfully happy. Sometimes she wondered if her grandmother had always been so judgemental and bitter: the photo albums showed her smiling and laughing with her daughter on the beach, on a prom, in the garden; but then people always put on a good face for sunshine and holiday photos. She was convinced that she was responsible for the air of impending gloom – she was born, her mother went away – had her grandmother's smile vanished at the same time? She was given the impression that her mother was dead.

She drew a line under the flood of memories as Anchorage Point rose above her: it was automatic for her to rerun her past as vividly as daylight when the present was anything less than comfortable. Josie hated meeting new people and tonight she'd have to meet David, an unknown in every way.

A man is only after one thing and he'll have no respect for the fool of a girl who gives in to him.

That was the entire content of her grandmother's sex education.

Only she would never have let the three letter word cross her lips. Sex was It or Something You Have to Know About. Once only she called it Carnal Knowledge and couldn't meet Josie's eyes as she told her that Men seem to enjoy It, and women have to endure It for the sake of Marriage and The Children.

That was the answer when she asked her grandmother what was a love child? A boy at school had jeered at her and called her a Bastard. Her best friend defended her, saying hotly that Josie was a Love Child, her mother had told her.

Love child, love child, never meant to be . . .

Secretly, she bought the Supremes record and learnt every word by heart. One day she came home from school and the record had disappeared. She knew there was nothing she could say.

What would this David be like? Caz was the most intolerant person Josie had ever met and she loved her for it. She wasn't afraid to say she didn't like someone: she delighted in parrying fools gladly. David would have to be all right – wouldn't he?

She was stunned when she saw him.

The first word that came to her mind was hippy, and she knew Caz's acid opinion of hippies. He was sprawled on the living room floor with cushions under his shoulder, smiling through his tangled beard and moustache. He was a bit drunk and offered her a can as soon as he'd said hello. She'd heard Caz's diatribe about space invading men who play host and charmer no matter whose house they're in: and Caz was just sitting with a smile, letting it happen under her own roof.

'I haven't told David about the project,' she said, 'we've been catching up on old times – haven't we?'

'Yes,' David said, 'I've not seen Caz for years, you see. I was one of the inmates of Trimdon House.'

'Oh, I see,' Josie said.

Trimdon House, the arty commune Caz spoke of only when she was drunk. The one time she talked with passion, the twin lenses of brandy and rosy nostalgia crumbling her severe and immaculate facade.

'It sounds wonderful,' Josie said. 'You must have hated leaving.'

'All good things come to an end,' David said. 'You don't recognise me, do you?'

'Josie doesn't read the Sundays, David,' Caz said, 'she only listens to Radio Three. He's disappointed really: David's also known as The Angry Man.'

'Of course I've heard of The Angry Man,' Josie said. 'That's you? I thought you'd be older.'

David laughed too loud. 'When I'm walking I'm as old as the hills,' he said, 'old enough to know better, whatever that means.'

'Listen to the boy,' Caz said with a Gloria Swanson toss of the head.

'Well,' Josie said, 'well. You must be really pleased, Caz. I mean, all these people coming from the past!'

'Yeah,' Caz said, 'can't get away from the buggers.'

'I don't know about this. Who else is there?' David said.

Josie saw Caz's face change. Her mouth went thin and her cheeks looked leaner; her eyes were light years distant. This was the face she'd worn when Josie first met her in the Lovenest.

'Charlotte,' she said crisply, 'she may be coming to visit.'

'Did you know Charlotte – you must have done. Or perhaps I've got it wrong,' Josie floundered, for the air was razor edged and chill. 'Wasn't she part of the commune?'

Caz's eyes froze and David was instantly unsmiling and sober. 'You didn't say she was coming, Caz.'

'No. It's only maybe – I didn't know if you'd want to know. She's not about to walk through the door.'

Shit, thought Josie, I shouldn't be here.

'Charlotte and I – were involved,' David said, 'married, if you like, only we didn't believe in it. I haven't seen her – oh, for almost as long as I haven't seen Caz. We parted badly. I was a shit.'

'I think – you don't have to explain,' Josie said, grasping at anything by way of oil on troubled waters. Caz just sat looking at him.

'It's OK,' she said after an ugly silence. 'That's just it. You were involved, you parted badly, you were a shit. I think that, although I wouldn't have missed it for the world, Trimdon House has a way of overshadowing everything. It's got a life of its own, so to speak. I keep going over it: I was never happier. It's as if my lifetime's happiness was totally there for five years and that's all folks. No more goodies.'

'Yes,' David said. 'Hey, Josie, this is a bit of open heart surgery. Caz and I have dispensed with the cocktail party approach to conversation. What did T. S. Eliot say: humankind cannot bear too much reality?'

'I could never trust a man whose name almost spells toilets backwards,' Caz quoted Ben and smiled.

'Have another can and tell me about the project,' David said, 'or tell me about you. A bit of hot air takes the bumps out of driving. Let's get present tense.'

'Be here now,' Caz said in soft Californianese, 'today is the first day of the blah of your etcetera.'

'Now is the only time we've got, folks, and I mean that most sincerely. I should have been a TV evangelist,' David relaxed back on to his cushions.

While there was silence, this time Caz's shoulders had gone down and her eyes unclouded as she put on more music. This time it was Bob Dylan, the unwashed guru of all their early years.

'You know you're getting old when you remember all the words to songs while the DJ tells you they came out twenty years ago,' David said.

'Yeah,' Caz said, 'there was a Janis Joplin bio on TV last week and the paper had two paragraphs explaining who she was. It felt weird: I lived on 'Summertime' and 'Maybe' for – Jesus – three years at least. Young and easy under the apple boughs.'

'You were never easy,' David said. 'It's the eyebrows. I used to breathe again when you smiled. Until I got to know you.'

'Caz has that effect,' Josie said. 'We were all terrified when she came up here.'

'Aw shucks,' Caz said. 'Sweet harmless little moi?'

'Beneath that marble exterior beats a heart of solid granite,' David said.

'It's dead 'andy,' Caz said, 'like having big fierce eyes on your tail if you're a soppy flit of a butterfly. No, let's talk about the project: I should have been model-making this evening, you see. You've blown me off me course, Master David. Come on, we'll show you the sketches. But first, children, I gotta line up *Kozmic Blues*.'

She riffled through the tapes, desperately seeking Janis. But even as she found them – *Pearl, Kozmic Blues, Cheap Thrills* – she knew she couldn't play them. Not now, with David and Josie.

When Ben died, she listened to nothing else: Janis was her lifebelt, a ring of jagged glass for sure, but it kept her floating.

60

Janis Joplin, born in 1947 in Port Arthur, Texas, born twenty-six years before she died.

She gave and gave, she ripped her guts out and spilled them on stage. They tried to say she was one of the boys off stage and on, but she wasn't.

She was one of the women.

No middle way for Janis: rage sandpapered her voice to fury, love stroked every vocal chord into passion, primeval cries snaked through her wild hippy hair, her whole body shook as she sang, her gold hippy shoes stamped and kicked against her pain, her voice grabbed a lyric by the scruff of its neck and rattled the teeth in its head.

After Ben, Caz watched every movie where there was a clip of Janis, she watched *Going Home*, she watched *Woodstock*, she watched *Monterey Pop*, she swapped an oil painting for a pirate video of *Janis*. She watched her sober until she was sweating, every muscle screaming as the music tore through her. She set up evenings where she and a bottle of brandy and a line of cigarettes paid homage in front of the screen, flipping to the floor to rewind, to absorb.

Not to *be* Janis. No, Janis had already done that. But to find a way of surviving through agony and come up kicking.

She pulled out the portfolio marked DREAMCHARE and resisted the urge to let the great woman take over the room. Sheer animal exuberance, her growl, snarl, whine, sometimes Janis was a she-wolf baying the moon. And then there were the songs where the drums and the bass marked time through the dull smash of bottles, the rasp of a cigarette, the manic giggle until Janis was ready. Good and ready to bad blues it with Snookie Flowers on saxophone – Snookie Flowers and all the boys. There was no way Caz could play those tapes without throwing her own agonised viscera on the floor and howling for Ben.

Let Bob Dylan cruise them down the familiar highways of safe pain, smart sneering words and raw riffs brought a feeling of living dangerously without getting your hands dirty. With Janis Joplin there was no technique to cushion you; no one could say anything smart about her, no one could stand back and be superior when a woman is flaying the skin from her breasts and breaking her own ribs apart to show you the pulsing muscle of her breaking heart.

She let Josie talk about the drawings, blanking out *it's all over now, baby blue,* while a torrent of *my lost, my lonely, my little little girl, little girl blue* drenched every cell in her body. Unless she could step aside from the torment, soon her mouth would start offering coffee in a bid to end the evening. The words would be distant and ridiculous.

Either that, or Janis would take over and Caz would find herself unstashing a bottle of brandy and tossing it down shot by shot, goading herself into a creature at bay, a wild-eyed thing with no skin to cover her.

Bob Dylan sang: *you shouldn't take it so personal* . . .

It was a lifebelt. She clutched at it and started breathing again.

Dylan sang *you just happened to be there, that's all* . . .

David went to the toilet. He felt like he should say something about the sketches he'd seen and the plans he'd heard, but what? The whole idea was pretty – no, beautiful – hell, what could he say? He'd known Caz would have changed over the years, but he'd imagined her still angry and ranting, if she was alive, living an austere life in minimalist surroundings. This Caz was quieter than he'd ever thought possible, she had a – sadness? No, more than that, an austerity of thought and a guarded self-assurance that was foreign to him. Everywhere in the flat he could see familiar touches: the roundabout horse, the pantomime dragon, her love of gold paint. All this said Trimdon House, for her – and Ben's – flat had been rococo wedding cake, kitsch, glitz. 'Our decor is a twin tribute to Mae West and Liberace!' That was Ben.

Here in Galleon Heights was a sophistication he'd never anticipated. If she'd had a pantomime horse back then, it would have been painted with roses and worn a hat Carmen Miranda would have been proud of. It would not have been perfectly restored, she would have made it camp and laughable. There had been dragons on the living room wall, he seemed to remember, but they were Disney lilac and pink . . . these dragons swirled from the spirit of ancient Japan, fierce and fine.

Yes. Caz wasn't angry and ranting: she was fierce and fine and serious. He envied the confidence and breadth of the project she was working on with her mousy little sidekick.

Steady, he told his lager-fuelled mind, you can't take it all out on them. This isn't a press call.

It depressed him that Charlotte was probably coming to visit, probably to make flags. To be a part of Caz's self-sufficient Now. He thought of Charlotte every day: she'd have changed as well. There would be no place for his ghost with her, the coward craving forgiveness. She'd always said he was her hero.

My hero!

Whatever he did: mend a fuse, make a meal, make tea, make jokes, make love. Even moaning about a hard day's work . . .

My hero!

The man from planning had asked if he was her husband and she laughed and said no . . . he's my hero. Well, he'd never be that again. No matter what he did. Caz said that Trimdon House still cast its long shadow and she had to live with it. His leaving Charlotte was his compass error and he'd just have to live with that. Strange, he'd almost felt happy a few times out on the road, when he forgot why he was there.

It was time to take his feet of clay back out into the dark streets, his head buzzing with the glut of words and warmth. There was no place for him here. It was time to go.

'Got to go,' he said.

'Yeah?'

'Yeah, man,' he said, leaning on the bannister, 'can't sleep indoors. I like your project. I envy your application. I wish you luck with it. I'll see you along the High Road, Caz. Josie. It's been different – nice.'

He nodded as Caz opened the front door for him.

'Goodnight,' he said and when she'd gone in, he rubbed the doorframe. 'Have a nice life,' he said and meant it.

He sat in the doorway of The Ritz: it was about six hours to daylight and he could get his things and move on. Or not.

Or not?

Dawn found him striding along a beach twenty miles north of the mouth of the Tyne. Miston was the sort of place where Dora at the Ritz would probably keep his things out the back for months, years even. And if ever he felt like it, he could go back and pick them up again and walk slow. Right now, he wanted to swim, so he rolled his clothes up on the sand and ran into the icy water.

61

'God,' Josie said, 'I thought he was going to hit you!'

'You felt that?' Caz said, lighting a cigarette. 'So did I. David wouldn't actually hit anyone. I don't think. Apart from himself. But I think the project really upset him. It's the sort of thing we used to plan way back then at Trimdon House. You know BC and AD? Before Trimdon House, we were just students. Now there's just ATH. Life is an aftermath. Oh dear, cue melodrama.'

'What happened?' Josie said. 'It feels like there was some huge row or something. He must have loved Charlotte a lot – were they the sort of centre of it?'

Caz had never heard Josie ask so many questions. And with so many layers peeled off, she was too tired to fence. 'Actually there was a fire,' she said – five words said it all? 'That's how Charlotte lost her legs. She was pregnant too – she lost the baby. Her spine's damaged. David just pissed off while she was still in a coma.'

'Oh dear,' Josie said, 'that's awful. You didn't get hurt?'

'No,' Caz said, wishing she could tell Josie everything. 'No, I got out.'

'God, and then you feel so guilty,' Josie said. 'That explains a lot, Caz, you know, I couldn't put my finger on it with David. Guilt. Remorse. Why didn't I and if only until you drive yourself mad. I know.'

'Do you?' Caz said, 'Do you really?'

'Yes,' Josie said. 'I don't discuss it. No one knows. Can you keep a secret?'

Caz nodded. Could she not!

'It was Miss Rainier,' Josie said. 'I worked for her – she was the owner of The Manse, and I was the gardener. She's the one who left me the cottage and the garden – in perpetuity. She did it before she died, she said, I want you where I can find you, Josephine. The cottage and boxes full of old papers. It's a bit fairytale, really, now I think of it, but I've always been looked after. I must have that Orphan Annie appeal. Anyway. She wasn't an easy person, Miss Rainier. I was terrified of her: *Why the hell can't I have hostas here, Josephine? Tell me that!* She was used to throwing money at things to get her own way, but you can't do it with plants.'

She lit a cigarette and sighed through the smoke. 'The first summer was awful. I'd done exactly what she said although I knew it wouldn't work and it looked appalling. Everything was sallow, burnt, bare. It all clashed. It was disgusting. She came down to the cottage shouting one day in July and told me to pack my bags. *If I wanted to live in scrub, Josephine, I would move back to Kenya! You're a charlatan! I shall have your name blacked in horticultural society!* I lost my temper.'

'And?' Caz couldn't imagine it.

'Well, I'd never lost my temper before. You know me. I told her she was an arrogant fool. I dragged out my plans for her garden and made her look at them. I dragged her up to the garden and told her exactly what I'd said about every bloody plant and bush and exactly what she'd said. I said I wouldn't have to pack my bags: I'd never unpacked properly because she was impossible. I said I wished I'd never met her let alone agreed to work for her.'

Caz laughed. 'I like it,' she said. 'And Miss Rainier?'

'She laughed – just like you! Only hers was a Wicked Witch of the North cackle. She took me into the big house and opened champagne. Now we can work together, she said, I can't be doing with mice! She said, had I noticed her housekeeper and her chauffeur were rude to her? She said she needed telling, all the wealth had made her life streamlined, she was a real jetsetter in her youth. When she had to slow down and decided to come and live in The Manse, it was the first time she had to think about bills and meals and housekeeping: she'd lived in hotels most of her life. *No regrets, Josephine!* she cried and opened more champagne and said could we salvage a) the garden, and b) a working arrangement? She said please – I'd never heard that from her before.'

'Wonderful,' Caz said. 'So what happened?'

'We toasted the future and made a list of her favourite plants. She wanted a waterfall and a lake and swans. We did it. We sat up all night and planned – oh, dozens of times. She never slept, you see, so I got to catnapping as well. *We'll hibernate in winter, Josephine!* she said, and we did. I got all the plants – it's fantastic when money is no object and you can send all over the world. All these weird coloured seeds dropping through the mail. All different shapes and sizes. Christmas all year round. I put them in the right places and the next year she was over the moon: she said it was a delight, never knowing what was going to appear where. The only thing we argued about was the bloody coat of arms she wanted in front of the house. She said it would be a hoot, but I'd done my time with the council, you see, and I hate all that. Plants in lines and squares. I had to change the date every day, uproot the poor little things just for the vanity of the town hall and I swore I'd never do that sort of thing again. But I gave in for Miss Rainier. I said I wouldn't and then I did one week when she was at Henley. Oh, you should have seen her face when she came back! She must have been a beauty in her youth, and she had this wrecked face with a thousand lines, like a relief map of the Andes. Her eyes were this wicked brown and they flashed when she was happy. That's when she made over the cottage and garden to me. Set me up for life: a real fairy godmother.'

'I can feel the bad bit coming,' Caz said.

'Well, she wanted to go out to the casino one evening and the chauffeur was off. She was a truly horrendous driver and asked me to go with her. To take the wheel. I didn't want to but I said I would. When I went up to the house, she'd already left. She left a note: "My dear Josephine, I've gone. Couldn't wait another minute. The buddleia has delighted me all day: red admirals and peacocks all over. What about peacocks? Do they *really* roost in trees? À demain – Fizzy." Her name was Felicity but no one ever called her that. It was Fizz, Fizzy, or Miss Rainier. Or Madam.'

'A car crash?' Caz asked.

'No,' said Josie, 'well, yes. She had a heart attack, doing a hundred along the Fossway. Way to go, the doctors said she wouldn't have felt a thing. Only if I'd been driving, we wouldn't have been doing a hundred. If she'd had a heart attack, I could have got her to hospital. And so on.'

'How long did you work for her?'

'Five years all but a few months,' Josie said. 'My best five years – when you've talked about Trimdon House, I've often thought of that. Maybe that was *my* happiness. After she died, I had to start living in the world again: getting work, listening to the silly things people want done with their gardens for tuppence ha'penny. The worst part was when they sold The Manse and the new people changed everything. As if they couldn't wait to wipe out every trace of her – which is ridiculous, they never knew her. I know my life changed completely knowing her: most people now seem like shadows, half life? Do you know what I mean?'

'Oh yes,' Caz said. 'Someone like that is so alive it brings out the best in you. You feel like you never want to waste a minute. You start taking risks and guess what, henny penny, the sky doesn't fall.'

'That's why I'm so fired about this project,' Josie said. 'It'll be like Miss Rainier's garden, but this time I know it's coming to an end, it's designed to last for a season, so I'll never be looking at where it was and fretting that it's gone.'

'Right,' Caz said. 'You know you'll have to let go. You even know when.'

'Exactly,' Josie said. 'The worst bit won't be a shock.'

'Shall we catnap here?' said Caz. 'Catnap and breakfast at Earl's, belt over to yours and work until it's done?'

Josie smiled. 'I'll take the couch,' she said.

62

Caz felt her stomach flutter as they reached the High Road. David would be there and she geared herself up for taking him for breakfast. Josie caught her look and they crossed the road, but David's bench by the phone box was occupied by a pensioner couple enjoying the sun.

The old man patted the old woman's knee. 'I'll be twenty minutes,' he said, standing up. 'Twenty minutes for I've a canny tip the day. Yer bus comes in half an hour and we'll dae the lot. My bonny horse and yer daft seaside and ice-creams too I shouldn't wonder. If me tip comes in, we'll gan tae the Grand for wor bit dinner. If it doesn't, it'll be fish and chips on the front. Have I got a wife the day or am I divorced again?'

'Ye're on trial,' she said severely. 'What'll I dae with ye! More than twenty minutes in that betting shop wi yer daft horses and ye can take that ring to the pa'n shop for it'll dae ye no good to wear it.'

'Ah, she's lovely,' he said, 'lovely.'

The old lady shook her head and grinned. 'Ye cannot give him an inch,' she said tenderly. 'Am I right, am I?'

'You're right,' Caz said.

'Have a canny day, lasses!'

Since David was nowhere in sight, they crossed over to The Ritz and looked through the windows. There were no customers, only a waitress dabbing the tables, her eyes on the door.

'Oh dear,' Josie said, 'what's happened to him, I wonder.'

Caz shrugged. She had a gut feeling that he'd left the High Road. He was gone, God knows where, and she'd maybe never see him again. But she must still have been looking for him, for a voice calling her and Josie took her by surprise.

The voice was dead ahead of them, three shops away.

'Oh, God,' Josie said, 'Sadie!'

What was she doing in Miston? Sadie in vampiric black bearing down on them – what was she doing in daylight? Her face was pancake white like a stage ghost, her full scarlet lips were a trap and her teeth looked huge. The people of Miston had seen most things but Sadie drew stares and nudges.

'Is it street theatre, like?'

Sadie had her pale retinue dragging along behind her, in their dreary livery of ripped black jeans, dog collars and handcuffs. It looked like costumes and the black bull-whip she had tucked in her elbow was a prop. They wore the same in the nightclub and Caz guessed they simply hadn't gone to bed last night. But what were they doing on her patch? She bristled.

'Caz, Josie, don't you look *purposeful*!' Sadie linked their names with a sub-text of facial innuendo. She tapped her chin with the whip handle.

'Hi, Sadie,' Caz said. 'Morning, boys.'

The retinue looked to Sadie – for permission to speak? She kept her eyes on Caz and they said nothing.

'Strange we should happen on you. Me and the Boys,' she said. 'I've been offered some work starting at nine in the morning – I'd forgotten that there is a nine in the morning. We don't generally do mornings, so we thought we'd try it out.'

'How do you find it?' Josie said.

'Bizarre!' Sadie's black gloved hand clawed the air and her face expressed fleeting bewilderment. 'All these peculiar people everywhere. All these weird bright clothes. Shopping! Someone thought I was in The Addams Family. You know the movie? I've given autographs! Morticia Addams! Moi? But I won't take the job, it's just too bright. Light doesn't suit me. But it has its pay-offs. Can I trust you?'

'With your soul,' Caz said.

'That's already been taken care of,' Sadie laughed and heads turned in alarm. 'Come up here! Boys!'

She took them past the building where the back end of an orange Mini stuck out of the wall. Kris's Car Shop: YOU BEND 'EM WE MEND 'EM.

'Crucial!' breathed Sadie.

Past New 2 U and Oxfam and the Weighhouse, past Iceland – Caz felt sure they were going to H. A. Fallows, Funeral Directors – *Economy with Refinement*. In the window was a dusty plastic bust of Beethoven on a bed of jade weatherproof chips, by way of illustration. Sadie swept past. Earl's Amusements was just opening next door and they walked another block before she stopped.

'Look,' she said intensely, 'I *want* it.'

They were at the windows of Spring Fisheries, under the beautifully italicised legend: *Exotic and Continental Pescatoria For Your Palate*. Someone had painted FISH SHOP in whitewash on the glass to avoid any confusion.

The trays in the window gleamed with tentacles and scales, fins and fillets and claws. Two black lobsters with yellow rubber bands on their claws heaved miserably along a cabbage leaf.

It took a moment for Caz to recognise the centrepiece of the display. It was a rough grey cone with a dark dull disc on either side. One slope of the cone was white at the base, and split on to teeth like sharpened stalagmites and stalactites in a miniature limestone cave. It was the decapitated head of a shark resting on ruffles of its own scarlet flesh.

'Ugh,' Josie said, 'I've never seen anything more revolting.'

'Don't be so predictable,' Sadie said savagely, 'it's stunning. Isn't it, Boys?'

'Stunning,' said the Boys obediently.

'Isn't it, Boys?' Sadie's heavily kohled eyelids drew back.

'Yes, mistress. Stunning.' This time the chorus rang with pride.

'And I want it, don't I, Boys?'

'Yes, mistress.'

'Then?'

'We'll get it, mistress.'

The Boys went into the shop.

Caz burst out laughing. 'Do you keep it up the whole time, Sadie?' she said.

'Of course,' Sadie's lips flickered a little.

'Do they?'

'Of course,' Sadie was matter of fact, 'it's the Rules.'

'Rules?' Josie was repelled and intrigued by the whole episode.

'You'll have to come and visit me, if you want to know more,' Sadie said, giving her the full benefit of a heavy-lidded stare, 'both of you.'

'Well, we've got work to do,' Caz said, 'otherwise we'd be charmed.'

Sadie snickered. 'I don't bite,' she said, clashing her teeth together, 'unless you want me to.'

One of her acolytes came out of the shop.

'Well?'

The acolyte closed his eyes and recited. 'He says it's part of the display, mistress. He says it's worth its weight in gold for the customers it brings in and he can't let it go. Until six tomorrow evening and it'll be pretty high by then. Mistress. And it won't be cheap.'

'We'll come back,' Sadie said, giving him a ten pound note. 'That's a down payment. Tell him to freeze it tonight.'

'Yes, mistress.'

'And . . .'

'Yes, mistress?'

'You're not to click your heels. Not this week.'

'No, mistress.'

'Don't you get bored?' Caz was determined to crack the mask.

'Never,' Sadie said serenely. 'And what work are you doing? I assume you landed the project?'

'Maybe,' Caz said. 'We're hoping.'

'Well now,' Sadie swept her eyelashes wide apart, 'the Boys and I might be able to help. We do the dirty work. Digging and clearing and so on. Take my card.'

'I've got your card,' Josie said.

'You kept it! How very sweet of you. How interesting,' Sadie sighed. '*This* card is different.'

As the acolytes came out and stood perfectly still, she clicked her fingers and one of them produced a card, reading THE CHAIN GANG and a telephone number.

'We're very good,' she said, 'very thorough. I guarantee satisfaction. Call me. I wouldn't know where to call you.'

'No phone,' said Caz, pocketing the card. 'We'll see you around, anyway.'

'No doubt,' Sadie licked her lips. 'See you. Around. Boys!'

The entourage moved down the street.

63

So that was their game!

Serena ducked into the funeral director's door-way as Sadie and the Boys went past. Up the street, that peculiar Caz was smiling, laughing with her scruffy friend, jeering outside the fish shop with blood on their hands. Poor Angry Man – murdered in a bed that wasn't his own, poor lamb, all those years of trying to do the right thing only to be snuffed out by two wicked women. It's jealousy, Caz and her paintbrushes – who did she think she was fooling? – she could tell he'd rather have gone with me, ah, jealousy is a terrible thing. And no one would know, their sort thought a toffy accent and living quietly had everyone fooled, did they!

Not me, thought Serena, I know about these things.

And to judge from the company they kept, they were in league with Satan. Orgies and sacrifices behind closed curtains – nothing would surprise her.

'My hair's white with it!'

For this was no chance meeting: the murderesses were too bold and familiar with what they chose as company for that! No doubt these evil people in black had arranged to do terrible things to the corpse! She'd seen it in the *Monthly News*: they drank blood and daubed themselves with the fat of innocent virgins. She crossed herself against Sadie's mockery of the crucifix and crept along the High Road, trailing Josie and Caz.

What were they at now? Going into Earl's as bold as daylight, well, their sort would finish a night of wickedness in that den of depravity and gambling.

'Police,' Serena said loudly. 'I shall go the police and see the chief inspector and put a stop to it, I shan't be here much longer, ah ha ha, no! And I shall demand security for myself, a safe house until I leave these shores!'

'You do that, lover,' said Beerbelly Billy, upending a bottle of tonic wine.

'Aah!' Serena screeched. 'I'll report you too, attacking a good woman in broad daylight!'

'Now then,' said the traffic warden, who'd really wanted to join the police, only she was three inches too short, 'now then, Billy, are ye making a nuisance of yourself?'

'You!' Serena backed away from the dark uniform and the cap with its yellow band like a streak of plague. 'Don't come near me! It won't be long before I have the telephone and then you'll see!'

She scuttled along the street before the diseased gaoler could clamp on a pair of handcuffs: nowhere was safe. And they wouldn't stop her doing her duty as a citizen! That was the trouble, too many people just stood by and said nothing. She stuck her head round the darkened glass of Earl's door and nodded. The murderesses were sitting in the café talking and laughing, she knew where to find them.

'Bread and water for you,' she crooned. 'Iron bars and water and a crust of bread.'

Josie scooped bacon, baked beans and egg yolk on to her fork. 'I always expect Sadie to get cross when you have a go at her,' she said.

'Have a go?' Caz snorted. 'That wasn't having a go. That was me trying to outcool her. Posers anonymous. I wanted her to crack, just a little, maybe even giggle at herself. I have this absurd suspicion – maybe it's hope – that once she and the Boys are indoors without an audience, they act normal.'

'They don't,' Josie said, 'I bet! They're never off stage. What do you think of this chain gang bit?'

'I don't know,' Caz said. 'I know George Tweddle will want to pull in every bit of local talent for the donkey work and he might be quite relieved to have Sadie doing something constructive and arts related. He's terrified of her – of course, he's terrified of me too – but it would be a way of siphoning money in her direction. She's been trying to get on the arty gravy train for ages.'

'Didn't she have an exhibition or something?'

'No,' Caz pushed her plate aside. 'I'm off me chips. I think it's the shark's head. No, she wanted to: she wanted inverted crucifixes along the Tyne Bridge, and a light display in that abandoned church – you know the one? Where the Mafia keep their horses and Rottweilers in the graveyard? Sadie wanted to open the graves and have a circus there: her and the Boys as Le Cirque Macabre. Sick. Sick but inventive.'

'Are they a circus as well?'

'Yes,' Caz said. 'They're very good. I saw them rehearse once. I hated what they were doing, all skeletal and violent, zombies and symbolic sex; hateful really, but they were very professional.'

'A circus,' Josie said. 'I dreamed of a circus on our project, but it was all beautiful bright colours and dazzle. Like butterflies. I think I know why Sadie doesn't ever laugh at herself: we'd all start laughing too. The way things are, we're all a bit in awe of her. Can you imagine? Sadie and her clowns coming into the Lovenest and the whole crowd sniggering and clapping her on the back, saying things like, Oo, that's a great Cruella de Ville impersonation, Sadie.'

'Or can I call you Morticia?' Caz nodded. 'I think you're right. Sadiekind cannot bear too much reality.'

'Like you and David were saying last night,' Josie said. 'I felt a bit lost some of the time, he's very clever, isn't he? So are you.'

'Of course we're *clever*,' Caz was dismissive. 'Clever and so what? *You're* clever. We were being clever clever last night, actually, it's a way of avoiding painful – reality! – my God, is reality this week's watchword?'

'After our mutual secret sharing and Sadie's shark's head, we could do with a dose of it.' Josie looked round Earl's. 'Let's play the machines. Maximum stake five pounds.'

'This is Miston, pet, make it two quid and you'll be the last of the high rollers.' Caz stood up. 'Let's get some change.'

64

An hour later, a taxi drew up at the gate of Josie's cottage. Exeunt Josie and her bike and Caz and her three carrier bags of bits for the model. Josie leant her bike against the hedge and hauled out the last passenger, which happened to be a four foot high china tiger with gilt stripes and a soppy grin on its pink-gummed mouth.

'Give us three pund,' said the cab driver. 'It's more, like, but Ah've nivver had a tiger in me tank before. Could be the start of something big!' He waved like an old friend as he turned the cab and drove away.

'Well,' Josie said, 'well!'

They wheeled and bumped along the path, giggling.

They'd been halfway through their maximum stake in Earl's, when Happy Henry summoned them to the lucky bingo hour. First they'd won a green fluffy duck, and gambled it for a plastic Teenage Mutant Ninja Hero turtle. That went west for a dubious crystal vase and the vase got them the kind of rococo urn that Madame de Pompadour might have considered an adequate spittoon. By this time they had gone from hysterics to amazement, and all their numbers came rattling home to a straight full house. Which brought them the star prize: the china tiger with a five pound note taped to its neck. And hence the taxi.

'We can't lose,' Caz said, dumping everything in the living room. Josie's cat Mint looked scornfully through her dirty-stop-out mistress and swooned in front of Caz as if they were new lovers.

'Harlot,' Caz said, rubbing the wanton fur of her tummy.

'She always does that when I've been out,' Josie said. 'Only usually it's just me coming back so she has to make love to the chair to punish me. I have to court her all over again every time.'

'I've often thought about pets,' Caz said, massaging Mint's sensuous spine. 'I had this idea that they were a tie, but as Carrie says, where do I go anyway. Maybe I'll turn Mint right off me and get a puppy. I like dogs. I had a stray once. He ate everything in sight. There was a chewed-up copy of *Dombey and Son* on the floor once and my visitor said, well, Caz, I've heard of digesting literature, but this is ridiculous! Isn't it, Mint, you hussy?'

Mint's golden eyes promised her a thousand and one nights of any kind of ecstasy she chose to name.

'I'll feed her,' Josie said. 'Well, put food down for her. She won't eat when I've been out unless I sort of grovel by the dish making yum yum noises. So don't assume that living alone has driven me round the twist. It's all perfectly reasonable as far as Madam's concerned.'

Suddenly the cat leapt up and froze.

'It's a tiger,' Caz said.

Mint looked at Caz as if she was an unsavoury groper and did a Mae West sashay towards the china beast.

'I give up,' Caz said. 'Fickle flirt! Oh look. You got everything ready for last night. Did I say I was sorry? I am.'

'You did. But everything has a purpose. I had a nice healthy bike ride – oh, did I say? – I jumped a red light up by the Lazerium without even noticing. How's that for brazen? I met David and got a bit more of your elusive past. You know about Miss Rainier, too. And we had breakfast and played bingo! And we won a tiger and it's only eleven o'clock. In the morning.'

'Not to mention Sadie and Co.'

'Exactly,' Josie said. 'The Unmentionables. Do you know, my

grandmother actually used to say that. For underwear and body parts. Anything below the first layer of clothing was simply Unmentionable.'

'In betweens,' Caz said. 'Wash your in-betweens. Down there. The rude bits. Your you-know-whats. Your back body. Your front bottom. The nicest bits. Daft, innit?'

'Now you're being Unnecessary,' Josie said. 'And being Unnecessary is Uncalled for. Frilly underwear, shop cake and swearing are both. I hope you're not being Ungrateful for your Unbearably Uncomfortable Undergarments!'

'Which you must understand I underpaid an underling to undersell from under the counter!'

'In my grandmother's case, that would have been Unthinkable,' Josie shook her head. 'Stop it, or we'll never get done and what will the bank manager do then, poor thing.'

'Yeah,' Caz said, 'this is a winner's day, Josie. We're seeing gorgeous George a week today. Let's work.'

65

The model split into seven sections for ease of transport. Even so, the first taxi driver radioed for help. It was Monday evening and the late porter at NACAD was less than delighted by yet another couple of arty types disturbing his tea. He inspected his clipboard and led them to the conference room. His look of boredom didn't flicker, but nothing could knock their excitement. He switched on the splendid deco chandeliers and told them to say when they were leaving.

They set it out on the golden gloss of the table and fixed the final and most fragile pieces into place. First, the glasshouse, where they'd decided to have a model Viking ship burgeoning with plants from all the wild and exotic parts of the globe visited by the early ships of the mighty Tyne.

'We can really sting them for those,' Josie said. 'I've got most of them in my greenhouse: when I saw what they were doing to Miss Rainier's garden I did midnight raids and rescued them. I was terrified – of course, what else – but I could hear Miss Rainier cackling and that ever so aristocratic ruined voice egging me on. *Take what you bloody well want, Josephine, you planted them for me and God knows I'm in no condition to appreciate them!* I can't be reverent about her just because she's dead. She would have hated hushed voices and hallowed tones. I went to a funeral with her once and she said, really loud, *I'd be six foot under now if I drank as much Scotch as him. Silly old bugger should have stuck to wine!* She did wait until the end of the service, but she had one of those strip-paint-at-five-hundred-yards voices. You know the way the wealthy have of Projecting their words? She'd love this project.'

Miss Rainier's ghost grinned wickedly from the crystal drops strung between tulip lightshades.

That's my gel! she said.

The longboat was pure Ben. Caz had dropped in that a friend used to make ships in bottles, when Josie noticed the ark with its clear dimpled skies. The idea of a boat in a glasshouse struck them both immediately. They'd made a last-minute trip to the model shop, amazed that there was a perfect replica of a Viking ship two inches long, but appalled that it was dull metal and there simply wasn't time to paint it. But the latter-day Viking at the counter threw in that there wasn't much call for them these days what with Dungeons and Dragons and Wrestlers and Gladiators and he'd be happy to paint it for them, say a fiver? His eyes burned with the manic blue of a faraway ocean and they left it with him. Now the sails had stripes of crimson and gold and every shield bore a beast from the mists of myth and magic. A dragon, a centaur, a kraken, a phoenix, a griffin, a mermaid, a unicorn, a hydra, a hippogriff. Kevin the Viking said he'd be happy to do the real thing, if it came off.

On the third day, while they'd been setting the tiny flowers and bricks, Josie stood back and swore softly. 'We haven't really used the river,' she said. 'Our bit goes right to the water's edge: we can't just ignore it.'

'True,' Caz said, squatting so that the model was at eye level. 'What is there on the other bank?'

'Warehouses,' Josie said, 'isn't it?'

They taxied back to the site.

'Cranes,' Caz said, 'a whole forest of disused cranes.'

'Insects. A praying mantis, dinosaurs,' Josie said, squinting. 'A flock of flamingos?'

They went to the water's edge and Caz thought of her dream and the lake in the sky. 'What about your circus?' she said suddenly.

'Here, right by the water? All busy and fun, like the Fish Quay Festival?'

'Yes,' Josie said. 'Well, that's solved.'

Now, a dozen cardboard tumblers and acrobats were frozen on the boards of the model, next to the green and grey acrylic squiggles of the Tyne. Caz took great delight in stringing a silver thread like a web between three sculpted oasis trees and gluing a monocyclist in mid-air. The circus of her dreams was alive behind her eyes and its radiance drove her to a perfectionism that made her spine tingle. And, of course, there was Carrie's carousel.

They'd slowed a little while setting up the burnt-out house. It was midnight and Josie opened a bottle of wine.

'We need a break,' she said and sat down. 'Cheers!'

Caz sipped and looked into the flames in the hearth.

'I understand why you went all weird when we went to the site,' Josie said. 'I thought you'd given up. I thought it was all too daunting and depressing, or maybe you suddenly decided it was stupid. I wish you'd said. I mean, I can see why you didn't.'

'Well, what's to say?' Caz drank more wine. 'Actually there was a fire. Actually I've never got over it? I wanted to tell you.'

'Well, now you have,' Josie said. 'And maybe this is good for getting over it. You know we said cottage garden? I think roses. I have some fabulous ones, what do you think?'

They poked around the garden with a torch. Carnival, Ena Harkness, Peace, Superstar . . . the lovely flowers floated out of the darkness.

Back in the cottage they sat and Josie poured more wine.

'Peace,' Caz said, 'for all sorts of reasons. And Rosa Mundi – did you know it's one of the oldest, it was bred as a lover's token? Let's have that – for all sorts of other reasons. Peace and love, if you'll pardon the expression.'

Silently she added: *for you, Ben*. The thought filled her with warmth.

Josie started to shred tissue under her magnifier stand. 'I like this bit,' she said. 'Cut and twirl and stick and *voilà*: a rose. So much easier than growing and pruning and making war on leaf mould and black fly. We have those pleasures to come.'

'Maybe we could have a little old lady in the garden,' Caz said.

'What, go and raid The Turk's Head?' Josie laughed. 'Hey, pet, have Ah got a job for ye the day! Come and potter round a garden in Dreamchare. Ye divent have to dae nowt, just look like ye're gardening. It's Art!'

'Oh, sod off!' Caz said. 'No, a model old lady. Maybe one with a tape in her head so she can be singing or talking about what it was like there?'

'One old lady,' Josie picked a doll's house figure from a box and stood her among the flowers.

The ghost of Miss Rainier strolled round the model and knocked over the homey old lady in her pinafore.

Remember an old girl with a bit of style! she said.

'I can't get our little old lady to stand up,' Josie said.

Miss Rainier's ghost laughed and the crystal chandelier tinkled. She went through the motions of lighting a cigarette.

'Maybe she's drunk,' Caz said. 'Old lady felled by gin in cottage garden: a sad sign of our times. Let me try. There.'

The old lady keeled over again.

'Spooky,' Josie said. 'You might think it's daft, but I'd like to put a sort of Fizz Rainier figure there instead of an apple-cheeked granny.'

'The Fizz Rainiers of this world would hardly hang out in Dreamchare,' Caz said drily. 'Unless we had her as the sort of healer, witch, fortune teller?'

'Miss Rainier used to read the Tarot,' Josie said. 'She was uncannily accurate. Yes, let's do that. Here – give me the gold paint.'

She added tiny hoops to the old lady's ears and brightened her shawl with gleaming flecks. Miss Rainier's ghost approved and this time, the figure stayed upright.

'Just the flags now,' Caz said, unreeling multicoloured bunting where each flag was smaller than a fingernail. At intervals there was a Chinese lantern.

'Yes,' Caz said, 'Charlotte's bit – hell, I'm jumping ahead. Charlotte's bit if we get the money.'

Money? Miss Rainier's ghost sighed: *of course you'll get the money, you silly pair, she thought, that has never been in question. This is your dream and there's a lot of us over here riding on it and living through it. We are the dreammakers and we're rooting for you!*

She chivvied them out of the door before they faffed and fidgeted themselves into anxiety.

'Here's to the project,' Caz said, raising her glass a while later in Galleon Heights. 'Is it bad luck to toast before we're sure?'

Josie clinked her glass. 'To Dreamchare,' she said, her skin rippling as if an exotic breeze had wandered in through the Tyneside darkness to caress her from head to toe.

66

'Complex,' said George Tweddle, walking round the model with bouncy little steps. His eyes darted from the table to Michael's face – looking for a cue?

'Complex,' said Michael, ducking down and rocking on his heels. He picked up the magnifying glass and studied the Viking ship.

These chaps appear to have a complex, Miss Rainier's ghost cackled. *Someone other than yourself should buy your ties, George Tweddle. That excrescence round your neck looks like an act of revenge. Crack your face, Michael, he can't read your mind! Look at it, you silly fellows: it's beyond your ken! Think of the glory that will come your way!*

A smile struggled through Michael's beard and moustache. George stopped bouncing and swept his small hands behind his back. 'There's a breadth here I hadn't hoped for,' he said. 'You've gone to a great deal of trouble.'

Did that mean it was time wasted? Josie's mind raced frantically between a gloomy grandmaternal *don't count your chickens* to Fizz's autocratic rasp: *why the hell not, Josephine, let's DO it!* Caz crossed her fingers, thumb gripping the crystal hidden in the deep pockets of her dark sweatpants. *Don't let them change a thing*, she thought, *it's bloody perfect*.

Michael put the magnifying glass down and leant on the edge of the table. 'I could have used you two in Berlin,' he said. 'It's perfect. Have you seen the shields, George? I was going to ask about them – but the creatures are already there. I was wondering about the river bank: you've done it. A sort of medieval minstrelsy, a riverside *busy*ness. I have no questions or suggestions. Except . . .'

This is it, thought Caz and Josie.

'What about lights? The festival will go on after dark, did you know?'

Caz pressed a switch and the Chinese lanterns lit up; the mosaicked paths sparkled with a pattern of light emitting diodes. It had all the glitz of a night-time city seen from an aeroplane window, when roundabouts are coronets of light and a flyover lies on the ground like a belt studded with diamonds.

'And there'll be a carousel,' Josie said, 'near the shore. Old fashioned roundabout horses and a calliope. There'll be music too, from the early radio days. The Bradford Brass Band, The Manchester Municipal Traders' Banjo Band. Then Reggae and Salsa and Cajun around the glasshouse. In tune with the plants in the boat. We thought we'd pipe old radio programmes from inside the cottage: Uncle Caractacus and the Cloud Lady, the shipping forecast . . .'

Michael bowed. 'Lunch?' he said. 'What do you think, George?'

'I'll send out for sandwiches,' George said, bustling out of the room.

Sandwiches! The ghost of Miss Rainier shuddered: *Surely my girls deserve champagne?*

'Sandwiches mean the great man is pleased,' Michael said with a hint of irony. 'Which only leaves the twin hurdles of How and How Much. I have no doubt you've got a few ideas which will cross them gracefully. Money isn't limitless, but this is going to be a showpiece – the whole festival is a kind of yah boo snubs to the south and its bulging coffers. To put it crudely.'

They sat round the model with a Marks and Spencer instant feast: George had let rip with the petty cash and splashed out on

Buck's Fizz. It was a celebration, even if they had to drink it from NACAD mugs.

'Obviously, the answer is yes,' he said, fastidiously wiping chicken tikka sauce from his lips. 'There have been other proposals, but theirs was a bulldozing approach. Pleasantly surreal – but a sort of imposition: the kind of thing that could simply be set anywhere. But you don't really want to know about your rivals, do you? Having said yes – and it's an unqualified yes, by the way – '

He paused.

'Unqualified means don't change a thing,' Michael said. 'A rare compliment.'

'Quite,' said George, dipping a sliver of carrot into some nameless white gunk. 'Having given you my unqualified yes, we shall need to discuss how? One benefit of the bulldozing approach is just that: it's simple to demolish and clear. I can't quite see Mr O'Hagan and his lads steering round a wreck of a cottage or leaving cobblestones remotely intact. And we do have a good relationship with Mr O'Hagan.'

Jeff O'Hagan was the biggest demolition contractor in the north east. It was advisable to be in with him.

'Ah,' Caz said, 'we'd thought of that. Have you heard of The Chain Gang?'

'Other than Jimmy Cagney, ha ha, I can't say I have,' said George, spearing a mini Scotch egg.

'Ah,' said Caz, 'the only connection is monochrome. No, this chain gang is Sadie and Co.'

George looked alarmed. 'Sadie,' he bleated.

Don't scare the chap, drawled Miss Rainier's ghost, *soothe him*.

'I know all that,' Caz said, 'but they do work hard and they don't charge much. They seem to enjoy physical exertion.'

'Sadie?' Michael looked puzzled.

'She's an artist,' George said unhappily.

'She looks like a vampire,' Josie said. 'She's always in the Lovenest with her – gang.'

'Pint of Bloody Mary,' Caz said, 'chalk white face and millions of teeth.'

Michael grimaced with recognition.

'I'm glad you said that,' George smiled, 'within these walls and all that. One can't er, be too condemnatory. One gets so many applications for funding. Some are quite unsuitable. One has to set aside personal taste and consider the general public of the region without falling into the trap of parochialism. Sometimes one simply has to say no: quite beyond the pale!'

Oh, does one, jeered the ghost of Miss Rainier.

'Well, behind the deathly pale mask, there's quite a brain,' Caz said. 'And even Sadie has to eat. I hate to think what. No, that's enough. It's just an idea: since we need people to clear the site, why not use The Chain Gang?'

George made notes. 'And the artefacts?' he said. 'You can't be planning to do them all yourselves?'

'No,' Josie said. 'We have people in mind for flags and ship-building, and maybe you could help us on circuses?'

'It would be your budget,' George said. 'Confidentially, there's a leeway: so don't cut any corners. Equally, gold leaf and a platinum frame for your – marvellous! – glasshouse would be pushing it. Even I have masters to account to. And I suppose that if Sadie and her cohorts put in the best bid then we should employ them.'

He wrote more notes on a fresh page and tore it off the pad. 'Dates. Budget. A few hints on obtaining quotations. You'll get all this formally in a week or so,' he said. 'Meanwhile, go ahead. Go ahead! Full steam ahead!'

Let's go on a river trip, urged the throaty voice of Fizz Rainier. *Survey your new kingdom, Josephine! Live your dreams! You'll never know how time flies – even if I could tell you!*

67

'Before we go and get drunk on our elegant barquentine,' Caz said, 'I want to send a telegram to Charlotte.'

'A telegram!' Josie said, 'that's very extravagant.'

'It's fun,' Caz said, 'and from now on, it's expenses all the way. Have you not sent a telegram before?'

'No,' Josie said, 'I've received them. Miss Rainier was addicted to them. She'd send them from Newcastle so I'd know what she was raving on about before she got home. *Josephine my dear stop what you are doing stop now imperial purple white striped yellow mauve marvellous crocuses that flower all winter stop think where maybe in the lawn stop back at two stop Fizz.* She used to use the word stop as many times as she could for economy, and to hell with the costly verbiage in between!'

'Let's start using our leeway,' Caz said.

But the post office didn't do telegrams any more, said the pink cheeked lad at the counter, scrubbing his imminent moustache with the tip of a biro. He wore a badge saying Matthew Boon, Post Office Counters.

'There's telemessages,' he said, shifting on his high stool. 'It's the same difference.'

Charlotte my dear come and make flags stop only your legless genius will do stop sane phonecall follows stop money even stop over the moon starry-eyed and witless Caz and Josie.

Matthew Boon Post Office Counters read it back to them – were they sure, like? – and dabbed at his calculator.

'Could we have a receipt?' Caz said, 'and a large brown envelope?'

'You're so efficient,' Josie giggled and linked arms with Caz.

'No,' Caz said, 'just trying to keep the chaos at bay. My life is filled with scraps of paper and newspaper clippings – tearings, more like – the thought of yet another set of paper swimming into the general mêlée! This way, at least we'll know where things are. Everything goes into the envelope.'

'A spike,' Josie said, 'we'll get a spike, it's the only way to keep things in chronological order. One spike for Galleon Heights, one for the cottage. Then we can number it all every month.'

'Lawks, missus, innit exciting! I think we've missed the boat trips. We'll go tomorrow. Let's coffee it chez moi!'

Serena flattened herself against the magazine shelves as they bought twin spikes and her eyes glittered. That was material evidence, just like the inspector said they'd need to proceed with anything more than preliminary enquiries. Thought she'd be put off with him being busy, did he? Thought the bare room with its one high window would intimidate her? Dear, she mouthed, I've been in darker rooms than yours with never a window in sight, you and your long words are ashes beneath my tongue. She wondered sometimes, honest to God, was there a brand on her head that people treated her like a leper? Well, Mr Dead Eyes Inspector, I'll tell you and you'll have to act and we can all sleep in our beds! She crept along the High Road, snickering all the way to the sign of the blue lamp.

68

'Ee, pet, come in a minute!' Carrie called Josie and Caz with an urgent wave. 'What a carry on! Sit yerselves doon. I'm demented wi it. It's *hor*. Serena.'

'Oh dear,' Caz said, 'what's been happening?'

'It was last Monday night – ye've been away, isn't it? I said ye were away working as far as I knew. It was the police.'

'Police?'

'Aye. They come knocking on your door, and Serena, she's laughing away like a mad thing. They come banging on her door and she wadn't answer it. Then they're banging on mine. I opens the door and says, well, lads, are ye after giving us a heart attack? What's yer trouble? I find ye have to be polite to them, it costs ye nowt and they're only doing their job. We're all people. When it comes to it. Ah said come in and sit doon, like I've done to ye the day.'

'What on earth did they want?'

'Well, it seems they're on to *hor*,' Carrie jerked her head at the wall. 'She's been down there making her mouth go. First there's Lennie. She's got him down as a missing person. Missing, Ah said to them, he does well to hev got hisself oot. They knew what I meant. Anyways, that's only the half of it. It seems Serena's been making a nuisance of herself about ye.'

'What am I supposed to have done?' Caz said.

'The both of yez,' Carrie said, chuckling. 'Serena says ye've murdered that friend of yours. David. Angus. The Angry Man.

She took quite a shine to him, I tellt ye, didn't I, owt in a pair of trousers, well, owt that's a man. She saw him go into yer flat and he never came oot. The pair of ye come oot laughing, and met yer accomplices up the High Road. That's what the police says Serena's told them and they knaa she's a crackerjack but they have to inquire. And that's not the last of it.'

'Go on,' Caz said.

'It seems the lass at the caffy, what is it, The Ritz? I never hev a meal there, it's a dirty place. Any road, this lass that works there has let yer friend leave his bits and pieces at the back of the caffy, in the yard? And he's not been back.'

'Oh, shit,' murmured Caz. 'So they think something's happened to him?'

'Ah says to them, he's a gentleman of the road, ye knaa all aboot his sort, here today and gone tomorrow and who knows where? They says, aye, but he's never been known to move so fast. Him and all his belongings, he takes a week to gan the length of the High Road. So where is he? I says I divent knaa.'

'He left us about midnight,' Caz said. 'I thought he'd be up the High Road the next day, but there was no sign of him.'

'Like I said,' Carrie nodded. 'Any road, the police says would ye be good enough to call in the station when ye get back and make a statement. In case there's any trouble. There, I've said me bit.'

'Well, I'll go in,' Caz said. 'There's not much to say. He was in a strange mood when he left, wasn't he, Josie? He was a bit drunk, but I wouldn't have let him go if I'd been worried.'

'Just tell them pet,' Carrie said. 'It was more Lennie they were interested in, and I says to them, I could write a book about that. I told them about the language and the bruises and him working nights and her gannin off it. The police says, aye, we've been rang up more times than a telephone exchange wi hor wanting him put away and him wanting her put away. She's got her own phone now, so there'll be no peace till the bill comes and she cannot pay it. They've driven the police ragged and the one police says, well, Mrs Ives, while we'd like to join ye and say good riddance to him, aye, and lock her up an all, we hev to look at every report as potentially serious. I says, I wouldn't have your job for me weight in gold. Oh, they were nice. I've always found the police is decent if ye're straight wi em. I've never had nowt to hide, me.'

'Me neither,' Caz said. 'Oh well, we'll go and give our statements.'

'There's no rush,' Carrie said. 'They knaa it's hor and hor mind twisting it all, but better be safe.'

'We'll do it now,' Caz said, 'get it out of the way. We've missed the boat trips this afternoon anyway.'

'I like a boat trip, me,' Carrie said.

'Come with us,' Josie said. 'We're going to look at the site from the river again. We've got the project.'

'Is it!' Carrie beamed. 'I wasn't dropping hints there, by the way. I'd never get doon to the quayside, I've not been there for years.'

'We'll get a taxi,' Caz said. 'Pick you up for ten?'

'Well, that's more like,' Carrie said. 'Have a bit fun, instead of *her* and her nonsense. I'd love it.'

69

Serena's telephone sat on a lace edged mat on the dining room table, flanked by a picture of Our Lady of Guadeloupe and a flaxen haired St Francis chucking a blue-eyed Disney bunny under the chin. A cup of tea steamed in front of the mat, the steam and the smoke from a cigarette curling up like incense. So far, she had rung nobody apart from the police and her MP: no doubt the phone was bugged and she wouldn't give them the satisfaction. That filthy bigamist, Mrs Purse Strings, had the nerve to tell her to watch her bills, ha ha, she'd never owed anybody.

The phone hadn't rung for all the four weeks it had been there, although she snatched it up from time to time, with a hoarse hello. Well, the operator had rung a few times, calling her back to check that it would ring. It did.

'But I am ex-directory, dear,' she told St Francis. 'A woman on her own doesn't like to be bothered.'

There was a new book in her flat, a big book that had been given to her free. The Yellow Pages. She glared at its fat spine. All very well to urge her to let her fingers do the walking, that was a fact of her life, her feet might as well wear a ball and chain these days. She'd been expecting it, but even so, it frightened her when she realised she wasn't allowed out of Miston. The prison officer in his bus driver's uniform had told her. All polite and smiling, but his words were terrible. 'This is where you get off, pet, this is your stop.'

Just this side of The Drop! She could have walked this far and had almost decided to take the risk of setting foot on the bridge and legging it to freedom. Then she noticed the traffic cones and a policeman and four people with clipboards stopping cars. If they could wave car drivers off the road for questioning, then what chance did she stand? She stood on the traffic island and howled, until the policeman came towards her and she dived through the impatient roundabout traffic, banging car bonnets with her fists, bashing doors with her bag.

Oh, it was becoming clearer every day. They watched her every move, they probably had her tagged and followed her on a computer, like she'd seen on the telly the other night.

Someone walked to her door and knocked. She sat completely still, glowering at the frosted glass. There was a loud noise, something dropped on the step, and the footsteps moved away. She let a whole cigarette burn down until she sneaked the door open a crack.

Another book! The phone directory. That was more like it, now she could get on to Hajid and his family and get her rights as a mother. But the map in the front showed Newcastle, Tynemouth, the coast, a thick black line wriggling round the area she was allowed to dial. It was too much to bear. Like giving you an empty oxygen cylinder, she'd seen them doing in the hospital, when they thought no one was watching.

'And then the poor lady died,' she wailed. 'Am I to be left to die here, left to rot until I die in this awful place?'

She flung the directory on the floor. It lurched open on the first section, pale blue pages, what was that about?

She knelt on the floor and read, swayed forwards and crouched, rocking back on her heels. This was better.

They were slipping, the fools, she'd got them this time. They might withhold every number in the United Kingdom from her, who would she want to talk to in this God-forsaken spot? But they hadn't thought of this.

She pulled the book on to the table and gulped her tea.

The blue pages opened up the whole globe to her. She could ring Albania, just dial 010355, followed by Durres 52, Elbasan 545, Korce 824, Tirana 42, followed by customer's number. She could ring Antigua, Aruba, Ascension Island and the Azores. Or the Bahamas, Bhutan and Burkina Faso – wherever they were. She scrabbled at the sea-blue pages, her mind racing.

Cocos Island, China. 'Christmas Island, did you ever?' she sat back and cackled.

Djibouti, Egypt. Maybe Hajid had gone home to Egypt and where was he hiding, she'd like to know. Aswan? Heliopolis? Luxor? Pyramids – no one lived in the pyramids, must be a mistake. Zagazig. Yes, he'd be in Zagazig, all the best places had a zed and a zig and a zag and a zoo. Him and his mother and all the family, happy families were they, they wouldn't be able to sleep in their beds for worrying, serve them right, nightmares in Zagazig, it was only right.

El Salvador, Equatorial Guinea. 'That sounds like a nice hot place. Guinea, they don't have them any more, guinea-fowl, guinea-pig, ah, the little guinea-pigs,' said Serena, underlining it. This was a marvellous book, one to keep hidden from Mrs Well-Wisher Wishing Well, waste of money, you silly girl, throwing it in the water. She put the chain on the door and pored over the book.

'French Polynesia – I'll wear a hula hula skirt and they'll call me madame,' she cried.

Gibraltar and the dirty monkeys, Greenland all covered in ice. The weather was bad enough here, thank you very much. Guam – they must think she was soft in the head, Guam, Guam, how did you even say it? Hungary.

'Yes, miss, I know it. Great big Italy kicked little Sicily into the Mediterranean Sea. Up jumped Austria, said I am Hungary, took a bite of Turkey, dipped in Greece,' Serena chanted, tapping her foot on the table leg, cuddling the magic book.

Inmarsat, well that was something, you could ring the Atlantic Ocean west and east, the Indian Ocean and the Pacific Ocean. If you knew a ship's identification number.

'A sailor boyfriend of mine,' she started, 'my gentleman friend is at sea at present, a life on the ocean wave!'

She put the book face down and made fresh tea with fresh milk, they'd returned her fridge from storage at last and not even asked her for money, no apologies but they knew they were in the wrong.

'We'll not bother with Iraq,' she said firmly. 'Tkrit . . . I live in Tkrit, me and my secret. Ah ha ha. Jordan – Zerqa. Zerqa.'

In the Lebanon, there was Zahle, Libya had Zawia and Zuara. Her head spun the words dreamily.

Midway Island, Mozambique. She flicked the M page quickly past. Miston wasn't there, Miston wasn't anywhere, Miston was just where she was forced to stay. Nowhere.

New Zealand, Niue, Norfolk Island, Northern Marianas, what a pretty place that must be. Pitcairn Island. Qatar, Rodriguez Island, St Helena: that was a prison too, she'd seen it on the telly. The poor man with arsenic in his wallpaper, she'd stripped all hers off the same night.

'No, thank you,' she said firmly.

Swaziland, Tanzania, Tonga where that lovely lady came from and got rained on all for nothing. Tuvalu.

'Uruguay,' Serena said, 'Vanuatu. Dear, I can telephone the Vatican City and speak to the Pope himself only I wouldn't stoop so low. Zingibar, Zanzibar, candy bar.' She was shaking as she reached Zimbabwe.

'Alleluia,' she whispered, 'alleluia.'

Somewhere on this earth there would be someone who could help her. Someone who would listen and understand and get her away from this life sentence. She'd committed no crime but being born a foundling, after all. You couldn't trust the past.

She sat bolt upright and closed her eyes.

'This is Serena McCulla – ah no, that's his filthy name. This is Serena Parra née Bolton and that isn't true either. Let me see now. Ahem. This is Serena Zachary, Serena Zachary, dialling the World.'

70

'That's your passport, Legless,' Daisy tossed the telemessage across the table. 'You're out of here.'

Charlotte looked at it again. She was sitting in an easy chair, her new legs propped up in front of her. But, being Charlotte, her wheelchair sat beside her.

'I'll wait for the phonecall,' she said.

'Well, that's you, isn't it?' Daisy laughed harshly. 'You'd wait for the pigeons to shit on your head, you would. Christ! I've only been here – coming up for a year, and I know freedom when I see it. But not you! You need a foot up your arse. Get on the phone now, sort it out! You'll sit around all day thinking about it and by the time your loony mate rings up, you'll have worked out all the reasons why a crip can't travel. Innit?'

'No,' Charlotte scowled. 'Yes, Daisy. Is that what I'm supposed to say? Sod you! It's just – it's Newcastle. It's the other end of the country. Where would I stay? Even supposing I can manage trains? I've only been on adapted coaches for the last five years. And that was only after you turned up.'

'Where's me bloody violin!' Daisy concentrated on getting a cigarette between her plastic fingers. 'Don't! I've told you! Your hands go on automatic to help poor little armless me! I don't want it. I'm going to get this bloody thing perfect, so I can do everything and maybe one day no one'll notice. That's what's wrong with this place. You think helping each other's the answer.

You've got no hands? Let me scratch your arse! I could walk over to the phone and make your call for you: you could wheel yourself there. It's not the point. Those legs are designed for walking! State of the art bionics! So bloody walk!'

She booted Charlotte's chair over to the other side of the room. 'You've got to *use* your legs, girl,' she said, raising her cigarette with sweat breaking out on her brow. 'And I've got to do matches. That's this morning's battle.'

'Bastard,' said Charlotte.

'That's me, folks,' Daisy grinned and swore as she knocked the matchbox to the floor.

'You think I should ring Caz?'

'My God, its ears are working,' Daisy picked up the matchbox and crushed it. 'Shit! These bionics! Lee Major never had this trouble.'

Charlotte laughed. 'The obvious solution is to give up smoking, Daisy,' she said, mimicking the rehab physio. 'The obvious solution is to give up. It's my mind that can't walk.'

'You control your mind,' Daisy frowned and inched the matchbox open.

'Anyway, what's put you in such a charming mood? Last night you were going to open a bar in Spain,' Charlotte said.

'Last night I poured a can of lager into a glass without spilling,' Daisy said, holding the matchbox down while she dragged the red tip across the rough side. 'Shit! Last night, I picked up a full glass of lager without breaking the glass or slopping it down me ballgown. That was yesterday's battle and I won. I was queen of the universe last night. This morning, my shoulders ache and it took forever to get this bloody thing on. One day at a time! Sweet Jesus! Then you get a telemessage, offering you work, escape, money, fun, LIFE – and you can't even be bothered to totter across the hall to make a phonecall. I'm the green-eyed monster this morning.'

'Well, why don't you come too – suppose it's for real?' Charlotte said. 'It would make a change from this dump.'

'Nah,' Daisy said, 'I'm shy. Anyway, I can't make flags.'

'You can pour drinks,' Charlotte said. 'You can keep me company. God knows what Caz is on about. There might be work for you too. Jobs for the girls.'

'Dream on, Legless,' Daisy said, frowning as she raised the lit match, 'dream on. I'm not one of your arty types, you know. You know what I done before I come here? I was a motorbike messenger, a waitress, a shelf-filler, market researcher, I've sold heavy breathing over the phone. I've done door-to-door encyclopaedias. That's my career: any bloody stupid job no bastard else will do because there's piss-all money in it for a start and you don't need any qualifications. I never went to college. I bunked off school all the time. I'm chronically unemployable – and that was when I had both arms! What can I do now?'

'Well, let me quote you to you,' Charlotte said, hauling herself upright on the arms of the chair. 'You can drown in self-pity, Legless, you said, or you can tell yourself that you can do anything and if you say it often enough and loud enough, you'll convince yourself and somewhere along the way, you'll convince some other bastard.'

'I said that?' Daisy shook her head. 'Bollocks, the way I feel this morning. Where are you running off to?'

'The phone,' Charlotte said. 'Make me a coffee while I'm away. This morning's challenge: you've done cigarettes and matches and it's only half-past ten. Stretch yourself! Fill a kettle and spoon coffee.'

'Aw, fuck off,' Daisy said. 'Milk and sugar? Or just milk – are we watching our figure today?'

Charlotte swung one leg in front of the other and flicked a V sign at Daisy's triumphant grin.

71

Josie sat beside the rockery outside her cottage, sipping coffee in the early morning light. *Live your dreams.* The project was a chimera with a gleam in its eye and a twist in its glittering tail. They had a free hand to construct all the wild and separate parts, to weave each fragile link: to create the whole just as they'd imagined it. It would be unique. The twist was that it would only last for a season – and Josie craved for ever.

Part of her had been geared up for argument and she was almost disappointed when George and Michael raised none of the points she'd expected. She'd enjoyed her assertive inner monologues: in fact, her blood had never flowed so urgently since that glorious row with Miss Rainier, the unchained outrage that had brought her everything she needed simply to live where she wanted and to do what she wanted. What she did best.

Josie knew she was excellent at her chosen work, although often she felt guilty that things had been handed her on a plate. Somewhere inside, her grandmother had embedded a seed of self-doubt that had sprouted with her young heartbeat and grew through every vein and nerve. *Life's a struggle, Josephine, you can only do your best.* The sub-text undermined the worth of everything she accomplished. It didn't occur to her with any reality that she had any struggles in her life. Living alone was a delight most of the time, loneliness was the price you paid sometimes. Being an orphan was nothing new to her. Not having much money was just the way it was: economising was as natural to her as breathing. Economy with refinement, like the slogan in the funeral parlour.

Most of the time she felt lucky. So many people she'd met had no idea what they wanted to do and life just happened to them. Then there were those who knew what they wanted to do, but couldn't get on with it, whether because they were bone idle like Mad Mark, or simply that they had chosen badly.

Gardening was a way of life: every season had its tasks, its rewards, its frustrations. Since she was meticulous and tireless, she could let her thoughts stray towards new challenges until she was ready to start the day-to-day work needed to achieve them.

It was one thing to plant a rosebush, tend it, protect it from blight and rust and aphids and bring it to flower. It was quite another to be certain of exactly where the buds would form, how many heads a stem would bear, how to clip and tease the plant so that perfect blooms followed each other in a cascade of petals and perfume all through the season. That sort of horticultural engineering delighted her.

She loved the result of bonsai, but couldn't bring herself to perform the root surgery it required. She wouldn't do it even though Fizz nagged and begged. 'I really am very keen on a Japanese garden,' she'd said. 'I bow to your expertise – as always. I've learnt not to cross my staff, particularly you. But . . .?'

Josie wouldn't budge, but she took the van and spent a week in the highlands of Scotland collecting natural bonsai, trees which would grow as best they could in spite of all the elements, with no chance of reaching their lofty wide-branched genetic destiny. She found a knotty mountain ash all of five inches high, clinging fiercely to a wind-blasted rock and trembling with the impossible fury of orange berries the size of love beads. There was an oak, too, a foot high, knotted and gnarled like the great-grandfather of an oak where Robin Hood hid out with his merry men. She found a grove of beech trees that scarcely reached her knees, their doughty trunks welded to a granite slab so high up that the wind whipped her ears scarlet.

Miss Rainier's eyes gleamed as she unloaded her treasures.

'Piracy on the high hills, Josephine!' she cried. 'Didn't your wretched little conscience prick you as you wrested these miracles from their native soil?'

'Yes,' Josie said, 'but it's better than mutilating roots. And I brought their rocks and heather and two sacks of soil. Here – I've done sketches of where they came from so we can reproduce the environment as near as dammit. Let's get indoors and look at them.'

'I take it I shall have to have a mountain built on the tennis courts?' Miss Rainier arched one painted eyebrow.

'I think there's enough of an arctic breeze blowing across the estate for five months of the year,' Josie said. 'These aren't hand-reared cute little hothouse numbers, these are rough tough gypsying trees. You can have your Japanese garden, only it will be on the Buddhist lines of minimalism, severe, sparse.'

'Then bugger the tennis courts,' said Miss Rainier. 'I'd worked out that each game of tennis costs about four thousand pounds, anyway. May I insist on a lily pond?'

'You may,' Josie said.

Of course, the new people had restored the tennis courts. But the oak, the mountain ash and the beeches were now the exquisite heart of a rockery in her own garden. She sat beside them, towering over the tree tops. She felt like an eagle, she felt like God.

She'd have to put her brakes on to complete the Dreamchare project – already her mind was searching for the next task.

She knew what it would be. First and for ever were the most important words Josie knew. She wondered sometimes if it was being brought up by her grandmother: it wasn't even like being a second child, but a motherless child of a second generation. She could never say that she wasn't wanted: but when she grew up a bit and started to think about people who had children, she wondered if her own mother had wanted her. Was she really dead? Her grandmother hedged and she didn't want to push it, afraid of hurting her, afraid that she too might go away.

Death had taken her, and her grandfather too, within three months. Then she knew she'd loved them. She'd loved Miss Rainier in a way that surprised her. At least she realised it before she died. Numb, all she could think was, well, that's what comes of loving older people. Maybe I should try loving someone my own age. But who?

Her mind baulked at the thought, changed gear and took her into her favourite daydream, one that involved both first and for ever.

She wanted to develop a new strain of a plant which would be named after her. Studying plant textbooks had given her the germ of this idea. She'd laughed aloud at the index of ordinary English names Latinised with a double ii, or -iensis. Her plant would be something Josephinae, or Blackia something. She dithered between roses and marguerites. Marguerita Josephina: it sounded like a Mexican cocktail, its petals a hectic shock of orange and crimson, with a heavy spicy perfume that spoke of heat and dust. Rosa Blackia: the elusive black rose? The nearest they'd got to that was a lacklustre magenta, virtually free of scent. Rosa Josephina – she inclined to the mad candy stripes of old English roses, their petals flirting like a Georgian lady's parasol, their perfumes soft, like talcum powder, sweet like Parma violets.

It took years to develop a new strain of any plant and perhaps that was the main appeal. A lifetime's work that would be planted all over the world wherever people love flowers, an italicised entry in a catalogue, a glossy photo with a note about Josephine Black, a date somewhere in her lifetime when she'd achieved something so new and lovely that no one could take it away.

72

'She's not in,' said Charlotte, collapsing back in the chair. 'Is that my coffee?'

'Well, it's not shit and sugar,' Daisy said. 'Sneaky one there, Legless, getting me to do the caff bit and then she's out. You'll get her later.'

'The physio says do a little more each day,' Charlotte groaned and dragged her legs up in front of her.

'Well, at least they're not Clearasil orange,' Daisy said, 'and at least they're not wooden. My uncle had a wooden leg when I was little, it was all leather straps and clump clump clump. Then they gave him a new one, lightweight, they said. Poor old bugger, it was so surgical. I mean, we thought a wooden leg was glamorous, you know, like a pirate? After that he was just any old man with an artificial limb. And he never got used to it being so light.'

'The first pair she showed me were blue,' Charlotte said, 'silicone, like false tits. These must be the de-luxe: I think my chronic depression made her give in at once. We don't want to discourage you, do we, Charlotte? Hell, if tears work, I'll cry on cue. They tried me before, oh, maybe three years ago, but I just couldn't face it.'

'Cry a lot, did you?'

'Rivers and oceans,' Charlotte said. 'I was stuck in it's not fair. It isn't fair. Life's a bitch. It was all too much.'

'My mum said, come home, Daisy, it's God's will and we'll look after you. I think she was quite relieved when I didn't. I haven't lived in her house since I was sixteen.'

'Mine are dead,' Charlotte said. 'A relief, really. I'd have had to cope with their grief as well: God, that sounds callous. Do you know what I mean?'

'Yeah,' Daisy said. 'Like they'd visit me in hospital and wind up eating all the grapes and chocolates and talking about their prostates and hip replacements. You feel cheated. That's what my old man did.'

'Your husband?'

'Good as. Bad as. Moaning on about how could he manage without me. I told him to piss off after a few months, go and be sorry for himself out of my sight.'

Charlotte thought of David. 'I didn't have that satisfaction,' she said, 'mine just never came near me.'

'That's better,' Daisy said. 'No, think about it. If they can't handle it, they should keep clear. At least then you know where you are. Mine was on his way out before I done this. I'm sick of fellas. If he'd stayed it would have been guilt and he'd have been off as soon as I didn't need him. What really gets my wild up is the thought of him poncing drinks for sympathy when it's my sodding stump. I can hear him laying it on with a bloody spade: he liked sympathy, my old man. Never happier than when he was ill. The day he broke his collarbone, you'd have thought he'd won the pools. Off his bloody rocker.'

'Fancy a walk?'

'Nice one, Legless, I do,' Daisy stretched. 'All the way to the games room. We'll play pool. Good for your balance, good for my comeback into the real world. I was dead good at pool.'

'I was lousy,' Charlotte said.

'Lousy? You want to see lousy?' Daisy flexed her fingers, 'I'll show you lousy.'

'We'll phone later,' Charlotte said. 'If it's true we'll celebrate, if it isn't, we'll drown a few more sorrows.'

'I'm drinking shorts tonight,' Daisy said. 'The challenge is small glasses.'

'You will come with me if Newcastle's on?'

'Twist me arm,' Daisy said. 'Any arm you like – only one of them comes off.'

73

Sadie yawned and shuffled to her desk, trailing a scarlet kimono and a cloud of smoke. Friday morning was when the Boys signed on, they weren't allowed back into the house until three: it was the time she reserved to write her memoirs.

There were sixty black-spined notebooks so far. Sadie had been writing for six years. She was thirty-one years old.

'Flukish Revelations of Ridicule', parts one through sixty, had been inspired by a firework display one November 5th. She hadn't bothered much with the glitzy explosions in the sky, just concentrated on the gleeful upturned faces. Why all this joy on November 5th – who cared about bloody Guy Fawkes? She just wondered that the human race measured its pleasures so meanly: why only November 5th? Why not fill your back yard with rockets and catherine wheels and volcanoes and webs of sparks any damn time you please!

She had come to the north quayside to kill herself that November 5th. School and art school saw her pass with flying colours and then she was out in a world where no one gave a toss for any word or sign that Sadie Hendricks was alive. She'd written applications for jobs and grants until her wrist ached. She'd hung around the places people like her were supposed to hang around and no one had noticed. She'd even stayed at home alone for months and no one had missed her.

When the barman at the Lovenest had failed – yet again! – to return her smile or remember what she drank, she decided to end it all.

The north quay was usually deserted, with puddles of oily water steaming under faint street lights: an eerie *cinéma noir* setting. Perfect for a little suicide. But that November 5th, just to thwart her, it was alive with the Guy Fawkes crowd, ringing with cheers and chat. She watched them eating hamburgers and hot dogs and chips and candy floss. She loitered by the bollards in front of the rotting timbers edging the quay and then went home.

That night she'd started her memoirs.

After a few weeks, she noticed patterns: in her thoughts, in her actions, in her days. Patterns like a laboratory rat, paths of safety, doors she avoided for fear of the electric shock of rejection. Just like a rat, she headed for food and sleep, and she scourged herself for playing so safe. Scuttle and hide, wash and dress and eat, whimper a little. No wonder no one noticed her, what was there to notice? There were millions of Minnie Mouse clones infesting the world of the arts: she'd wasted enough time being a good listener, a polite hopeful hovering on the fringes. Life had not let her go gently into the anonymous ripples on the surface of the Tyne. She took November 5th as her official birthday, quelling a giggle. Save the lash of ridicule for the rest of the human race.

Sadie became her own special creation.

She called her first notebook Chrysalis, and with the second, she started to invent herself.

Tonight I went to the Lovenest. The usual crowd, George Tweddle leering, but I won't have his fantasies dictate that I wear a yashmak. Mark begs me to join him on a mural project, but his fundamental idea is way off beam. A fascinating stranger took me home in a taxi. Fabulous sex until the birds were singing. No names, no words. Home before the milkman, all bodily fluids washed away before nine.

Reading it back thrilled her. Months of anonymous and wonderful sex, work spurned for the loftiest reasons, she was both siren and genius between the covers of her diary. She set her mind to making it reality.

A new wardrobe was essential. She found a near perfect dress-shop mirror in a skip and the distortion of its one jagged crack delighted her. She dressed like a silent movie vamp – as close as Oxfam permits – and examined the result: her new self. She practised walking in these clothes, lighting cigarettes, leaning against doorframes and the line she'd painted at bar height on her bedroom wall. Stilettos were *de rigueur*.

Her make-up took a week to devise and another week under a spotlight beside the mirror to carry off. She studied Theda Bara, Yvonne de Carlo and Joan Crawford. Her voice dropped an octave and her words slowed on every syllable. Her smile was the greatest achievement: she emphasised its curve in scarlet and never let it reach her eyes. Her dress rehearsal took her as far as the shop for a pint of milk.

'I've not seen ye before,' said the woman who'd sold her milk and bread almost every day for two years. 'Have ye just moved in, like?'

'Yes,' Sadie said, making of the word a loaded tri-syllabic sigh, 'up the street. My sister used to live there.'

'Oh, I think I remember,' the woman said. 'She was a student or summat, wasn't she?'

'Yes,' Sadie said.

'Are ye just visiting, like?'

'No,' Sadie said, 'I've moved in. I'm an artist.'

'Aye,' the woman looked relieved. 'Ye'll be at the college too?'

'Lecturing,' Sadie said. 'I'm older than I look.'

'Ah, ye cannot tell wi young uns,' the woman said. 'Listen to me, the whole world looks young when ye're my age. Ye'll like it round here. Folk are geet friendly.'

Sadie vamp-walked home: the time was ripe to try the Lovenest.

74

Since then, Sadie's diaries had careered more or less along the path of truth. If her thwarted suicide was a crossroads, then her revamped image was the sliproad on to life's highway. No exits from now on. She pasted lurid newspaper stories and stolen phrases into the pages. Every week she included a polaroid of herself. She had cultivated various phrases she considered to be a knockout and a shorthand for the people she met. People who were like she had been before The Change were Aspirants, those in positions of power were Robots and most of the human race were Zombies. The handful of people she truly admired were Banshees and those she half-admired were Trolls. Those she surrounded herself with were Geeks. She believed her memoirs to be a work of art *per se*, and she now wrote with the confidence of one who has a familiar and enthusiastic audience. She unscrewed the cap of her squat steel pen.

I have, as you will have realised, a tangential relationship with reality.

She drew on her cigarette.

When I choose to interact with other human beings, I am always aware of the layer upon layer of trust and suspicion which grow symbiotically. Sometimes I am the mistletoe and suck the sap while people kiss each other under my berries.

*Sometimes I am oak. Oak so strong that they may suck my sap
until I scream. Orgasm. Death.*

That was this week's teaching and she read it through, nodding
with satisfaction.

*A double Troll happening this week. At a most unnaturally
Banshee non-hour, I discovered an exhibit for the show to end
the World. (cf. January–June.) A shark's head, perfectly dead
and now in my icy vaults. Straightaway a meeting with Banshee
Caz and her Troll Josie. They are an instrument of Money and
work without which the World and all its people will collapse.*

The World was her house and the People were her Boys, every
one a Geek. The Creation of the World had come about quite –
flukishly – !

This flukish floating World.

She'd had – yet another – one night stand involving a pleasingly
inventive Zombie. But the Zombie had trailed her and pursued
her beyond her Banshee limits. One day he'd 'bumped into her'
on her doorstep and come in. He wanted coffee and she stared at
him and said: 'Go and buy it. Make it yourself.'

Something in his eyes changed and she felt a power possess her
spine. By the end of the day he'd cleaned the bathroom with a
toothbrush and washed all the windows with his handkerchief.
He'd done everything there is to do in a house several times until
she was satisfied. And then he called her Mistress.

She led him to the nightclub on a doglead and allowed him to
sleep on the kitchen floor. As sex disappeared from their contact,
her hold on him became absolute. He was her creature, he was a
Geek. After a month or so, she was bored and so she chose another
Zombie. Amazingly, the Geek begged her to let him stay and
the Zombie turned into the second Geek.

And so on until there were seven, sleeping wherever she told them and obeying her every word. She didn't understand it, she didn't choose to think about it, whatever they were to her, she knew that she was their Mistress, their Dominatrix. Her Rules were the Law and her Presence sat at the centre of their World. The show to end the World was her ultimate threat. There would be a show. They would all work towards it. They would achieve it and then they would have to go. For ever.

Outer darkness, weeping and wailing and gnashing of teeth.

Any time she felt a frisson of ennui, she would summon the Geeks and have them sit in silence while Baby Jane Hudson and Lucretia Borgia met in her smile.

'I've been thinking about The Show. And my wish is for your thoughts.'

They were pledged to do her wishes without question and now her wishes threatened their World. Her ennui vanished as she watched them floundering. They became the Lost Boys – and Sadie despised Peter Pan.

She was always looking for new challenges: Caz was one. She had been for four years. Caz was a Banshee from the moment she cooled it into the Lovenest. The only true Banshee Sadie had ever met. She knew them to be twin spirits from before the dawn of time, split by Fate. In fact, Caz dominated her thoughts and her greatest fantasy was to hand all the tools of her office to Caz and to grovel like a Geek at her feet.

I left the freaks and the Banshee left her Troll and took me to her World. She stood over me, leather boots muscled up her thighs, and stroked me with her whip. I begged her for release and she left me bound until my whole body wept and sweated with longing. She told me to go from her World and she will only ring me to summon me when I have stopped thinking of her. I hear and obey.

She ground out her cigarette on the page and added splashes of scarlet to the singed grey mark. A good morning's work?

'Excellent,' she said aloud.

But goddammit, would the telephone ever ring?

Part five

75

'What's the matter wi *hor*?' Carrie nudged Caz, rolling her eyes towards Sadie.

It was a dank November morning and they were on the site, after a boat ride that felt like crossing the Channel when the twentieth century was new. They hadn't told Sadie they were coming – it was morning as well, and Sadie and her Boys didn't emerge before noon. But Sadie had been popping up all over the place since Caz had rung her to ask for a job quote: here she was again, like a ghoulish jack in a box. And she was alone, which made her even more bizarre.

'Caz, Josie, how unexpected,' she said, picking her way over the rubble with one black gloved hand extended.

'This is Carrie,' Caz said, 'this is Sadie.'

'Isn't it spectacular,' cried Sadie, 'all this decay and destruction . . .'

'It's a reet clarty mess,' Carrie said, and as Sadie leapt towards a fallen chimney, she whispered: 'Is she reet in the head?'

'Tell you later,' Caz said.

'I love the end of autumn,' Sadie swam towards them with closed eyes. 'It's the dead season. No more pretty leaves, a time without sunshine, an uneasy pause before the pretty snow. Death. I love it.'

Carrie pushed her glasses up her nose. 'Ye're ower young to be moithering on aboot death,' she said, 'Ah knaa it comes tae us all, but it's wicked to wish it before yer time.'

'Troll,' murmured Sadie, her teeth gleaming.

'I knaa it's true,' Carrie said. 'There's been times I've wished meself six feet under, but ye divent stay that way. It can be a week later, sometimes years, and ye say tae yersel, who was that fool as looked like me wishing herself dead? It's never as bad as ye think.'

Sadie sighed. 'Usually it's worse,' she said, intensely.

'Ah, divent let yerself get miserable, pet,' Carrie said, 'a bonny lass like ye! Mind ye will wear black, won't ye? All on ye. That was mourning when I was a lass. Widow's weeds.'

'I've splashed out on colour,' Caz said, unzipping her jacket. 'Look. A tropical forest with parrots.'

'That's more like,' Carrie said. 'Ah cannot see the sense in black all the time. Ye'd think ye'd get bored wi it, wadn't ye?'

Sadie was silent, her lips twitching.

'Texture,' she said finally, 'texture. I must go and devour that cottage. Ciao.'

Carrie winked knowingly at Caz. 'That one's cut from the same bolt of cloth as wor Serena,' she said. 'Crackers. De-vour a cottage! Whatever next? Is she a friend of yours, Caz? I hope I've said nowt out of turn.'

'She might be clearing the site for us,' Josie said.

'Her?' Carrie laughed. 'She'd never get her sleeves rolled up and get her hands dirty. Howay, ye're having us on.'

'She's more the – supervisor,' Caz said, trying to find a way to explain Sadie and her Boys. 'She works with a group of lads who do that sort of thing.'

'Like a placement,' Carried nodded. 'They do say it's the daftest ones that can understand them sort of lads. Ye have to be a few shillings short of a pund tae get on their wavelength. Is it rehabilitation, like – ee, there's a big word – is it?'

'Sort of,' Caz said.

'Aye, well, I've heard there's grants for them these days,' Carrie said. 'Grants for this and grants for that, the money can always be found for grants for the *less fortunate* wi this government. I'd like to be on one of the boards that decides who's less fortunate. I would! Everyone was less fortunate when I was a lass so ye never even thought of it. It was normal. They divent knaa they're born these days. I hope they're good, mind: that one's away wi the fairies. *I love death* – listen to her!'

'She's very strict with her boys,' Caz said.

'Aye, and she'd need to be,' Carrie said. 'Them sorts of lads is in trouble every time ye turn yer back. I never had that sort of trouble wi mine. It's the parents is responsible, they has bairns these days and they divent want them. Then they say it's not their responsibility and hand them over for fostering, give their bairns to some daft social worker. It's the do-gooders messes it all up. We never heard the like in our day. Look at that one – she'll have had a mother and father as daft as she's turned out. All out to put the world to rights and cannot be seeing after their own homes.'

Sadie wandered back towards them, gesticulating. 'It's too much,' she said. 'Which means we can handle it, I enjoy pushing the Boys. It's good for them.'

'It's what they need,' Carrie said.

Sadie raised an eyebrow and looked at Caz.

'I've told Carrie what we have in mind for your little lot,' she said. 'You feel confident?'

'Supremely so,' Sadie smiled and her eyes almost twinkled. 'I shall lick them into shape, bring out the whips if necessary. That is, of course, if my quote is accepted.'

'Send it in,' Caz said. 'We have to do that. Don't underprice yourselves.'

'Naturally,' Sadie said, her tongue exloring her upper lip. 'Well, I must go home. I believe the Boys are cooking my dinner.'

'Does she live wi them, like?' Carrie said.

'Yes,' Josie said, thinking, whoops!

'Ah've misjudged her,' Carrie said. 'It takes the patience of a saint to be wi those sort of lads. It'll be a hostel, will it, and her the warden? Nae wonder she's demented. Ye grow like them as ye lives with. Either that or it kills your spirit. I should know, the life I had wi my husband. Me spirit was choked wi him, but he never turned a bone of my body mean and cruel like he was. Now yer loopy mate's gone, tell us what ye're ganna dee here.'

She nodded approval as Josie described the fairground and circus and squeezed Caz's arm when she heard about the round-about with all its horses. She nodded ah ha, ah ha when Caz talked about the restored and embellished pavements. Josie spoke of the space-age greenhouse and the ship they'd put there.

Carrie shook her head. 'Well, ah nivver,' she said. 'And ye're getting well paid for this, lasses? It'll be a lot of work.'

'We're contracting some of it out,' Caz said. 'We've got the lad in the model shop to build us the boat and decorate it. I've got a friend – two friends – coming up to make the flags. We've written to half a dozen circuses and fairgrounds – it'll be the best we can afford.'

'I wish ye well wi it,' Carrie said. 'Ye'll have to ask us to the opening and have a party. Here's me getting cheeky! That lad in the model shop, ye're not meaning Kevin?'

'That's him,' Caz said.

'Ye'll hev to watch him,' Carrie said knowingly. 'I knew his mam and his nanna. He was always a handful, Kevin. He went off to do engineering and had a breakdown. He was in and out of St Zach's for close to two year. He's a great one for starting owt, but as for finish! His nanna, that's Pearl – ye'll hev seen her at The Turk's Head – she says he started her kitchen three year gone and she's still waiting on him for her borders. Watch him. He's a good lad, but there's summat not right about him. A lad his age mad about models, Ah divent knaa!'

'Well, I'm freezing,' Josie said, noticing Carrie's cheeks. 'Shall we go back to the landing stage and get home? They do hot toddies on the boats in the winter. Can I tempt you?'

'I'm not a drinking woman,' Carrie said, 'but mine's a double. Medicinal of course. I'm getting as bad as ye!'

'Of course, Carrie, we'll not let on,' Caz said.

They each took an arm and crossed back over the site.

'Me mind's easier now,' Carrie said. 'Ye'll be getting a lot of money from the health. What wi her – the daft one in the hostel – and Kevin, ye'll be providing work for them as cannot dae a proper job.'

'Artists and painters included?' Caz said.

Carrie laughed at her. 'Whey aye, pet,' she said comfortably. 'Is there any other way a scatty pair like yez two can earn a crust?'

They were the only people on the boat up river.

'Divent worry about the commentary,' Carrie said to the steward, 'Ah was born here and ye'll only get us upset talking about the history of it. Ye get half of it wrong, any road.'

'Are you after my job?' he said.

'I could dae it an all,' Carrie told him. 'Nah. Get yerself busy wi hot toddies. I've a pair of alcofrolics wi us the day and Ah cannot let 'em drink alone!'

76

The calendar said January and the cold floor of King's Cross Station was streaked with mud and footprints etched in slush. Charlotte and Daisy sat on a red metal bench on platform 7, a wheelchair and a pile of bags beside them. Charlotte sipped a polystyrene beaker of coffee and Daisy held a can of Coke in her gloved bionic fingers.

'Is this wise?' Charlotte said.

'Which bit?' Daisy snorted. 'Me wearing both gloves? You wearing boots? Your belt and braces wheelchair? Newcastle? Us going up early in a great bid for independence?'

'Any of it,' Charlotte crossed her legs.

'Nice one,' Daisy said. 'I think we're bloody marvellous, me. We pass – didn't you see how pissed off that porter was with the pair of us? He wasn't happy about the wheelchair. *He didn't notice!* It worked.'

'We've worked,' Charlotte said.

'Ain't that the truth!'

They'd sweated for months. Not just to get the hang of their new limbs, but to pass, as Daisy put it. One evening she'd taken Charlotte to the TV room.

'Look at this video,' she said. 'I've been out doing me Spielberg. It's just people – lots of ordinary people doing ordinary things. Watch the arms and legs. It's amazing. That physio's stuck in kindergarten. It's not just walking, it's not just lifting – look at all the daft things people do without even noticing. Look at that geezer scratching, putting his hands in his pockets! And his mate – stretching, fiddling with his clothes. And that blonde there, leaning on her elbow, that bloke banging the table, the old girl there messing her hair around. They just do it naturally, all the time!'

'Yes, don't they just!' Charlotte said. 'Tapping their heels, swinging their legs from the knee and leaning against a wall. I wish! Bouncing their knees in time to the muzak. Kicking chair legs. Hopping from one foot to the other – it's endless!'

They studied people in cafés and pubs, at bus stops, in shops: Daisy was riveted by the thousand and one arm movements that most of the human race considers run of the mill, every day.

Charlotte's eyes drank in the casual tireless leg and foot movements. 'It's exhausting,' she said, after a morning in a shopping arcade in Kingston.

'Yes,' Daisy said, 'but we've got to do it. This is what's kept you away from the physio, Legless. You won't settle for Barbie goes walking, one foot in front of the other, and I won't settle for Action Man and the automatic arm swing. It's not good enough.'

'No,' Charlotte said, 'I don't want to be a ballerina, but I want to feel like I could be.'

'I want to play the piano,' Daisy said, 'or make mosaics. I want to be precise. Ambidextrous.'

They'd taught themselves through the days, becoming mistresses of all the casual and useless gestures most of the human race takes for granted. Daisy felt like she'd won the pools when she could scratch her shoulders and fiddle with a shoelace. Bloody velcro? – what am I, a nursery schoolkid? Charlotte was absurdly proud of hooking one leg round a chair leg and tapping the other heel at the same time. The first time she'd forgotten and knocked the chair over when she stood up. Now, people seldom noticed and that meant triumph. The day they were jostled aside in a shopping queue was a turning point: up till then, people had drawn aside and pulled children out of their way as if they were contaminated. Mostly they looked over your head or through you, they smiled with an uncomfortable blend of compassion and embarrassment. Daisy called it the *you poor thing and thank God it's not me* syndrome.

When they shopped for boots and gloves, it had all the thrill of dressing for an illicit nightclub.

Sometimes, these days, they'd get a wistful smile from an old lady as they collapsed in giggles. *You young girls!* Maybe Charlotte had crossed her legs three times both ways for the hell of it, maybe Daisy had balanced a spoon and thrown it from one hand to the other: everything was sheer delight.

'We'd better not overdo it, Legless,' Daisy said. 'It's only loonies who throw themselves about a lot.'

'Less of the legless,' Charlotte said, 'you'll have to come up with something more appropriate.'

'Oh, get her!' Daisy was sarcastic, 'I'll think of something.'

'And the armless,' Charlotte said. 'It's either Arnie or Lee at the moment. Did you know that Schwarzenegger means blackhead?'

'I'll call you Betty,' said Daisy. 'Nothing to do with Michael bloody Crawford either, it's Betty Grable, the girl with the million dollar legs.'

A few days later, Charlotte was reading a magazine. 'Hey, Daisy,' she said, 'I've got it. Listen. *Cane-toting oldster Twyla Dolan was alone when a burly bandit walked in, drew a gun and demanded money. So spitfire Twyla offered to arm-wrestle the creep for the cash – and whipped him so bad he shuffled off without a dime!*'

'You're making it up,' Daisy said. 'Arm-wrestling!'

'I am not! Listen. *Said Twyla: What he didn't know was I drove big old trucks and worked in the shipyards most of my life and I can take care of myself pretty good, even if I am seventy-nine years old.* I'm calling you Twyla from now on.'

'Twyla, Twyla,' Daisy tried it out. 'It's a weird name. I like it.'

She cut out the story, complete with its picture of the 'seventy-nine-year-old powerhouse' and tacked it to the noticeboard, adding a felt-tip message. THIS IS MY GRAN, DON'T MESS WITH ME! DAISY.

Caz was expecting them on January 15th, but they booked train tickets for the 12th and rang ahead to the Y, determined to find their own way round Newcastle for a couple of days.

'I know Caz'll do everything to make life easy,' Charlotte said. 'It's things like finding public loos on the flat. The little things. Our blow for freedom!'

'Like I said,' Daisy lit a cigarette and waved the match-flame out, 'we're a bloody miracle.'

77

Daisy was reading a copy of the *Daily Telegraph* some commuter had abandoned in the train. She whimpered like an animal in pain.

'I feel like a martian, Betty,' she said. 'Whoever writes this stuff don't live on the same planet as me. You know what? No wonder Tory politicians think there's some sort of plot going on, if they believe this crap. Listen: they're talking about the travellers, the tepee people. They say there's "undeniable signs of a sinister Mr Big to mastermind such a large organisation". Bollocks! I met them lot once, they couldn't organise their way out of a paper bag. Bloody hell!'

'They're neurotic,' Charlotte said. 'They thought that Black Triangle, Pink Triangle, Rainbow Pentacle, the gallery where Caz had her first big show, was a front for communists.'

'They're bloody paranoid. Can't they suss that most people are just trying to get by and squeeze as much fun out of life as they can?' Daisy shook her head. 'They don't know what it is to sweat when the bills come through the door, that's the trouble. Give one of them a week's dole – no, let's be good to them. Give them an average wage for a month and let them get on with it.'

'That Tory MP did it,' Charlotte said. 'Just for a week, he lived on the dole. No credit cards. Nothing. He was in debt by the end of the week and he started off with years of good living and good clothes on his back.'

'What happened to him?'

'He got cold-shouldered in the House, my dear, he was an embarrassment. He resigned.'

'Cop out!' Daisy turned the page. 'This is doing my head in. Reds under the beds, anarchists behind the aspidistra. I can feel it turning my brain inside out. Oh Betty, what's happening to me? I want to be a stockbroker. I need a mortgage. I want to be normal! And that's only two pages in.'

'Don't read any more,' Charlotte said. 'Rip it to bits, Twyla. What are you getting all uptight about, anyway?'

'Well, it's meeting your friend Caz,' Daisy said. 'I mean, I'd never have got to know you if we hadn't been in hospital together. You're posh, Betty. I ain't. No, don't go all like that. It's true. I don't meet people who do arty things. What if she thinks I'm a wally?'

'If she does,' Charlotte said, 'she'll have changed. Caz is just not like that. She mouths off a lot, we all do, but she's nice.'

'Nice. Nice? NICE! That's what I mean. Nice people don't hang out with people like me,' Daisy stared at Charlotte.

'Bloody hell!' Charlotte rolled her eyes upwards. 'Now who's paranoid? I can understand you being nervous about meeting someone new, but this is just ridiculous.'

'I'm not nervous. I'm shitting myself. I'll let you down,' Daisy said. 'I mean I'm mouthy, streetwise, I'm a cocky little sod. You're used to me, Betty, I don't want to show you up.'

'What's a nice girl like me doing with scum like you?' Charlotte mocked. 'That's what you're saying, isn't it? Well, you're not scum. You're my mate. You're the one who got my lazy butt out of bed, out of a wheelchair after five years. You're magic. Caz already likes you for that. And she's expecting me still to be helpless. I think she has an idea that we'll take taxis everywhere and she'll find a chair for me behind a table and I'll sit and sew a fine seam until it's time to get wheeled back to the taxi. She's going to be gob-smacked when she sees it's not like that. And it's all down to you. You're an angel.'

'Piss off!' Daisy said.

'Can't take it, can you?' Charlotte laughed. 'Any time I say anything good about you, it's piss off, leave it out. You have to make a joke of it. Take a compliment, Twyla. You've changed my life. I really admire you.'

'All right,' Daisy said, 'all right. That's enough. God's truth, I never thought you'd do it. You had that look that says I've given up, when I first seen you. It really got to me. I thought, shit, if I don't keep it together I'm going to give up too. That's why I took the mick out of you all the time, I was scared bloody stiff. You remember the first time you told me to eff off? I was over the moon, I thought, hey, we're going to make it.'

'I didn't know it showed,' Charlotte said. 'It was bad.'

'It was like a bloody neon sign,' Daisy said. 'You were like a leper with a bloody bell round your neck. Unclean! Unclean! Lose hope, all ye that enter here. You were dying, Charlotte. It had me shitting myself.'

'Dying,' Charlotte said. 'I suppose I was. Well, that's changed. Look at me now and here I am . . .'

78

Carrie and Rose were on the High Road, reading the postcards in the newsagent's window.

'Listen to this!' Carrie said. ' "Mature Lady Charity Entertainer – piano – seeks similar. Banjo, ukelele, guitar, percussion – anything considered, even mouth organ. Please apply Mrs Cornelia Glazebrook, within." '

'Well, there's a job for ye, pet,' Rose shifted her handbag on to her hip. 'Ye're mature. That's what we used to call ower the hill, mind. Lady, Ah divent knaa. And entertainer? Can ye get a tune out of a mouth organ?'

'I'll tune ye,' Carrie said, 'and I'll mouth-organ ye, Rose Easton! Ah divent need a job. Caz and Josie has one all lined up for us at the festival. Ah dare say ye could come and be me assistant.'

'Never!' Rose laughed comfortably. 'Gan on then, what's yer job?'

'I've tae sit in a garden two three days in a week, fanning meself and chatting to folk,' Carrie said. 'Ah've tae have a basket wi flowers and gardening tools in beside us, but Ah divent hev to dae nowt in the garden. I get me dinner and taxis both ways and a bit extra. Ye can come along, Ah'm sure it'll be nae bother and it'll give us a bit company.'

'That's a job?' Rose shook her head.

'That's what Ah said. Caz says they're having a model there and all, for when it's raining or cold. It's like lifesize, geet old fashioned wi gold earrings and scarves an that. Like one of them Town Moor gypsies as reads yer palm. She'll hev a tape playing in her head, ye knaa, the history of Dreamchare and the Tyne and what not. But it's my voice on the tape. Caz paid us just for talking! I says to her, Caz, I'm not a charity, ye knaa. She's employing all sorts on the project, boys as has been in trouble, and Kevin, Pearl's daft grandbairn – ye knaa him in the model shop? Him. She just laughs and says to us, Carrie, ye've more wisdom and history in yer little finger than ye could find in a whole library. There now.'

'It'll be geet expensive tae get tickets for the festival,' Rose said. 'Ah've heard it on the radio. Eight pund for a day! Five if ye're on a pension. And they say it'd take more than a week to see the half of it. Ah divent knaa!'

'Well,' Carrie said, leaning close, 'that's part of me perks as an employee, pet. *Ah* get a pass for the festival. *Ah* can walk through the gates any day and it won't cost us a penny piece. But that's not the best bit. The best bit is me pass admits meself and a friend. Caz says what's the use of trailing round it all by yerself, bring yer company wi ye.'

'Ee!'

'So ye'd best mind yer manners and stay friends with us.'

'Ah will!'

'She treats us lovely, mind, Caz. And Josie. I think of them as bairns, Ah know they've both seen thirty come and go, but people is getting younger these days.'

'Ah think it's us getting older,' said Rose. 'Although ye're right. By their age us'd had wor bairns and was raising them. There's a lot more fun for lasses these days. Think of it, in our day, we'd hev thought Caz and Josie was on the shelf. These days, they've got careers.'

'Aye, they has their bairns late these days, gets in a bit of living first. Mebbe it's better that way, by the time ye picks yer man ye've seen a few bad uns come and go.'

'Is wor Caz having a bairn now?'

'Ah wadn't put nowt past her. Mind, she's not one for the men so I divent knaa.'

'Hev ye got tae get dressed up for this job, like?'

'Oh aye,' Carrie said. 'Caz hasn't said nowt, but I've been going through me costumes. Ah'm getting me cruise clothes let out – ye knaa the suits and dresses I bought for me Christmas cruise? Ah ha. Them. Folks treats you better if ye're well dressed. It'll be a change, like.'

'We got some lovely things at Blackpool last year and all,' Rose said. 'That one ye wore for the nightclub, all ower flowers. Ye look geet bonny in that, lass.'

'We'll get wor hair done,' Carrie said. 'Caz says they'll *cover all me expenses*, Ah says, what, a trip to the beauty salon? She says owt ye like, Carrie, just give us the receipts and I'll see ye reet.'

'Well, will we gan ower the road for our bit dinner?' said Rose. 'The Raby does a canny good meal, like ye'd make yerself if ye could be bothered.'

'We will,' Carrie said, 'and we'll call on Caz and I'll tell her ye daen't mind helping us oot.'

'Ah'm looking forward to it,' Rose said. 'D'ye think we'll get our picture in the papers?'

'Get away wi ye!'

79

For so long now, Caz had woken without a shred of a dream in her mind, that the land of lake and mountains in the sky was more like a cherished memory of somewhere she had actually visited. It was as if she and Ben had really been there together: she could see them walking together, holding hands, pointing things out with a smile, a laugh – even a kiss. She could feel them both riding through the magical caves and hear Tom's bare feet kicking along the tunnel roof. She could see Ben's smile behind her eyes and her ears rang with the joy of Ben's voice.

One day Caz was at Dreamchare, trying to explain to Sadie just how it would look when it was finished and she realised that she was talking about the magic kingdom inside the mountain and the fair by the lake shore.

'I can't picture it,' Sadie said, 'a little too Over the Rainbow for moi. I don't have to, but the Boys like to imagine a finished result as they break their backs. Feet in the mud, heads in the stars. Poor Geeks.'

'Are they always this depressed?' Caz said.

'Depressed?' Sadie was surprised. 'As a Rule, we don't use facial enthusiasm. Do you think they're depressed? I wonder.'

She watched their pale blank faces and thought, maybe she's right. Maybe they're frightened. But why? They were working, there was money, she was there, in charge. It occurred to her that this project might actually be The Show To End The World, or at least, that was what they were afraid of. The End of the World had been an idle whim of hers: she was astonished when they took it so seriously. But as she watched them scraping weeds and grass from the cobbles, she knew she was right.

Part of her wanted to say: 'Hey, guys, there is no End of the World.'

She could hear her voice using the words, but it wasn't the Joan Crawford/Cloris Leachman dominatrix tone. No, it was – how strange – her old voice, the voice of the loser she'd been before her Metamorphosis. I've been getting too much fresh air, she thought, nudging one of the Boys with the toe of her boot.

'With care!'

'Yes, mistress.'

That was more like it. Let them think they were working towards their ultimate destruction! She swaggered along the line, a caustic syllable or two dropping on each bent shaven head. Let the threat hang over them: it was, after all, she who'd raised them from Zombies to Geeks. Her word was Law.

Well, Law within the World. Here on the muddy banks of the Tyne, there was a subtle difference. Caz the Banshee ruled Dreamchare, Caz and her Troll, Josie. Sadie deferred utterly to Caz: perhaps that was the source of these flukish stirrings. Mistress of the World and would-be Acolyte to Caz – the strain of playing a dual role had her feeling edgy. It is very difficult when your elected Dominatrix smiles at you and wants to discuss things, when she asks for – and heeds! – your opinion. She'd even said to Caz: 'Give me orders. I will obey them beyond the letter.'

Caz had just laughed. 'Ideas, not orders,' she said. 'This is a democracy, Sadie, your voice is needed. I'll make the final decisions, but informed decisions! I want lots of input first.'

Sadie had done everything she could think of to get Caz to make a move on her. Everything short of flinging herself naked at her feet and saying *I am your creature*. No, Caz simply didn't play the game, she didn't know the Rules, she operated in a way Sadie simply couldn't get her head around.

You'd have thought she would be strutting around and mopping up the lavish praise flying around the arts scene. Sadie would have killed for it! Caz didn't strut. She shrugged it all off. She'd talk passionately about the festival, her hands flying to illustrate her words; she'd listen intently to suggestions. Zombies and Aspirants bombarded her with half-baked notions about thematic street theatre, kites, balloons, old fashioned playground toys. Caz lapped it up *and meant it*!

The other night it was street names. Some Blob had cornered her and was firing a litany of words her way. 'Cushycow Lane. Penny Pie Steps. Jarrow Slack. Cobble Dene. Blink Bonny Avenue. Voltage Terrace. Pontop Pike? Magic, isn't it?'

Caz grinned like an idiot child and wrote them all down, asked the Blob if he did sign-painting and gave him her phone number when he said he did. And this was in the nightclub, when Sadie had engineered to be *à deux* in a dark private corner. She'd even banished all the Geeks to the dance floor.

'Then there's Tyzack Crescent, Saffron Place, Tarragon Way – see, all the herbs. Topaz Street, Ruby Street, Jade Close – that must have been when they started sailing to China. I could go on for hours, me, I'll definitely ring you.'

The Blob stood to leave.

'What are you drinking, Caz?' Sadie said, loading each syllable with louche longing.

'Oh – Coke and ice,' Caz said. 'Thanks, Sadie. Don't go, Ted, tell me more streets. It's wonderful!'

The Blob grinned and sat down again.

Sadie seethed a path to the bar.

Coke and ice for chrissakes!

It was hopeless! Caz's whole being was concentrated on the Project, she brushed aside any hint of personal glory, impatient to get on, as if she had a religious vision.

It was all very puzzling. Today, for example, she was going to meet a couple of friends who'd come from the south to make flags and you'd have thought it was a royal visit. It was only flags, for God's sake! Sadie wandered to the burnt-out shell of the cottage and sat on a rock, brooding.

The whole thing was unsettling: perhaps it should be the End of the World. Perhaps she'd have to admit she was bored. Was she? *I am bored?* Or perhaps she was ready for change, for a long solitary period when she could pursue an artistic vision the way she'd imagined all those years ago. Maybe she could edit and polish her memoirs. Her memoirs! Come up 'n see my memoirs, Caz. She practised the invitation.

That was an angle she hadn't tried.

And here was Caz, striding through the mud, talking to the Geeks as she went. Telling them what a fine job they were doing. Sadie winced. Praise should be strictly measured!

'I'm off to the station,' Caz said, 'I might be back straight away, but if they're tired, it'll be tomorrow. There's plenty to keep you going anyway. Bye!'

She half-raised one hand as Caz turned away.

This year, next year . . .

Come up 'n see me sometime.

Never?

80

'Hotchpudding Place, Dumpling Hall Drive,' thought Caz, easing her scrapyard van on to the road. 'Pease Pudding Avenue, Stottie Cake View, you can do anything with names up here.'

She was thrilled at the way everything was slotting into place, like a multidimensional jigsaw. There were trays and troughs of seedlings exploding all over Josie's greenhouses and half of her garden boasted a small forest of trees and bushes only days from being transplanted into their summer palace.

'I love it,' Josie said, simply. 'Some of these have been lying around for years. It's like seeds in the desert sands, they can lie for a hundred years before it rains and then they grow and bloom overnight. If it wasn't for the festival, these would still be dark and dry and waiting.'

Kevin the Viking and a pile of seasoned timber had taken over the back yard of Toyz 4 Boyz 'n Gurlz. His hands shook with excitement as he showed Caz blueprints for the ship and stencils for the shields. He was building in hidden recesses for plant pots: the effect would be of a ship that has trawled slowly through tight-knit jungle where seeds and plants drop to the deck and put down roots between the curbed timbers. A voyage of metamorphosis: the ship turned into a floating garden, as if the deck and mast had come to hectic life, like St Christopher's gnarled staff and its miraculous roses. Perfect blooms after the dangerous turbulence of dark flood waters. The boat would rest on the ground as if its crew had dragged it from the Tyne then simply vanished. An enigma, where people could only stare and wonder at the clear glass panels rising around it like a shrine. Kevin and Caz called it Waelwaegsdottir: the daughter of the whale road, the old name for the ocean.

Ben would like that.

Then there was Ted, the amateur geographical etymologist. He made his money working for the Inland Revenue and had begged her not to let on.

'Me brother's a traffic warden, Caz,' he said, laughing ruefully. 'The big sister's a social worker, and the little sister works at Holloway Prison down in London. Me mam says, well, ye've all got work, and I suppose I should be glad, but I wish ye had jobs I could tell me friends about. Of a Christmas, she looks at us and says, well, here's a house full of the most unpopular people in the country.'

His life's work was exploring every stratum of Newcastle since its proud beginnings in 1079. His eyes burned when he talked about all the layers of meaning trapped in street names. The poets and composers and writers and statesmen; the lords and ladies who lent their names to esplanades and crescents. The decades when coal was King, the foundries that sprang up in times of war and prosperity. Pit Place, Pipeswellgate, Vulcan Place. The Neptune years when Britannia ruled the waves and rows of houses were named for heroes and distant lands: Horatio Street, Raleigh Square, Tel-El-Kebir Road, Cuba Street. There had been multiple christenings of brick and stone in honour of the age of steam: Stephenson Street, Rocket Way, Engine Inn Road. In Newcastle, 'railway' prefixed everything from cottages to cuttings. The ironic optimism that called slum dwellings Arcadia, Paradise, Halcyon, Sunnyside. And everywhere the presence of the docks and the sea, its myriad islands and its darling Grace honoured in lofty avenues and cul-de-sacs.

'I can go on for weeks, Caz,' he said. 'I know that there's not many interested, so tell us to shut up when you've had enough.'

'No,' Caz said, 'I'm fascinated. We want twenty-one names that encapsulate Dreamchare and the Tyne and its history.'

'Twenty-one!' Ted said. 'That's like asking me for a bottle of brown ale when I've got the rights on Newcastle Breweries! Nowt's a bother! And the actual street signs – will I do them all the same, or would you like them in the style of the times they were put up? That'd be better, like.'

'It would,' Caz said. 'Just keep your receipts. It's in your hands. *Carte blanche*, Ted!'

The most astonishing thing so far was the meticulous dedication of The Chain Gang. It wasn't just that they did everything they were asked, but they did it immediately and worked until it was too dark to see, and started again as soon as it was light. Caz might have wished for – what did Sadie call it? – facial enthusiasm but she was getting used to their deadpan pallor. Even Sadie was melting a little. She was friendly in a way Caz hadn't hoped for, she seemed eager to please in every detail.

Caz took a ticket from the man in the station booth and parked. Time to saunter around the hall and have a fag, standing under the clock until the train pulled in.

Charlotte and Daisy, two more oddball jigsaw pieces come to play their part in making the picture complete.

81

They were hiding in the Ladies on platform 4A, hoping to mix with the crowds from the London train. Charlotte thought they shouldn't bother, but Daisy said Caz wouldn't like them coming earlier than they were supposed to. Charlotte couldn't see why, she thought it was quite funny, really.

'It's manners, innit, Betty,' Daisy insisted.

'You don't know Caz, Twyla,' Charlotte said. 'She doesn't give a bugger. She'll only mind that we paid out for the Y when she could have been putting us up.'

'Nah,' Daisy said, 'I'm not convinced.'

Charlotte shrugged, willing Daisy to feel easy, knowing that she wouldn't – until she met Caz. Hopefully.

The lavatory attendant mopped the cubicles, staring at them. They weren't lipstick and hairdo sort of ladies, checking their appearance in the dull vandal-proof mirror. They weren't teenagers having an illicit smoke. Students, she thought, giggling like bairns, just let them try injecting their marijuana in here! Then the sight of the wheelchair softened her: they must be here to meet a friend and maybe they weren't all bad.

When the train pulled in, they waited for a moment and joined the steady trickle of passengers. Charlotte spotted Caz first and nudged Daisy. 'That's her.'

Daisy looked over. Caz was leaning on a trolley, scanning every face. She hadn't seen them.

'Caz!'

She sauntered over, smiling. She and Charlotte stood for a few seconds, then hugged each other. They loaded the trolley.

'Smart wheels,' Caz said, lifting the chair. 'Do you . . .?'

'Not often,' Charlotte said. 'Emergencies and heavy drinking sessions only.'

'Well, you're looking wonderful,' Caz said. 'Hello, Daisy, I presume.'

'Hello,' Daisy said. 'Presume away. Nice place you got here.'

'Whey aye, pet,' Caz said. 'It's not all Spender and pitheads and whippets and leeks. I've got a van outside and if we're quick I don't have to pay a parking fee. Can you . . .?'

'Sprint?' Charlotte said. 'Almost.'

'I don't know what you want to do,' Caz said. 'We can dump your stuff at my flat – which is yours while you're here, by the way. We can go and see the site. We can go and see Josie and have a look at the model and have a drink. We can do anything you want, really.'

'What about dump our stuff and go and see Josie?' Charlotte said.

'I could murder a drink,' Daisy said.

'Yeah,' Caz said, loading the van. 'Well, what about this. Dump your stuff, hit an offie, go see Josie and hang out. Then later we can go to poser's paradise. Hit the Lovenest so you can see what sort of idiots there are on the arts scene. No, that's a bit harsh. You know what I mean, love 'em and hate 'em. A wee spot of disco the night away and home?'

'Fine,' Daisy said, relaxing a little. Caz was enough like Charlotte for her to feel comfortable. Posh but ordinary. Ish. 'Hey, I'll take the back of the van. Betty here can have the lady's seat.'

'Betty?'

'Betty Grable,' Charlotte said, 'for my lovely legs. I can't say I'm keen on it.'

'Of course,' Caz said. 'Mind, Marlene Dietrich had lovely legs too.'

'She never insured them for a million,' Daisy said.

'That's true. Betty, huh? I'll have to show you round,' Caz said, 'tho you'll probably want to find your own way.'

Charlotte laughed. 'Well, we've done that bit,' she said. 'Oh, belt up, Twyla, it's ridiculous.'

'Twyla?' Caz asked.

'Twyla Dolan,' Charlotte said. 'Arm-wrestling geriatric – I'll show you the cutting. God, it's good to see you.'

'Fine,' Caz said, 'afternoon, Twyla. What do you mean – you've done that bit?'

'We came up here three days ago,' Charlotte said. 'We stayed at the Y and had a mini recce. You know?'

'You didn't need to do that,' Caz said. 'Got money to burn, have you? You could have stayed at mine and done that. I don't want to be the guided tour babysitting bit. I gather – from your letters – you've been nannied a bit too long, Charlotte. I mean, I can't begin to know what it's like, losing your arm or your legs. I wouldn't pretend to. But I'd imagine people either look through you or fall over themselves being helpful – yeah? And help is only help if it's what you want. I really don't want to do either of those. So you'll have to tell me if you need anything done. Just say what you want.'

'We will,' Charlotte said, turning to meet Daisy's smile.

'Blimey,' Daisy said, as they turned into the massive gates of the estate, 'is your mate Josie loaded or something?'

'No,' Caz said, 'just bloody lucky. I'll let her tell you about it. It's all down to an ancient aristocrat type called Fiz Rainier. It's a brilliant story. Let's go meet Josie.'

82

Josie took a back seat the way you do when two old friends meet after a long time and you're not one of them. She liked Charlotte on sight, and realised she hadn't a clear picture of her until now. Charlotte had shoulder length hair, blonde and dark blonde, like the lady on the cereal packet when Josie was a child. Cornflake coloured hair. Her eyes were a surprising hazel, and she had a sprinkle of freckles. Her smile was a living thing, shifting through her whole face: she was utterly beautiful in a sort of robust pre-Raphaelite way. A wistful maiden who went for healthy walks and ate her greens. Josie couldn't help but look at her legs, but there was only a slight awkwardness in the way she walked. She dressed with style, a cape flung round her shoulders, her elegant black skirt brushing the top of her stylish boots. She kept her eyes on Caz most of the time, with an expression of real tenderness.

Josie had never seen Caz so – animated? No, she'd been sparky ever since George gave them his unqualified yes. Warm? Maybe that was it, warm and soft in a gallant way. You could always tell shades of mood from her cheeks and lips and now, her mouth was relaxed and her cheeks rounded. When Caz was happy, she looked like a child. As if she was on her best behaviour but with none of the stiffness that implies. But if either she or Charlotte mentioned Trimdon House, the other would skate away at a tangent with a joke. A little like Caz had been with David, but much easier. Josie surmised that the fire was the last time they'd really seen each other, and she tried to imagine what they were feeling and thinking. It was impossible to guess. There was a deep bond there, but at the same time, the way they linked included Daisy and herself.

They sat drinking wine and the small talk slowed down. Josie felt that Charlotte and Caz needed to talk on their own. What, for example, about David? Surely Caz would have to say something.

'Can we look at the greenhouses?' Caz said. 'I can't think about anything much beyond this project, tell the truth. It's so amazing to see you again.'

'What did you expect?' Charlotte said. 'Twyla and I thought of doing a double act to wind you up. A modern *Whatever Happened to Baby Jane*? You didn't finish your lager, Blanche, so you can't have a short . . . Only I've given up the wheelchair and she doesn't drink enough gin.'

'I didn't fancy the overall either,' said Daisy, 'far too girly girly for me. It's more Laurel and Hardy, really, only we don't have the right figures for it.'

'Take Charlotte round the greenhouses,' Josie said, 'I'll show Daisy the model.' That way they could talk and she could try and put Daisy at her ease.

'Right,' Caz said, 'let's go. Save the model for when we get back. Tell Daisy about Miss Fizz Rainier. She thinks you must be loaded, living here.' Charlotte took her arm and they went outside.

'Good move,' Daisy said, 'they've got a lot to catch up on. You know, I used to think posh people had it all. Till I met her. Legless. Betty. Charlotte. I thought they didn't feel like I do. Where I come from, if you're pissed off, you shout about it and thump someone. The most I thought posh people did was swear a bit, you know, *oh dash it, what a damned nuisance*, maybe, and keep a stiff upper lip.'

'Yes,' Josie said. 'It's a weird thing, this class system everyone pretends we haven't got, well, they'd rather not talk about it. My grandparents were working class, but they wanted to better themselves, slide into the lower middle classes. Mayonnaise not salad cream. Brighton not Blackpool. They were always trying to do the right thing, but they were never sure of the rules.'

Daisy laughed. 'Tell us about this Miss Fizz Rainier,' she said, 'I like a mystery.'

The ghost of Miss Rainier drifted through the open French doors and she perched on the sofa next to Daisy, watching Josie with the laughter of the spheres bubbling all around her. It is the – sometimes doubtful – privilege of the dead to hear exactly what people think of them. Miss Rainier was eternally humbled by how many people genuinely liked her. Even admired her! She'd suspected that most people she dealt with had put up with her, deferring to her wealth and position in her presence and bad-mouthing her once she was gone.

'Well,' Josie said, 'Miss Fizz Rainier. Where do I begin?'

At the beginning, the ghost suggested, *it's so much easier that way.*

'It's a bit like a fairytale,' Josie said. 'Once upon a time, as far as I know, Felicity Rainier was born to parents of high degree. Stinking rich, had been for centuries, probably rewarded by Henry VIII for scourging peasants, I imagine.'

Miss Rainier's ghost nodded. *Absolute swine, the lot of them*, she agreed, *but by God, the money was useful!*

'Anyway,' Josie said, 'she did the usual aristocratic things and lived in the south of France most of her young life. It was all champagne and parties and dashing young men and yachts. Then she vamped around Kenya for a while. She got bored before it was too late, though, and came back to England. I'm not sure how old she was then, but she got involved in a strange secret society. They called themselves Ferguson's Gang – I think one of them had relations in the Wild West and they saw themselves as latter-day highwaymen, rather Robin Hood-ish.'

Dear girl, the ghost smiled, *you bothered reading my papers. I thought you'd just leave them to mildew away.*

'Go on,' Daisy said, 'I like stories. She sounds like a right headcase.'

Miss Rainier's ghost gave a wicked smile.

'Well, Ferguson's Gang,' Josie said, 'they took on different names. There was Mad Moll, Dick Turpin, Sally Blood, Marion Hood, Greybeard, Zorro and Guy Fawkes. Guy Fawkes was Miss Rainier. They were interested in Merrie England, guts and gusto, they had the idea that rural life was the answer to most of this century's problems and cities were The Octopus which would strangle everything good about England. This must have been – oh, early twenties, thirties?'

'They ought to come down to Deptford,' Daisy said. 'It's all NF now, and the estates! Man, even the fire brigade won't go in most of them now. I was brought up there. You feel like a zombie in a morgue.'

'Yes,' Josie said. 'They thought it was bad all those years ago. Anyway, the aims of this Ferguson's Gang were to buy up land and stop developers. Buy old buildings and keep them lived in. Plant trees and keep flower meadows. Make it worth people's while to stay in villages. They wanted to revive old crafts and keep traditions alive, country festivals and local songs, that sort of thing.'

'Sounds like the National Trust and the Green Party,' Daisy said. 'Bit do-goody, but good, you know what I mean?'

'Yes,' Josie said. 'Sort of keep the peasants peasants but give them decent money and bathrooms. They knew that the only way to keep the land halfway intact was to own it, and they had enough money to put it into action. They gave a lot to the National Trust, set up funds to preserve it and that sort of thing.'

Miss Rainier's ghost sighed. *Wish I'd told you all about it when I still could,* she said. *You'll never know how it felt, being in Ferguson's Gang. Damn that vow of secrecy, someone should have written a book! But it seemed – ostentatious. We wanted to do so much more.*

'So where do you come in?' Daisy said.

'I came in in the Indian summer of Fizz Rainier's life. That's what she used to say,' Josie smiled. 'She said her spring had been total self-indulgence, wandering round as if the world was the Garden of Eden and gorging herself on every tree. Her summer was Ferguson's Gang, trying to do something worthwhile with her life. They split up after the last war, no, about the fifties. Some of them were tired and everything they'd done seemed like a drop in the ocean. Some of them wanted to do other things. Mad Moll bought a desert island and lived there. Dick Turpin went to live on an island off the coast of Ireland. Marion Hood went into politics. Guy Fawkes – Fizz Rainier – decided to return to the crumbling family pile in Northumberland and put her own house and garden in order. I was her gardener. She left me this house and garden in perpetuity. There was a great furore over her will and some awful people bought the big house and I think they were turning it into a hotel, but the money's running out. They kept finding massive structural faults, underground streams and dry rot. It's all over scaffolding now.'

And they will lose it, said the ghost crisply. *My will was crystal clear. My damned stubborn great-niece should be living there. Stupid girl lives in the middle of a desert in Australia and they simply haven't found her yet. Lawyers!*

'So she's dead?' Daisy said, pouring more wine. 'I think I'd have liked her. Miss Fizz Rainier! When you're that upper, money doesn't matter.'

'You couldn't help but like her,' Josie said. 'This is part of her wine cellar we're drinking now, by the way. She sounded awful – almost Lady Bracknell – really bossy, but once you got past that, she was so real and alive. Yes, she died in a road crash. She was eighty-four, doing a hundred in her Rolls Royce on the Fossway. They say she had a heart attack and lost control.'

Lady Bracknell indeed! Actually, the ghost twinkled, *I felt the heart attack and I knew what it was, so I put my foot down as far as it would go. It was better than sex.*

'Way to go!' Daisy said. 'Here's to her, old Fizz, Guy Fawkes, whoever she was. Nice taste in booze – and the rest!'

So glad you approve, the ghost commented drily.

83

Between the cottage door and the greenhouse, Charlotte and Caz could see the chill smoke of their breath in the air. Once the glass doors were closed behind them, they relaxed. In the steamy warmth, the smells of earth and leaves wrapped round them. Caz flicked the light switch and they were in a jungle where great fleshy leaves carved shadows like animals waiting for danger to pass.

'It's wonderful to see you,' Caz said again, squeezing Charlotte's arm. 'Christ, I feel weepy, it's been so long.'

'Bubbly baby,' Charlotte said. 'I know what you mean. Your friend Josie's lovely. It's weird, Caz, just weird, I never thought I'd see you again, to be honest. Not all the time. Only in the darkest bits. At least you always wrote. I feel like I've been in a cocoon for years. Very shaky.'

'Are your wings still wet?' Caz said. 'You know, I feel like I've been frozen for years. Like a mammoth. I'd forgotten what it is to be happy, until – oh, about a year ago, I guess.'

'Go on,' Charlotte said. 'You tell me your turning point and I'll tell you mine.'

'Whoo!' Caz said, 'there's been more than a few. I think there's been possible turning points all along the years only I wasn't in the space to – use them. This lot was a series that I just couldn't ignore. I think it started in Miston with the flat. My place, not just some rented set of rooms. Yes. Then Carrie – she's a neighbour. She's eighty-three and she just has this twinkling serenity after a hell of a life. Stuff you just wouldn't believe, only it's true. I could listen to her for hours.'

'Makes you humble, doesn't it?' Charlotte said. 'Daisy talked about her life when I first knew her and it made mine seem like a privileged bed of roses. As if I was happily sleepwalking until the fire. Totally unaware of how lucky I was. Go on, I'm interrupting.'

'Then I had that dream,' Caz said, laughing. '*I have a dream today!* I told you about it – it was a land, a land of mountains and a lake, and in the dream, I got there by climbing up through the spine of Galleon Heights. It was so real I keep looking at the boarded-up corner of my living room. In the dream, there's a ladder inside and I climb it. It's actually too small for that in real life, and there's just two massive pipes and telephone wires there. But it was so real I had to check – you know what I mean? I could feel the rungs under my feet. Let's find a seat.'

'You said a bit about it,' Charlotte said. 'Tell me more.'

They sat on milk crates under a sinfully beautiful orchid.

'Yes,' Caz said. 'Well, this land. I felt like I'd been there before, or at least, that I could stay there quite happily. There wasn't a sign of modern life. The nearest I can get to it is the Lake District if you took away all the tourist bits and towns. The second time I dreamed about it, there was a sort of circus there, an old fashioned horses and rounded caravans circus. I met a woman there – well, I would, wouldn't I? – her name was Joy and she just knew everything about me. She even mentioned Ben. But I've told you that bit, haven't I?'

Charlotte held her hand and touched her forehead with her own.

'You're still in love with her, aren't you?' she said.

'Yes,' Caz said, 'I'll always be in love with her.'

'I'm glad,' Charlotte said. 'I believe in love, you see, in spite of David and the baby and this bloody leg situation. I wondered if you'd got hard and cynical about it. You've got your guard up, but it's still soppy roses and kisses Caz underneath.'

'Oh yes,' Caz said, 'I think I'm lucky to have known it. I wouldn't even let myself think about it for years, not unless I was on my own. The temptation to get drunk and stay that way! That's what Jay does.'

'Oh, have you kept in touch with her?' Charlotte said.

'Not a lot,' Caz said. 'We met a few times – afterwards – but it was too painful. For both of us. We'd drink and play pool and go dancing, but then there was going home. She'd ask me to stay with her, she hates being on her own, but I couldn't bear being with anyone. I think she saw me and Ben as somehow – the perfect couple – and she wanted to talk about it. I just couldn't. We ring each other up sometimes. She seems busy, lots of work, but she's drinking all the time, too much. It's not making her happy.'

'She came to see me – about every month, two months until a couple of years ago,' Charlotte said. 'I was so miserable I think she felt awful. She kept saying I could go and live at her place, and she meant it, but I was welded to my institutional four walls. I'd given up. Lady Lazarus. I wondered if Jay was coming up for this amazing festival of yours.'

'Well, I thought of it,' said Caz. 'Only at the moment she's In Love in that widescreen early Technicolor way she's addicted to. Sensurround. The Beloved hasn't got a clue, of course, but there's no way Jay can wrest herself from the Maybe – maybe this time, I'll be lucky? She lives for the precious moments spent in the Beloved's presence. She even laughs about it, she knows it's probably hopeless, but it's a challenge.'

'That's one thing none of us lost,' Charlotte said. 'How we loved a challenge! I did for a while, you did too, from the sound of it, but we're picking up. I can feel your dreamland. Tell me more.'

'The best thing – well, Joy was the best thing. Talking about Ben as if it was a natural thing to do. There was another amazing thing. I went through underground caves in a sort of exotic pleasure gondola,' Caz said. 'It was all tricks of the light, caves with Egyptian figures and jungles and diamonds and a waterfall. This boy, Tom, took me through. Thinking about it, he was just like Ben. So joyful.'

'You and Ben were always like children,' Charlotte said. 'So brilliant and just laughing it off. Clever happy children. I thought you'd lose that. I don't think you have.'

'Well,' Caz said, 'Ben wouldn't have liked my company the way things were for the first few years. That sort of slapped me in the face after the second dream. It was all very well getting on with things, but deep down I was mourning and hanging on. It gives you a sort of detachment. Nothing really matters. The so what syndrome.'

'Ben would have gone apeshit,' Charlotte said. 'She couldn't stand cynicism.'

'Quite,' Caz said. 'So I started – dunno, sounds corny – but I started caring again. Just little things. Fixing Carrie's door. Listening to Josie. She sort of whitters on a lot and you can tune out, and I'd got into the habit of half-listening. So I made this real effort and listened and responded. That's how this project really started. She wouldn't have done it on her own, and I thought I'd get her going and drift out of it. But then I found I really was interested. It's Newcastle as well. People do things here, mad things like happenings on ancient sites and situationist exhibitions in old churches. And The Turk's Head – you'll have to come to the piano bar, Miston style. Like if you ask why all the time you do nothing. Here it's more, well why not? Fun.'

'I know you saw David,' Charlotte said. 'I got a postcard from Glasgow just before Christmas. He's going to the States.'

'Oh good, he's alive,' Caz said. 'He was camping out on Miston High Road and I bumped into him. He came over for a strange evening and vanished around midnight. My loony neighbour thought Josie and I had killed him and we had to go and make a police statement. The police were really apologetic, but they had to follow it up.'

'What do you mean, camping out?' Charlotte said.

'He's The Angry Man,' Caz said. 'Didn't you know?'

'Bloody hell!' Charlotte pursed her lips. 'You know, I've felt every emotion there is about David. Love, passion, reverence, warmth, hate, fury, rage. I felt so abandoned, Caz. It was Daisy who snapped me out of that. Probably about the same time as you were moving. A bit before. I realised I was developing a saintly smile, wrapping myself in self-pity like a thermal blanket. Waiting for Godot. God only knows what. Five minutes with Daisy on her old man and I started laughing. My bloody prodigal hero – The Angry Man! Did he ask about me?'

'Oh, yes,' Caz said. 'He said he'd been a real shit, he just couldn't handle it, man, and so on. He sounded very seventies. The Angry Man bit was just his way of escaping. So he's going to the States?'

'They're welcome to him,' Charlotte said. 'I've often thought, could I forgive him, then I thought, well, he'd have to be sorry first. Even then I couldn't. I wouldn't have made him stay for ever, you know. But it would have been nice to have him to come round to.'

Caz rubbed her hand. 'He said we were all casualties. The walking wounded. Or I did. We are.'

'I've had for ever to think about it,' Charlotte said. 'Life's not the way we were brought up to believe it should be. It's messy, it's supremely unfair, there's no tidy endings, but it's all we've got. The walking wounded, huh? Well, goddamm it, I'm walking, Caz. Eighteen months ago, I'd have been bawling my eyes out. And if you get all the bits of glass out, wounds heal.'

They walked along the slats between the plants, reading the tags that said ship, pergola, face-garden, cottage.

'That's where they're going,' Caz said, 'and it'll mean nothing to you without that model. Let's join the girls and we can tell you about the flags.'

'There's a name for studying flags,' Charlotte said. 'Vexillology.

I'm a vexillologist. That would look good on a passport. Mummy, what did you do in the Great War? I was a vexillologist, my child, and the King's Navy sailed under my flags.'

84

Caz felt responsible for her guests' happiness, and tonight that involved deflecting the collective misbehaviour of the arty crowd in the Lovenest. At times like this she wished she was six foot three. She was embarrassed by George Tweddle's ridiculous cravat and Michael's precious way of speaking so quietly that you had to move close to hear him. She just about managed to keep Mad Mark and his real ale real male lechery at bay with the leather jacket glowering across her shoulders. Mad Mark had taken to kissing women's hands as a greeting, and Charlotte's blonde hair guaranteed the full treatment: a handclasp, a moustached kiss and a burning look that travelled up the arm and lingered somewhere around the cleavage. Undesirable.

Dreary Desirée and the faded henna of her mane were being Unnecessary, it was only nine o'clock and she was weeping mascara from pink eyes and wiping spit from her lips. She lurched upright, waving her arms like a drowning person and howling between vodkas. The gin-swilling clone at her side pulled green crumpled toilet paper from a squashed handbag like a second-rate magician caught on the hop. Unsavoury.

The brothers McVey had declared UDI around a toffee-coloured pole that went from floor to ceiling, punctuated by a circular shelf which held glasses, an ashtray, dead cigarette packets and their immaculate linen elbows. Their twin mops of blonde curls recalled Medusa, and their eyes slithered venomously past Caz's *hi there, boys.* They bit half inches from the clear liquid in their glasses, their lips spinning dangerous webs of scorn. Ungracious.

Hell hath no fury like a queen scorned, Caz thought, a sceen quorned, a squean corned, well, what did I expect. None of this crowd had the grace to be pleased with anyone's success – apart from their own.

'What you drinking then,' Daisy said.

'Brandy,' Caz said. At least that guaranteed inner warmth.

She almost added I'll get them, but Daisy was gone, elbowing through the crowd, her height and leather jacket made it easy. Oh shit, Sadie and the Boys made their entrance and lined the bar like a South American death squad.

'Scuse,' Daisy called and landed her elbows between Sadie's black satin gloves and the scarred pallor of a Geek's arm.

Sadie turned her Draculesque grin to inspect her and ran her tongue round her lips. Put that away, thought Caz, you know where it's been. Sadie's head swivelled and her eyes met Caz. She raised one dull black hand and wiggled the fingers. Caz smiled back and nodded. Soon Sadie would be scything her way through the baggy knitwear and crumpled cotton to join them.

And she did. Plan 97 phase 1 had dropped into her mind when she saw the scenario of Daisy with Caz, and she dispensed coins to the Geeks with orders to fill the juke-box and empty the fruit machines.

'Caz,' she said, the loaded word swinging like a B-movie scythe over the hairless sweating chest of Our Bound Hero, 'how *flukish* to find you here. Such a busy bee! Josie. Hi.'

'Well, hey, Sadie,' Caz said, 'this is Charlotte and this is Daisy. Our vexillologists.'

'Vexillologists,' Sadie's voice crackled on the x. 'Is this something I should add to my repertoire? Is it fun? Does it hurt? Both?'

'It's making flags,' Daisy said. 'Her not me really. Christ, they're never playing The Grateful Dead, Betty! It's a bloody time warp in here, innit?'

'It's the In place,' Caz said.

'*Avant garde*,' Sadie said, '*nouveau riche*, they should be so lucky. Myself, I favour *fin de siècle*.'

'Wassat then,' Daisy said, oblivious to the fire hose of seduction Sadie was gushing her way.

'A *plaisanterie*,' Sadie said. She'd been struggling with Proust in the original all afternoon.

'It's yer actual French,' Caz said, 'since Europe is upon us.'

'That bleeding tunnel,' Daisy said, 'I hope the bugger falls in before they try using it.'

'Why?' Sadie said.

'You like it?' Daisy swigged enough lager in one go to underline her contempt.

'I despise it,' Sadie told her, 'but if it falls in before they use it, they'll repair it and we'll be stuck with it. Let it implode when it's packed with traffic.'

'Ugh,' Daisy said, 'that's disgusting.'

Sadie smirked. 'They only take notice of disaster if it involves death,' she said, sniggering. 'Ecological disaster doesn't even merit a headline.'

'All right,' Daisy bartered. 'Only let it be a goods train with one driver who miraculously staggers along and crawls out at Dover, or wherever it ends. Human interest: *I'll never drive through there again*, says white-faced father of three. *It's a miracle*, sobs vigil wife after night-long ordeal.'

Sadie looked disappointed. 'Too neat,' she said dismissively, 'I like bangs not whimpers.'

Daisy laughed wildly. 'Have a gang bang and you get both,' she said loudly.

Sadie's teeth gleamed. '*Tell* me about yourself,' she said.

Caz grinned and slipped away. Daisy was well able to chew up and spit out the likes of Sadie.

'That's our resident dominatrix,' she told Charlotte. 'Daisy appears to be making mincemeat of her. I think they're both enjoying it.'

'This is like the end of art school party,' Charlotte said. 'Everyone out to impress and everyone knows everyone too well to be impressed. You must have made quite a stir.'

'I think I did,' Caz said. 'Hell, I know I did. They see a new face and it's an unbent pair of ears and, potentially, a new pair of willing arms. Since I've lent neither I'm still new. It's offputting. Even if I wanted a romance, the thought of the 40 per cent proof post mortem is enough to put me off.'

'No romance?' Charlotte asked.

'No,' Caz said. 'I've had offers. Sadie wishing to experiment. Dyke didn't put off Mad Mark. Dreary Desirée, the resident bisexual. A poet. Self-styled.'

'Anyone interesting?'

'Well, everyone assumes I'm Doing It with Josie. She's virgin territory for this lot too. We're each other's beard.'

'She is lovely,' Charlotte said, 'the rescue-me type. God help us if Jay was here.'

Caz groaned. 'No,' she said, 'Josie's a friend and that's pretty rare. Like me and you. I love Josie. I love you, but there's no undercurrent. None of that maybe Jay seems to thrive on.'

'You're gorgeous,' Charlotte said and hugged her.

Ooh, look at that, said half the Lovenest, what's Josie going to do about that, is that Caz's bit from the south, ooh that explains a lot, ooh, look, she's not even embarrassed.

Ooh!

'Can I join you?' Josie escaped from Michael's intense monotone, pleading dipsomania and incontinence.

Caz flung an arm round her shoulder.

'Isn't it awful,' she said, laughing.

Ooh! *Now* look!

'We were just talking about you,' Charlotte said. 'I have mother-hen in my genes and I'm so pleased you've taken care of Caz. She's such a softie.'

A softie! Josie was amazed: Charlotte was serious.

'And she's so cuddly,' Charlotte said, wrapping an arm round Caz's waist.

Cuddly? Josie looked at Caz's face, laughing at her, blushing a little, one arm round each of their shoulders. She was a softie, a cuddly softie, tender and gallant and, now that her old friend was here, confident enough to be both.

'Can I come in on this old hippy's hug-in?' Daisy laced her bionic arm round Charlotte and rested her hand on Josie's shoulder.

Well, did you see that, God, there's a story, *gets you right in the gonads*, that blonde one looks so feminine, *makes you feel like someone's performed a cockectomy when you weren't looking* ha ha, squelchy dykes! have you ever watched – you know? you can get videos, *I've got them, my son, I've got them*.

Said Desirée, Mad Mark, the brothers McVey, even the Geeks were moved to monosyllabic speech: every cuckoo in the Lovenest chipped in with a beakful of cheap twitters.

'Brandy,' Sadie's lips rolled out the word, 'a triple. Lager. Twice. Bloody Mary with an iceberg drowning in it. And a tray.'

She bore down on Caz and her company. It was time to orchestrate plan 97, phase 2.

85

'Y̲our friend Daisy's fascinating,' Sadie told Caz under the smoky strobes of The Generator. 'So raw. So powerful. And yet, such an *air de tristesse!*'

Caz was unnerved by how close Sadie was sitting, one shoulder grazing her cheek. She could feel her heartbeat, for goodness' sake – was she surprised that Sadie had a heartbeat? It was more that her body was soft under the stiff black jacket, and Caz imagined her naked body, bloodless and pale. She realised with a jolt that Sadie was coming on to her – for heaven's sake! It is always a compliment when someone desires you, but Caz felt herself stiffening, every pore in her body shrinking in on itself. It wasn't even that Sadie was drunk. She never got drunk so you'd notice. Or was Sadie's ooze of desire directed towards Daisy? Am I supposed to be some sort of go-between? thought Caz. She felt a sudden revulsion.

'My round,' she said and ducked out of Sadie's reach.

'Oo, Caz,' said Desirée, lolling at the bar, 'you're a dark horse. You've got the bloody lot now, haven't you?'

'Leave it, Desirée,' said her clone. 'Sorry Caz, she's really down. She's so smashed.'

'I'm still conscious,' said Desirée and slid to the floor.

'Blimey,' Daisy said, 'this is like the Walworth Road at chucking out time. Only this lot just got let in.'

'Hello,' Caz said. 'Say when you want to leave. You've made

quite an impression on Sadie. I think I'm supposed to say my friend Sadie fancies you.'

'She'll have to join the queue,' Daisy said. 'She's off her bleeding rocker. I've had to take her paws off me twice already. She just swoons and goes, oh, Daisy, you're so strong. She's mental.'

'Take her with a handful of salt,' Caz said.

'I wouldn't take her with salt and vinegar and brown sauce slathered from head to foot,' Daisy said. 'She spent the whole time telling me how talented you were, how much she admired you, I reckon she's after you, Caz.'

Caz closed her eyes and blew smoke. 'No chance,' she said.

'I'll look after you,' Daisy said, and shot her arm out to stop the twinkletoed barperson ignoring them yet again.

'You dykes!' he said, 'I'll do you for GBH.'

'How dare you assume I'm sexual?' Daisy said. 'Pint of lager – in a can. And a double brandy for her. Only I want to see the bottle it comes out of.'

'Is she a friend of yours?' the barperson twirled in his ripped denim shorts.

'You have to check,' Daisy said. 'What is it? Two shots for a quid? That means it's poison. They'll have a good bottle under the bar. See?'

Twinkletoes pouted and poured, lizard eyes clocking every face along the bar.

'And a Bloody Mary – Sadie's size,' said Caz.

'*She* likes it out of the optics,' he told them. 'More of a kick, dear.'

'She would,' Daisy said. 'Here, Caz, leave it to me.'

She led the way back to the dark corner where Sadie smouldered and sat down.

'You chatting me up?' she said.

'The question direct!' Sadie laughed. '*J'accuse!* How refreshing. Are you interested?'

'Are you asking?'

'I'm asking,' Sadie blinked slowly. Plan 97, phase 2 was showing promise.

'No,' Daisy said. 'Thanks all the same. Right. You chatting her up?'

'Caz?' Sadie twinkled.

'Caz.'

'Yes,' Sadie said. 'I'm crazy about you, Caz.' What the hell. 'You interested, Caz?'

'No,' Caz said. 'Flattered. Thank you, Sadie, but no thanks.'

'Flattered?' Sadie's eyes vamped her through cigarette smoke. 'How *gamine*!'

'Don't give her straws,' Daisy said, 'I just like to get things straight. You could have been buggering about for weeks wondering. She ain't interested. Now you know.'

'Do I? Must freshen my *maquillage*,' Sadie murmured and left them. *Merde* and double *merde*!

'Is it me deodorant?' Daisy said.

'No,' Caz said. 'Sadie likes buggering about, Daisy. She enjoys playing at chatting people up. Now I think about it, she's been doing it with me ever since I got here.'

'Well, it's bloody stupid,' Daisy said. 'You want to or you don't. She got right on my nerves in that hole we just came from. Lovenest? More like a flaming rat's nest. I told her about me arm cuz she kept clutching me and I don't like it. Then she wanted to see it. I know what she wanted. She wanted to see the stump and where it joins. I would have clocked her one only I'm a stranger in town and her sort! – she'd probably have thought I was making a pass. Bloody dog!'

Caz looked at her. 'I'm sorry about that,' she said. 'I guess I'm used to Sadie – she gave me the creeps when I first met her. I just keep her at arm's length, laugh at her. And she's been brilliant on the project.'

'She'd have done cartwheels with no knickers on all down the High Street if you wanted her to,' Daisy said. 'Anything for a conquest, that one. I hate her sort. Come on with a gobful of long words trying to make you feel stupid. You're too polite, Caz. Most of the world is as far as I can see. You've got to say what you want, come out with it and then everyone knows where they are.'

Say what you want.

Caz already liked Daisy from the afternoon they'd all spent together. She liked her humour, her way of protecting Charlotte. Now, in the floating fruit gum lights and lasers of The Generator, her words echoed Joy and her firelight wisdom beside the lake in the sky. Charlotte kept confidences so she couldn't know about the dream – or could she?

86

'**B**romeliads,' Charlotte said, turning to Josie in the dank early spring garden.

Josie was delighted. 'Do you like them?'

'Love them,' Charlotte said. 'They look like some genius child's papier mâché creation. Before Teacher gets her hands on the imagination and dictates limits on what's possible.'

'I pinched this lot,' Josie said. 'The one unlawful act my grandmother sanctioned. She said nothing grows so well as something you pinch. I was embarrassed of course – every stately home and municipal garden, there was Granny, solid woollen bum in the air, snipping off bits and stuffing them into plastic bags in her handbag. These were in a lakeside arbour I made for Miss Rainier.'

'Who designed it?' Charlotte laughed. She would have liked to meet Fizz Rainier.

'She did,' Josie said. 'Well – her design was as vague and vivid as always. How did it go? *I was in South America, Josephine. Where they make love like angels. Possibly it's the climate. Do you imagine a little more sunshine might unleash the tweedy libido of the English Male? No matter. Even I will admit that octogenarianism precludes the likelihood of an affaire de coeur. I was staying in a marvellous villa in the mountains and, my dear, they had a garden I would cheerfully murder for! Lush foliage, a waterfall like an Escher lithograph, orchids growing like weeds, do you see? Of course, we can forget a lot of it, given the prevailing clime of Northumberland. I am a realist. But.*'

Josie giggled.

'Then she gave me that pleading twinkle that meant she was damn well going to have her way. Bring on the empty horses! I had to pretend to be severe and down to earth. I asked her to describe it in detail. She waved her hands around and said: *There was a columned area in the garden. Almost a temple only more abstract. Marvellous columns alive with mosses and plants, a sort of jungle with the added flair of an Ascot milliner. I think there's some good stone lying around. Roderigo – the landscape chap – was a master. I'll invite him here some time, you'd love to meet him. His genius stroke was to plant living antlers on the peak of each column. It was a pagan festival, russet, green, pink, rough as the flanks of Pan, stems smooth as young flesh. Don't ask for their name, Josephine, that's your department.*'

The ghost of Miss Rainier ruffled her hair. *Dear girl!* she said, *we had such fun!*

Josie smiled and dragged on her cigarette. 'Her only other instructions were called from the car window as she was driven to the airport. *Please, not bloody Greek or Italian! I have the utmost confidence in you! Put your foot down, man, I have a plane to catch. One of the Gang imagines that her time has come! Again! Best!*'

'Best what?' Charlotte laughed.

'Best,' Josie shrugged. 'She liked to use that instead of goodbye. Do your best? You're the best? All of that. I almost saluted as the Rolls crunched away. Then I was off to the library, ploughing through the botanical section and I decided she must mean bromeliads. They grow from bare stone, wet or dry, apparently living on fresh air. And she was right: there was some 'good stone' lying around, the debris from an eighteenth-century Rainier folly. The sort of thing a museum would go into debt for. I sketched and measured and brought in a branch of Jeff O'Hagan's empire to build it.'

She smiled and thought back. Jeff O'Hagan and his men had been sceptical.

'Are ye sure now?' That was the man himself, inspecting the result. 'It looks cock-eyed to me. Rough.'

'It's what Miss Rainier wants,' she'd told him.

'Say no more,' he said, getting into his BMW. 'We'll be pulling it to bits until her ladyship's happy with it, but she never minds paying.'

With the same cheerfulness, Jeff O'Hagan had undone all Miss Rainier's vision, following the orders given by the new people until their cashflow became a trickle. His men had carried the top stones and their rejected bromeliads into Josie's garden as they prepared to fill the lake.

'If there's anything else ye're after, give us a shout,' they said. 'Them buggers wants it all changed.'

Miss Rainier would turn in her grave if she could see it now.

Wrong, the ghost said. *What use is turning in one's grave? I've put a stop to it, that's all. And you didn't pinch them, Josephine, if you care for something that its owners neglect, it's yours.*

'Bromeliads,' Josie said. 'I've been racking my brains to think where they could go at the festival.'

'In the river?' Charlotte suggested. 'Could you sink columns for them – they need height.'

'Of course!' Josie said. 'Or I could just recreate Miss Rainier's arbour by the shore, maybe have one column in the tidal ooze. The Vikings are coming!'

Quite, Miss Rainier's ghost lent her approval.

They had fallen into a pattern of work: Charlotte spent her mornings stencilling the flags with coats of arms and names of merchants and pictures of their goods. She'd asked Caz about a budget, but Caz just laughed and said George was on their side and she could let rip.

Caz was painting a backdrop for the Viking ship and murals for the burnt-out cottage. Daisy had decided she was Twyla the Gopher and one day she would be combing Fenwick's and Bainbridge's for fabrics for Charlotte; the next would find her planting out with Josie, using her bionic hand as a trowel. Then she would help Caz with tins of paint and hold stencils in place. Anything, in fact.

'You're my right arm,' Caz said one day, then winced, but Daisy only laughed.

'My right's better than my left,' she said, 'as the actress said to the bishop. I love it. I can crush a full can of beer open with it, you know. I can do more now than before the bloody accident. But I'm not bloody sewing, Caz! That's my last word. I can't ruin me street cred.'

Afternoons Charlotte went through a gruelling physio routine and rested. Caz and Josie were at the site and Twyla the Gopher would join them, or go off on her own, exploring the many faces of Tyneside. The back streets of Miston with their threadbare junkshops, the funfairs and arcades on the coast: sunny days would find her in a park, watching the mothers and children in pushchairs and prams throwing bread at city-sleek ducks. Daisy had lived all her life in London and she couldn't get over how easy it was to get around in the north east: the buses ran on time, the metro was clean, crossing the river was easy. Pick a bridge, any bridge.

'It's like Newcastle was built for people,' she said. 'London must have been at one time, only they've forgotten that people live there. Forgotten or don't give a shit. You feel like you're some sort of raving loony anarchist cuz you want to get home after midnight without taking out a loan for a cab.'

Mainly, they spent evenings together: close knit in the Lovenest and The Generator. Sometimes they'd take a ride into the hills for a drink, a drive up the coast for fish and chips with a sea view.

'It's like being on holiday,' Daisy said, watching a ship surge towards the mouth of the Tyne, bright as a Christmas display waltzing past the twin lighthouses winking in the dark.

Caz grinned. 'That's why I live here,' she said. 'I'm good at holidays.'

Charlotte needed fewer painkillers these days. Only once had her spine convulsed in a blinding spasm of agony. Five minutes of 4 a.m. terror was nothing to her.

Caz basked in their company as they planned a dress-rehearsal party. The festival opened in a month's time.

87

'It's like the last stages of decorating,' Josie said. 'Like when we were doing your flat. Rooms all bare and painted, waiting for pictures and photos and furniture.'

'All those personal touches that make a house a home!' Caz squeezed her. 'It's wonderful, isn't it?'

They were on the site as the clear panels of the greenhouse were slotted into place. Kevin the Viking had spent the night assembling his ship: his greeting was a wild whoop.

'Waelwaegsdottir is about ready to have a bottle of something cracked across her bows,' Caz said. 'Champagne seems too modern and decadent. I can't see Erik the Red with a crystal flute in his gauntlet somehow.'

'Dragon's Blood,' Kevin said, pointing to an earthenware flagon on the ground.

'Dragon's Blood?' Caz looked at him.

'I made it myself,' he said. 'It's a real headbanger.'

'Can we wait for the foliage?' Josie asked him. 'The blokes with the greenhouse are just coming.'

'Of course,' Kevin said. 'Dragon's Blood has to be drunk when you can just lie down straight afterwards.'

'Now then, our Kevin,' Charlotte said, 'let's put this homebrew somewhere safe.'

'Here's one I made earlier,' Daisy murmured. 'Blue Peter for loony adults, this, Caz.'

'Ain't that the truth,' Caz was pleased. 'Come and help me

with the gazebo, duck, I've been saving the insides of toilet rolls and egg boxes all my life.'

They strolled away. Kevin blushed and decided to help Ted with the street signs. Dragons and dungeons, said Kevin, history and mystery, said Ted. Men's talk.

Sadie stood on a pile of stone like a Hollywood queen bidding her native land adieu for ever. A black swathed figurehead, she directed the Boys' painstaking construction of the temple.

'Bromeliads,' thought Sadie, tonguing the word. 'Maybe I should have a conservatory. The Geeks could build it.'

She blotted out the instant picture of Mr and Mrs Normal prospecting at a DIY megastore, exclaiming over clean-cut creations of glass and timber and sub-deco panels. Her conservatory would be gothic and gloomy, a steamy tangle where spiked succulents and fungi like deformed brains sweltered around her. A place where no one would be surprised to come across the mottled corpse of Mrs Bates or even the bones of her psychotic son Norman. Plants that drew their sap from flies drowned in small vats of siren-scented poison. Huge dull green leaves dripping with moisture, lukewarm drops gathering in stagnant puddles.

She had thrilled at the winter decay of the festival site, but the cheery garishness of spring left her feeling drained. Caz and her trio of Trolls bounced around like kids on holiday and she could find no enthusiasm for the maypole celebration of the carousel or any of Josie's absurdly healthy plants. All things bright and beautiful – it was turning into a Sunday school picnic. She toyed with the idea of the sunny months becoming her hibernation period. That meant reverting to complete nocturnalism and her need to see Caz was as powerful as an opiate. Sure, she could mock herself and Caz when she was alone. Her diaries sneered: *wide-eyed as a marigold, my little ray of sunshine, Jesus wants me for a sunbeam, the Banshee has become a butterfly* . . . Jeered phrases which crumbled to dust at the sight of her. Damn the woman for being so bright!

'Roughly!' she ordered. 'You're getting symmetrical – this isn't the bloody Home and Garden exhibition! Do it again!'

Daisy nudged Caz and jerked her head towards the voice.

'Still coming on like Rosa Klebb,' she said. 'I had a games mistress like Sadie. But the Boys like it. Christ! She gives me the creeps.'

'She is a games mistress,' Caz said. 'A mistress of games. I always start thinking of cosy tea and toast by the fire when she starts. Bunny slippers and hot water bottles.'

'You what?' Daisy looked back at Sadie. 'I think of Bluebeard.'

'I think mine's like the marshmallow man in *Ghostbusters*,' Caz said. 'Casting up everything soft and gentle and soppy like a barricade.'

'Well, you would,' Daisy said. 'Where I come from, Sadie'd have her lights put out in five minutes flat. Either that or she'd be running every backstairs massage parlour south of the river. I'm no prude, but I can't get my head round her stuff.'

'Oh, bugger Sadie!' Caz said. 'Or not. As you choose. I'm sure it's been done a thousand times. We have a gazebo to construct, my girl, there are *trompe-l'oeil* panels to place. I need your hands and eyes, Twyla. Your judgement. Your flair!'

'*All of me, why not take all of me?*' Daisy sang in a camp falsetto. '*Can't you see I'm crazy over you?*'

'*But you took the part that once was my heart,*' Caz scolded her.

'*So why not take all of me?*' Daisy finished, basso profundo. 'Hey, what about Caz and Daze? I'll do the piano.'

'Let's not give up the day job, Daisy,' Caz said.

Watching them laugh together, Charlotte wondered.

'Penny?' Josie said.

'Caz,' Charlotte turned to her. 'Sorry. I'm just having a little snuffle. I haven't seen her like this for years. This is the way she was around Ben, you know, bubbling with it all, nothing was impossible. They were like *wunderkinder* brilliant joyful kids, every day an adventure. It's nice to see she hasn't lost it.'

'Ben?' Josie said. 'Who's Ben?'

Charlotte looked straight at her. 'My God,' she said, 'you don't know, do you?'

'No,' Josie said. 'Maybe it's none of my business.'

'Balls to that, my dear,' Charlotte said, sitting on a deckchair. 'Would you pour me some coffee? Have a break. I knew Ben too, so Caz can't say it's a secret. I'm just gob-smacked she hasn't told you.'

Josie sat next to her and they sipped coffee.

'Give me a fag,' Charlotte said. 'I don't much but I will now. Who's Ben. I can't believe you know Caz and you don't know about Ben. My goodness.'

She smoked for a while then sat forward. 'Ben lived at Trimdon House like we all did. She and Caz were lovers, each other's one and only. Like me and David, only I think theirs would have lasted. Ben died in the fire. She and Caz were trying to get out and let go of each other's hands. Caz got out. Ben didn't. I didn't know until I came round and we started writing to each other. That was months later and there was piss all I could do. My spine was damaged and I couldn't move at all for – for bloody ever. Caz lived for Ben. Ben lived for Caz. What you saw in their eyes was this pure burning passion – it was magic. True love like – oh hell – like you see in the movies. Caz blames herself even though she's got no reason.'

'Poor Caz,' Josie said. 'I wish she'd told me. God I wish she'd told me, but what could I have said or done? I could have stopped teasing her about her nunnish lifestyle. Although I didn't do that much.'

'Teasing's no bad thing,' Charlotte said. 'In fact taking the piss, even being savage, can be excellent. I'd never have risen from my sickbed without Daisy's sarky mouth. I hadn't realised how much Caz hides. She never used to. It's as if she came up here and shut all the doors on the past.'

'No,' Josie said, 'she didn't. I mean, only the ones she had to.

And it's different now you're here. The only closed door is that one, and who can blame her?'

'Well, I'm going to Spanish Inquisition young Twyla,' Charlotte said firmly. 'Even if there's nothing in it, and Daisy's like a porcupine at bay when it comes to affairs of the heart. No, a good flirt does wonders in the way of healing.'

88

'To your left, you can see Longstone Lighthouse where Grace Darling and her family lived. The night she rowed through the storm with her father to rescue the crew of the Forfarshire gave her a place in history for her outstanding courage, but she didn't live long enough to enjoy it, and died at the age of twenty-six on October the 20th, 1842. We shall now proceed to the Inner Farnes where I hope we'll be able to show you some seals.'

The invisible captain of the Britannia crackled into silence and the engines roared into throaty life. It was early in the season so the boat was half-empty: a middle-aged couple in matching anoraks, a young couple sharing binoculars and a tartan blanket and Caz, Josie, Daisy and Charlotte on a day trip. Morning had found them stiff and jaded so they tore themselves from the festival site for a long overdue day off.

'The sea!' Caz said. 'Let's be tourists.'

The van rattled on to the quay at Seahouses fifteen minutes before the next sailing for the Farnes.

'Ice-cream and pop,' Josie said. 'I know it's freezing, but that's what tourists do.'

'Ice-cream,' Daisy concentrated on holding a wafer in her right hand.

Black waves washed at the scrub-tipped islands. Longstone Lighthouse shone briefly under a watery ray of sunshine, but the cliffs were weatherbeaten after a long winter, collapsed columns of rock with a slapdash whitewash of guano.

'People lived here?' Daisy shook her head. 'Not much of a life, was it? They didn't have phones then, did they? They didn't even have the telly.'

'Bloody southerners!' Caz mocked her. 'No one had the telly, Daisy. No electricity, dear. They used to get over to the mainland regularly, you know. That amazes me, reading about history: the seas were as busy as motorways. You got a boat to London even. Everything took longer. Letters not phonecalls.'

'It's what you get used to,' Josie said. 'If you don't have electricity, candlelight's normal. I read a thing about St Kilda – bang in the middle of the ocean. They had a whole different culture there – quite pagan to start with. Then the church moved in and expressed horror at them dancing naked on the shore and generally communing with nature. Crinolines and liberty bodices all round! They lived on puffins and fulmars and had tiny sheep – the size of collies, with sooty wool that you just combed off instead of shearing.'

'Oh, rural ocean-bound bliss!' Caz said. 'And Grace Darling is a footnote in history, a splendid tomb in a windy churchyard, a dozen portraits in a tiny museum at the hem of Bamburgh Castle.'

'Bit lyrical, Caz,' Daisy said. 'My gran says you're only dead when no one remembers you any more.'

How cheering, said the ghost of Miss Rainier, hovering over the waves. *Not strictly speaking true. One's spirit is never snuffed out, but it is a constant pleasure to be remembered fondly.*

The engines of the boat cut out and they rode the waves a dozen feet from the rocks. A troupe of seals bobbed up obligingly to have their photos taken. Some lounged like Roman emperors on wave-washed couches of rock and waved a flipper.

'It's like a gentleman's club,' Charlotte said. 'Morning, old boy, how's tricks? Can't grumble, dear chap. The fishin' is awfully damn good this season. Shame about the tourists gawpin' around the old family pile. Still, it pays the taxes.'

'Well, that one's a queen,' Caz said. 'Look at the elegant flip of the flipper, and the seductive twirl of the tail. Look at me, aren't I handsome?'

'There is a thriving colony of shags on your right,' said the commentator. 'Shags have a greenish bronze plumage and a crest which distinguishes them from cormorants.'

'Shag?' Daisy said. 'Bit basic, innit?'

'Shag,' Josie said. 'There's one, flying – over there!'

'A flying fuck,' Daisy roared with laughter. 'Like, I don't give a flying fuck? Just me sense of humour.'

Caz laughed. Ben and she had both liked playing with the nonsense of Rude Words. What do you call two burglars? A pair of (k)nickers. So adult.

'If it wasn't for bums and sex, we'd have nothing to laugh at,' she quoted. 'Hey, Charlotte, we'd better get you a new bum. Your old one's got a hole in it.'

Charlotte sniggered. 'Isn't it nice being grown up,' she said. 'No one can tell you off for talking dirty. Or leaving your crusts.'

'I tried telling that to my little sister,' Daisy said. 'Wait till you're grown up and you can do what you like.'

She cast her eyes to heaven. 'It was as much use as telling me at her age. Or now, come to that. You've got to live it and make your own mistakes before you realise your mum and your gran and your moany old aunties were bloody right, after all.'

'The price of eggs!' Josie bleated, wringing her hands. 'I remember when they were threepence a dozen and you young ones don't even know what a thru'penny bit looks like! And now I'm the one who remembers when you got half an ounce of tobacco for twenty p, four shillings old money and now it's nearly three flaming quid and I used to get that for a week's paper round.'

'Are we getting old?' Caz said softly. 'I remember, I remember? I'm not even angry about most things any more, they just seem so ludicrous. Political shenanigans – they have this *déjà vu* ring about them. Can't take it seriously.'

'Oh, I almost forgot,' Josie said, 'I had a phonecall yesterday. You know the street theatre and circus bits we've been looking for? Well, we've got The Panhaggerty Women's Morris Dancing Team. They rang from Chopwell and they sound amazing. They could do a show? – a morris? a dance? whatever – for us every Saturday morning throughout the festival.'

'Panhaggerty?' Caz asked. 'This is getting surreal.'

'It's a dish you make in a frying pan with layers of cheese and potato,' Josie said. 'Why are they named after it? Don't ask!'

'Out of the frying pan?' Caz mused. 'Book them, Josephine!'

'I already did,' Josie said. 'They're the first and only women's Morris team. I couldn't resist it!'

89

When Caz woke, she knew her dreams had taken her back to the shore of the lake, under a sky promising dawn or nightfall. She closed her eyes to drift there for a few moments longer. But she felt restless, even sad, as the details of her dream came clear.

Yes, she had been there when she thought it was lost to her, but this time she'd been pacing the shore, anxious, impatient, waiting for someone. She was sure that they weren't coming, but equally sure that the moment she gave up and left, they'd be there and she'd have missed them for ever. She backed away from the water's edge as the light grew stronger: it was dawn and she had the gut feeling that it was too late. She'd started running over the grass, running away towards the Hole, looking back, pausing, stopping to rake her eyes all over the empty landscape. Nervously closing her eyes and giving it a count of ten, fifteen, crossing her fingers like a child willing away ill fortune, wishing for magic. Still no one came. She wasn't at all clear who she was waiting for, even.

Now that she was fully awake she could find no memory of the ritual of climbing up the hidden ladder, or her heart racing with anticipation as she pushed aside the wooden cover. It was as if she'd simply been dumped there and her waking body felt numb with a lack of remembered feeling: the land in the sky had always been so vivid. The resilient grass and its green smell, the chill breeze from the lake, the bird cries, the shifting clouds: they were living things but this time, it was as if she'd seen it all on a cinema screen. Flat and hasty, like the view through a train window on a dull day. As if she'd been detached, walking above the grass, like a ghost haunting a house where the floor levels have been changed, and still she makes her nightly trek on the invisible boards of used to be. Yes, that was it: if she'd bent to touch the grass, her fingers would have slipped through the blades, and stayed dry even in the dew or the waters of the lake. Somehow she had slipped out of time with the land in the sky.

She'd wanted to see Joy, and Joy wasn't there: had she been waiting for her so that the longing forced the dream, making the magical land no more than a backdrop for their meeting?

Why had she wanted to see Joy? Clarity? Resolution? Absolution? In the limbo between dream-sleep and daylight she knew it was all three and more: she wanted answers only Joy could give. Answers to questions she didn't even know how to phrase. Didn't know or didn't dare? Joy wouldn't need to hear questions to tell her everything: Joy could read her whole being without a word.

Maybe it was a flashback. Caz had a deep-ingrained mental habit of looking for stumbling blocks and tripwires when there weren't any. Two, twenty, even two hundred people could tell her a picture was marvellous and complete and still she'd hover beside it, fretting. When life was good and flowed sure as a river she was afraid of unseen currents, sudden bends and dangerous white water. After all, everything was going her way. It was a beautiful morning. There was a bright golden haze on the tree tops, a bright golden haze in the valley. New leaves uncurled in front of her eyes all along the cherry branches. A little brown sparrow dipped and preened, a cheeky swagger in its song.

Tomorrow was the party before the festival and everyone was coming. Faff and fuss as she might, there was nothing else to be done. Maybe she'd just wanted Joy's seal of approval . . .?

Well, she could have a last-minute panic about clothes.

The idea took her to Miston High Road and as she mooched, she wanted to tell everyone about the festival, see her enthusiasm mirrored in their faces, share it, wear it, stand on a soapbox and gather pennies in a cap as she raved.

Oyez! Oyez! Oyez! A scarlet livery of Dickensian splendour and a bell to ring to gather the crowds! Hear ye, hear ye, hear ye: I'm here and we've done it, alleluia! Now, where on Miston High Road could she find a frogged and gilt-buttoned greatcoat to match her mood? Maybe she'd mooch along Delaval Avenue, the street of a thousand junkshops, comb the bric-à-brac backrooms of Wyndytop Place, gleaning dusty treasures from Bedknobs and Broomsticks and Aladdin's Cave.

But it was Thursday and the windows of every second-hand emporium were boarded and wired for protection. Bedknobs and Broomsticks hadn't bothered to flip over the OPEN sign hanging above the letterbox. If you stood inside the unlit shop, the street outside would be CLOSED.

She dithered between going home and taking a bus to town. She decided to take the scenic route home and change before meeting the others in The Frog and Nightgown for a pre-party bracer. They'd adopted the pub because of the name, its red plush velvet and golden anaglyptaed ordinariness belonged on Any Street, Any Town, England, nineteen ninety-something.

Bedknobs and Broomsticks was on a corner halfway down Wyndytop Place and when she stood back from trying to see inside, she noticed that the other dusty window belonged to Pendragon Street. She pictured a fierce old lady novelist rattling wild tales across yellowing paper with a dark-nibbed claw of a pen. Ethel Pendragon, thirteen Pendragon Street, eccentric and recluse, white hair streaked with nicotine, smoke turning one eye scarlet behind raddled nets in a bay window. Her novelist's view of the world tarnished by groundsel and thistles head-butting the windowsill; her rusty gate tethered open by sinewed dandelions as big as swamp lilies. Ethel would stump along the pavement after dark to scrabble coins from a flat purse and exchange them for a restorative bottle of gin, waving a stick and muttering at lamp-posts. A mad forgotten great-aunt . . .

Don't go near number thirteen, children, she's a witch!

Caz grinned. She'd have to check it out. She had never walked along this street before and a dilly dallying exploration would do very well to chip away some more bits of anxious waiting time. Caz: a professional moocher.

90

The garden at number thirteen was four tubs of French marigolds and the door was buttercup yellow. There was a mobile in the bay window: Bo-Peep in pink and white gingham and seven sheep fluffy as summer clouds. Most of the street was fresh as paint, and there wasn't a whiff of gin-sodden ancient literateuse until Caz reached number seventy-seven. Both sevens hung sideways weeping rust on to the peeling olive-green door. The wall was collapsed on a crop of thistles and bindweed that any night-hag would be proud of. A faded FOR SALE sign had fallen into the leafy clutches of neglect and lay in a pale green embrace. Cracks scarred every window and the chimney wore a plume of purple buddleia. The melancholy spirit of Ethel Pendragon hovered around yellowing envelopes stuffed in the gap-tooth letterbox.

Caz wondered if the number of a house affected its character: the maverick thirteen was obvious and anyone living there would keep a weather eye for rot, be it wet or dry, and develop a sixth sense about sinister cracks in the structure. Seventy-seven Pendragon Street was abandoned and no one would be surprised to wake up one day and find it had simply collapsed into rubble. Come to that, her own flat had been on the skids when she took it over. Maybe the next owners of this sad shell would revamp it into a thing of living beauty. Given the recession, it would go for a song: 'in need of modernisation' as the optimistic estate agent's jargon might read.

Well, this is first class mooching, she told herself, buying a house now, are we? A shame they don't take bottle tops these days.

Caz liked the idea of choosing exactly where you live, but for the moment, given the circs of an income as reliable as an ancient rollercoaster, she was happy with her lifetime tenancy of Galleon Heights. That was more permanency than she'd ever dreamed of. Bricks and mortar the mortgage way felt like a ball and chain: with monthly payments or repossession hanging over her, how could she take off for her world cruise? Just in case she wanted to.

She reached a T junction and dithered. Left or right would be an uncharted loop along Jellicoe Terrace: left looked slightly longer, so she took it. Using left and right alternately made a zig-zag of terraces: Ingoe Place, Polinaize Bank, Staynebrigg Chare and then a wide road of Victorian opulence called the Sheriff's Highway. Houses big enough for maids in the attic and family retainers below stairs and a dozen children: so big that these days they were sliced into flats or offices, to let, to let, to let again.

Except for one, number thirty-seven, painted white like a brick of ice-cream, criss-crossed with trellises swirling with vines and clematis, studded with Mediterranean plaques of fishermen and dolphins. Close to, she saw that the brilliant flowerbeds in the garden held plastic blooms alongside real; three jaunty gnomes were fishing in a mirror and the figurehead of a ship was planted in an arbour of psychedelic pink wisteria, with a bunch of silk roses against her ample pink bosom.

The plaque by the door read MADAME JOY: CLAIRVOYANT.

Caz's skin prickled: the street seemed suddenly quiet and empty, and time stood still. No cars, no children or dogs, every window blank, not even a breeze to stir the trees. Only the riot of garish tat was real – like the sudden burst of Technicolor in *The Wizard of Oz* when the twister has torn Dorothy from monochrome Kansas to land her somewhere over the rainbow.

She walked up the garden path and rang the brass doorbell. A woman in a flowered overall opened the door, clutching a duster.

'Ee, you give us a turn, pet,' she said. 'Did you ring the bell? Only it doesn't work, you see, I was just coming out to do the brasses.'

'Yeah, I rang the bell,' Caz said. Somehow she couldn't see this bright and busy woman as Madame Joy.

'Well, she's in,' the woman said doubtfully. 'Have you got an appointment? Madame Joy doesn't usually do Thursdays.'

'Oh well,' Caz said, ready to leave.

'But I can ask her for you,' the woman said. 'You never know your luck. Just wait a minute.'

She went back into the house and Caz looked along the hallway. Madame Joy had a taste for the gothic: the hall went on for ever, its walls lined with gilt hands holding orbs of light. Twin chandeliers gave the impression of a ballroom. No, it was one chandelier and there was a mirror at the end of the passage. What Caz had taken for a statue was herself in near silhouette. The carpet was damask pink with black stylised arrows leading into the house – walk this way? Somehow the arrows led into the reflection without a break. She was intrigued.

The bright breezy woman came out of a door next to the mirror and smiled at Caz. 'Well, pet,' she said, 'the angels are looking after you today! I'm to get you a cup of tea and Madame Joy will see you in twenty minutes. Come and have a sit down in here.'

Caz guessed she was in a waiting room from the number of seats and a tatty pile of magazines on a coffee table in the middle of the room. A wide electric blue sofa went along one wall and she picked up a *Woman's Own* from June 1986 and sat down. A wooden fireplace dominated the space, with a vase of dried flowers in all shades of flame standing in the grate. The walls were covered with pictures: a bizarre mix of cutesy bunnies and puppies and kittens and beautiful photographs bearing comforting adages in the style of Patience Strong. *The darkest hour is just before dawn. I love you because you understand. Do not be afraid of what you love, be afraid of not loving*: that was two rumpled bulldog puppies looking helpless, adorable and puzzled.

'Oh dear,' thought Caz, noticing a three-dimensional picture of 'The Last Supper', 'religion I don't need.'

But then she saw a reassuring gallery of children's pictures and faded photos. A statue of Krishna, an ashtray that was a present from Malta, a boomerang, a bullfighting poster proclaiming Madame Joy's prowess in Seville, a Japanese courtesan contemplating one bare nipple. To confuse her utterly, there was a lifesize velvet flag of Elvis Presley in startling white hanging over the mantelpiece, with glittering jewels on every cuff and lapel.

Madame Joy was certainly eclectic. How could you describe the room – early wedding cake, Samarkand bazaar – bizarre? – nursery school, Hollywood back lot? If these were props then what on earth was the play? She closed her eyes and when she opened them, Elvis the King caught her eye, with the cheeky grin of assured genius. Elvis and the velvet folds of baby bulldog wisdom. *Do not be afraid of what you love, be afraid of not loving*.

Caz had been to a fortune teller just before she left London. He wore a silk cravat fastened with a ring that looked like it had come out of a Christmas cracker, and he read her life from a dozen or so Tarot packs. He told her she was looking for love and would soon find it; he said she would be moving, he told her that her heart was too soft and open. All very general and since it had taken her six months to get up the nerve to go and see him, she was disappointed. He was nice enough, but his silky fingers flicked the cards as softly as his voice and it felt like visiting a cosy old auntie who half listens, half agrees and makes comforting noises. A pastel interlude. She wanted someone as primary and abrasive as Fizz Rainier and she had the feeling that Madame Joy could at best, offer a bright enthusiastic muddle.

Still, it would be interesting.

'adame Joy will see you now. You can bring your tea if you're not done, pet.'

The cleaning lady led her down the corridor and she caught her own look as they reached the mirror. It was what the *Newcastle Thunderer* had described as lofty and fierce. It was her armour.

Madame Joy sat behind a desk in a bay window. Clever, thought Caz, put yourself in imposing silhouette. The door clicked softly behind her.

'Sit yourself down,' said Madame Joy.

There was only one chair and it was directly in front of the desk. Caz sat and crossed her legs. OK, Madame Joy, Clairvoyant, impress me! She met her eyes and was startled by the cheerful impudence of a naughty child. They were a vivid blue, kind eyes, eyes that see everything in a twinkling. Caz steeled herself against the challenge, determined to give nothing away.

'Have a shuffle of these,' said Madame Joy, handing her a set of Tarot cards. The Major Arcana.

'I don't really know why I'm here,' Caz said, suddenly depressed: Tarot cards again. And the walls of the room covered with look-for-the-silver-lining mottos; Elvis Presley again, the King in a dozen hip-thrust poses alongside the Virgin Mary, lacy fans from Spain, brass tongs from Tunisia. It was as arbitrary as the junk in Bedknobs and Broomsticks, ten minutes' walk away.

'Give me the cards,' said Madame Joy briskly, 'and suppose you just keep quiet and listen to me. You're paying to listen to me, you can get the sound of your own voice any time. There'll be a reason you're here.'

She laid the cards out as she spoke, nodding a couple of times.

'Well, I got told,' Caz thought and leant back in her chair.

'Well, there's no fellas round you, is there?' Madame Joy smiled. 'Not what you'd call close, it's all women with you. No, I cannot see a fella at all.'

'I've got male friends,' Caz said.

'We're not talking about that, *are we?*' Madame Joy looked right inside her. 'Ee, lass, there's been rivers of tears in your life. For about six years. You've been crying inside and it's all *I am the great I am* when you're out, isn't it?'

'I suppose,' Caz said. It could be a lucky guess.

'I know,' said Madame Joy, 'I'm telling you. Just listen. You're right mouthy when you start, I'd not like to be on the rough side of your tongue. You're just as hard on yourself, mind. You're working, aren't you? I cannot figure it out, me. You've got a paintbrush in your hand, sometimes it's like decorating, but mainly it's pictures. Beautiful. You're a very talented lass and you don't know it. It's the best way to be. But you're doing an awful lot of faffing around too. You're driving, you've got a hammer and all sorts of tools, you're digging and having a high old time with the drink and dancing. Parties every night and about time too. You've been on your own too long a time. You thought it was for ever, didn't you?'

Caz nodded, feeling tears on the edge of her eyes.

'And then there's gardens,' Madame Joy looked over Caz's left shoulder and nodded. 'Beautiful plants, like something out of a botanical garden. You surround yourself with beauty. It comes from inside. And who's – Fizz? That's the name I'm getting.'

Caz was astonished. 'Fizz Rainier,' she said. 'She's dead.'

'I know she's dead,' Madame Joy said, smiling patiently, 'she's here. She's telling me about a friend of yours, a lass Josie who does gardening? You work with her?'

Caz nodded.

'Well, whatever you're working on will be fine,' Madame Joy said. 'It's more fun than you thought you'd a right to. You and your friend Josie are too serious by half most of the time, she says, this Fizz. She's holding a glass of champagne up, like toasting the pair of you.'

'That's amazing,' Caz said. 'What does she look like?'

'Geet ould fashioned,' Madame Joy smiled, 'like something off one of those period plays on the telly, she's a very elegant lady. She was a right bugger in this world, but she always had a good heart. She was very rich but she knew that means nothing well before she passed over. She says she's proud of you both. Josie's like a daughter to her and you're the friend who looks after her. You're not from around here, are you? I feel London. Ah hah. It'll be Fizz Rainier brought you up here: she's been in the spirit world for just over five years. She was frightened that Josie couldn't manage on her own. Josie needs a foot up her arse. That's what you're here for.'

'Well, I did come up here five years ago,' Caz said.

'That's what I'm telling you,' the blue eyes searched her face. 'And now you've gone and done it again, haven't you? Little Orphan Annie, you think you count for nothing with a word, you. It was you she brought here to do the job and you've done it well. But Josie'll be going abroad later this year – something to do with gardening. Don't! You're not the lass the world forgot, you know. You'll be all right.'

Again she looked over Caz's left shoulder.

'Has there never been a fella?' she said suddenly. 'I'm getting someone you loved a lot who worshipped the ground you walked on. Ben?'

Caz went cold.

'Ben,' said Madame Joy. 'Died in a fire, I'm being told, and you blame yourself. Ben's saying you shouldn't, there was nothing you could have done. But this Ben was a lass.'

Tears flowed down Caz's cheeks. Hot salt tears she'd never dreamt she could shed.

'Ben was a woman,' she said. 'Bernadette, but no one called her that. How do you know?'

'She's here telling me, lass. Have a bit weep,' said Madame Joy, handing her a tissue from an inlaid box which read Tears Wash The Hurt Away. 'You've never stopped loving her, have you. And you've never told anyone much about her either. Well, she says it's time to cry until you're all cried out and then you can start smiling again from inside of yourself. She says she lost your hand in the smoke but she saw you fighting to get back in to save her. She was gone by then, though, it wouldn't have been any use.'

'Oh, Christ,' Caz said.

'It's Ben who's brought you here to see me, my love,' Madame Joy said. 'It's time to start healing. And this I don't understand. Often enough someone from the spirit world will come with a gift for their loved ones. A freesia for love, a golden key for wisdom, a bonnet for a new baby. But Ben's standing there holding an armful of flowers and she keeps picking out a marguerite to give you.'

'A marguerite?' Caz said.

'Yes. Just like a geet big daisy. She's got – like, a beautiful rosebush beside her, lovely old fashioned blooms, and that's for the love that bloomed between you and her. That's your past. But your future is this marguerite. Does that make sense to you? She says she's bringing someone new into your life. Maybe a Margaret? No, I cannot get the sense of it. But you should see her smile and her geet bonny eyes!'

'I don't know,' Caz said, 'I've sort of given up on romance and all that jazz.'

'No one can live alone,' said Madame Joy. 'Oh, you can wing it, you can fake it and wall yourself up in an ivory tower, but your eyes are forever on the gates and the road to see who's coming to light up your loneliness. *I know.* And there's someone coming for you. Ben's telling you it would be all right. True love cannot die but there has to be an end to mourning. Time you unwrapped the black ribbons from your heart and let the poor thing breathe again.'

Caz looked into the willow-pattern glow of her eyes and got the same wonderful feeling she had when Joy in the sky spoke with her. It was like having a mother who likes you: someone who knows everything about you, even the worst bits, things you lie about for fear of people not liking you: everything. Someone who makes no judgements at all. Who tells you the truth and wishes you nothing but good.

'Is there anything you want to ask me?' Madame Joy's blue eyes were deep as lapis lazuli.

'I don't know,' Caz said. 'There'll be a million things the minute I leave. I'm just – knocked out.'

Madame Joy laughed. 'You take care,' she said. 'You've got Ben and Fizz Rainier looking after you. Come back any time and see me and tell me how it all works out. Love go with you.'

Caz was out in the street and it felt like a hundred years later. The sun was blazing off every surface and she felt as if she could run all the way to the coast and do cartwheels right across the ocean.

92

Back at the flat, Caz clipped a spotlight on the frame and looked in the mirror. She could see the shadow of a line above her eyebrow, echoed in another line from her left nostril to the corner of her mouth. The legacy of the quizzical, half-smiling mask she'd been wearing for years. As her face relaxed, she felt her shoulders go soft and start a wholly pleasant ache like blood flowing free after being trapped. There was even a guarded sparkle in her eyes and she smiled at herself, shy, like a child who desperately wants you to like her.

Be gentle with me, her eyes said, poised to flicker back to the safety of distant self-mocking.

'Gentle? I'll spoil you rotten,' she promised aloud.

As always she saw Ben beside her, only this time she dared to picture her face and Ben was smiling too, daring her to laugh and get down, get fine, and get out there. She had about an hour to go before meeting Charlotte and Josie and Daisy.

And Daisy? Hell, was it possible to blush and look away from your own reflection?

It was. She felt her heart beating and a fizzy curiosity surging through her. Fizzy, *fizzy*! Hmm. She opened her wardrobe and untied a dustbin bag of clothes she hadn't even thought of for a long time. In and out of five outfits and back to her habitual black, she sat again in front of the mirror rolling a cigarette as her palms sweated. Every word Madame Joy had spoken was clear in her mind.

She stood up and deliberately pulled her sweatshirt off, dumping it and her jeans in the Ali Baba washing basket. She stood naked and took a polaroid of Ben from the top drawer. Yes, their love was an eternal rose and she stuck the photo in the corner of the mirror. She smiled. Ben smiled back.

As surely as if scripted and rehearsed, she poured a glass of wine, put on the Pointer Sisters – *I'm so excited and I just can't hide it!* – and dressed with a hypnotised confidence, the disco beat colonising her whole body. Get *down!*

The bus pulled up to the stop just as she got there and the roads were clear over The Drop and all the way to town. She strolled into The Frog and Nightgown as if she was walking on stage.

'My, my, Caz! That's wonderful! Have you been shopping?' Josie took in her highwayman's hat, pirate's shirt and boots and the razzmatazz of her gypsy waistcoat.

'Oh, these old things?' Caz threw the words out with a show of ennui. 'I've had them for ages.'

'She has,' Charlotte said. 'What's the occasion?'

'Pre-festival nerves – what are you drinking?' Caz said, not daring to look at Daisy.

A flashbulb popped.

'Gotcha!' Daisy said. 'I like the drag. Pint for me if you're buying.'

'I am,' Caz said, feeling dashing and gallant. She darted a glance towards Daisy and smiled briefly. I'm no good at this, she thought, and what if I've got it wrong? Ben might send you a margeurite-daisy, this might be *the* Daisy, but what if she doesn't know about it? Or what if this Daisy doesn't feel the same way? The brakes were off, but she wished someone else was driving – Madame Joy?

'Do you think they've noticed the *love thang*?' Charlotte murmured to Josie from where they sat.

'I've never seen Caz look so amazing,' Josie said. 'It's obvious to me and you. Daisy's face lit up like Santa's grotto the minute she walked in the joint.'

'And Caz is doing the mile a minute I don't care chat,' Charlotte said. 'Did you see – she blushed when she asked Daisy if she wanted a drink. Oh, I feel like a matchmaker! Only I don't have a lot of experience.'

'Well, we're either chaperones or wallflowers, you and I,' Josie said. 'A twentieth-century chaperone should disappear discreetly up her own rectitude, but what on earth does a wallflower do?'

'You're the gardener,' Charlotte said. 'Personally speaking myself, I think they haven't noticed. All we can do is act naturally. Caz doesn't need more than a thread of third party innuendo to put the barriers up again.'

'It would be nice,' Josie said, 'especially after that phonecall today. I'd feel I was abandoning her.'

'She'll be happy for you,' Charlotte said, 'happy for both of us. Watch out, they're coming back.'

'It'll be mega,' said Josie loudly, as Caz and Daisy came back from the bar. 'The party tomorrow, we were talking about. What do you think?'

'Here's to it,' Caz said, clinking glasses.

'So what have you been up to today? Who is this international woman of mystery?' Daisy asked her. 'I missed you.'

'I got my fortune told,' Caz said. *She missed me!* Why couldn't I say something straightforward and simple like that?

'And?' Daisy challenged her. 'Come on, Mona Lisa, crack the painted enigmatic smile. You can't just leave it there!'

'No, I can't, can I?' Caz nodded. 'Yes. Well. I was walking down the street – like you do – quite a lot of streets actually. Anyway, this street. This house. This sign: Madame Joy, Clairvoyant. So I went in and got a reading. Like you do.'

'And? This is like getting blood out of a stone,' Daisy said.

'Well, I'm shy,' Caz said.

'You're among friends,' said Charlotte. 'We all love you, girl. Now GIVE!'

Daisy patted her knee and Caz found herself squeezing her

hand. *We all love you* – it was true. Then she was just holding Daisy's hand with wonder that its warmth stayed there while she spoke.

'I'm a cynic,' she said, 'which is just a disappointed optimist. Only this Madame Joy is the biz. She knew my life. All of it. No kidding. Names, places, people – alive and dead – she knew the lot. I felt a million times lighter when I came away. You know I've always been afraid of dying in my sleep, every day a shock, a surprise, good days a bonus – you know. She's made me feel peaceful somehow. It sounds daft, but now I know there's a future out there and it's got my name written on it.'

Charlotte sat back, relieved. Caz's voice was soft and confident, a tone she hadn't heard since coming to Newcastle. A lightness, a cheekiness, where at first there was a mannered courtesy scoring a space around her. Caz was really talking, not parrying from behind a shield.

'Maybe I should go and see her,' Daisy said. 'Did she have a crystal ball? What did she say?'

'Well, I didn't see a crystal ball,' Caz said, 'but she had these incredible eyes. She can see right inside you. Madame Joy! She brings you joy, just talking. She made me set out some Tarot cards but she didn't look at them hardly. She was talking to Fizz Rainier.'

'Good God,' Josie said. 'How did you know it was really her?'

'She told me,' Caz said, 'Her name, what she looked like. What was it – she said Fizz Rainier was very elegant, like something off a period drama on the telly. Just like the photo you showed me.'

'Weren't you scared?' Josie said.

'No,' Caz said, 'anything but. It all seemed completely natural. She said Fizz wished us well and she was proud of us.'

'I think I'm going to cry,' Josie said. 'All the time we've been doing this project I've felt her around me, and she was such a taskmaster, it's made me really push myself. I'd better go and see Madame Joy.'

'So you've got a future, Caz,' Charlotte said. 'I suppose it's too much to hope you'll tell us what it is?'

'Get your own future!' Caz said, laughing. 'I'm telling you nothing!'

'The artist is not at home,' Daisy said. 'I know that steel trap of a mouth. You'll have to be well pissed before we get the rest, Caz. Sod you! We're not interested.'

She squeezed Caz's hand and giggled.

'Anyway,' she said to Charlotte, 'what are you looking cat that got the cream for, Betty? I'll set me granny Twyla on you if you go all secretive too.'

'We got a phonecall today,' Josie said. 'Beardy Michael.'

'He's fallen in love with you,' Daisy said. 'Can I be bridesmaid?'

'Balls,' Josie said. 'No. He wants me and Charlotte to go to Berlin to help him with the Unity Park. He said he felt bad about not asking all of us, but . . .'

'I know,' Caz said, 'Madame Joy said you'd be going abroad, something to do with gardening.'

'She can't have!' Josie said. 'He only rang two hours ago. Oh, God, I was afraid of telling you, Caz.'

'Don't be daft,' Caz said, 'we're not Siamese twins. I mean, I love you to bits, but I've got the feeling my place is here. Miston. Newcastle. Me and Daisy can mind the shop while you go gallivanting.'

'Yeah,' Daisy said, 'you need a bit of muscle, Caz.'

'My hero!' said Caz. 'It's your round, Josie. Come on, I'll give you a hand.'

'You see?' Charlotte said to Daisy as soon as they'd gone. 'You don't have to piss off back to London. Caz wants you to stay here.'

'Oh, that's just polite,' Daisy said. 'Nah. You and Josie are all set up for international fame, Caz'll go back to painting and – what the hell do I do? I mean, this has been fun. Really fun. I've never done anything like this before, but I don't expect Caz to go on dreaming up Noddy jobs for me. I'll find something, but it'll be London. That's my gaff.'

'You're wrong,' Charlotte said. 'Caz needs looking after. I never thought of it that way before, but we have to take care of each other. That's what friends do.'

'Caz doesn't need anyone,' Daisy said, blowing smoke. 'Anyway, Betty, I don't know if I could hack it, being just good friends with Caz.'

'Is that a blush?' Charlotte said.

'All right,' Daisy said quietly. 'Don't say a word, Betty, but I think I'm falling head over heels. Probably fallen. All right? I've always said I must be bent, it always went wrong with blokes, but I never met a woman to feel like this about before. And how the hell do you tell someone like Caz? She never even thinks about love, Betty, we've been here four months and aside from that prat Sadie and her bullwhip bullshit crap in the nightclub, there's never been a word about love, romance or even basic sex. Caz is one of those artistic types, it's all in her head. Married to her work. I'm not going to blow a friendship and get a polite thanks but no thanks. A girl has her pride. Anyway, there's my arm. Well, there isn't. You should bloody know. It knocks you, that. You know, would she be all nice because she felt sorry for me? Leave me out.'

'I think you're wrong,' Charlotte said. 'She was very hurt, you know.'

'Leave it,' Daisy said. 'I've picked up bits but it's none of my business unless she wants to tell me. I might just do a bit of a flirt, see what happens. But I don't need any back-up, right? None of this my friend fancies you number, OK?'

'OK,' Charlotte said. 'I'll just watch and hold up score cards from time to time. Subtle, like. Talk to Josie, see what she thinks.'

'I might at that,' Daisy said. 'Beats trying to talk to Caz. Christ! Sarf London gob goes silent – could this be Love?'

Much later on in The Generator, Charlotte and Josie swapped notes while Caz and Daisy danced under the rainbow lights and strobes. Disco-danced, then slow-danced, smiling then drawing apart.

'I'm fed up with being a wallflower,' Charlotte said. 'I could knock their heads together.'

'No,' Josie said. 'Wallflowers provide a very pleasing backdrop. And I have a date with Daisy tomorrow in the greenhouse.'

'Tell me!'

'Well now,' Josie said, 'it's like this . . .'

93

The day dawned grey and drizzly, but so what, said Caz, this near the coast, it never lasts.

Sure enough by eleven o'clock, a no-nonsense wind ushered the clouds out to sea. When they arrived at Dreamchare, sunlight burned the raindrops from the mosaic paths, flashing off the golden chips that made dolphin's eyes and mermaid's scales under their feet.

The burnt-out cottage was alive with flowers like flames, dazzling an autumn richness against the vines and curls of bright green leaves. The waters of the Tyne slipped silver and grey behind Miss Rainier's grotto and its primeval bromeliad antlers. Michael and George picked their way over stepping stones in the spring green lawn sculpted into the contours of a face gazing peacefully up at the heavens.

'Truly magical,' George said. 'The TV crew will be arriving soon – could you manage a bit of a chat?'

'With your help, of course,' Caz said, amused at his pompous delight.

'Why, certainly,' said he, clasping his hands behind his back. 'And there'll be quite a spin-off in terms of future projects, you know. One is torn between sitting on one's laurels and the uneasy flatness of accomplishment. Which can be dispelled only by thinking – what next?'

'Yes,' Caz said, astonished that he – of all people! – knew.

'Of course, Michael's borrowing Josie for a while,' he said hesitantly, 'and your flag-making friend.'

'I wanted to commission all of you,' Michael said, 'but even the Eurocrats have a ceiling to their budget. But who knows? If I corner the international market, we'll all be in clover!'

'It's wonderful,' Caz said. She hadn't credited either of them with this kind of sensitivity. 'I'm thrilled for Josie – and Charlotte. But I'll be around sunny Tyneside for a good long time, and I think Daisy will too. Give us a nice muriel, George, do, and we'll knock you for six.'

Daisy smiled and caught Josie's eye. She slipped away as the TV North East van arrived.

Ted appeared with a dumpy grey woman on his arm. 'Me mam,' he said proudly.

'Ee, has he been behaving himself?' Ted's mum shook her head. 'His dad was a great one for do it yourself. Always down in the shed making things, wasn't he, Dad? Aye. Well, give us the guided tour, Teddy, I've got me camera.'

Ted's forty years of Inland Revenue officialdom melted away as he showed his mum his beloved signs and he was as proud as a five year old on parents' evening at school.

And then came Kevin's custom-painted Transit – the chariot of Asgard, he called it. He opened the back doors – splitting a cartoon Thor's ferocious grin in half – and helped his precious passengers to the ground. Pearl, his nanna, and his mother Maudie, all done up like it was Easter Sunday. And Carrie and Rose in brilliant flowered silk. Divent get us another taxi, Caz, save yersel the fare, pet!

'Ee, there's the telly, Carrie!' Rose said, waving her arm. Carrie gave a regal nod and nudged her.

'That's wor bench, Rose,' she said. 'Come and try it for size.'

'Carrie!' Caz said. 'What do you think?'

'Well, it's very nice,' Carrie said. 'Ye'll have to do something about that roundabout, though.'

'Gawd!' Caz said. 'What's wrong with the roundabout, Mrs Ives, ma'am?'

'Well, it's not switched on,' Carrie said. 'Mind you, when it is, I'm having the first ride, else there'll be war, mind.'

'Don't you start,' Caz said. 'Rose, can't you make her behave?'

'I wouldn't have the nerve, pet,' Rose said. 'She's an aggravating divil, wor Carrie.'

'I'm having the first ride,' Carrie said serenely. 'And I'm having as many rides as I want, just like I always wished for when I was a bairn. I'll stay on that horse till I've got saddle sores, so I will!'

'Pet,' Pearl said, 'yez two are Josie and Caz, isn't it? Aye. I'm reet pleased wi what ye've done for our Kevin. He's sensitive, ye see, and not everyone can have the patience wi him. Come and have your photo took – yez two and Maudie – that's his mum, and me and me laddo himself. Up beside his daft boat, mind, he's done it lovely, hasn't he?'

'Mam!' said Kevin, blushing.

'Well, ye have,' Maudie patted his arm. 'Pipe us aboard, son, or whatever yer daft Vikings used to do.'

'Isn't it fabulous?' Josie said. 'We did it!'

'We did, didn't we?' Caz turned slowly to take it all in. 'All of us.'

Yes, you did, the ghost of Miss Rainier drifted beside them. *It's better than I could have imagined or hoped for.*

Does she know everything's going to be all right from now on? Ben's ghost hovered beside her, caressing Caz's face, drinking in her smile.

She will, Miss Rainier twinkled, *now that you've made contact. Thank God for the channel of Madame Joy! Caz is beginning to realise she will never have to live without you. And it's the same for you, Ben, you can start your spirit life now.*

Let's fly, Ben said. *I can't get over being able to have a bird's eye view any time I choose.*

And that's only the beginning!

The wild and restless spirit of Miss Rainier soared over the greenhouse, Ben with her, casting their blessing, celebrating the scene. And with them danced the spirits of everyone whose life was filled with love for gardens, for festivals, for life. The eighteenth-century propriety of Batty Langley approved every vista. King Sennacherib of Nineveh strolled around the spaceship greenhouse, marvelling at the miracle of glass. *Look*, he said, *the air has walls!* Vita Sackville-West tipped her hat to Caz and Josie: the islands of flowers pleased her; one colour, a spectrum of shapes and textures. Where there was white, there were *boule de neige* roses, sleek rays of marguerite, butterfly scented sweet peas. *And so much passion yet to come*, she murmured. *Enjoy!*

Sadie had engaged the Geeks in a conference every night of the last week. It was murder trying to get them to express an opinion, but she'd finally convinced them that it was her Wish.

'You are off the leash, figuratively speaking,' she told them. 'You are to contrive our celebration for this party.'

They'd come up trumps and travelled to the site by way of a black stretch limousine with smoked windows.

'That has to be Sadie,' Josie said. 'It's as close to a hearse as you can get! Hold your hats! It's Munster time!'

But the neo-hearse disgorged a raggle-taggle crew bright as medieval players. The Boys with rainbow mohicans like parrots, for plumage they'd found folds of brocade and scarlet silk like Shakespearian trollops – over their DMs. Of course. The skip-diving splendour of pantomime drag. They carried juggling clubs, fire-eaters' batons and pitchblende hoops to set alight and leap through.

Sadie swaggered behind them, her habitual black jazzed up with a vermilion boa and fake roses glittering with sequins. Even her whip was transformed, the handle all tinselled, the leather painted silver. Unseen, the irreverent genius of Grimaldi swaggered among them.

'A circus for you all,' Sadie smirked at George Tweddle, 'at no extra cost. The Boys devised it themselves!'

'Now that's better, pet,' Carrie said to her, then whispered to Rose, 'that's the daft one I told ye about. Them lads is all like borstal and she's the warden. Would ye look at them! Cartwheels and handstands, I nivver would have guessed they had it in them. And look at that fella juggling! She should be proud of them!'

'Let me get you a drink,' George said. 'We'll have to have a chat about your project, Sadie.'

'Which one, George?' she said, 'there have been so many! *Mon Dieu!* Have we grabbed your imagination at last? Don't tell me we have a chance of eating courtesy of knackered!'

George came back with two glasses of wine.

'It's the submission you made last year,' he said. 'With a little modification . . .'

'Oh, we're *very* good at modifying,' Sadie said, lighting a dark cheroot. '*Santé!*'

Caz sat on the wall between the giant earthenware pots of nasturtiums, watching everyone. The generator roared into life and beat a smoky rhythm to the calliope tiddley-pom of 'Me and My Gal'. She saw Carrie ascend the carousel steps like a queen and sit on Merrilegs's golden back, her smiling face glowing younger with every carnival turn. The ride slowed and Carrie nodded regally to stay on. Rose struggled up to ride Lightning and Josie and Charlotte mounted Dobbin and Dapple and bobbed up and down behind them.

Last night was fun, Caz told herself, she and Daisy would be friends, have a drink and a disco and work together. OK, she'd hoped for something more – something different – but it takes two to turn a bop into an all night tango. Maybe Ben just wanted her to have a buddy. It was a nice thought. Where was Daisy, anyway? She couldn't see her anywhere.

Down by the gates on the ground, Daisy took a damp ended parcel from the back of the van. 'Just hope you're right, Josie,' she said, tearing off brown paper and hiding something behind her back as she wandered back to the party crowd clustered around the carousel. She looked forward, frowning. When she saw Caz up on the wall, she smiled and raised one arm, wagging her fingers.

'Showing off!' she called.

Caz gave no sign. She probably hadn't seen or heard her. Typical of Caz to slip away and hide. Daisy walked along the mosaic street, suede boots taking her from whalespout to the sure curve of a dolphin's back by way of a bright midday sun. Wish me luck, she told the silent model in the cottage garden. Then she was knee deep in leafy green wheels of nasturtium leaves; trumpets of red, gold and orange scented the air as she ducked into the overgrown bower of the burnt-out house.

Suddenly she was standing still, framed by red hot pokers, looking up at Caz. 'Thought I'd lost you there,' she said, and started to climb the ladder. Caz shifted over so there was room for her. Daisy swung from the top of the ladder and sat for a moment, swinging her legs.

Charlotte nudged Josie. 'Don't be too obvious, but look over there,' she said, her eyes dancing. 'Up on the wall. Beware, my foolish heart! Do you think it's courtship?'

'I don't know,' Josie said. 'Keep your fingers crossed. Nothing would surprise me. That's my catch phrase, by the way, Charlotte, after this lot – here, and Berlin – nothing would surprise me.'

'I'll drink to that,' Charlotte said, never taking her eyes from the two figures on the wall.

Dark against the sun, they sat between the urns with a wild tumble of plants rampant over twin bellies of glazed clay. Caz turned her head and smiled at Daisy. 'Hello, you,' she said.

'Hello, there,' said Daisy.

She looked at Caz through her fringe as she brought her bionic arm from behind her back. Between the thumb and first finger she held a rose.

'Rosa Mundi,' she said, her eyebrows quizzical. 'It's for you.'

'Rosa Mundi,' Caz said, 'for me?'

'I don't see anyone else up here, do you?' Daisy challenged her. 'Just thee and me?'

And all the dreamers who live and love . . .

Caz smiled and took the rose.